12 YEARS A SLAVE

A TRUE STORY

Solomon Northup

COLLINS
CLASSICS

William Collins
An imprint of HarperCollins*Publishers*
77–85 Fulham Palace Road,
Hammersmith, London W6 8JB
WilliamCollinsBooks.com

This edition published in Great Britain in 2014

5

A catalogue record for this book
is available from the British Library

ISBN 978-0-00-758042-2

Printed and bound in Great Britain by
Clays Ltd, St Ives plc

MIX
Paper from
responsible sources
FSC™ C007454

FSC™ is a non-profit international organisation established to promote the
responsible management of the world's forests. Products carrying the FSC label
are independently certified to assure consumers that they come
from forests that are managed to meet the social, economic and
ecological needs of present and future generations,
and other controlled sources.

Find out more about HarperCollins and the environment at
www.harpercollins.co.uk/green

Life & Times section © HarperCollins*Publishers* Ltd
Silvia Crompton asserts her moral rights as author of the Life & Times section
Classic Literature: Words and Phrases adapted from
Collins English Dictionary
Typesetting in Kalix by Palimpsest Book Production Limited,
Falkirk, Stirlingshire

History of Collins

In 1819, millworker William Collins from Glasgow, Scotland, set up a company for printing and publishing pamphlets, sermons, hymn books, and prayer books. That company was Collins and was to mark the birth of HarperCollins Publishers as we know it today. The long tradition of Collins dictionary publishing can be traced back to the first dictionary William published in 1824, *Greek and English Lexicon*. Indeed, from 1840 onwards, he began to produce illustrated dictionaries and even obtained a licence to print and publish the Bible.

Soon after, William published the first Collins novel, *Ready Reckoner*; however, it was the time of the Long Depression, where harvests were poor, prices were high, potato crops had failed, and violence was erupting in Europe. As a result, many factories across the country were forced to close down and William chose to retire in 1846, partly due to the hardships he was facing.

Aged 30, William's son, William II, took over the business. A keen humanitarian with a warm heart and a generous spirit, William II was truly "Victorian" in his outlook. He introduced new, up-to-date steam presses and published affordable editions of Shakespeare's works and *The Pilgrim's Progress*, making them available to the masses for the first time. A new demand for educational books meant that success came with the publication of travel books, scientific books, encyclopedias, and dictionaries. This demand to be educated led to the later publication of atlases, and Collins also held the monopoly on scripture writing at the time.

In the 1860s Collins began to expand and diversify

and the idea of "books for the millions" was developed. Affordable editions of classical literature were published, and in 1903 Collins introduced 10 titles in their Collins Handy Illustrated Pocket Novels. These proved so popular that a few years later this had increased to an output of 50 volumes, selling nearly half a million in their year of publication. In the same year, The Everyman's Library was also instituted, with the idea of publishing an affordable library of the most important classical works, biographies, religious and philosophical treatments, plays, poems, travel, and adventure. This series eclipsed all competition at the time, and the introduction of paperback books in the 1950s helped to open that market and marked a high point in the industry.

HarperCollins is and has always been a champion of the classics, and the current Collins Classics series follows in this tradition – publishing classical literature that is affordable and available to all. Beautifully packaged, highly collectible, and intended to be reread and enjoyed at every opportunity.

Life & Times

12 Years a Slave is a tale of deception, violence and callous disregard for the human rights we now take for granted. It is a true story, and over a century and a half after it was published it still has the power to shock and shame. But perhaps the greatest tragedy of Solomon Northup's memoir is that his experiences were not unique. He was simply one of the fortunate few who survived to tell the tale.

Until 1841 Solomon Northup could barely have imagined he might ever become the property of another man. He was a self-made success, a celebrated violinist, a homeowner and a family man – but a lapse in judgement, a misplaced trust, turned his American dream into a living nightmare. For twelve long years Solomon Northup was a slave in his own land.

The Last Years of the Slave Trade

When we think of slavery in the United States we tend to picture the barbarous trafficking of Africans across the Atlantic, but by Solomon Northup's time this was no longer the case. In 1808, the year of Northup's birth, the Act

Prohibiting Importation of Slaves came into force. It was not until the end of the Civil War in 1865 that slavery within the United States was definitively abolished – and along with it the appalling physical, mental and sexual abuse endured at the hands of cruel masters – but the Act at least put an end to the forced transportation of Africans. It had been a long time coming: by 1808, the transatlantic slave trade had been in operation for almost 200 years, bringing an estimated 11 million Africans to the United States. Slaves may still have been seen as possessions to be bought and exploited by their masters, but it was becoming increasingly hard to deny that they too were Americans.

The War of Independence, or Revolutionary War (1775–83), played a decisive role in turning the tide against slavery. Perhaps inspired by their own newfound freedom from colonial subjugation, many American landowners freed their slaves, many of whom had fought alongside their masters against the British. Often this emancipation was granted in masters' wills – as was the case with Solomon's father, Mintus. Born into slavery in the United States, he ultimately found a sympathetic master in Captain Henry Northup of New York. In 1798, as stipulated in the captain's will, Mintus became a freedman. In gratitude he took his former master's family name.

A Country Divided

Solomon Northup was born in the relatively enlightened state of New York, which had abolished slavery in 1799, and he grew up as a free black American. His father had by this time built up a successful farming business and was able to provide an education, and music lessons, for his sons; Solomon, who in this memoir describes playing the violin as 'the ruling passion of my youth', ultimately became a professional musician. Mintus was even registered to vote.

Life was quite different in the Southern states, where lucrative sugar, cotton and tobacco plantations maintained a high demand for slaves throughout the first half of the nineteenth century. Even the nation's capital, Washington DC, retained its thriving slave trade until 1862. And it was to Washington DC that Solomon Northup was lured in 1841 on the pretext of a well-paid fiddling contract. Northup knew the dangers of travelling into slave territory but he took the precaution of carrying his official identity papers with him. Thanks in large part to his privileged New York upbringing, he felt secure enough in his status as a free man to make the brief trip without even telling his wife, Anne, where he was going. He had not counted on the duplicitousness of his money-grabbing employers, who drugged him, stole his papers and sold him to a slave-catcher.

As late as 1850 new laws were being passed that made escape from slave states to free states almost impossible. If a black man in a free state was discovered to be a fugitive slave – or, as in the case of Solomon Northup, was simply suspected of being a fugitive slave – any person preventing his return to servitude was liable for a hefty fine. Slaves had no right to trial by jury and were not allowed to testify against whites. Northup came up against this unjust system himself when, even after the great success and widespread publicity of his tell-all memoir, he tried to sue those responsible for selling him into slavery and saw them all acquitted.

Literary Sensations

12 Years a Slave, published in 1853 – the year of Solomon Northup's rescue – was not the first exposé written by a former slave. In 1825 fugitive slave William Grimes had published his story in order to raise the money to buy his way out of servitude, while perhaps the most famous slave memoir of them all, *Narrative of the Life of Frederick Douglass, an American Slave*, had appeared in 1845. But the timing of Northup's revelations meant that his book became a crucial document for abolitionists in the last decade of American slavery.

One year earlier, in 1852, a white abolitionist author named Harriet Beecher Stowe had published *Uncle Tom's Cabin*, a novel that exposed the harsh truth of life as a slave in the Southern states. It became an instant bestseller on both sides of the Atlantic and prompted further debate about slavery – so much so that it is anecdotally credited with instigating the Civil War of 1861–5. Northup's first-hand account corroborated much of what Beecher Stowe had written in her novel, and was reviewed and written about in major newspapers including the *New York Times*. Over the next few years, as political divisions between North and South became ever more violent, Northup became a figurehead of the abolitionist movement and travelled around the free states and Canada giving lectures.

Solomon Northup disappeared from the public arena as suddenly as he had been thrust into it; there is little evidence of his whereabouts after 1857. He is not recorded in the census of 1860 and it is unlikely he lived to see the end of slavery in 1865. His memoir might likewise have vanished after it went out of print had historian Sue Eakin not happened upon the book in a bargain store in 1936 and recognised from her childhood a number of the families and plantations Northup mentions. After extensive research by Eakin and others, *12 Years a Slave* was reissued in the 1960s and went on to become a bestseller once more. We may never know the end of Solomon Northup's life story, but there is little doubt that his written legacy inspired his country's greatest revolution, saving countless other black Americans from the same unspeakable fate.

12 YEARS A
SLAVE

"It is a singular coincidence, that Solomon Northup was carried to a plantation in the red river country— that same region where the scene of Uncle Tom's captivity was laid—and his account of the plantation, and the mode of life there, and some incidents which he describes, form a striking parallel to that history."

—Key to Uncle Tom's Cabin

To Harriet Beecher Stowe:

Whose name, throughout the World, is identified with the Great Reform: This narrative, affording another Key to Uncle Tom's Cabin, *is respectfully dedicated*

Such dupes are men to custom, and so prone
To reverence what is ancient, and can plead
A course of long observance for its use,
That even servitude, the worst of ills,
Because delivered down from sire to son
Is kept and guarded as a sacred thing!
But is it fit, or can it bear the shock
Of rational discussion, that a man
Compounded and made up like other men
Of elements tumultuous, in whom lust
And folly in as ample measure meet
As in the bosom of the slave he rules,
Should be a despot absolute, and boast
Himself the only freeman of his land?

—Cowper

CONTENTS

EDITOR'S PREFACE

When the editor commenced the preparation of the following narrative, he did not suppose it would reach the size of this volume. In order, however, to present all the facts which have been communicated to him, it has seemed necessary to extend it to its present length.

Many of the statements contained in the following pages are corroborated by abundant evidence—others rest entirely upon Solomon's assertion. That he has adhered strictly to the truth, the editor, at least, who has had an opportunity of detecting any contradiction or discrepancy in his statements, is well satisfied. He has invariably repeated the same story without deviating in the slightest particular, and has also carefully perused the manuscript, dictating an alteration wherever the most trivial inaccuracy has appeared.

It was Solomon's fortune, during his captivity, to be owned by several masters. The treatment he received while at the 'Pine Woods' shows that among slaveholders there are men of humanity as well as of cruelty. Some of them are spoken of with emotions of gratitude – others in a spirit of bitterness. It is believed that the following account of his experience on Bayou Boeuf presents a correct picture of slavery, in all its lights and shadows, as it now exists in that locality. Unbiased, as he conceives, by any prepossessions or prejudices, the only object of the editor has been to give a faithful history of Solomon Northup' s life, as he received it from his lips.

In the accomplishment of that object, he trusts he has succeeded, notwithstanding the numerous faults of style and expression it may be found to contain.

David Wilson, Whitehall, New York, May 1853

CHAPTER 1

Having been born a freeman, and for more than thirty years enjoyed the blessings of liberty in a free state—and having at the end of that time been kidnapped and sold into slavery, where I remained, until happily rescued in the month of January, 1853, after a bondage of twelve years—it has been suggested that an account of my life and fortunes would not be uninteresting to the public.

Since my return to liberty, I have not failed to perceive the increasing interest throughout the northern states, in regard to the subject of slavery. Works of fiction, professing to portray its features in their more pleasing as well as more repugnant aspects, have been circulated to an extent unprecedented, and, as I understand, have created a fruitful topic of comment and discussion.

I can speak of slavery only so far as it came under my own observation—only so far as I have known and experienced it in my own person. My object is, to give a candid and truthful statement of facts: to repeat the story of my life, without exaggeration, leaving it for others to determine, whether even the pages of fiction present a picture of more cruel wrong or a severer bondage.

As far back as I have been able to ascertain, my ancestors

on the paternal side were slaves in Rhode Island. They belonged to a family by the name of Northup, one of whom, removing to the state of New York, settled at Hoosic, in Rensselaer county. He brought with him Mintus Northup, my father. On the death of this gentleman, which must have occurred some fifty years ago, my father became free, having been emancipated by a direction in his will.

Henry B. Northup, Esq., of Sandy Hill, a distinguished counselor at law, and the man to whom, under Providence, I am indebted for my present liberty, and my return to the society of my wife and children, is a relative of the family in which my forefathers were thus held to service, and from which they took the name I bear. To this fact may be attributed the persevering interest he has taken in my behalf.

Sometime after my father's liberation, he removed to the town of Minerva, Essex county, N.Y., where I was born, in the month of July, 1808. How long he remained in the latter place I have not the means of definitely ascertaining. From thence he removed to Granville, Washington county, near a place known as Slyborough, where, for some years, he labored on the farm of Clark Northup, also a relative of his old master; from thence he removed to the Alden farm, at Moss Street, a short distance north of the village of Sandy Hill; and from thence to the farm now owned by Russel Pratt, situated on the road leading from Fort Edward to Argyle, where he continued to reside until his death, which took place on the twenty-second day of November, 1829. He left a widow and two children—myself, and Joseph, an elder brother. The latter is still living in the county of Oswego, near the city of that name; my mother died during the period of my captivity.

Though born a slave, and laboring under the disadvantages to which my unfortunate race is subjected, my father was a man respected for his industry and integrity, as many now living, who well remember him, are ready to testify. His whole life was passed in the peaceful pursuits of agriculture, never seeking employment in those more menial positions, which seem to be especially allotted to the children of Africa. Besides giving us an education surpassing that ordinarily bestowed upon children in our condition, he acquired, by his diligence and economy, a sufficient property qualification to entitle him to the right of suffrage. He was accustomed to speak to us of his early life; and although at all times cherishing the warmest emotions of kindness, and even of affection towards the family, in whose house he had been a bondsman, he nevertheless comprehended the system of slavery, and dwelt with sorrow on the degradation of his race. He endeavored to imbue our minds with sentiments of morality, and to teach us to place our trust and confidence in Him who regards the humblest as well as the highest of his creatures. How often since that time has the recollection of his paternal counsels occurred to me, while lying in a slave hut in the distant and sickly regions of Louisiana, smarting with the undeserved wounds which an inhuman master had inflicted, and longing only for the grave which had covered him, to shield me also from the lash of the oppressor. In the churchyard at Sandy Hill, a humble stone marks the spot where he reposes, after having worthily performed the duties appertaining to the lowly sphere wherein God had appointed him to walk.

Up to this period I had been principally engaged with my father in the labors of the farm. The leisure hours allowed me were generally either employed over my books, or playing on the violin—an amusement which was the ruling passion of my youth. It has also been the source of consolation since, affording pleasure to the simple beings with whom my lot was cast, and beguiling my own thoughts, for many hours, from the painful contemplation of my fate.

On Christmas day, 1829, I was married to Anne Hampton, a colored girl then living in the vicinity of our residence. The ceremony was performed at Fort Edward, by Timothy Eddy, Esq., a magistrate of that town, and still a prominent citizen of the place. She had resided a long time at Sandy Hill, with Mr. Baird, proprietor of the Eagle Tavern, and also in the family of Rev. Alexander Proudfit, of Salem. This gentleman for many years had presided over the Presbyterian society at the latter place, and was widely distinguished for his learning and piety. Anne still holds in grateful remembrance the exceeding kindness and the excellent counsels of that good man. She is not able to determine the exact line of her descent, but the blood of three races mingles in her veins. It is difficult to tell whether the red, white, or black predominate. The union of them all, however, in her origin, has given her a singular but pleasing expression, such as is rarely to be seen. Though somewhat resembling, yet she cannot properly be styled a quadroon, a class to which, I have omitted to mention, my mother belonged.

I had just now passed the period of my minority, having reached the age of twenty-one years in the month of July previous. Deprived of the advice and assistance of my father, with a wife dependent upon me for support, I resolved to enter upon a life of industry; and notwithstanding the obstacle of color, and the consciousness of my lowly state, indulged in pleasant dreams of a good time coming, when the possession of some humble habitation, with a few surrounding acres, should reward my labors, and bring me the means of happiness and comfort.

From the time of my marriage to this day the love I have borne my wife has been sincere and unabated; and only those who have felt the glowing tenderness a father cherishes for his offspring, can appreciate my affection for the beloved children which have since been born to us. This much I deem appropriate and necessary to say, in order that those who read these pages, may comprehend the poignancy of those sufferings I have been doomed to bear.

Immediately upon our marriage we commenced housekeeping, in the old yellow building then standing at the southern extremity of Fort Edward village, and which has since been transformed into a modern mansion, and lately occupied by Captain Lathrop. It is known as the Fort House. In this building the courts were sometime held after the organization of the county. It was also occupied by Burgoyne in 1777, being situated near the old Fort on the left bank of the Hudson.

During the winter I was employed with others repairing the Champlain Canal, on that section over which William Van Nortwick was superintendent. David McEachron had the immediate charge of the men in whose company I labored. By the time the canal opened in the spring, I was enabled, from the savings of my wages, to purchase a pair of horses, and other things necessarily required in the business of navigation.

Having hired several efficient hands to assist me, I entered into contracts for the transportation of large rafts of timber from Lake Champlain to Troy. Dyer Beckwith and a Mr. Bartemy, of Whitehall, accompanied me on several trips. During the season I became perfectly familiar with the art and mysteries of rafting a knowledge which afterwards enabled me to render profitable service to a worthy master, and to astonish the simple-witted lumbermen on the banks of the Bayou Boeuf.

In one of my voyages down Lake Champlain, I was induced to make a visit to Canada. Repairing to Montreal, I visited the cathedral and other places of interest in that city, from whence I continued my excursion to Kingston and other towns, obtaining knowledge of localities, which was also of service to me afterwards, as will appear towards the close of this narrative.

Having completed my contracts on the canal satisfactorily to myself and to my employer, and not wishing to remain idle, now that the navigation of the canal was again suspended, I entered into another contract with Medad Gunn, to cut a large quantity of wood. In this business I was engaged during the winter of 1831–32.

With the return of spring, Anne and myself conceived the project of taking a farm in the neighborhood. I had been accustomed from earliest youth to agricultural labors, and it was an occupation congenial to my tastes. I accordingly entered into arrangements for a part of the old Alden farm, on which my father formerly resided. With one cow, one swine, a yoke of fine oxen I had lately purchased of Lewis Brown, in Hartford, and other personal property and effects, we proceeded to our new home in Kingsbury. That year I planted twenty-five acres of corn, sowed large fields of oats, and commenced farming upon as large a scale as my utmost means would permit. Anne was diligent about the house affairs, while I toiled laboriously in the field.

On this place we continued to reside until 1834. In the winter season I had numerous calls to play on the violin. Wherever the young people assembled to dance, I was almost invariably there. Throughout the surrounding villages my fiddle was notorious. Anne, also, during her long residence at the Eagle Tavern, had become somewhat famous as a cook. During court weeks, and on public occasions, she was employed at high wages in the kitchen at Sherrill's Coffee House.

We always returned home from the performance of these services with money in our pockets; so that, with fiddling, cooking, and farming, we soon found ourselves in the possession of abundance, and, in fact leading a happy and prosperous life. Well, indeed, would it have been for us had we remained on the farm at Kingsbury; but the time came when the next step was to be taken towards the cruel destiny that awaited me.

In March, 1834, we removed to Saratoga Springs. We occupied a house belonging to Daniel O'Brien, on the north side of Washington Street. At that time Isaac Taylor kept a large boarding house, known as Washington Hall, at the north end of Broadway. He employed me to drive a hack, in which capacity I worked for him two years. After this time I was generally employed through the visiting season, as also was Anne, in the United States Hotel, and other public houses of the place. In winter seasons I relied upon my violin, though during the construction of the Troy and Saratoga railroad, I performed many hard days labor upon it.

I was in the habit, at Saratoga, of purchasing articles necessary for my family at the stores of Mr. Cephas Parker and Mr. William Perry, gentlemen towards whom, for many acts of kindness, I entertained feelings of strong regard. It was for this reason that, twelve years afterwards, I caused to be directed to them the letter, which is hereinafter inserted, and which was the means, in the hands of Mr. Northup, of my fortunate deliverance.

While living at the United States Hotel, I frequently met with slaves, who had accompanied their masters from the South. They were always well dressed and well provided for, leading apparently an easy life, with but few of its ordinary troubles to perplex them. Many times they entered into conversation with me on the subject of slavery. Almost uniformly I found they cherished a secret desire for liberty. Some of them expressed the most ardent anxiety to escape, and consulted me on the best method of effecting it. The fear of punishment, however, which they knew was certain to attend their re-capture and return, in all cases proved suffi-cient to deter them from the experiment. Having all my life breathed the free air of the North, and conscious that I possessed the same feelings and affections that find a place in the white man's breast; conscious, moreover, of an intel-ligence equal to that of some men, at least, with a fairer skin, I was too ignorant, perhaps too independent, to conceive how anyone could be content to live in the abject condition of a slave. I could not comprehend the justice of that law, or that religion, which upholds or recognizes the principle of slavery; and never once I am proud to say, did I fail to counsel anyone who came to me, to watch his opportunity, and strike for freedom.

I continued to reside at Saratoga until the spring of 1841. The flattering anticipations which, seven years before, had seduced us from the quiet farmhouse, on the east side of the Hudson, had not been realized. Though always in comfortable circumstances, we had not prospered. The society and associations at that world-renowned watering place, were not calculated to preserve the simple habits of industry and economy to which I had been accustomed, but, on the contrary, to substitute others in their stead, tending to shift-lessness and extravagance.

At this time we were the parents of three children—Elizabeth, Margaret, and Alonzo. Elizabeth, the eldest, was in her tenth year; Margaret was two years younger, and little Alonzo had just passed his fifth birthday. They filled our house with gladness. Their young voices were music in our ears. Many an airy castle did their mother and myself build for the little innocents. When not at labor I was always walking with them, clad in their best attire, through the streets and groves of Saratoga. Their presence was my delight; and I clasped them to my bosom with as warm and tender love as if their clouded skins had been as white as snow.

Thus far the history of my life presents nothing whatever unusual—nothing but the common hopes, and loves, and labors of an obscure colored man, making his humble progress in the world. But now I had reached a turning point in my existence—reached the threshold of unutterable wrong, and sorrow, and despair. Now had I approached within the shadow of the cloud, into the thick darkness whereof I was soon to disappear, thenceforward to be hidden from the eyes of all my kindred, and shut out from the sweet light of liberty, for many a weary year.

CHAPTER 2

One morning, towards the latter part of the month of March, 1841, having at that time no particular business to engage my attention, I was walking about the village of Saratoga Springs, thinking to myself where I might obtain some present employment, until the busy season should arrive. Anne, as was her usual custom, had gone over to Sandy Hill, a distance of some twenty miles, to take charge of the culinary department at Sherrill's Coffee House, during the session of the court. Elizabeth, I think, had accompanied her. Margaret and Alonzo were with their aunt at Saratoga.

On the corner of Congress Street and Broadway, near the tavern, then, and for aught I know to the contrary, still kept by Mr. Moon, I was met by two gentlemen of respectable appearance, both of whom were entirely unknown to me. I have the impression that they were introduced to me by some one of my acquaintances, but who, I have in vain endeavored to recall, with the remark that I was an expert player on the violin.

At any rate, they immediately entered into conversation on that subject, making numerous inquiries touching on my proficiency in that respect. My responses being to all appearances satisfactory, they proposed to engage my services for a short period, stating, at the same time, I was just such a person as their business required. Their names, as they afterwards gave them to me, were Merrill Brown and Abram Hamilton, though whether these were their true appellations, I have strong reasons to doubt. The former was a man apparently forty years of age, somewhat short and thick-set, with a countenance indicating shrewdness and intelligence. He wore a black frock coat and black hat, and said he resided either at Rochester or at Syracuse. The latter was a young man of fair complexion and light eyes, and, I should judge, had not passed the age of twenty-five. He was tall and slender, dressed in a snuff-colored coat, with glossy hat, and vest of elegant pattern. His whole apparel was in the extreme of fashion. His appearance was somewhat effeminate, but prepossessing, and there was about him an easy air, that showed he had mingled with the world. They were connected, as they informed me, with a circus company, then in the city of Washington; that they were on their way thither to rejoin it, having left it for a short time to make an excursion northward, for the purpose of seeing the country, and were paying their expenses an occasional exhibition. They also remarked that they had found much difficulty in procuring music for their entertainments, and that if I would accompany them as far as New York, they would give me one dollar for each day's services, and three dollars in addition for every night I played at their performances, besides sufficient to pay the expense of my return from New York to Saratoga.

I at once accepted the tempting offer, both for the reward it promised, and from a desire to visit the metropolis. They were anxious to leave immediately. Thinking my absence would be brief, I did not deem it necessary to write to Anne whither I had gone; in fact supposing that my return, perhaps, would be as soon as hers. So taking a change of linen and my violin, I was ready to depart. The carriage was brought round a covered one, drawn by a pair of noble bays, altogether forming an elegant establishment. Their baggage, consisting of three large trunks, was fastened on the rack, and mounting to the driver's seat, while they took their places in the rear, I drove away from Saratoga on the road to Albany, elated with my new position, and happy as I had ever been, on any day in all my life.

We passed through Ballston, and striking the ridge road, as it is called, if my memory correctly serves me, followed it direct to Albany. We reached that city before dark, and stopped at a hotel southward from the Museum.

This night I had an opportunity of witnessing one of their performances the only one, during the whole period I was with them. Hamilton was stationed at the door; I formed the orchestra, while Brown provided the entertainment. It consisted in throwing balls, dancing on the rope, frying pancakes in a hat, causing invisible pigs to squeal, and other like feats of ventriloquism and legerdemain. The audience was extraordinarily sparse, and not of the selectest character at that, and Hamilton's report of the proceeds presented but a "beggarly account of empty boxes."

Early next morning we renewed our journey. The burden of their conversation now was the expression of an anxiety to reach the circus without delay. They hurried forward, without again stopping to exhibit, and in due course of time, we reached New York, taking lodgings at a house on the west side of the city, in a street running from Broadway to the river. I supposed my journey was at an end, and expected in a day or two at least, to return to my friends and family at Saratoga. Brown and Hamilton, however, began to importune me to continue with them to Washington. They alleged that immediately on their arrival, now that the summer season was approaching, the circus would set out for the north. They promised me a situation and high wages if I would accompany them. Largely did they expatiate on the advantages that would result to me, and such were the flattering representations they made, that I finally concluded to accept the offer.

The next morning they suggested that, inasmuch as we were about entering a slave state, it would be well, before leaving New York, to procure free papers. The idea struck me as a prudent one, though I think it would scarcely have occurred to me, had they not proposed it. We proceeded at once to what I understood to be the Custom House. They made oath to certain facts showing I was a free man. A paper was drawn up and handed us, with the direction to take it to the clerk's office. We did so, and the clerk having added something to it, for which he was paid six shillings, we returned again to the Custom House. Some further formalities were gone through with before it was completed, when, paying the officer two dollars, I placed the papers in my pocket, and started with my two friends to our hotel. I thought at the time, I must confess, that the papers were scarcely worth the cost of obtaining them—the apprehension of danger to my personal safety never having suggested itself to me in the remotest manner. The clerk, to whom we were directed, I remember, made a memorandum in a large book, which, I presume, is in the office yet. A reference to the entries during the latter part of March, or first of April, 1841, I have no doubt will satisfy the incredulous, at least so far as this particular transaction is concerned.

With the evidence of freedom in my possession, the next day after our arrival in New York, we crossed the ferry to Jersey City, and took the road to Philadelphia. Here we remained one night, continuing our journey towards Baltimore early in the morning. In due time, we arrived in the latter city, and stopped at a hotel near the railroad depot, either kept by a Mr. Rathbone, or known as the Rathbone House. All the way from New York, their anxiety to reach the circus seemed to grow more and more intense. We left the carriage at Baltimore, and entering the cars, proceeded to Washington, at which place we arrived just at nightfall, the evening previous to the funeral of General Harrison, and stopped at Gadsby's Hotel, on Pennsylvania Avenue.

After supper they called me to their apartments, and paid me forty-three dollars, a sum greater than my wages amounted to, which act of generosity was in consequence, they said, of their not having exhibited as often as they had given me to anticipate, during our trip from Saratoga. They moreover informed me that it had been the intention of the circus company to leave Washington the next morning, but that on account of the funeral, they had concluded to remain another day. They were then, as they had been from the time of our first meeting, extremely kind. No opportunity was omitted of addressing me in the language of approbation while, on the other hand, I was certainly much prepossessed in their favor. I gave them my confidence without reserve, and would freely have trusted them to almost any extent. Their constant conversation and manner towards me—their foresight in suggesting the idea of free papers, and a hundred other little acts, unnecessary to be repeated all indicated that they were friends indeed, sincerely solicitous for my welfare. I know not but they were. I know not but they were innocent of the great wickedness of which I now believe them guilty. Whether they were accessory to my misfortunes—subtle and inhuman monsters in the shape of men—designedly luring me away from home and family, and liberty, for the sake of gold—those who read these pages will have the same means of determining as myself. If they were innocent, my sudden disappearance must have been unaccountable indeed; but revolving in my mind all the attending circumstances, I never yet could indulge, towards them, so charitable a supposition.

After receiving the money from them, of which they appeared to have an abundance, they advised me not to go into the streets that night, inasmuch as I was unacquainted with the customs of the city. Promising to remember their advice, I left them together, and soon after was shown by a colored servant to a sleeping room in the back part of the hotel, on the ground floor. I laid down to rest, thinking of home and wife, and children, and the long distance that stretched between us, until I fell asleep. But no good angel of pity came to my bedside, bidding me to fly—no voice of mercy forewarned me in my dreams of the trials that were just at hand.

The next day there was a great pageant in Washington. The roar of cannon and the tolling of bells filled the air, while many houses were shrouded with crape, and the streets were black with people. As the day advanced, the procession made its appearance, coming slowly through the Avenue, carriage after carriage, in long succession, while thousands upon thousands followed on foot—all moving to the sound of melancholy music. They were bearing the dead body of Harrison to the grave.

From early in the morning, I was constantly in the company of Hamilton and Brown. They were the only persons I knew in Washington. We stood together as the funeral pomp passed by. I remember distinctly how the window glass would break and rattle to the ground, after each report of the cannon they were firing in the burial ground. We went to the Capital, and walked a long time about the grounds. In the afternoon, they strolled towards the President's House, all the time keeping me near to them, and pointing out various places of interest. As yet, I had seen nothing of the circus. In fact, I had thought of it but little, if at all, amidst the excitement of the day.

My friends, several times during the afternoon, entered drinking saloons, and called for liquor. They were by no means in the habit, however, so far as I knew them, of indulging to excess. On these occasions, after serving themselves, they would pour out a glass and hand it to me. I did not become intoxicated, as may be inferred from what subsequently occurred. Towards evening, and soon after partaking of one of these potations, I began to experience most unpleasant sensations. I felt extremely ill. My head commenced aching— a dull, heavy pain, inexpressibly disagreeable. At the supper table, I was without appetite; the sight and flavor of food was nauseous. About dark the same servant conducted me to the room I had occupied the previous night. Brown and Hamilton advised me to retire, commiserating me kindly, and expressing hopes that I would be better in the morning. Divesting myself of coat and boots merely, I threw myself upon the bed. It was impossible to sleep. The pain in my head continued to increase, until it became almost unbearable. In a short time I became thirsty. My lips were parched. I could think of nothing but water of lakes and flowing rivers, of brooks where I had stooped to drink, and of the dripping bucket, rising with its cool and overflowing nectar, from the bottom of the well. Towards midnight, as near as I could judge, I arose, unable longer to bear such intensity of thirst. I was a stranger in the house, and knew nothing of its apartments. There was no one up, as I could observe. Groping about at random, I knew not where, I found the way at last to a kitchen in the basement. Two or three colored servants were moving through it, one of whom, a woman, gave me two glasses of water. It afforded momentary relief, but by the time I had reached my room again, the same burning desire of drink, the same tormenting thirst, had again returned. It was even more torturing than before, as was also the wild pain in my head, if such a thing could be. I was in sore distress—in most excruciating agony! I seemed to stand on the brink of madness! The memory of that night of horrible suffering will follow me to the grave.

In the course of an hour or more after my return from the kitchen, I was conscious of someone entering my room. There seemed to be several—a mingling of various voices,—but how many, or who they were, I cannot tell. Whether Brown and Hamilton were among them, is a mere matter of conjecture. I only remember, with any degree of distinctness, that I was told it was necessary to go to a physician and procure medicine, and that pulling on my boots, without coat or hat, I followed them through a long passage-way, or alley, into the open street. It ran out at right angles from Pennsylvania Avenue. On the opposite side there was a light burning in a window. My impression is there were then three persons with me, but it is altogether indefinite and vague, and like the memory of a painful dream. Going towards the light, which I imagined proceeded from a physician's office, and which seemed to recede as I advanced, is the last glimmering recollection I can now recall. From that moment I was insensible. How long I remained in that condition—whether only that night, or many days and nights—I do not know; but when consciousness returned, I found myself alone, in utter darkness, and in chains.

The pain in my head had subsided in a measure, but I was very faint and weak. I was sitting upon a low bench, made of rough boards, and without coat or hat. I was handcuffed. Around my ankles also were a pair of heavy fetters. One end of a chain was fastened to a large ring in the floor, the other to the fetters on my ankles. I tried in vain to stand upon my feet. Waking from such a painful trance, it was some time before I could collect my thoughts. Where was I? What was the meaning of these chains? Where were Brown and Hamilton? What had I done to deserve imprisonment in such a dungeon? I could not comprehend. There was a blank of some indefinite period, preceding my awakening in that lonely place, the events of which the utmost stretch of memory was unable to recall. I listened intently for some sign or sound of life, but nothing broke the oppressive silence, save the clinking of my chains, whenever I chanced to move. I spoke aloud, but the sound of my voice startled me. I felt of my pockets, so far as the fetters would allow—far enough indeed, to ascertain that I had not only been robbed of liberty, but that my money and free papers were also gone! Then did the idea begin to break upon my mind, at first dim and confused, that I had been kidnapped. But that I thought was incredible. There must have been some misapprehension—some unfortunate mistake. It could not be that a free citizen of New York, who had wronged no man, nor violated any law, should be dealt with thus inhumanly. The more I contemplated my situation, however, the more I became confirmed in my suspicions. It was a desolate thought, indeed. I felt there was no trust or mercy in unfeeling man; and commending myself to the God of the oppressed, bowed my head upon my fettered hands, and wept most bitterly.

CHAPTER 3

Some three hours elapsed, during which time I remained seated on the low bench, absorbed in painful meditations. At length I heard the crowing of a cock, and soon a distant rumbling sound, as of carriages hurrying through the streets, came to my ears, and I knew that it was day. No ray of light, however, penetrated my prison. Finally, I heard footsteps immediately overhead, as of someone walking to and fro. It occurred to me then that I must be in an underground apartment, and the damp, mouldy odors of the place confirmed the supposition. The noise above continued for at least an hour, when, at last, I heard footsteps approaching from without. A key rattled in the lock—a strong door swung back upon its hinges, admitting a flood of light, and two men entered and stood before me. One of them was a large, powerful man, forty years of age, perhaps, with dark, chestnut-colored hair, slightly interspersed with gray. His face was full, his complexion flush, his features grossly coarse, expressive of nothing but cruelty and cunning. He was about five feet ten inches high, of full habit, and, without prejudice, I must be allowed to say, was a man whose whole appearance was sinister and repugnant. His name was James H. Burch, as I learned afterwards—a well-known slave-dealer in Washington; and then, or lately, connected in business, as a partner, with Theophilus Freeman, of New Orleans. The person who accompanied him was a simple lackey, named Ebenezer Radburn, who acted merely in the capacity of turnkey. Both of these men still live in Washington, or did, at the time of my return through that city from slavery in January last.

The light admitted through the open door enabled me to observe the room in which I was confined. It was about twelve feet square—the walls of solid masonry. The floor was of heavy plank. There was one small window, crossed with great iron bars, with an outside shutter, securely fastened.

An iron-bound door led into an adjoining cell, or vault, wholly destitute of windows, or any means of admitting light. The furniture of the room in which I was, consisted of the wooden bench on which I sat, an old-fashioned, dirty box stove, and besides these, in either cell, there was neither bed, nor blanket, nor anything whatever. The door, through which Burch and Radburn entered, led through a small passage, up a flight of steps into a yard, surrounded by a brick wall ten or twelve feet high, immediately in rear of a building of the same width as itself. The yard extended rearward from the house about thirty feet. In one part of the wall there was a strongly ironed door, opening into a narrow, covered passage, leading along one side of the house into the street. The doom of the colored man, upon whom the door leading out of that narrow passage closed, was sealed. The top of the wall supported one end of a roof, which ascended inwards, forming a kind of open shed. Underneath the roof there was a crazy loft all round, where slaves, if so disposed, might sleep at night, or in inclement weather seek shelter from the storm. It was like a farmer's barnyard in most respects, save it was so constructed that the outside world could never see the human cattle that were herded there.

The building to which the yard was attached, was two stories high, fronting on one of the public streets of Washington. Its outside presented only the appearance of a quiet private residence. A stranger looking at it, would never have dreamed of its execrable uses. Strange as it may seem, within plain sight of this same house, looking down from its commanding height upon it, was the Capitol. The voices of patriotic representatives boasting of freedom and equality, and the rattling of poor slave's chains, almost commingled. A slave pen within the very shadow of the Capitol!

Such is a correct description as it was in 1841, of Williams' slave pen in Washington, in one of the cellars of which I found myself so unaccountably confined.

"Well, my boy, how do you feel now?" said Burch, as he entered through the open door. I replied that I was sick, and inquired the cause of my imprisonment. He answered that I was his slave—that he had bought me, and that he was about to send me to New Orleans. I asserted, aloud and boldly, that I was a free man—a resident of Saratoga, where I had a wife and children, who were also free, and that my name was Northup. I complained bitterly of the strange treatment I had received, and threatened, upon my liberation, to have satisfaction for the wrong. He denied that I was free, and with an emphatic oath, declared that I came from Georgia. Again and again I asserted I was no man's slave, and insisted upon his taking off my chains at once. He endeavored to hush me, as if he feared my voice would be overheard. But I would not be silent, and denounced the authors of my imprisonment, whoever they might be, as unmitigated villains. Finding he could not quiet me, he flew into a towering passion. With blasphemous oaths, he called me a black liar, a runaway from Georgia, and every other profane and vulgar epithet that the most indecent fancy could conceive.

During this time Radburn was standing silently by. His business was, to oversee this human, or rather inhuman stable, receiving slaves, feeding and whipping them, at the rate of two shillings a head per day. Turning to him, Burch ordered the paddle and cat-o'-ninetails to be brought in. He disappeared, and in a few moments returned with these instruments of torture. The paddle, as it is termed in slave-beating parlance, or at least the one with which I first became acquainted, and of which I now speak, was a piece of hard-wood board, eighteen or twenty inches long, moulded to the shape of an old-fashioned pudding stick, or ordinary oar. The flattened portion, which was about the size in circum-ference of two open hands, was bored with a small auger in numerous places. The cat was a large rope of many strands—the strands unraveled, and a knot tied at the extremity of each.

As soon as these formidable whips appeared, I was seized by both of them, and roughly divested of my clothing. My feet, as has been stated, were fastened to the floor. Drawing me over the bench, face downwards, Radburn placed his heavy foot upon the fetters, between my wrists, holding them painfully to the floor. With the paddle, Burch commenced beating me. Blow after blow was inflicted upon my naked body. When his unrelenting arm grew tired, he stopped and asked if I still insisted I was a free man. I did insist upon it, and then the blows were renewed, faster and more energetically, if possible, than before. When again tired, he would repeat the same question, and receiving the same answer, continue his cruel labor. All this time, the incarnate devil was uttering most fiendish oaths. At length the paddle broke, leaving the useless handle in his hand. Still I would not yield. All his brutal blows could not force from my lips the foul lie that I was a slave. Casting madly on the floor the handle of the broken paddle, he seized the rope. This was far more painful than the other. I struggled with all my power, but it was in vain. I prayed for mercy, but my prayer was only answered with imprecations and with stripes. I thought I must die beneath the lashes of the accursed brute. Even now the flesh crawls upon my bones, as I recall the scene. I was all on fire. My sufferings I can compare to nothing else than the burning agonies of hell!

At last I became silent to his repeated questions. I would make no reply. In fact, I was becoming almost unable to speak. Still he plied the lash without stint upon my poor body, until it seemed that the lacerated flesh was stripped from my bones at every stroke. A man with a particle of mercy in his soul would not have beaten even a dog so cruelly. At length Radburn said that it was useless to whip me anymore—that I would be sore enough. Thereupon, Burch desisted, saying, with an admonitory shake of his fist in my face, and hissing the words through his firm-set teeth, that if ever I dared to utter again that I was entitled to my freedom, that I had been kidnapped, or anything whatever of the kind, the castigation I had just received was nothing in comparison with what would follow. He swore that he would either conquer or kill me. With these consolatory words, the fetters were taken from my wrists, my feet still remaining fastened to the ring; the shutter of the little barred window, which had been opened, was again closed, and going out, locking the great door behind them, I was left in darkness as before.

In an hour, perhaps two, my heart leaped to my throat, as the key rattled in the door again. I, who had been so lonely, and who had longed so ardently to see someone, I cared not who, now shuddered at the thought of man's approach. A human face was fearful to me, especially a white one. Radburn entered, bringing with him, on a tin plate, a piece of shriveled fried pork, a slice of bread and a cup of water. He asked me how I felt, and remarked that I had received a pretty severe flogging. He remonstrated with me against the propriety of asserting my freedom. In rather a patronizing and confidential manner, he gave it to me as his advice, that the less I said on that subject the better it would be for me. The man evidently endeavored to appear kind—whether touched at the sight of my sad condition, or with the view of silencing, on my part, my further expression of my rights, it is not necessary now to conjecture. He unlocked the fetters from my ankles, opened the shutters of the little window, and departed, leaving me again alone.

By this time I had become stiff and sore; my body was covered with blisters, and it was with great pain and difficulty that I could move. From the window I could observe nothing but the roof resting on the adjacent wall. At night I laid down upon the damp, hard floor, without any pillow or covering whatever. Punctually, twice a day, Radburn came in, with his pork, and bread, and water. I had but little appetite, though I was tormented with continual thirst. My wounds would not permit me to remain but a few minutes in any one position; so, sitting, or standing, or moving slowly round, I passed the days and nights. I was heartsick and discouraged. Thoughts of my family, of my wife and children, continually occupied my mind. When sleep overpowered me I dreamed of them—dreamed I was again in Saratoga—that I could see their faces, and hear their voices calling me. Awakening from the pleasant phantasms of sleep to the bitter realities around me, I could but groan and weep. Still my spirit was not broken. I indulged the anticipation of escape, and that speedily. It was impossible, I reasoned, that men could be so unjust as to detain me as a slave, when the truth of my case was known. Burch, ascertaining I was no runaway from Georgia, would certainly let me go. Though suspicions of Brown and Hamilton were not infrequent, I could not reconcile myself to the idea that they were instrumental to my imprisonment. Surely they would seek me out—they would deliver me from thraldom. Alas! I had not then learned the measure of "man's inhumanity to man," nor to what limitless extent of wickedness he will go for the love of gain.

In the course of several days the outer door was thrown open, allowing me the liberty of the yard. There I found three slaves—one of them a lad of ten years, the others young men of about twenty and twenty-five. I was not long in forming an acquaintance, and learning their names and the particulars of their history.

The eldest was a colored man named Clemens Ray. He had lived in Washington; had driven a hack, and worked in a livery stable there for a long time. He was very intelligent, and fully comprehended his situation. The thought of going south overwhelmed him with grief. Burch had purchased him a few days before, and had placed him there until such time as he was ready to send him to the New Orleans market. From him I learned for the first time that I was in Williams' slave pen, a place I had never heard of previously. He described to me the uses for which it was designed. I repeated to him the particulars of my unhappy story, but he could only give me the consolation of his sympathy. He also advised me to be silent henceforth on the subject of my freedom for, knowing the character of Burch, he assumed that it would only be attended with renewed whipping. The next eldest was named John Williams. He was raised in Virginia, not far from Washington. Burch had taken him in payment of a debt, and he constantly entertained the hope that his master would redeem him—a hope that was subsequently realized. The lad was a sprightly child, that answered to the name of Randall. Most of the time he was playing about the yard, but occasionally would cry, calling for his mother, and wondering when she would come. His mother's absence seemed to be the great and only grief in his little heart. He was too young to realize his condition, and when the memory of his mother was not in his mind, he amused us with his pleasant pranks.

At night, Ray, Williams, and the boy, slept in the loft of the shed, while I was locked in the cell. Finally we were each provided with blankets, such as are used upon horses—the only bedding I was allowed to have for twelve years afterwards. Ray and Williams asked me many questions about New York—how colored people were treated there; how they could have homes and families of their own, with none to disturb and oppress them; and Ray, especially, sighed continually for freedom. Such conversations, however, were not in the hearing of Burch, or the keeper Radburn. Aspirations such as these would have brought down the lash upon our backs.

It is necessary in this narrative, in order to present a full and truthful statement of all the principal events in the history of my life, and to portray the institution of slavery as I have seen and known it, to speak of well-known places, and of many persons who are yet living. I am, and always was, an entire stranger in Washington and its vicinity—aside from Burch and Radburn, knowing no man there, except as I have heard of them through my enslaved companions. What I am about to say, if false, can be easily contradicted.

I remained in Williams' slave pen about two weeks. The night previous to my departure a woman was brought in, weeping bitterly, and leading by the hand a little child. They were Randall's mother and half-sister. On meeting them he was overjoyed, clinging to her dress, kissing the child, and exhibiting every demonstration of delight. The mother also clasped him in her arms, embraced him tenderly, and gazed at him fondly through her tears, calling him by many an endearing name.

Emily, the child, was seven or eight years old, of light complexion, and with a face of admirable beauty. Her hair fell in curls around her neck, while the style and richness of her dress, and the neatness of her whole appearance indicated she had been brought up in the midst of wealth.

She was a sweet child indeed. The woman also was arrayed in silk, with rings upon her fingers, and golden ornaments suspended from her ears. Her air and manners, the correctness and propriety of her language—all showed, evidently, that she had sometime stood above the common level of a slave. She seemed to be amazed at finding herself in such a place as that. It was plainly a sudden and unexpected turn of fortune that had brought her there. Filling the air with her complainings, she was hustled, with the children and myself, into the cell. Language can convey but an inadequate impression of the lamentations to which she gave incessant utterance. Throwing herself upon the floor, and encircling the children in her arms, she poured forth such touching words as only maternal love and kindness can suggest. They nestled closely to her, as if *there* only was there any safety or protection. At last they slept, their heads resting upon her lap. While they slumbered, she smoothed the hair back from their little foreheads, and talked to them all night long. She called them her darlings—her sweet babes—poor innocent things that knew not the misery they were destined to endure. Soon they would have no mother to comfort them— they would be taken from her. What would become of them? Oh! she could not live away from her little Emmy and her dear boy. They had always been good children, and had such loving ways. It would break her heart, God knew, she said, if they were taken from her; and yet she knew they meant to sell them, and, maybe, they would be separated, and could never see each other anymore. It was enough to melt a heart of stone to listen to the pitiful expressions of that desolate and distracted mother. Her name was Eliza; and this was the story of her life, as she afterwards related it:

She was the slave of Elisha Berry, a rich man, living in the neighborhood of Washington. She was born, I think she said, on his plantation. Years before, he had fallen into dissipated habits, and quarreled with his wife. In fact, soon after the birth of Randall, they separated. Leaving his wife and daughter in the house they had always occupied, he erected a new one nearby, on the estate. Into this house he brought Eliza; and, on condition of her living with him, she and her children were to be emancipated. She resided with him there nine years, with servants to attend upon her, and provided with every comfort and luxury of life. Emily was his child! Finally, her young mistress, who had always remained with her mother at the homestead, married a Mr. Jacob Brooks. At length, for some cause, (as I gathered from her relation,) beyond Berry's control, a division of his property was made. She and her children fell to the share of Mr. Brooks. During the nine years she had lived with Berry, in consequence of the position she was compelled to occupy, she and Emily had become the object of Mrs. Berry and her daughter's hatred and dislike. Berry himself she represented as a man of naturally a kind heart, who always promised her that she should have her freedom, and who, she had no doubt, would grant it to her then, if it were only in his power. As soon as they thus came into the possession and control of the daughter, it became very manifest they would not live long together. The sight of Eliza seemed to be odious to Mrs. Brooks; neither could she bear to look upon the child, half-sister, and beautiful as she was!

The day she was led into the pen, Brooks had brought her from the estate into the city, under pretense that the time had come when her free papers were to be executed, in fulfillment of her master's promise. Elated at the prospect of immediate liberty, she decked herself and little Emmy in their best apparel, and accompanied him with a joyful heart. On their arrival in the city, instead of being baptized into the family of freemen, she was delivered to the trader Burch. The paper that was executed was a bill of sale. The hope of years was blasted in a moment. From the height of most exulting happiness to the utmost depths of wretchedness, she had that day descended. No wonder that she wept, and filled the pen with wailings and expressions of heartrending woe.

Eliza is now dead. Far up the Red River, where it pours its waters sluggishly through the unhealthy, low lands of Louisiana, she rests in the grave at last—the only resting place of the poor slave! How all her tears were realized—how she mourned day and night and never would be comforted—how, as she predicted, her heart did indeed break, with the burden of maternal sorrow, will be seen as the narrative proceeds.

CHAPTER 4

At intervals during the first night of Eliza's incarceration in the pen, she complained bitterly of Jacob Brooks, her young mistress' husband. She declared that had she been aware of the deception he intended to practice upon her, he never would have brought her there alive. They had chosen the opportunity of getting her away when Master Berry was absent from the plantation. He had always been kind to her. She wished that she could see him; but she knew that even he was unable now to rescue her. Then would she commence weeping again—kissing the sleeping children—talking first to one, then to the other, as they lay in their unconscious slumbers, with their heads upon her lap. So wore the long night away; and when the morning dawned, and night had come again, still she kept mourning on, and would not be consoled.

About midnight following, the cell door opened, and Burch and Radburn entered, with lanterns in their hands. Burch, with an oath, ordered us to roll up our blankets without delay, and get ready to go on board the boat. He swore we would be left unless we hurried fast. He aroused the children from their slumbers with a rough shake, and said they were d—d sleepy, it appeared. Going out into the yard, he called Clem

Ray, ordering him to leave the loft and come into the cell, and bring his blanket with him. When Clem appeared, he placed us side by side, and fastened us together with handcuffs—my left hand to his right. John Williams had been taken out a day or two before, his master having redeemed him, greatly to his delight. Clem and I were ordered to march, Eliza and the children following. We were conducted into the yard, from thence into the covered passage, and up a flight of steps through a side door into the upper room, where I had heard the walking to and fro. Its furniture was a stove, a few old chairs, and a long table, covered with papers. It was a white-washed room, without any carpet on the floor, and seemed a sort of office. By one of the windows, I remember, hung a rusty sword, which attracted my attention. Burch's trunk was there. In obedience to his orders, I took hold of one of its handles with my unfettered hand, while he taking hold of the other, we proceeded out of the front door into the street in the same order as we had left the cell.

It was a dark night. All was quiet. I could see lights, or the reflection of them, over towards Pennsylvania Avenue, but there was no one, not even a straggler, to be seen. I was almost resolved to attempt to break away. Had I not been handcuffed the attempt would certainly have been made, whatever consequence might have followed. Radburn was in the rear, carrying a large stick, and hurrying up the children as fast as the little ones could walk. So we passed, handcuffed and in silence, through the streets of Washington— through the Capital of a nation, whose theory of government, we are told, rests on the foundation of man's inalienable right to life, LIBERTY, and the pursuit of happiness! Hail! Columbia, happy land, indeed!

Reaching the steamboat, we were quickly hustled into the hold, among barrels and boxes of freight. A colored servant brought a light, the bell rung, and soon the vessel started down the Potomac, carrying us we knew not where. The bell tolled as we passed the tomb of Washington! Burch, no doubt, with uncovered head, bowed reverently before the sacred ashes of the man who devoted his illustrious life to the liberty of his country.

None of us slept that night but Randall and little Emmy. For the first time Clem Ray was wholly overcome. To him the idea of going south was terrible in the extreme. He was leaving the friends and associations of his youth—everything that was dear and precious to his heart—in all probability never to return. He and Eliza mingled their tears together bemoaning their cruel fate. For my own part, difficult as it was, I endeavored to keep up my spirits. I resolved in my mind a hundred plans of escape, and fully determined to make the attempt the first desperate chance that offered. I had by this time become satisfied, however, that my true policy was to say nothing further on the subject of my having been born a freeman. It would but expose me to maltreatment, and diminish the chances of liberation.

After sunrise in the morning we were called up on deck to breakfast. Burch took our handcuffs off, and we sat down to table. He asked Eliza if she would take a dram. She declined, thanking him politely. During the meal we were all silent—not a word passed between us. A mulatto woman who served at table seemed to take an interest in our behalf—told us to cheer up, and not to be so cast down. Breakfast over, the handcuffs were restored, and Burch ordered us out on the stern deck. We sat down together on some boxes, still saying nothing in Burch's presence. Occasionally a passenger would walk out to where we were, look at us for a while, then silently return.

It was a very pleasant morning. The fields along the river were covered with verdure, far in advance of what I had been accustomed to see at that season of the year. The sun shone out warmly; the birds were singing in the trees.

The happy birds—I envied them. I wished for wings like them, that I might cleave the air to where my birdlings waited vainly for their father's coming, in the cooler region of the North.

In the forenoon the steamer reached Aquia Creek. There the passengers took stages—Burch and his five slaves occupying one exclusively. He laughed with the children, and at one stopping place went so far as to purchase them a piece of gingerbread. He told me to hold up my head and look smart. That I might, perhaps, get a good master if I behaved myself. I made him no reply. His face was hateful to me, and I could not bear to look upon it. I sat in the corner, cherishing in my heart the hope, not yet extinct, of some day meeting the tyrant on the soil of my native state.

At Fredericksburgh we were transferred from the stage coach to a car, and before dark arrived in Richmond, the chief city of Virginia. At this city we were taken from the cars, and driven through the street to a slave pen, between the railroad depot and the river, kept by a Mr. Goodin. This pen is similar to Williams' in Washington, except it is somewhat larger; and besides, there were two small houses standing at opposite corners within the yard. These houses are usually found within slave yards, being used as rooms for the examination of human chattels by purchasers before concluding a bargain. Unsoundness in a slave, as well as in a horse, detracts materially from his value. If no warranty is given, a close examination is a matter of particular importance to the negro jockey.

We were met at the door of Goodin's yard by that gentleman himself—a short, fat man, with a round, plump face, black hair and whiskers, and a complexion almost as dark as some of his own negroes. He had a hard, stern look, and was perhaps about fifty years of age. Burch and he met with great cordiality. They were evidently old friends. Shaking each other warmly by the hand, Burch remarked he had brought some company, inquired at what time the brig would leave, and was answered that it would probably leave the next day at such an hour. Goodin then turned to me, took hold of my arm, turned me partly round, looked at me sharply with the air of one who considered himself a good judge of property, and as if estimating in his own mind about how much I was worth.

"Well, boy, where did you come from?"

Forgetting myself, for a moment, I answered, "From New York."

"New York! H—l! What have you been doing up there?" was his astonished interrogatory.

Observing Burch at this moment looking at me with an angry expression that conveyed a meaning it was not difficult to understand, I immediately said, "O, I have only been up that way a piece," in a manner intended to imply that although I might have been as far as New York, yet I wished it distinctly understood that I did not belong to that free state, nor to any other.

Goodin then turned to Clem, and then to Eliza and the children, examining them severally, and asking various questions. He was pleased with Emily, as was everyone who saw the child's sweet countenance. She was not as tidy as when I first beheld her; her hair was now somewhat disheveled; but through its unkempt and soft profusion there still beamed a little face of most surpassing loveliness. "Altogether we were a fair lot—a devilish good lot," he said, enforcing that opinion with more than one emphatic adjective not found in the Christian vocabulary. Thereupon we passed into the yard. Quite a number of slaves, as many as thirty I should say, were moving about, or sitting on benches under the shed. They were all cleanly dressed—the men with hats, the women with handkerchiefs tied about their heads.

Burch and Goodin, after separating from us, walked

up the steps at the back part of the main building, and sat down upon the door sill. They entered into conversation, but the subject of it I could not hear. Presently Burch came down into the yard, unfettered me, and led me into one of the small houses.

"You told that man you came from New York," said he.

I replied, "I told him I had been up as far as New York, to be sure, but did not tell him I belonged there, nor that I was a freeman. I meant no harm at all, Master Burch. I would not have said it had I thought."

He looked at me a moment as if he was ready to devour me, then turning round went out. In a few minutes he returned. "If ever I hear you say a word about New York, or about your freedom, I will be the death of you—I will kill you; you may rely on that," he ejaculated fiercely.

I doubt not he understood then better than I did the danger and the penalty of selling a free man into slavery. He felt the necessity of closing my mouth against the crime he knew he was committing. Of course, my life would not have weighed a feather, in any emergency requiring such a sacrifice. Undoubtedly, he meant precisely what he said.

Under the shed on one side of the yard, there was constructed a rough table, while overhead were sleeping lofts—the same as in the pen at Washington. After partaking at this table of our supper of pork and bread, I was hand-cuffed to a large yellow man, quite stout and fleshy, with a countenance expressive of the utmost melancholy. He was a man of intelligence and information. Chained together, it was not long before we became acquainted with each other's history. His name was Robert. Like myself, he had been born free, and had a wife and two children in Cincinnati. He said he had come south with two men, who had hired him in the city of his residence. Without free papers, he had been seized at Fredericksburgh, placed in confinement, and beaten until he had learned, as I had, the necessity and the policy of silence. He had been in Goodin's pen about three weeks. To this man I became much attached. We could sympathize with, and understand each other. It was with tears and a heavy heart, not many days subsequently, that I saw him die, and looked for the last time upon his lifeless form!

Robert and myself, with Clem, Eliza and her children, slept that night upon our blankets, in one of the small houses in the yard. There were four others, all from the same plantation, who had been sold, and were now on their way south, who also occupied it with us. David and his wife, Caroline, both mulattoes, were exceedingly affected. They dreaded the thought of being put into the cane and cotton fields; but their greatest source of anxiety was the apprehension of being separated. Mary, a tall, lithe girl, of a most jetty black, was listless and apparently indifferent. Like many of the class, she scarcely knew there was such a word as freedom. Brought up in the ignorance of a brute, she possessed but little more than a brute's intelligence. She was one of those, and there are very many, who fear nothing but their master's lash, and know no further duty than to obey his voice. The other was Lethe. She was of an entirely different character. She had long, straight hair, and bore more the appearance of an Indian than a negro woman. She had sharp and spiteful eyes, and continually gave utterance to the language of hatred and revenge. Her husband had been sold. She knew not where she was. An exchange of masters, she was sure, could not be for the worse. She cared not whither they might carry her. Pointing to the scars upon her face, the desperate creature wished that she might see the day when she could wipe them off in some man's blood!

While we were thus learning the history of each other's wretchedness, Eliza was seated in a corner by herself, singing hymns and praying for her children. Wearied from the loss of so much sleep, I could no longer bear up against the advances of that "sweet restorer," and laying down by the side of Robert, on the floor, soon forgot my troubles, and slept until the dawn of day.

In the morning, having swept the yard, and washed ourselves, under Goodin's superintendence, we were ordered to roll up our blankets, and make ready for the continuance of our journey. Clem Ray was informed that he would go no further, Burch, for some cause, having concluded to carry him back to Washington. He was much rejoiced. Shaking hands, we parted in the slave pen at Richmond, and I have not seen him since. But, much to my surprise, since my return, I learned that he had escaped from bondage, and on his way to the free soil of Canada, lodged one night at the house of my brother-in-law in Saratoga, informing my family of the place and the condition in which he left me.

In the afternoon we were drawn up, two abreast, Robert and myself in advance, and in this order, driven by Burch and Goodin from the yard, through the streets of Richmond to the brig *Orleans*. She was a vessel of respectable size, full rigged, and freighted principally with tobacco. We were all on board by five o'clock. Burch brought us each a tin cup and a spoon. There were forty of us in the brig, being all, except Clem, that were in the pen.

With a small pocket knife that had not been taken from me, I began cutting the initials of my name upon the tin cup. The others immediately flocked round me, requesting me to mark theirs in a similar manner. In time, I gratified them all, of which they did not appear to be forgetful.

We were all stowed away in the hold at night, and the hatch barred down. We laid on boxes, or where ever there was room enough to stretch our blankets on the floor.

Burch accompanied us no farther than Richmond, returning from that point to the capital with Clem. Not until the lapse of almost twelve years, to wit, in January last, in the Washington police office, did I set my eyes upon his face again.

James H. Burch was a slave trader—buying men, women and children at low prices, and selling them at an advance. He was a speculator in human flesh—a disreputable calling— and so considered at the South. For the present he disappears from the scenes recorded in this narrative, but he will appear again before its close, not in the character of a man-whipping tyrant, but as an arrested, cringing criminal in a court of law, that failed to do him justice.

CHAPTER 5

After we were all on board, the brig *Orleans* proceeded down James River. Passing into Chesapeake Bay, we arrived next day opposite the city of Norfolk. While lying at anchor, a lighter approached us from the town, bringing four more slaves. Frederick, a boy of eighteen, had been born a slave, as also had Henry, who was some years older. They had both been house servants in the city. Maria was a rather genteel looking colored girl, with a faultless form, but ignorant and extremely vain. The idea of going to New Orleans was pleasing to her. She entertained an extravagantly high opinion of her own attractions. Assuming a haughty mien, she declared to her companions, that immediately on our arrival in New Orleans, she had no doubt, some wealthy single gentleman of good taste would purchase her at once!

But the most prominent of the four, was a man named Arthur. As the lighter approached, he struggled stoutly with his keepers. It was with main force that he was dragged aboard the brig. He protested, in a loud voice, against the treatment he was receiving, and demanded to be released. His face was swollen, and covered with wounds and bruises, and, indeed, one side of it was a complete raw sore. He was forced, with all haste, down the hatchway into the hold. I caught an outline of his story as he was borne struggling along, of which he afterwards gave me a more full relation, and it was as follows: He had long resided in the city of Norfolk, and was a free man. He had a family living there, and was a mason by trade. Having been unusually detained, he was returning late one night to his house in the suburbs of the city, when he was attacked by a gang of persons in an unfrequented street. He fought until his strength failed him. Overpowered at last, he was gagged and bound with ropes, and beaten, until he became insensible. For several days they secreted him in the slave pen at Norfolk—a very common establishment, it appears, in the cities of the South. The night before, he had been taken out and put on board the lighter, which, pushing out from shore, had awaited our arrival. For some time he continued his protestations, and was altogether irreconcilable. At length, however, he became silent. He sank into a gloomy and thoughtful mood, and appeared to be counseling with himself. There was in the man's determined face, something that suggested the thought of desperation.

After leaving Norfolk the handcuffs were taken off, and during the day we were allowed to remain on deck. The captain selected Robert as his waiter, and I was appointed to superintend the cooking department, and the distribution of food and water. I had three assistants, Jim, Cuffee and Jenny. Jenny's business was to prepare the coffee, which consisted of corn meal scorched in a kettle, boiled and sweetened with molasses. Jim and Cuffee baked the hoecake and boiled the bacon.

Standing by a table, formed of a wide board resting on the heads of the barrels, I cut and handed to each a slice of meat and a "dodger" of the bread, and from Jenny's kettle also dipped out for each a cup of the coffee. The use of plates was dispensed with, and their sable fingers took the place of knives and forks. Jim and Cuffee were very demure and attentive to business, somewhat inflated with their situation as second cooks, and without doubt feeling that there was a great responsibility resting on them. I was called steward—a name given me by the captain.

The slaves were fed twice a day, at ten and five o' clock—always receiving the same kind and quantity of fare, and in the same manner as above described. At night we were driven into the hold, and securely fastened down.

Scarcely were we out of sight of land before we were overtaken by a violent storm. The brig rolled and plunged until we feared she would go down. Some were seasick, others on their knees praying, while some were fast holding to each other, paralyzed with fear. The seasickness rendered the place of our confinement loathsome and disgusting. It would have been a happy thing for most of us—it would have saved the agony of many hundred lashes, and miserable deaths at last—had the compassionate sea snatched us that day from the clutches of remorseless men. The thought of Randall and little Emmy sinking down among the monsters of the deep, is a more pleasant contemplation than to think of them as they are now, perhaps, dragging out lives of unrequited toil.

When in sight of the Bahama Banks, at a place called Old Point Compass, or the Hole in the Wall, we were becalmed three days. There was scarcely a breath of air. The waters of the gulf presented a singularly white appearance, like lime water.

In the order of events, I come now to the relation of an occurrence, which I never call to mind but with sensations of regret. I thank God, who has since permitted me to escape from the thralldom of slavery, that through his merciful interposition I was prevented from imbruing my hands in the blood of his creatures. Let not those who have never been placed in like circumstances, judge me harshly. Until they have been chained and beaten—until they find them, in the situation I was, borne away from home and family towards a land of bondage let them refrain from saying what they would not do for liberty. How far I should have been justified in the sight of God and man, it is unnecessary now to speculate upon. It is enough to say that I am able to congratulate myself upon the harmless termination of an affair which threatened, for a time, to be attended with serious results.

Towards evening, on the first day of the calm, Arthur and myself were in the bow of the vessel, seated on the windlass. We were conversing together of the probable destiny that awaited us, and mourning together over our misfortunes. Arthur said, and I agreed with him, that death was far less terrible than the living prospect that was before us. For a long time we talked of our children, our past lives, and of the probabilities of escape. Obtaining possession of the brig was suggested by one of us. We discussed the possibility of our being able, in such an event, to make our way to the harbor of New York. I knew little of the compass; but the idea of risking the experiment was eagerly entertained. The chances, for and against us, in an encounter with the crew, was canvassed. Who could be relied upon, and who could not, the proper time and manner of the attack, were all talked over and over again. From the moment the plot suggested itself I began to hope. I revolved it constantly in my mind. As difficulty after difficulty arose, some ready conceit was at hand, demonstrating how it could be overcome. While others slept, Arthur and I were maturing our plans. At length, with much caution, Robert was gradually made acquainted with our intentions. He approved of them at once, and entered into the conspiracy with a zealous spirit. There was not another slave we dared to trust. Brought up in fear and ignorance as they are, it can scarcely be conceived how servilely they will cringe before a white man's look. It was not safe to deposit so bold a secret with any of them, and finally we three resolved to take upon ourselves alone the fearful responsibility of the attempt.

At night, as has been said, we were driven into the hold,

and the hatch barred down. How to reach the deck was the first difficulty that presented itself. On the bow of the brig, however, I had observed the small boat lying bottom upwards. It occurred to me that by secreting ourselves underneath it, we would not be missed from the crowd, as they were hurried down into the hold at night. I was selected to make the experiment, in order to satisfy ourselves of its feasibility. The next evening, accordingly, after supper, watching my opportunity, I hastily concealed myself beneath it. Lying close upon the deck, I could see what was going on around me, while wholly unperceived myself. In the morning, as they came up, I slipped from my hiding place without being observed. The result was entirely satisfactory.

The captain and mate slept in the cabin of the former. From Robert, who had frequent occasion, in his capacity of waiter, to make observations in that quarter, we ascertained the exact position of their respective berths. He further informed us that there were always two pistols and a cutlass lying on the table. The crew's cook slept in the cook galley on deck, a sort of vehicle on wheels, that could be moved about as convenience required, while the sailors, numbering only six, either slept in the forecastle, or in hammocks swung among the rigging.

Finally our arrangements were all completed. Arthur and I were to steal silently to the captain's cabin, seize the pistols and cutlass, and as quickly as possible dispatch him and the mate. Robert, with a club, was to stand by the door leading from the deck down into the cabin, and, in case of necessity, beat back the sailors, until we could hurry to his assistance. We were to proceed then as circumstances might require. Should the attack be so sudden and successful as to prevent resistance, the hatch was to remain barred down; otherwise the slaves were to be called up, and in the crowd, and hurry, and confusion of the time, we resolved to regain our liberty or lose our lives. I was then to assume the unaccustomed place of pilot, and, steering northward, we trusted that some lucky wind might bear us to the soil of freedom.

The mate's name was Biddee, the captain's I cannot now recall, though I rarely ever forget a name once heard. The captain was a small, genteel man, erect and prompt, with a proud bearing, and looked the personification of courage. If he is still living, and these pages should chance to meet his eye, he will learn a fact connected with the voyage of the brig, from Richmond to New Orleans, in 1841, not entered on his logbook.

We were all prepared, and impatiently waiting an opportunity of putting our designs into execution, when they were frustrated by a sad and unforeseen event. Robert was taken ill. It was soon announced that he had the smallpox. He continued to grow worse, and four days previous to our arrival in New Orleans he died. One of the sailors sewed him in his blanket, with a large stone from the ballast at his feet, and then laying him on a hatchway, and elevating it with tackles above the railing, the inanimate body of poor Robert was consigned to the white waters of the gulf.

We were all panic-stricken by the appearance of the smallpox. The captain ordered lime to be scattered through the hold, and other prudent precautions to be taken. The death of Robert, however, and the presence of the malady, oppressed me sadly, and I gazed out over the great waste of waters with a spirit that was indeed disconsolate.

An evening or two after Robert's burial, I was leaning on the hatchway near the forecastle, full of desponding thoughts, when a sailor in a kind voice asked me why I was so down-hearted. The tone and manner of the man assured me, and I answered, because I was a freeman, and had been kidnapped. He remarked that it was enough to make any one down-hearted, and continued to interrogate me until he learned the particulars of my whole history. He was evidently much interested in my behalf, and, in the blunt speech of a sailor, swore he would aid me all he could, if it "split his timbers." I requested him to furnish me pen, ink and paper, in order that I might write to some of my friends. He promised to obtain them—but how I could use them undiscovered was a difficulty. If I could only get into the forecastle while his watch was off, and the other sailors asleep, the thing could be accomplished. The small boat instantly occurred to me. He thought we were not far from the Balize, at the mouth of the Mississippi, and it was necessary that the letter be written soon, or the opportunity would be lost. Accordingly by arrangement, I managed the next night to secret myself again under the longboat. His watch was off at twelve. I saw him pass into the forecastle, and in about an hour followed him. He was nodding over a table, half asleep, on which a sickly light was flickering, and on which also was a pen and sheet of paper. As I entered he aroused, beckoned me to a seat beside him, and pointed to the paper. I directed the letter to Henry B. Northup, of Sandy Hill—stating that I had been kidnapped, was then on board the brig *Orleans*, bound for New Orleans; that it was then impossible for me to conjecture my ultimate destination, and requesting he would take measures to rescue me. The letter was sealed and directed, and Manning, having read it, promised to deposit it in the New Orleans post office. I hastened back to my place under the longboat, and in the morning, as the slaves came up and were walking round, crept out unnoticed and mingled with them.

My good friend, whose name was John Manning, was an Englishman by birth, and a noble-hearted generous sailor as ever walked a deck, he had lived in Boston—was a tall, well-built man, about twenty four years old, with a face somewhat pock-marked, but full of benevolent expression.

Nothing to vary the monotony of our daily life occurred, until we reached New Orleans. On coming to the levee, and before the vessel was made fast, I saw Manning leap on shore and hurry away into the city. As he started off he looked back over his shoulder significantly, giving me to understand the object of his errand. Presently he returned, and passing close by me, hunched me with his elbow, with a peculiar wink, as much as to say, "it is all right."

The letter, as I have since learned, reached Sandy Hill. Mr. Northup visited Albany and laid it before Governor Seward, but inasmuch as it gave no definite information as to my probable locality, it was not, at that time, deemed advisable to institute measures for my liberation. It was concluded to delay, trusting that a knowledge of where I was might eventually be obtained.

A happy and touching scene was witnessed immediately upon our reaching the levee. Just as Manning left the brig, on his way to the post office, two men came up and called aloud for Arthur. The latter, as he recognized them, was almost crazy with delight. He could hardly be restrained from leaping over the brig's side; and when they met soon after, he grasped them by the hand, and clung to them a long, long time. They were men from Norfolk, which had come on to New Orleans to rescue him. His kidnappers, they informed him, had been arrested, and were then confined in the Norfolk prison. They conversed a few moments with the captain, and then departed with the rejoicing Arthur.

But in all the crowd that thronged the wharf, there was no one who knew or cared for me. Not one. No familiar voice greeted my ears, nor was there a single face that I had ever seen. Soon Arthur would rejoin his family, and have the satisfaction of seeing his wrongs avenged; my family, alas, should I ever see them more? There was a feeling of utter desolation in my heart, filling it with a despairing and regretful sense, that I had not gone down with Robert to the bottom of the sea.

Very soon traders and consignees came on board. One, a tall, thin-faced man, with light complexion and a little bent, made his appearance, with a paper in his hand. Burch's gang, consisting of myself, Eliza and her children, Harry, Lethe, and some others, who had joined us at Richmond, were consigned to him. This gentleman was Mr. Theophilus Freeman. Reading from his paper, he called, "Platt." No one answered. The name was called again and again, but still there was no reply. Then Lethe was called, then Eliza, then Harry, until the list was finished, each one stepping forward as his or her name was called.

"Captain, where's Platt?" demanded Theophilus Freeman.

The captain was unable to inform him, no one being on board answering to that name.

"Who shipped *that* nigger?" he again inquired of the captain, pointing to me.

"Burch," replied the captain.

"Your name is Platt—you answer my description. Why don't you come forward?" he demanded of me, in an angry tone.

I informed him that was not my name; that I had never been called by it, but that I had no objection to it as I knew of.

"Well, I will learn you your name," said he; "and so you won't forget it either, by—," he added.

Mr. Theophilus Freeman, by the way, was not a whit behind his partner, Burch, in the matter of blasphemy. On the vessel I had gone by the name of "Steward," and this was the first time I had ever been designated as Platt—the name forwarded by Burch to his consignee. From the vessel I observed the chain gang at work on the levee. We passed near them as we were driven to Freeman's slave pen. This pen is very similar to Goodin's in Richmond, except the yard was enclosed by plank, standing upright, with ends sharpened, instead of brick walls.

Including us, there were now at least fifty in this pen. Depositing our blankets in one of the small buildings in the yard, and having been called up and fed, we were allowed to saunter about the enclosure until night, when we wrapped our blankets round us and laid down under the shed, or in the loft, or in the open yard, just as each one preferred.

It was but a short time I closed my eyes that night. Thought was busy in my brain. Could it be possible that I was thousands of miles from home—that I had been driven through the streets like a dumb beast—that I had been chained and beaten without mercy—that I was even then herded with a drove of slaves, a slave myself? Were the events of the last few weeks realities indeed?—or was I passing only through the dismal phases of a long, protracted dream? It was no illusion. My cup of sorrow was full to overflowing. Then I lifted up my hands to God, and in the still watches of the night, surrounded by the sleeping forms of my companions, begged for mercy on the poor, forsaken captive. To the Almighty Father of us all—the freeman and the slave—I poured forth the supplications of a broken spirit, imploring strength from on high to bear up against the burden of my troubles, until the morning light aroused the slumberers, ushering in another day of bondage.

CHAPTER 6

The very amiable, pious-hearted Mr. Theophilus Freeman, partner or consignee of James H. Burch, and keeper of the slave pen in New Orleans, was out among his animals early in the morning. With an occasional kick of the older men and women, and many a sharp crack of the whip about the ears of the younger slaves, it was not long before they were all astir, and wide awake. Mr. Theophilus Freeman bustled about in a very industrious manner, getting his property ready for the salesroom, intending, no doubt, to do that day a rousing business.

In the first place we were required to wash thoroughly, and those with beards, to shave. We were then furnished with a new suit each, cheap, but clean. The men had hat, coat, shirt, pants and shoes; the women frocks of calico, and handkerchiefs to bind about their heads. We were now conducted into a large room in the front part of the building to which the yard was attached, in order to be properly trained, before the admission of customers. The men were arranged on one side of the room, the women on the other. The tallest was placed at the head of the row, then the next tallest, and so on in the order of their respective heights. Emily was at the foot of the line of women. Freeman charged us to remember our places; exhorted us to appear smart and lively,—sometimes threatening, and again, holding out various inducements. During the day he exercised us in the art of "looking smart," and of moving to our places with exact precision.

After being fed, in the afternoon, we were again paraded and made to dance. Bob, a colored boy, who had some time belonged to Freeman, played on the violin. Standing near him, I made bold to inquire if he could play the "Virginia Reel." He answered he could not, and asked me if I could play. Replying in the affirmative, he handed me the violin. I struck up a tune, and finished it. Freeman ordered me to continue playing, and seemed well pleased, telling Bob that I far excelled him—a remark that seemed to grieve my musical companion very much.

Next day many customers called to examine Freeman's "new lot." The latter gentleman was very loquacious, dwelling at much length upon our several good points and qualities. He would make us hold up our heads, walk briskly back and forth, while customers would feel of our hands and arms and bodies, turn us about, ask us what we could do, make us open our mouths and show our teeth, precisely as a jockey examines a horse which he is about to barter for or purchase. Sometimes a man or woman was taken back to the small house in the yard, stripped, and inspected more minutely. Scars upon a slave's back were considered evidence of a rebellious or unruly spirit, and hurt his sale.

One old gentleman, who said he wanted a coachman, appeared to take a fancy to me. From his conversation with Freeman, I learned he was a resident in the city. I very much desired that he would buy me, because I conceived it would not be difficult to make my escape from New Orleans on some northern vessel. Freeman asked him fifteen hundred dollars for me. The old gentleman insisted it was too much, as times were very hard. Freeman, however, declared that I was sound and healthy, of a good constitution, and intelligent. He made it a point to enlarge upon my musical attainments. The old gentleman argued quite adroitly that there was nothing extraordinary about the nigger, and finally, to my regret, went out, saying he would call again. During the day, however, a number of sales were made. David and Caroline were purchased together by a Natchez planter. They left us, grinning broadly, and in the most happy state of mind, caused by the fact of their not being separated. Lethe was sold to a planter of Baton Rouge, her eyes flashing with anger as she was led away.

The same man also purchased Randall. The little fellow was made to jump, and run across the floor, and perform many other feats, exhibiting his activity and condition. All the time the trade was going on, Eliza was crying aloud, and wringing her hands. She besought the man not to buy him, unless he also bought herself and Emily. She promised, in that case, to be the most faithful slave that ever lived. The man answered that he could not afford it, and then Eliza burst into a paroxysm of grief, weeping plaintively. Freeman turned round to her, savagely, with his whip in his uplifted hand, ordering her to stop her noise, or he would flog her. He would not have such work—such snivelling; and unless she ceased that minute, he would take her to the yard and give her a hundred lashes. Yes, he would take the nonsense out of her pretty quick—if he didn't, might he be d—d. Eliza shrunk before him, and tried to wipe away her tears, but it was all in vain. She wanted to be with her children, she said, the little time she had to live. All the frowns and threats of Freeman, could not wholly silence the afflicted mother. She kept on begging and beseeching them, most piteously, not to separate the three. Over and over again she told them how she loved her boy. A great many times she repeated her former promises how very faithful and obedient she would be; how hard she would labor day and night, to the last moment of her life, if he would only buy them all together. But it was of no avail; the man could not afford it. The bargain was agreed upon, and Randall must go alone. Then Eliza ran to him; embraced him passionately; kissed him again and again; told him to remember her—all the while her tears falling in the boy's face like rain.

Freeman damned her, calling her a blubbering, bawling wench, and ordered her to go to her place, and behave herself, and be somebody. He swore he wouldn't stand such stuff but a little longer. He would soon give her something to cry about, if she was not mighty careful, and *that* she might depend upon.

The planter from Baton Rouge, with his new purchases, was ready to depart.

"Don't cry, mama. I will be a good boy. Don't cry," said Randall, looking back, as they passed out of the door.

What has become of the lad, God knows. It was a mournful scene indeed. I would have cried myself if I had dared.

That night, nearly all who came in on the brig *Orleans*, were taken ill. They complained of violent pain in the head and back. Little Emily—a thing unusual with her— cried constantly. In the morning a physician was called in, but was unable to determine the nature of our complaint. While examining me, and asking questions touching my symptoms, I gave it as my opinion that it was an attack of smallpox—mentioning the fact of Robert's death as the reason of my belief. It might be so indeed, he thought, and he would send for the head physician of the hospital. Shortly, the head physician came—a small, light-haired man, whom they called Dr. Carr. He pronounced it smallpox, whereupon there was much alarm throughout the yard. Soon after Dr. Carr left, Eliza, Emmy, Harry and myself were put into a hack and driven to the hospital—a large white marble building, standing on the outskirts of the city. Harry and I were placed in a room in one of the upper stories. I became very sick. For three days I was entirely blind. While lying in this state one day, Bob came in, saying to Dr. Carr that Freeman had sent him over to inquire how we were getting on. Tell him, said the doctor, that Platt is very bad, but that if he survives until nine o'clock, he may recover.

I expected to die. Though there was little in the prospect before me worth living for, the near approach of death appalled me. I thought I could have been resigned to yield up my life in the bosom of my family, but to expire in the midst of strangers, under such circumstances, was a bitter reflection.

There were a great number in the hospital, of both sexes, and of all ages. In the rear of the building coffins were manufactured. When one died, the bell tolled—a signal to the undertaker to come and bear away the body to the potter's field. Many times, each day and night, the tolling bell sent forth its melancholy voice, announcing another death. But my time had not yet come. The crisis having passed, I began to revive, and at the end of two weeks and two days, returned with Harry to the pen, bearing upon my face the effects of the malady, which to this day continues to disfigure it. Eliza and Emily were also brought back next day in a hack, and again were we paraded in the salesroom, for the inspection and examination of purchasers. I still indulged the hope that the old gentleman in search of a coachman would call again, as he had promised, and purchase me. In that event I felt an abiding confidence that I would soon regain my liberty. Customer after customer entered, but the old gentleman never made his appearance.

At length, one day, while we were in the yard, Freeman came out and ordered us to our places, in the great room. A gentleman was waiting for us as we entered, and inasmuch as he will be often mentioned in the progress of this narrative, a description of his personal appearance, and my estimation of his character, at first sight, may not be out of place.

He was a man above the ordinary height, somewhat bent

and stooping forward. He was a good-looking man, and appeared to have reached about the middle age of life. There was nothing repulsive in his presence; but on the other hand, there was something cheerful and attractive in his face, and in his tone of voice. The finer elements were all kindly mingled in his breast, as anyone could see. He moved about among us, asking many questions, as to what we could do, and what labor we had been accustomed to; if we thought we would like to live with him, and would be good boys if he would buy us, and other interrogatories of like character.

After some further inspection, and conversation touching prices, he finally offered Freeman one thousand dollars for me, nine hundred for Harry, and seven hundred for Eliza. Whether the smallpox had depreciated our value, or from what cause Freeman had concluded to fall five hundred dollars from the price I was before held at, I cannot say. At any rate, after a little shrewd reflection, he announced his acceptance of the offer.

As soon as Eliza heard it, she was in an agony again. By this time she had become haggard and hollow-eyed with sickness and with sorrow. It would be a relief if I could consistently pass over in silence the scene that now ensued. It recalls memories more mournful and affecting than any language can portray. I have seen mothers kissing for the last time the faces of their dead offspring; I have seen them looking down into the grave, as the earth fell with a dull sound upon their coffins, hiding them from their eyes forever; but never have I seen such an exhibition of intense, unmeasured, and unbounded grief, as when Eliza was parted from her child. She broke from her place in the line of women, and rushing down where Emily was standing, caught her in her arms. The child, sensible of some impending danger, instinctively fastened her hands around her mother's neck and nestled her little head upon her bosom. Freeman sternly ordered her to be quiet, but she did not heed him. He caught her by the arm and pulled her rudely, but she only clung the closer to the child. Then, with a volley of great oaths, he struck her such a heartless blow, that she staggered backward, and was like to fall. Oh! how piteously then did she beseech and beg and pray that they might not be separated. Why could they not be purchased together! Why not let her have one of her dear children! "Mercy, mercy, master!" she cried, falling on her knees. "Please, master, buy Emily. I can never work any if she is taken from me: I will die."

Freeman interfered again, but, disregarding him, she still plead most earnestly, telling how Randall had been taken from her—how she never would see him again, and now it was too bad—oh, God! it was too bad, too cruel, to take her away from Emily—her pride—her only darling, that could not live, it was so young, without its mother!

Finally, after much more of supplication, the purchaser of Eliza stepped forward, evidently affected, and said to Freeman he would buy Emily, and asked him what her price was.

"What is her *price*? *Buy* her?" was the responsive interrogatory of Theophilus Freeman. And instantly answering his own inquiry, he added, "I won't sell her. She's not for sale."

The man remarked he was not in need of one so young— that it would be of no profit to him, but since the mother was so fond of her, rather than see them separated, he would pay a reasonable price. But to this humane proposal Freeman was entirely deaf. He would not sell her then on any account whatever. There were heaps and piles of money to be made of her, he said, when she was a few years older. There were men enough in New Orleans who would give five thousand dollars for such an extra, handsome, fancy piece as Emily would be, rather than not get her. No, no, he would not sell her then. She was a beauty—a picture—a doll—one of the regular bloods—none of your thick-lipped, bullet-headed, cotton-picking niggers—if she was might he be d—d.

When Eliza heard Freeman's determination not to part with Emily, she became absolutely frantic.

"I will *not* go without her. They shall not take her from me," she fairly shrieked, her shrieks commingling with the loud and angry voice of Freeman, commanding her to be silent.

Meantime Harry and myself had been to the yard and returned with our blankets, and were at the front door ready to leave. Our purchaser stood near us, gazing at Eliza with an expression indicative of regret at having bought her at the expense of so much sorrow. We waited some time, when, finally, Freeman, out of patience, tore Emily from her mother by main force, the two clinging to each other with all their might.

"Don't leave me, mama—don't leave me," screamed the child, as its mother was pushed harshly forward; "Don't leave me—come back, mama," she still cried, stretching forth her little arms imploringly. But she cried in vain. Out of the door and into the street we were quickly hurried. Still we could hear her calling to her mother, "Come back—don't leave me—come back, mama," until her infant voice grew faint and still more faint, and gradually died away, as distance intervened, and finally was wholly lost.

Eliza never after saw or heard of Emily or Randall. Day nor night, however, were they ever absent from her memory. In the cotton field, in the cabin, always and everywhere, she was talking of them—often *to* them, as if they were actually present. Only when absorbed in that illusion, or asleep, did she ever have a moment's comfort afterwards.

She was no common slave, as has been said. To a large share of natural intelligence which she possessed, was added a general knowledge and information on most subjects. She had enjoyed opportunities such as are afforded to very few of her oppressed class. She had been lifted up into the regions of a higher life. Freedom—freedom for herself and for her offspring, for many years had been her cloud by day, her pillar of fire by night. In her pilgrimage through the wilderness of bondage, with eyes fixed upon that hope-inspiring beacon, she had at length ascended to "the top of Pisgah," and beheld "the land of promise." In an unexpected moment she was utterly overwhelmed with disappointment and despair. The glorious vision of liberty faded from her sight as they led her away into captivity. Now "she weepeth sore in the night, and tears are on her cheeks: all her friends have dealt treacherously with her: they have become her enemies."

CHAPTER 7

On leaving the New Orleans slave pen, Harry and I followed our new master through the streets, while Eliza, crying and turning back, was forced along by Freeman and his minions, until we found ourselves on board the steamboat *Rodolph*, then lying at the levee. In the course of half an hour we were moving briskly up the Mississippi, bound for some point on Red River. There were quite a number of slaves on board beside ourselves, just purchased in the New Orleans market. I remember a Mr. Kelsow, who was said to be a well-known and extensive planter, had in charge a gang of women.

Our master's name was William Ford. He resided then in the "Great Pine Woods," in the parish of Avoyelles, situated on the right bank of Red River, in the heart of Louisiana. He is now a Baptist preacher. Throughout the whole parish of Avoyelles, and especially along both shores of Bayou Boeuf, where he is more intimately known, he is accounted by his fellow-citizens as a worthy minister of God. In many northern minds, perhaps, the idea of a man holding his brother man in servitude, and the traffic in human flesh, may seem altogether incompatible with their conceptions of a moral or religious life. From descriptions of such men as Burch and Freeman, and others hereinafter mentioned, they are led to despise and execrate the whole class of slaveholders, indiscriminately. But I was sometime his slave, and had an opportunity of learning well his character and disposition, and it is but simple justice to him when I say, in my opinion, there never was a more kind, noble, candid, Christian man than William Ford. The influences and associations that had always surrounded him, blinded him to the inherent wrong at the bottom of the system of slavery. He never doubted the moral right of one man holding another in subjection. Looking through the same medium with his fathers before him, he saw things in the same light. Brought up under other circumstances and other influences, his notions would undoubtedly have been different. Nevertheless, he was a model master, walking uprightly, according to the light of his understanding, and fortunate was the slave who came to his possession. Were all men such as he, slavery would be deprived of more than half its bitterness.

We were two days and three nights on board the steamboat *Rodolph*, during which time nothing of particular interest occurred. I was now known as Platt, the name given me by Burch, and by which I was designated through the whole period of my servitude. Eliza was sold by the name of "Dradey." She was so distinguished in the conveyance to Ford, now on record in the recorder's office in New Orleans.

On our passage I was constantly reflecting on my situation, and consulting with myself on the best course to pursue in order to effect my ultimate escape. Sometimes, not only then, but afterwards, I was almost on the point of disclosing fully to Ford the facts of my history. I am inclined now to the opinion it would have resulted in my benefit. This course was often considered, but through fear of its miscarriage, never put into execution, until eventually my transfer and his pecuniary embarrassments rendered it evidently unsafe. Afterwards, under other masters, unlike William Ford, I knew well enough the slightest knowledge of my real character would consign me at once to the remoter depths of slavery. I was too costly a chattel to be lost, and was well aware that I would be taken farther on, into some by-place, over the Texan border, perhaps, and sold; that I would be disposed of as the thief disposes of his stolen horse, if my right to freedom was even whispered. So I resolved to lock the secret closely in my heart—never to utter one word or syllable as to who or what I—trusting in Providence and my own shrewdness for deliverance.

At length we left the steamboat *Rodolph* at a place called Alexandria, several hundred miles from New Orleans. It is a small town on the southern shore of Red River. Having remained there over night, we entered the morning train of cars, and were soon at Bayou Lamourie, a still smaller place, distant eighteen miles from Alexandria. At that time it was the termination of the railroad. Ford's plantation was situated on the Texas road, twelve miles from Lamourie, in the Great Pine Woods. This distance, it was announced to us, must be traveled on foot, there being public conveyances no farther. Accordingly we all set out in the company of Ford. It was an excessively hot day. Harry, Eliza, and myself were yet weak, and the bottoms of our feet were very tender from the effects of the smallpox. We proceeded slowly, Ford telling us to take our time and sit down and rest whenever we desired—a privilege that was taken advantage of quite frequently. After leaving Lamourie and crossing two plantations, one belonging to Mr. Carnell, the other to a Mr. Flint, we reached the Pine Woods, a wilderness that stretches to the Sabine River.

The whole country about Red River is low and marshy. The Pine Woods, as they are called, is comparatively upland, with frequent small intervals, however, running through them. This upland is covered with numerous trees—the white oak, the chincopin, resembling chestnut, but principally the yellow pine. They are of great size, running up sixty feet, and perfectly straight. The woods were full of cattle, very shy and wild, dashing away in herds, with a loud snuff, at our approach. Some of them were marked or branded, the rest appeared to be in their wild and untamed state. They are much smaller than northern breeds, and the peculiarity about them that most attracted my attention was their horns. They stand out from the sides of the head precisely straight, like two iron spikes.

At noon we reached a cleared piece of ground containing three or four acres. Upon it was a small, unpainted, wooden house, a corn crib, or, as we would say, a barn, and a log kitchen, standing about a rod from the house. It was the summer residence of Mr. Martin. Rich planters, having large establishments on Bayou Boeuf, are accustomed to spend the warmer season in these woods. Here they find clear water and delightful shades. In fact, these retreats are to the planters of that section of the country what New Port and Saratoga are to the wealthier inhabitants of northern cities.

We were sent around into the kitchen, and supplied with sweet potatoes, corn-bread, and bacon, while Master Ford dined with Martin in the house. There were several slaves about the premises. Martin came out and took a look at us, asking Ford the price of each, if we were green hands, and so forth, and making inquiries in relation to the slave market generally.

After a long rest we set forth again, following the Texas road, which had the appearance of being very rarely traveled. For five miles we passed through continuous woods without observing a single habitation. At length, just as the sun was sinking in the west, we entered another opening, containing some twelve or fifteen acres.

In this opening stood a house much larger than Mr. Martin's. It was two stories high, with a piazza in front. In the rear of it was also a log kitchen, poultry house, corn cribs, and several negro cabins. Near the house was a peach orchard, and gardens of orange and pomegranate trees. The space was entirely surrounded by woods, and covered with a carpet of rich, rank verdure. It was a quiet, lonely, pleasant place—literally a green spot in the wilderness. It was the residence of my master, William Ford.

As we approached, a yellow girl—her name was Rose—was standing on the piazza. Going to the door, she called her mistress, who presently came running out to meet her lord. She kissed him, and laughingly demanded if he had bought "those niggers." Ford said he had, and told us to go round to Sally's cabin and rest ourselves. Turning the corner of the house, we discovered Sally washing—her two baby children near her, rolling on the grass. They jumped up and toddled towards us, looked at us a moment like a brace of rabbits, then ran back to their mother as if afraid

Sally conducted us into the cabin, told us to lay down our bundles and be seated, for she was sure that we were tired. Just then John, the cook, a boy some sixteen years of age, and blacker than any crow, came running in, looked steadily in our faces, then turning round, without saying as much as "how d'ye do," ran back to the kitchen, laughing loudly, as if our coming was a great joke indeed.

Much wearied with our walk, as soon as it was dark, Harry and I wrapped our blankets round us, and laid down upon the cabin floor. My thoughts, as usual, wandered back to my wife and children. The consciousness of my real situation; the hopelessness of any effort to escape through the wide forests of Avoyelles, pressed heavily upon me, yet my heart was at home in Saratoga.

I was awakened early in the morning by the voice of Master Ford, calling Rose. She hastened into the house to dress the children, Sally to the field to milk the cows, while John was busy in the kitchen preparing breakfast. In the meantime Harry and I were strolling about the yard, looking at our new quarters. Just after breakfast a colored man, driving three yoke of oxen, attached to a wagon load of lumber, drove into the opening. He was a slave of Ford's, named Walton, the husband of Rose. By the way, Rose was a native of Washington, and had been brought from thence five years before. She had never seen Eliza, but she had heard of Berry, and they knew the same streets, and the same people, either personally, or by reputation. They became fast friends immediately, and talked a great deal together of old times, and of friends they had left behind.

Ford was at that time a wealthy man. Besides his seat in the Pine Woods, he owned a large lumbering establishment on Indian Creek, four miles distant, and also, in his wife's right, an extensive plantation and many slaves on Bayou Boeuf.

Walton had come with his load of lumber from the mills on Indian Creek. Ford directed us to return with him, saying he would follow us as soon as possible. Before leaving, Mistress Ford called me into the store-room, and handed me, as it is there termed, a tin bucket of molasses for Harry and myself.

Eliza was still wringing her hands and deploring the loss of her children. Ford tried as much as possible to console her—told her she need not work very hard; that she might remain with Rose, and assist the madam in the house affairs.

Riding with Walton in the wagon, Harry and I became quite well acquainted with him long before reaching Indian Creek. He was a "born thrall" of Ford's, and spoke kindly and affectionately of him, as a child would speak of his own father. In answer to his inquiries from whence I came, I told him from Washington. Of that city, he had heard much from his wife, Rose, and all the way plied me with many extravagant and absurd questions.

On reaching the mills at Indian Creek, we found two more of Ford's slaves, Sam and Antony. Sam, also, was a Washingtonian, having been brought out in the same gang with Rose. He had worked on a farm near Georgetown. Antony was a blacksmith, from Kentucky, who had been in his present master's service about ten years. Sam knew Burch, and when informed that he was the trader who had sent me on from Washington, it was remarkable how well we agreed upon the subject of his superlative rascality. He had forwarded Sam, also.

On Ford's arrival at the mill, we were employed in piling lumber, and chopping logs, which occupation we continued during the remainder of the summer.

We usually spent our Sabbaths at the opening, on which days our master would gather all his slaves about him, and read and expound the Scriptures. He sought to inculcate in our minds feelings of kindness towards each other, of dependence upon God—setting forth the rewards promised unto those who lead an upright and prayerful life. Seated in the doorway of his house, surrounded by his manservants and his maidservants, who looked earnestly into the good man's face, he spoke of the loving kindness of the Creator, and of the life that is to come. Often did the voice of prayer ascend from his lips to heaven, the only sound that broke the solitude of the place.

In the course of the summer Sam became deeply convicted, his mind dwelling intensely on the subject of religion. His mistress gave him a Bible, which he carried with him to his work. Whatever leisure time was allowed him, he spent in perusing it, though it was only with great difficulty that he could master any part of it. I often read to him, a favor which he well repaid me by many expressions of gratitude. Sam's piety was frequently observed by white men who came to the mill, and the remark it most generally provoked was, that a man like Ford, who allowed his slaves to have Bibles, was "not fit to own a nigger."

He, however, lost nothing by his kindness. It is a fact I have more than once observed, that those who treated their slaves most leniently, were rewarded by the greatest amount of labor. I know it from my own experience. It was a source of pleasure to surprise Master Ford with a greater day's work than was required, while, under subsequent masters, there was no prompter to extra effort but the overseer's lash.

It was the desire of Ford's approving voice that suggested to me an idea that resulted to his profit. The lumber we were manufacturing was contracted to be delivered at Lamourie. It had hitherto been transported by land, and was an important item of expense. Indian Creek, upon which the mills were situated, was a narrow but deep stream emptying into Bayou Boeuf. In some places it was not more than twelve feet wide, and much obstructed with trunks of trees. Bayou Boeuf was connected with Bayou Lamourie. I ascertained the distance from the mills to the point on the latter bayou, where our lumber was to be delivered, was but a few miles less by land than by water. Provided the creek could be made navigable for rafts, it occurred to me that the expense of transportation would be materially diminished.

Adam Taydem, a little white man, who had been a soldier in Florida, and had strolled into that distant region, was foreman and superintendent of the mills. He scouted the idea; but Ford, when I laid it before him, received it favorably, and permitted me to try the experiment.

Having removed the obstructions, I made up a narrow raft, consisting of twelve cribs. At this business I think I was quite skillful, not having forgotten my experience years before on the Champlain canal. I labored hard, being extremely anxious to succeed, both from a desire to please my master, and to show Adam Taydem that my scheme was not such a visionary one as he incessantly pronounced it. One hand could manage three cribs. I took charge of the forward three, and commenced poling down the creek. In due time we entered the first bayou, and finally reached our destination in a shorter period of time than I had anticipated.

The arrival of the raft at Lamourie created a sensation, while Mr. Ford loaded me with commendations. On all sides I heard Ford's Platt pronounced the "smartest nigger in the

Pine Woods"—in fact I was the Fulton of Indian Creek. I was not insensible to the praise bestowed upon me, and enjoyed, especially, my triumph over Taydem, whose half-malicious ridicule had stung my pride. From this time the entire control of bringing the lumber to Lamourie was placed in my hands until the contract was fulfilled.

Indian Creek, in its whole length, flows through a magnificent forest. There dwells on its shore a tribe of Indians, a remnant of the Chickasaws or Chickopees, if I remember rightly. They live in simple huts, ten or twelve feet square, constructed of pine poles and covered with bark. They subsist principally on the flesh of the deer, the coon, and opossum, all of which are plenty in these woods. Sometimes they exchange venison for a little corn and whisky with the planters on the bayous. Their usual dress is buckskin breeches and calico hunting shirts of fantastic colors, buttoned from belt to chin. They wear brass rings on their wrists, and in their ears and noses. The dress of the squaws is very similar. They are fond of dogs and horses—owning many of the latter, of a small, tough breed—and are skillful riders. Their bridles, girths and saddles were made of raw skins of animals; their stirrups of a certain kind of wood. Mounted astride their ponies, men and women, I have seen them dash out into the woods at the utmost of their speed, following narrow winding paths, and dodging trees, in a manner that eclipsed the most miraculous feats of civilized equestrianism. Circling away in various directions, the forest echoing and re-echoing with their whoops, they would presently return at the same dashing, headlong speed with which they started. Their village was on Indian Creek, known as Indian Castle, but their range extended to the Sabine River. Occasionally a tribe from Texas would come over on a visit, and then there was indeed a carnival in the "Great Pine Woods." Chief of the tribe was Cascalla; second in rank, John Baltese, his son-in-law; with both of whom, as with many others of the tribe, I became acquainted during my frequent voyages down the creek with rafts. Sam and myself would often visit them when the day's task was done. They were obedient to the chief; the word of Cascalla was their law. They were a rude but harmless people, and enjoyed their wild mode of life. They had little fancy for the open country, the cleared lands on the shores of the bayous, but preferred to hide themselves within the shadows of the forest. They worshiped the Great Spirit, loved whisky, and were happy.

On one occasion I was present at a dance, when a roving herd from Texas had encamped in their village. The entire carcass of a deer was roasting before a large fire, which threw its light a long distance among the trees under which they were assembled. When they had formed in a ring, men and squaws alternately, a sort of Indian fiddle set up an indescribable tune. It was a continuous, melancholy kind of wavy sound, with the slightest possible variation. At the first note, if indeed there was more than one note in the whole tune, they circled around, trotting after each other, and giving utterance to a guttural, sing-song noise, equally as nondescript as the music of the fiddle. At the end of the third circuit, they would stop suddenly, whoop as if their lungs would crack, then break from the ring, forming in couples, man and squaw, each jumping backwards as far as possible from the other, then forwards—which graceful feat having been twice or thrice accomplished, they would form in a ring, and go trotting round again. The best dancer appeared to be considered the one who could whoop the loudest, jump the farthest, and utter the most excruciating noise. At intervals, one or more would leave the dancing circle, and going to the fire, cut from the roasting carcass a slice of venison.

In a hole, shaped like a mortar, cut in the trunk of a fallen tree, they pounded corn with a wooden pestle, and of the meal made cake. Alternately they danced and ate. Thus were the visitors from Texas entertained by the dusky sons and daughters of the Chicopees, and such is a description, as I saw it, of an Indian ball in the Pine Woods of Avoyelles.

In the autumn, I left the mills, and was employed at the opening. One day the mistress was urging Ford to procure a loom, in order that Sally might commence weaving cloth for the winter garments of the slaves. He could not imagine where one was to be found, when I suggested that the easiest way to get one would be to make it, informing him at the same time, that I was a sort of "Jack at all trades," and would attempt it, with his permission. It was granted very readily, and I was allowed to go to a neighboring planter's to inspect one before commencing the undertaking. At length it was finished and pronounced by Sally to be perfect. She could easily weave her task of fourteen yards, milk the cows, and have leisure time besides each day. It worked so well, I was continued in the employment of making looms, which were taken down to the plantation on the bayou.

At this time one John M. Tibeats, a carpenter, came to the opening to do some work on master's house. I was directed to quit the looms and assist him. For two weeks I was in his company, planning and matching boards for ceiling, a plastered room being a rare thing in the parish of Avoyelles.

John M. Tibeats was the opposite of Ford in all respects. He was a small, crabbed, quick-tempered, spiteful man. He had no fixed residence that I ever heard of, but passed from one plantation to another, wherever he could find employment. He was without standing in the community, not esteemed by white men, nor even respected by slaves. He was ignorant, withal, and of a revengeful disposition. He left the parish long before I did, and I know not whether he is at present alive or dead. Certain it is, it was a most unlucky day for me that brought us together. During my residence with Master Ford I had seen only the bright side of slavery. His was no heavy hand crushing us to the earth. *He* pointed upwards, and with benign and cheering words addressed us as his fellow mortals, accountable, like himself, to the Maker of us all. I think of him with affection, and had my family been with me, could have borne his gentle servitude, without murmuring all my days. But clouds were gathering in the horizon—forerunners of a pitiless storm that was soon to break over me. I was doomed to endure such bitter trials as the poor slave only knows, and to lead no more the comparatively happy life which I had led in the "Great Pine Woods."

CHAPTER 8

William Ford unfortunately became embarrassed in his pecuniary affairs. A heavy judgment was rendered against him in consequence of his having become security for his brother, Franklin Ford, residing on Red River, above Alexandria, and who had failed to meet his liabilities. He was also indebted to John M. Tibeats to a considerable amount in consideration of his services in building the mills on Indian Creek, and also a weaving house, corn mill and other erections on the plantation at Bayou Boeuf, not yet completed. It was therefore necessary, in order to meet these demands, to dispose of eighteen slaves, myself among the number. Seventeen of them, including Sam and Harry, were purchased by Peter Compton, a planter also residing on Red River.

I was sold to Tibeats, in consequence, undoubtedly, of my slight skill as a carpenter. This was in the winter of 1842. The deed of myself from Freeman to Ford, as I ascertained from the public records in New Orleans on my return, was dated June 23rd, 1841. At the time of my sale to Tibeats, the price agreed to be given for me being more than the debt, Ford took a chattel mortgage of four hundred dollars. I am indebted for my life, as will hereafter be seen, to that mortgage.

I bade farewell to my good friends at the opening, and departed with my new master Tibeats. We went down to the plantation on Bayou Boeuf, distant twenty-seven miles from the Pine Woods, to complete the unfinished contract. Bayou Boeuf is a sluggish, winding stream—one of those stagnant bodies of water common in that region, setting back from Red River. It stretches from a point not far from Alexandria, in a south-easterly direction, and following its tortuous course, is more than fifty miles in length. Large cotton and sugar plantations line each shore, extending back to the borders of interminable swamps. It is alive with alligators, rendering it unsafe for swine, or unthinking slave children to stroll along its banks. Upon a bend in this bayou, a short distance from Cheneyville, was situated the plantation of Madam Ford—her brother, Peter Tanner, a great landholder, living on the opposite side.

On my arrival at Bayou Boeuf, I had the pleasure of meeting Eliza, whom I had not seen for several months. She had not pleased Mrs. Ford, being more occupied in brooding over her sorrows than in attending to her business, and had, in consequence, been sent down to work in the field on the plantation. She had grown feeble and emaciated, and was still mourning for her children. She asked me if I had forgotten them, and a great many times inquired if I still remembered how handsome little Emily was—how much Randall loved her—and wondered if they were living still, and where the darlings could then be. She had sunk beneath the weight of an excessive grief. Her drooping form and hollow cheeks too plainly indicated that she had well-nigh reached the end of her weary road.

Ford's overseer on this plantation, and who had the exclusive charge of it, was a Mr. Chapin, a kindly-disposed man, and a native of Pennsylvania. In common with others, he held Tibeats in light estimation, which fact, in connection with the four hundred dollar mortgage, was fortunate for me.

I was now compelled to labor very hard. From earliest dawn until late at night, I was not allowed to be a moment idle. Notwithstanding which, Tibeats was never satisfied. He was continually cursing and complaining. He never spoke to me a kind word. I was his faithful slave, and earned him large wages every day, and yet I went to my cabin nightly, loaded with abuse and stinging epithets.

We had completed the corn mill, the kitchen, and so forth, and were at work upon the weaving house, when I was guilty of an act, in that state punishable with death. It was my first fight with Tibeats. The weaving house we were erecting stood in the orchard a few rods from the residence of Chapin, or the "great house," as it was called. One night, having worked until it was too dark to see, I was ordered by Tibeats to rise very early in the morning, procure a keg of nails from Chapin, and commence putting on tin clapboards. I retired to the cabin extremely tired, and having cooked a supper of bacon and corn cake, and conversed a while with Eliza, who occupied the same cabin, as also did Lawson and his wife Mary, and a slave named Bristol, laid down upon the ground floor, little dreaming of the sufferings that awaited me on the morrow. Before daylight I was on the piazza of the "great house," awaiting the appearance of overseer Chapin. To have aroused him from his slumbers and stated my errand, would have been an unpardonable boldness. At length he came out. Taking off my hat, I informed him Master Tibeats had directed me to call upon him for a keg of nails. Going into the store-room, he rolled it out, at the same time saying, if Tibeats preferred a different size, he would endeavor to furnish them, but that I might use those until further directed. Then mounting his horse, which stood saddled and bridled at the door, he rode away into the field, whither the slaves had preceded him, while I took the keg on my shoulder, and proceeding to the weaving house, broke in the head, and commenced nailing on the clapboards.

As the day began to open, Tibeats came out of the house to where I was, hard at work. He seemed to be that morning even more morose and disagreeable than usual. He was my master, entitled by law to my flesh and blood, and to exercise over me such tyrannical control as his mean nature prompted; but there was no law that could prevent my looking upon him with intense contempt. I despised both his disposition and his intellect. I had just come round to the keg for a further supply of nails, as he reached the weaving house.

"I thought I told you to commence putting on weather boards this morning," he remarked.

"Yes, master, and I am about it," I replied.

"Where?" he demanded.

"On the other side," was my answer.

He walked round to the other side, examined my work for a while, muttering to himself in a fault-finding tone.

"Didn't I tell you last night to get a keg of nails of Chapin?" he broke forth again.

"Yes, master, and so I did; and overseer said he would get another size for you, if you wanted them, when he came back from the field."

Tibeats walked to the keg, looked a moment at the contents, then kicked it violently. Coming towards me in a great passion, he exclaimed,

"G—d d—n you! I thought you *knowed* something."

I made answer: "I tried to do as you told me, master. I didn't mean anything wrong. Overseer said—" But he interrupted me with such a flood of curses that I was unable to finish the sentence. At length he ran towards the house, and going to the piazza, took down one of the overseer's whips. The whip had a short wooden stock, braided over with leather, and was loaded at the butt. The lash was three feet long, or thereabouts, and made of rawhide strands.

At first I was somewhat frightened, and my impulse

was to run. There was no one about except Rachel, the cook, and Chapin's wife, and neither of them were to be seen. The rest were in the field. I knew he intended to whip me, and it was the first time anyone had attempted it since my arrival at Avoyelles. I felt, moreover, that I had been faithful—that I was guilty of no wrong whatever, and deserved commendation rather than punishment. My fear changed to anger, and before he reached me I had made up my mind fully not to be whipped, let the result be life or death.

Winding the lash around his hand, and taking hold of the small end of the stock, he walked up to me, and with a malignant look, ordered me to strip.

"Master Tibeats, said I, looking him boldly in the face, "I will *not*." I was about to say something further in justification, but with concentrated vengeance, he sprang upon me, seizing me by the throat with one hand, raising the whip with the other, in the act of striking. Before the blow descended, however, I had caught him by the collar of the coat, and drawn him closely to me. Reaching down, I seized him by the ankle, and pushing him back with the other hand, he fell over on the ground. Putting one arm around his leg, and holding it to my breast, so that his head and shoulders only touched the ground, I placed my foot upon his neck. He was completely in my power. My blood was up. It seemed to course through my veins like fire. In the frenzy of my madness I snatched the whip from his hand. He struggled with all his power; swore that I should not live to see another day, and that he would tear out my heart. But his struggles and his threats were alike in vain. I cannot tell how many times I struck him. Blow after blow fell fast and heavy upon his wriggling form. At length he screamed—cried murder—and at last the blasphemous tyrant called on God for mercy. But he who had never shown mercy did not receive it. The stiff stock of the whip warped round his cringing body until my right arm ached.

Until this time I had been too busy to look about me. Desisting for a moment, I saw Mrs. Chapin looking from the window, and Rachel standing in the kitchen door. Their attitudes expressed the utmost excitement and alarm. His screams had been heard in the field. Chapin was coming as fast as he could ride. I struck him a blow or two more, then pushed him from me with such a well-directed kick that he went rolling over on the ground.

Rising to his feet, and brushing the dirt from his hair, he stood looking at me, pale with rage. We gazed at each other in silence. Not a word was uttered until Chapin galloped up to us.

"What is the matter?" he cried out.

"Master Tibeats wants to whip me for using the nails you gave me," I replied.

"What is the matter with the nails?" he inquired, turning to Tibeats.

Tibeats answered to the effect that they were too large, paying little heed, however, to Chapin's question, but still keeping his snakish eyes fastened maliciously on me.

"I am overseer here," Chapin began. "I told Platt to take them and use them, and if they were not of the proper size I would get others on returning from the field. It is not his fault. Besides, I shall furnish such nails as I please. I hope you will understand *that*, Mr. Tibeats."

Tibeats made no reply, but, grinding his teeth and shaking his fist, swore he would have satisfaction, and that it was not half over yet. Thereupon he walked away, followed by the overseer, and entered the house, the latter talking to him all the while in a suppressed tone, and with earnest gestures.

I remained where I was, doubting whether it was better to fly or abide the result, whatever it might be. Presently Tibeats came out of the house, and, saddling his horse, the only property he possessed besides myself, departed on the road to Cheneyville.

When he was gone, Chapin came out, visibly excited, telling me not to stir, not to attempt to leave the plantation on any account whatever, he then went to the kitchen, and calling Rachel out, conversed with her some time. Coming back, he again charged me with great earnestness not to run, saying my master was a rascal; that he had left on no good errand and that there might be trouble before night. But at any events, he insisted upon it, I must not stir.

As I stood there, feelings of unutterable agony overwhelmed me. I was conscious that I had subjected myself to unimaginable punishment. The reaction that followed my extreme ebullition of anger produced the most painful sensations of regret. An unfriended, helpless slave—what could I *do*, what could I *say*, to justify, in the remotest manner, the heinous act I had committed, of resenting a *white* man's contumely and abuse. I tried to pray—I tried to beseech my Heavenly Father to sustain me in my sore extremity, but emotion choked my utterance, and I could only bow my head upon my hands and weep. For at least an hour I remained in this situation, finding relief only in tears, when, looking up, I beheld Tibeats, accompanied by two horsemen, coming down the bayou. They rode into the yard, jumped from their horses, and approached me with large whips, one of them also carrying a coil of rope.

"Cross your hands," commanded Tibeats, with the addition of such a shuddering expression of blasphemy as is not decorous to repeat. "You need not bind me, Master Tibeats, I am ready to go with you anywhere," said I.

One of his companions then stepped forward, swearing if I made the least resistance he would break my head—he would tear me limb from limb—he would cut my black throat—and giving wide scope to other similar expressions. Perceiving any importunity altogether vain, I crossed my hands, submitting humbly to whatever disposition they might please to make of me. Thereupon Tibeats tied my wrists, drawing the rope around them with his utmost strength. Then he bound my ankles in the same manner. In the meantime the other two had slipped a cord within my elbows, running it across my back, and tying it firmly. It was utterly impossible to move hand or foot. With a remaining piece of rope Tibeats made an awkward noose, and placed it about my neck.

"Now, then," inquired one of Tibeats' companions, "where shall we hang the nigger?"

One proposed such a limb, extending from the body of a peach tree, near the spot where we were standing. His comrade objected to it, alleging it would break, and proposed another. Finally they fixed up on the latter.

During this conversation, and all the time they were binding me, I uttered not a word. Overseer Chapin, during the progress of the scene, was walking hastily back and forth on the piazza. Rachel was crying by the kitchen door, and Mrs. Chapin was still looking from the window. Hope died within my heart. Surely my time had come. I should never behold the light of another day—never behold the faces of my children—the sweet anticipation I had cherished with such fondness. I should that hour struggle through the fearful agonies of death! None would mourn for me—none revenge me. Soon my form would be mouldering in that distant soil, or, perhaps, be cast to the slimy reptiles that filled the stagnant waters of the bayou! Tears flowed down my cheeks, but they only afforded a subject of insulting comment for my executioners.

At length, as they were dragging me towards the tree, Chapin, who had momentarily disappeared from the piazza, came out of the house and walked towards us. He had a pistol in each hand, and as near as I can now recall to mind, spoke in a firm, determined manner, as follows:

"Gentlemen, I have a few words to say. You had better listen to them. Whoever moves that slave another foot from where he stands is a dead man. In the first place, he does not deserve this treatment. It is a shame to murder him in this manner. I never knew a more faithful boy than Platt. You, Tibeats, are in the fault yourself. You are pretty much of a scoundrel, and I know it, and you richly deserve the flogging you have received. In the next place, I have been overseer on this plantation seven years, and, in the absence of William Ford, am master here. My duty is to protect his interests, and that duty I shall perform. You are not responsible—you are a worthless fellow. Ford holds a mortgage on Platt of four hundred dollars. If you hang him he loses his debt. Until that is canceled you have no right to take his life. You have no right to take it anyway. There is a law for the slave as well as for the white man. You are no better than a murderer.

"As for you," addressing Cook and Ramsay, a couple of overseers from neighboring plantations, "as for you—begone! If you have any regard for your own safety, I say, begone."

Cook and Ramsay, without a further word, mounted their horses and rode away. Tibeats, in a few minutes, evidently in fear, and overawed by the decided tone of Chapin, sneaked off like a coward, as he was, and mounting his horse, followed his companions.

I remained standing where I was, still bound, with the rope around my neck. As soon as they were gone, Chapin called Rachel, ordering her to run to the field, and tell Lawson to hurry to the house without delay, and bring the brown mule with him, an animal much prized for its unusual fleetness. Presently the boy appeared.

"Lawson," said Chapin, "you must go to the Pine Woods. Tell your master Ford to come here at once and that he must not delay a single moment. Tell him they are trying to murder Platt. Now hurry, boy. Be at the Pine Woods by noon if you kill the mule."

Chapin stepped into the house and wrote a pass. When he returned, Lawson was at the door, mounted on his mule.

Receiving the pass, he plied the whip right smartly to the beast, dashed out of the yard, and turning up the bayou on a hard gallop, in less time than it has taken me to describe the scene, was out of sight.

CHAPTER 9

As the sun approached the meridian that day it became insufferably warm. Its hot rays scorched the ground. The earth almost blistered the foot that stood upon it. I was without coat or hat, standing bare-headed, exposed to its burning blaze. Great drops of perspiration rolled down my face, drenching the scanty apparel wherewith I was clothed. Over the fence, a very little way off, the peach trees cast their cool, delicious shadows on the grass. I would gladly have given a long year of service to have been enabled to exchange the heated oven, as it were, wherein I stood, for a seat beneath their branches. But I was yet bound, the rope still dangling from my neck, and standing in the same tracks where Tibeats and his comrades left me. I could not move an inch, so firmly had I been bound. To have been enabled to lean against the weaving house would have been a luxury indeed. But it was far beyond my reach, though distant less than twenty feet. I wanted to lie down, but knew I could not rise again. The ground was so parched and boiling hot I was aware it would but add to the discomfort of my situation. If I could have only moved my position, however slightly, it would have been relief unspeakable. But the hot rays of a southern sun, beating all the long summer day on my bare head, produced not half the suffering I experienced from my aching limbs. My wrists and ankles, and the cords of my legs and arms began to swell, burying the rope that bound them into the swollen flesh.

All day Chapin walked back and forth upon the stoop, but not once approached me. He appeared to be in a state of great uneasiness, looking first towards me, and then up the road, as if expecting some arrival every moment. He did not go to the field, as was his custom. It was evident from his manner that he supposed Tibeats would return with more and better armed assistance, perhaps, to renew the quarrel, and it was equally evident he had prepared his mind to defend my life at whatever hazard. Why he did not relieve me—why he suffered me to remain in agony the whole weary day, I never knew. It was not for want of sympathy, I am certain. Perhaps he wished Ford to see the rope about my neck, and the brutal manner in which I had been bound; perhaps his interference with another's property in which he had no legal interest might have been a trespass, which would have subjected him to the penalty of the law. Why Tibeats was all day absent was another mystery I never could divine. He knew well enough that Chapin would not harm him unless he persisted in his design against me. Lawson told me afterwards, that, as he passed the plantation of John David Cheney, he saw the three, and that they turned and looked after him as he flew by. I think his supposition was, that Lawson had been sent out by Overseer Chapin to arouse the neighboring planters, and to call on them to come to his assistance. He, therefore, undoubtedly, acted on the principle, that "discretion is the better part of valor," and kept away.

But whatever motive may have governed the cowardly and malignant tyrant, it is of no importance. There I still stood in the noon-tide sun, groaning with pain. From long before daylight I had not eaten a morsel. I was growing faint from pain, and thirst, and hunger. Once only, in the very hottest portion of the day, Rachel, half fearful she was acting contrary to the overseer's wishes, ventured to me, and held a cup of water to my lips. The humble creature never knew, nor could she comprehend if she had heard them, the blessings I invoked upon her, for that balmy draught. She could only say, "Oh, Platt, how I do pity you," and then hastened back to her labors in the kitchen.

Never did the sun move so slowly through the heavens— never did it shower down such fervent and fiery rays, as it did that day. At least, so it appeared to me. What my meditations were—the innumerable thoughts that thronged through my distracted brain—I will not attempt to give expression to. Suffice it to say, during the whole long day I came not to the conclusion, even once, that the southern slave, fed, clothed, whipped and protected by his master, is happier than the free colored citizen of the North. To that conclusion I have never since arrived. There are many, however, even in the northern states, benevolent and well-disposed men, who will pronounce my opinion erroneous, and gravely proceed to substantiate the assertion with an argument. Alas! They have never drunk, as I have, from the bitter cup of slavery. Just at sunset my heart leaped with unbounded joy, as Ford came riding into the yard, his horse covered with foam. Chapin met him at the door, and after conversing a short time, he walked directly to me.

"Poor Platt, you are in a bad state," was the only expression that escaped his lips.

"Thank God!" said I, "thank God, Master Ford, that you have come at last."

Drawing a knife from his pocket, he indignantly cut the cord from my wrists, arms, and ankles, and slipped the noose from my neck. I attempted to walk, but staggered like a drunken man, and fell partially to the ground.

Ford returned immediately to the house, leaving me alone again. As he reached the piazza, Tibeats and his two friends rode up. A long dialogue followed. I could hear the sound of their voices, the mild tones of Ford mingling with the angry accents of Tibeats, but was unable to distinguish what was said. Finally the three departed again, apparently not well pleased.

I endeavored to raise the hammer, thinking to show Ford how willing I was to work, by proceeding with my labors on the weaving house, but it fell from my nerveless hand. At dark I crawled into the cabin, and laid down. I was in great misery—all sore and swollen— the slightest movement producing excruciating suffering. Soon the hands came in from the field. Rachel, when she went after Lawson, had told them what had happened. Eliza and Mary broiled me a piece of bacon, but my appetite was gone. Then they scorched some corn meal and made coffee. It was all that I could take. Eliza consoled me and was very kind. It was not long before the cabin was full of slaves. They gathered round me, asking many questions about the difficulty with Tibeats in the morning— and the particulars of all the occurrences of the day. Then Rachel came in, and in her simple language, repeated it over again—dwelling emphatically on the kick that sent Tibeats rolling over on the ground— whereupon there was a general titter throughout the crowd. Then she described how Chapin walked out with his pistols and rescued me, and how Master Ford cut the ropes with his knife, just as if he was mad.

By this time Lawson had returned. He had to regale them with an account of his trip to the Pine Woods—how the brown mule bore him faster than a "streak o' lightnin'"—how he astonished everybody as he flew along—how Master Ford started right away—how he said Platt was a good nigger, and they shouldn't kill him, concluding with pretty strong intimations that there was not another human being in the wide world, who could have created such a universal sensation on the road, or performed such a marvelous John Gilpin feat, as he had done that day on the brown mule.

The kind creatures loaded me with the expression of

their sympathy—saying, Tibeats was a hard, cruel man, and hoping "Massa Ford" would get me back again. In this manner they passed the time, discussing, chatting, talking over and over again the exciting affair, until suddenly Chapin presented himself at the cabin door and called me.

"Platt," said he, "you will sleep on the floor in the great house tonight; bring your blanket with you."

I arose as quickly as I was able, took my blanket in my hand, and followed him. On the way he informed me that he should not wonder if Tibeats was back again before morning—that he intended to kill me—and that he did not mean he should do it without witnesses. Had he stabbed me to the heart in the presence of a hundred slaves, not one of them, by the laws of Louisiana, could have given evidence against him. I laid down on the floor in the great house—the first and the last time such a sumptuous resting place was granted me during my twelve years of bondage—and tried to sleep. Near midnight the dog began to bark. Chapin arose, looked from the window, but could discover nothing. At length the dog was quiet. As he returned to his room, he said,

"I believe, Platt, that scoundrel is skulking about the premises somewhere. If the dog barks again, and I am sleeping, wake me."

I promised to do so. After the lapse of an hour or more, the dog recommenced his clamor, running towards the gate, then back again, all the while barking furiously.

Chapin was out of bed without waiting to be called. On this occasion, he stepped forth upon the piazza, and remained standing there a considerable length of time. Nothing, however, was to be seen, and the dog returned to his kennel. We were not disturbed again during the night. The excessive pain that I suffered, and the dread of some impending danger, prevented any rest whatever. Whether or not Tibeats did actually return to the plantation that night, seeking an opportunity to wreak his vengeance upon me, is a secret known only to himself, perhaps. I thought then, however, and have the strong impression still, that he was there. At all events, he had the disposition of an assassin—cowering before a brave man's words, but ready to strike his helpless or unsuspecting victim in the back, as I had reason afterwards to know.

At daylight in the morning, I arose, sore and weary, having rested little. Nevertheless, after partaking breakfast, which Mary and Eliza had prepared for me in the cabin, I proceeded to the weaving house and commenced the labors of another day. It was Chapin's practice, as it is the practice of overseers generally, immediately on arising, to bestride his horse always saddled and bridled and ready for him—the particular business of some slave—and ride into the field. This morning, on the contrary, he came to the weaving house, asking if I had seen anything of Tibeats yet. Replying in the negative, he remarked there was something not right about the fellow—there was bad blood in him—that I must keep a sharp watch of him, or he would do me wrong some day when I least expected it.

While he was yet speaking, Tibeats rode in, hitched his horse, and entered the house. I had little fear of him while Ford and Chapin were at hand, but they could not be near me always.

Oh! How heavily the weight of slavery pressed upon me then. I must toil day after day, endure abuse and taunts and scoffs, sleep on the hard ground, live on the coarsest fare, and not only this, but live the slave of a blood-seeking wretch, of whom I must stand henceforth in continued fear and dread. Why had I not died in my young years—before God had given me children to love and live for? What unhappiness and suffering and sorrow it would have prevented. I sighed for liberty; but the bondman's chain was round me, and could not be shaken off. I could only gaze wistfully towards the North, and think of the thousands of miles that stretched between me and the soil of freedom, over which a *black* freeman may not pass.

Tibeats, in the course of half an hour, walked over to the weaving house, looked at me sharply, then returned without saying anything. Most of the forenoon he sat on the piazza, reading a newspaper and conversing with Ford. After dinner, the latter left for the Pine Woods, and it was indeed with regret that I beheld him depart from the plantation.

Once more during the day Tibeats came to me, gave me some order, and returned.

During the week the weaving house was completed— Tibeats in the meantime making no allusion whatever to the difficulty—when I was informed he had hired me to Peter Tanner, to work under another carpenter by the name of Myers. This announcement was received with gratification, as any place was desirable that would relieve me of his hateful presence.

Peter Tanner, as the reader has already been informed, lived on the opposite shore, and was the brother of Mistress Ford. He is one of the most extensive planters on Bayou Boeuf, and owns a large number of slaves.

Over I went to Tanner's, joyfully enough. He had heard of my late difficulties—in fact, I ascertained the flogging of Tibeats was soon blazoned far and wide. This affair, together with my rafting experiment, had rendered me somewhat notorious. More than once I heard it said that Platt Ford, now Platt Tibeats—a slave's name changes with his change of master— was "a devil of a nigger." But I was destined to make a still further noise, as will presently be seen, throughout the little world of Bayou Boeuf.

Peter Tanner endeavored to impress upon me the idea that he was quite severe, though I could perceive there was a vein of good humor in the old fellow, after all.

"You're the nigger," he said to me on my arrival—"You're the nigger that flogged your master, eh? You're the nigger that kicks, and holds carpenter Tibeats by the leg, and wallops him, are ye? I'd like to see you hold me by the leg—I should. You're a 'portant character—you're a great nigger—very remarkable nigger, ain't ye? *I'd* lash you—*I'd* take the tantrums out of ye. Jest take hold of my leg, if you please. None of your pranks here, my boy, remember *that*. Now go to work, you *kickin'* rascal," concluded Peter Tanner, unable to suppress a half-comical grin at his own wit and sarcasm.

After listening to this salutation, I was taken charge of by Myers, and labored under his direction for a month, to his and my own satisfaction.

Like William Ford, his brother-in-law, Tanner was in the habit of reading the Bible to his slaves on the Sabbath, but in a somewhat different spirit. He was an impressive commentator on the New Testament. The first Sunday after my coming to the plantation, he called them together, and began to read the twelfth chapter of Luke. When he came to the 47th verse, he looked deliberately around him, and continued— "And that servant which knew his lord's *will*"—here he paused, looking around more deliberately than before, and again proceeded —"which knew his lord's *will*, and *prepared* not himself"—here was another pause— "*prepared* not himself, neither did *according* to his will, shall be beaten with many *stripes*."

"D'ye hear that?" demanded Peter, emphatically. "*Stripes*," he repeated, slowly and distinctly, taking off his spectacles, preparatory to making a few remarks.

"That nigger that don't take care—that don't obey his lord—that's his master— d'ye see?— that *'ere* nigger shall be beaten with many stripes. Now, many signifies a *great* many— forty, a hundred, a hundred and fifty lashes. *That's* Scripter!" and so Peter continued to elucidate the subject for a great length of time, much to the edification of his sable audience.

At the conclusion of the exercises, calling up three of his slaves, Warner, Will and Major, he cried out to me—

"Here, Platt, you held Tibeats by the legs; now I'll see

if you can hold these rascals in the same way, till I get back from meetin'."

Thereupon he ordered them to the stocks—a common thing on plantations in the Red River country. The stocks are formed of two planks, the lower one made fast at the ends to two short posts, driven firmly into the ground. At regular distances half circles are cut in the upper edge. The other plank is fastened to one of the posts by a hinge, so that it can be opened or shut down, in the same manner as the blade of a pocketknife is shut or opened. In the lower edge of the upper plank corresponding half circles are also cut, so that when they close, a row of holes is formed large enough to admit a negro's leg above the ankle, but not large enough to enable him to draw out his foot. The other end of the upper plank, opposite the hinge, is fastened to its post by lock and key. The slave is made to sit upon the ground, when the uppermost plank is elevated, his legs, just above the ankles, placed in the sub-half circles, and shutting it down again, and locking it, he is held secure and fast. Very often the neck instead of the ankle is enclosed. In this manner they are held during the operation of whipping.

Warner, Will and Major, according to Tanner's account of them, were melon-stealing, Sabbath-breaking niggers, and not approving of such wickedness, he felt it his duty to put them in the stocks. Handing me the key, himself, Myers, Mistress Tanner and the children entered the carnage and drove away to church at Cheneyville. When they were gone, the boys begged me to let them out. I felt sorry to see them sitting on the hot ground, and remembered my own sufferings in the sun. Upon their promise to return to the stocks at any moment they were required to do so, I consented to release them. Grateful for the lenity shown them, and in order in some measure to repay it, they could do no less, of course, than pilot me, to the melon patch. Shortly before Tanner's return, they were in the stocks again. Finally he drove up, and looking at the boys, said, with a chuckle,—

"Aha! ye haven't been strolling about much today, anyway. *I'll* teach you what's what. *I'll* tire ye of eating watermelons on the Lord's day, ye Sabbath-breaking niggers."

Peter Tanner prided himself upon his strict religious observances: he was a deacon in the church.

But I have now reached a point in the progress of my narrative, when it becomes necessary to turn away from these light descriptions, to the more grave and weighty matter of the second battle with Master Tibeats, and the flight through the great Pacoudrie Swamp.

CHAPTER 10

At the end of a month, my services being no longer required at Tanner's I was sent over the bayou again to my master, whom I found engaged in building the cotton press. This was situated at some distance from the great house, in a rather retired place. I commenced working once more in company with Tibeats, being entirely alone with him most part of the time. I remembered the words of Chapin, his precautions, his advice to beware, lest, in some unsuspecting moment he might injure me. They were always in my mind, so that I lived in a most uneasy state of apprehension and fear. One eye was on my work, the other on my master. I determined to give him no cause of offence, to work still more diligently, if possible, than I had done, to bear whatever abuse he might heap upon me, save bodily injury, humbly and patiently, hoping thereby to soften in some degree his manner towards me, until the blessed time might come when I should be delivered from his clutches.

The third morning after my return, Chapin left the plantation for Cheneyville, to be absent until night. Tibeats, on that morning, was attacked with one of those periodical fits of spleen and ill-humor to which he was frequently subject, rendering him still more disagreeable and venomous than usual.

It was about nine o'clock in the forenoon, when I was busily employed with the jack-plane on one of the sweeps. Tibeats was standing by the workbench, fitting a handle into the chisel, with which he had been engaged previously in cutting the thread of the screw.

"You are not planing that down enough," said he.

"It is just even with the line," I replied.

"You're a d—d liar," he exclaimed passionately.

"Oh, well, master," I said, mildly, "I will plane it down more if you say so," at the same time proceeding to do as I supposed he desired. Before one shaving had been removed, however, he cried out, saying I had now planed it too deep— it was too small—I had spoiled the sweep entirely. Then followed curses and imprecations. I had endeavored to do exactly as he directed, but nothing would satisfy the unreasonable man. In silence and in dread I stood by the sweep, holding the jack-plane in my hand, not knowing what to do, and not daring to be idle. His anger grew more and more violent, until, finally, with an oath, such a bitter, frightful oath as only Tibeats could utter, he seized a hatchet from the workbench and darted towards me, swearing he would cut my head open.

It was a moment of life or death. The sharp, bright blade of the hatchet glittered in the sun. In another instant it would be buried in my brain, and yet in that instant—so quick will a man's thoughts come to him in such a fearful strait—I reasoned with myself. If I stood still, my doom was certain; if I fled, ten chances to one the hatchet, flying from his hand with a too-deadly and unerring aim, would strike me in the back. There was but one course to take. Springing towards him with all my power, and meeting him full half-way, before he could bring down the blow, with one hand I caught his uplifted arm, with the other seized him by the throat. We stood looking each other in the eyes. In his I could see murder. I felt as if I had a serpent by the neck, watching the slightest relaxation of my grip, to coil itself round my body, crushing and stinging it to death. I thought to scream aloud, trusting that some ear might catch the sound—but Chapin was away; the hands were in the field; there was no living soul in sight or hearing.

The good genius, which thus far through life has saved me from the hands of violence, at that moment suggested a lucky thought. With a vigorous and sudden kick, that brought him on one knee, with a groan, I released my hold upon his throat, snatched the hatchet, and cast it beyond reach.

Frantic with rage, maddened beyond control, he seized a white oak stick, five feet long, perhaps, and as large in circumference as his hand could grasp, which was lying on the ground. Again he rushed towards me, and again I met him, seized him about the waist, and being the stronger of the two, bore him to the earth. While in that position I obtained possession of the stick, and rising, cast it from me, also.

He likewise arose and ran for the broadaxe, on the workbench. Fortunately, there was a heavy plank lying upon its broad blade, in such a manner that he could not extricate it, before I had sprung upon his back. Pressing him down closely and heavily on the plank, so that the axe was held more firmly to its place, I endeavored, but in vain, to break his grasp upon the handle. In that position we remained some minutes.

There have been hours in my unhappy life, many of them, when the contemplation of death as the end of earthly sorrow—of the grave as a resting place for the tired and worn out body—has been pleasant to dwell upon. But such contemplations vanish in the hour of peril. No man, in his full strength, can stand undismayed, in the presence of the "king of terrors." Life is dear to every living thing; the worm that crawls upon the ground will struggle for it. At that moment it was dear to me, enslaved and treated as I was.

Not able to unloose his hand, once more I seized him

by the throat, and this time, with a vice-like grip that soon relaxed his hold. He became pliant and unstrung. His face, that had been white with passion, was now black from suffocation. Those small serpent eyes that spat such venom, were now full of horror—two great white orbs starting from their sockets!

There was "a lurking devil" in my heart that prompted me to kill the human bloodhound on the spot—to retain the grip on his accursed throat till the breath of life was gone! I dared not murder him, and I dared not let him live. If I killed him, my life must pay the forfeit—if he lived, my life only would satisfy his vengeance. A voice within whispered me to fly. To be a wanderer among the swamps, a fugitive and a vagabond on the face of the earth, was preferable to the life that I was leading.

My resolution was soon formed, and swinging him from the workbench to the ground, I leaped a fence nearby and hurried across the plantation, passing the slaves at work in the cotton field. At the end of a quarter of a mile I reached the wood pasture, and it was a short time indeed that I had been running it. Climbing on to a high fence, I could see the cotton press, the great house, and the space between. It was a conspicuous position, from whence the whole plantation was in view. I saw Tibeats cross the field towards the house, and enter it—then he came out carrying his saddle, and presently mounted his horse and galloped away.

I was desolate, but thankful. Thankful that my life was spared,—desolate and discouraged with the prospect before me. What would become of me? Who would befriend me? Whither should I fly? Oh, God! Thou who gavest me life, and implanted in my bosom the love of life—who filled it with emotions such as other men, thy creatures, have, do not forsake me. Have pity on the poor slave—let me not perish. If thou dost not protect me, I am lost—lost! Such supplications, silently and unuttered, ascended from my inmost heart to

Heaven. But there was no answering voice—no sweet, low tone, coming down from on high, whispering to my soul, "It is I, be not afraid." I was the forsaken of God, it seemed—the despised and hated of men!

In about three-fourths of an hour several of the slaves shouted and made signs for me to run. Presently, looking up the bayou, I saw Tibeats and two others on horse-back, coming at a fast gait, followed by a troop of dogs. There were as many as eight or ten. Distant as I was, I knew them. They belonged on the adjoining plantation. The dogs used on Bayou Boeuf for hunting slaves are a kind of bloodhound, but a far more savage breed than is found in the northern states. They will attack a negro, at their master's bidding, and cling to him as the common bulldog will cling to a four-footed animal. Frequently their loud bay is heard in the swamps, and then there is speculation as to what point the runaway will be overhauled—the same as a New York hunter stops to listen to the hounds coursing along the hillsides, and suggests to his companion that the fox will be taken at such a place. I never knew a slave escaping with his life from Bayou Boeuf. One reason is, they are not allowed to learn the art of swimming, and are incapable of crossing the most inconsiderable stream. In their flight they can go in no direction but a little way without coming to a bayou, when the inevitable alternative is presented, of being drowned or overtaken by the dogs. In youth I had practiced in the clear streams that flow through my native district, until I had become an expert swimmer and felt at home in the watery element.

I stood upon the fence until the dogs had reached the cotton press. In an instant more, their long, savage yells announced they were on my track. Leaping down from my position, I ran towards the swamp. Fear gave me strength, and I exerted it to the utmost. Every few moments I could hear the yelpings of the dogs. They were gaining upon me. Every howl was nearer and nearer. Each moment I expected they would spring upon my back—expected to feel their long teeth sinking into my flesh. There were so many of them, I knew they would tear me to pieces, that they would worry me, at once, to death. I gasped for breath—gasped forth a half-uttered, choking prayer to the Almighty to save me—to give me strength to reach some wide, deep bayou where I could throw them off the track, or sink into its waters. Presently I reached a thick palmetto bottom. As I fled through them they made a loud rustling noise, not loud enough, however, to drown the voices of the dogs.

Continuing my course due south, as nearly as I can judge, I came at length to water just over shoe. The hounds at that moment could not have been five rods behind me. I could hear them crashing and plunging through the palmettoes, their loud, eager yells making the whole swamp clamorous with the sound. Hope revived a little as I reached the water. If it were only deeper, they might lose the scent, and thus disconcerted, afford me the opportunity of evading them. Luckily, it grew deeper the farther I proceeded—now over my ankles now half-way to my knees—now sinking a moment to my waist, and then emerging presently into more shallow places. The dogs had not gained upon me since I struck the water. Evidently they were confused. Now their savage intonations grew more and more distant, assuring me that I was leaving them. Finally I stopped to listen, but the long howl came booming on the air again, telling me I was not yet safe. From bog to bog, where I had stepped, they could still keep upon the track, though impeded by the water. At length, to my great joy, I came to a wide bayou, and plunging in, had soon stemmed its sluggish current to the other side. There, certainly, the dogs would be confounded—the current carrying down the stream all traces of that slight, mysterious scent, which enables the quick-smelling hound to follow in the track of the fugitive.

After crossing this bayou the water became so deep I

could not run. I was now in what I afterwards learned was the "Great Pacoudrie Swamp." It was filled with immense trees—the sycamore, the gum, the cotton wood and cypress, and extends, I am informed, to the shore of the Calcasieu river. For thirty or forty miles it is without inhabitants, save wild beasts—the bear, the wildcat, the tiger, and great slimy reptiles, that are crawling though it everywhere. Long before I reached the bayou, in fact, from the time I struck the water until I emerged from the swamp on my return, these surrounded me. I saw hundreds of moccasin snakes. Every log and bog—every trunk of a fallen tree over which I was compelled to step or climb, was alive with them. They crawled away at my approach, but sometimes in my haste, I almost placed my hand or foot upon them. They are poisonous serpents—their bite more fatal than the rattlesnakes. Besides, I had lost one shoe, the sole having come entirely off, leaving the upper only dangling to my ankle.

I saw also saw many alligators, great and small, lying in the water, or on pieces of flood-wood. The noise I made usually startled them, when they moved off and plunged into the deepest places. Sometimes, however, I would come directly upon a monster before observing it. In such cases, I would start back, run a short way round, and in that manner shun them. Straight forward, they will run a short distance rapidly, but do not possess the power of turning. In a crooked race, there is no difficulty in evading them.

About two o'clock in the afternoon, I heard the last of the hounds. Probably they did not cross the bayou. Wet and weary, but relieved from the sense of instant peril, I continued on, more cautious and afraid, however, of the snakes and alligators than I had been in the earlier portion of my flight. Now, before stepping into a muddy pool, I would strike the water with a stick. If the waters moved, I would go around it, if not, would venture through.

At length the sun went down, and gradually night's

trailing mantle shrouded the great swamp in darkness. Still I staggered on, fearing every instant I should feel the dreadful sting of the moccasin, or be crushed within the jaws of some disturbed alligator. The dread of them now almost equaled the fear of the pursuing hounds. The moon arose after a time, its mild light creeping through the overspreading branches, loaded with long, pendent moss. I kept traveling forwards until after midnight, hoping all the while that I would soon emerge into some less desolate and dangerous region. But the water grew deeper and the walking more difficult than ever. I perceived it would be impossible to proceed much farther, and knew not, moreover, what hands I might fall into, should I succeed in reaching a human habitation. Not provided with a pass, any white man would be at liberty to arrest me, and place me in prison until such time as my master should "prove property, pay charges, and take me away." I was an estray, and if so unfortunate as to meet a law-abiding citizen of Louisiana, he would deem it his duty to his neighbor, perhaps, to put me forthwith in the pound. Really, it was difficult to determine which I had most reason to fear—dogs, alligators or men!

After midnight, however, I came to a halt. Imagination cannot picture the dreariness of the scene. The swamp was resonant with the quacking of innumerable ducks! Since the foundation of the earth, in all probability, a human footstep had never before so far penetrated the recesses of the swamp. It was not silent now—silent to a degree that rendered it oppressive—as it was when the sun was shining in the heavens. My midnight intrusion had awakened the feathered tribes, which seemed to throng the morass in hundreds of thousands, and their garrulous throats poured forth such multitudinous sounds—there was such a fluttering of wings—such sullen plunges in the water all around me—that I was affrighted and appalled. All the fowls of the air, and all the creeping things of the earth appeared to have assembled together in that particular place, for the purpose of filling it with clamor and confusion. Not by human dwellings—not in crowded cities alone, are the sights and sounds of life. The wildest places of the earth are full of them. Even in the heart of that dismal swamp, God had provided a refuge and a dwelling place for millions of living things.

The moon had now risen above the trees, when I resolved upon a new project. Thus far I had endeavored to travel as nearly south as possible. Turning about I proceeded in a north-west direction, my object being to strike the Pine Woods in the vicinity of Master Ford's. Once within the shadow of his protection, I felt I would be comparatively safe.

My clothes were in tatters, my hands, face, and body covered with scratches, received from the sharp knots of fallen trees, and in climbing over piles of brush and flood-wood. My bare foot was full of thorns. I was besmeared with muck and mud and the green slime that had collected on the surface of the dead water, in which I had been immersed to the neck many times during the day and night. Hour after hour, and tiresome indeed had they become, I continued to plod along on my north-west course. The water began to grow less deep and the ground more firm under my feet. At last I reached the Pacoudrie, the same wide bayou I had swum while "outward bound." I swam it again, and shortly after thought I heard a cock crow, but the sound was faint, and it might have been a mockery of the ear. The water receded from my advancing footsteps—now I had left the bogs behind me— now I was on dry land that gradually ascended to the plain, and I knew I was somewhere in the "Great Pine Woods."

Just at daybreak I came to an opening—a sort of small plantation—but one I had never seen before. In the edge of the woods I came upon two men, a slave and his young master, engaged in catching wild hogs. The white man I knew would demand my pass, and not able to give him one, would take me into possession. I was too wearied to run again, and too desperate to be taken, and therefore adopted a ruse that proved entirely successful. Assuming a fierce expression, I walked directly towards him, looking him steadily in the face. As I approached, he moved backwards with an air of alarm. It was plain he was much affrighted—that he looked upon me as some infernal goblin, just arisen from the bowels of the swamp!

"Where does William Ford live?" I demanded, in no gentle tone.

"He lives seven miles from here," was the reply.

"Which is the way to his place?" I again demanded, trying to look more fiercely than ever.

"Do you see those pine trees yonder?" he asked pointing to two, a mile distant, that rose far above their fellows, like a couple of tall sentinels, overlooking the broad expanse of forest.

"I see them," was the answer.

"At the feet of those pine trees," he continued "runs the Texas road. Turn to the left, and it will lead you to William Ford's."

Without further parley, I hastened forward, happy as he was, no doubt, to place the widest possible distance between us. Striking the Texas road, I turned to the left hand, as directed, and soon passed a great fire, where a pile of logs were burning. I went to it, thinking I would dry my clothes; but the gray light of the morning was fast breaking away—some passing white man might observe me; besides, the heat over-powered me with the desire of sleep: so, lingering no longer, I continued my travels, and finally, about eight o'clock, reached the house of Master Ford.

The slaves were all absent from the quarters, at their work. Stepping on to the piazza, I knocked at the door, which was soon opened by Mistress Ford. My appearance was so changed—I was in such a woebegone and forlorn condition, she did not know me. Inquiring if Master Ford was at home, that good man made his appearance, before the question could be answered. I told him of my flight, and ail the particulars connected with it. He listened attentively, and when I had concluded, spoke to me kindly and sympathetically, and taking me to the kitchen, called John, and ordered him to prepare me food. I had tasted nothing since daylight the previous morning.

When John had set the meal before me, the madam came out with a bowl of milk, and many little delicious dainties, such as rarely please the palate of a slave. I was hungry, and I was weary, but neither food nor rest afforded half the pleasure as did the blessed voices speaking kindness and consolation. It was the oil and the wine which the Good Samaritan in the "Great Pine Woods" was ready to pour into the wounded spirit of the slave, who came to him, stripped of his raiment and half-dead.

They left me in the cabin, that I might rest. Blessed be sleep! It visiteth all alike, descending as the dews of heaven on the bond and free. Soon it nestled to my bosom, driving away the troubles that oppressed it, and bearing me to that shadowy region, where I saw again the faces, and listened to the voices of my children, who, alas, for aught I knew in my waking hours, had fallen into the arms of that *other* sleep, from which they *never* would arouse.

CHAPTER 11

After a long sleep, sometime in the afternoon I awoke, refreshed, but very sore and stiff. Sally came in and talked with me, while John cooked me some dinner. Sally was in great trouble, as well as myself, one of her children being ill, and she feared it could not survive. Dinner over, after walking about the quarters for a while, visiting Sally's cabin and looking at the sick child, I strolled into the madam's garden. Though it was a season of the year when the voices of the birds are silent, and the trees are stripped of their summer glories in more frigid climes, yet the whole variety of roses were then blooming there, and the long, luxuriant vines creeping over the frames. The crimson and golden fruit hung half hidden amidst the younger and older blossoms of the peach, the orange, the plum, and the pomegranate; for, in that region of almost perpetual warmth, the leaves are falling and the buds bursting into bloom the whole year long.

I indulged the most grateful feelings towards Master and Mistress Ford, and wishing in some manner to repay their kindness, commenced trimming the vines, and afterwards weeding out the grass from among the orange and pomegranate trees. The latter grows eight or ten feet high, and its fruit, though larger, is similar in appearance to the jelly-flower. It has the luscious flavor of the strawberry. Oranges, peaches, plums, and most other fruits are indigenous to the rich, warm soil of Avoyelles; but the apple, the most common of them all in colder latitudes, is rarely to be seen.

Mistress Ford came out presently, saying it was praise-worthy in me, but I was not in a condition to labor, and might rest myself at the quarters until master should go down to Bayou Boeuf, which would not be that day, and it might not be the next. I said to her—to be sure, I felt bad, and was stiff, and that foot pained me, the stubs and thorns having so torn it, but thought such exercise would not hurt me, and that it was a great pleasure to work for so good a mistress. Thereupon she returned to the great house, and for three days I was diligent in the garden, cleaning the walks, weeding the flower beds, and pulling up the rank grass beneath the jessamine vines, which the gentle and generous hand of my protectress had taught to clamber along the walls.

The fourth morning, having become recruited and refreshed, Master Ford ordered me to make ready to accompany him to the bayou. There was but one saddle horse at the opening, all the others with the mules having been sent down to the plantation. I said I could walk, and bidding Sally and John good-bye, left the opening, trotting along by the horse's side.

That little paradise in the Great Pine Woods was the oasis in the desert, towards which my heart turned lovingly, during many years of bondage. I went forth from it now with regret and sorrow, not so overwhelming, however, as if it had then been given me to know that I should never return to it again.

Master Ford urged me to take his place occasionally on the horse, to rest me; but I said no, I was not tired, and it was better for me to walk than him. He said many kind and cheering things to me on the way, riding slowly, in order that I might keep pace with him. The goodness of God was mani-fest, he declared, in my miraculous escape from the swamp. As Daniel came forth unharmed from the den of lions, and as Jonah had been preserved in the whale's belly, even so had I been delivered from evil by the Almighty. He interrogated me in regard to the various fears and emotions I had experienced during the day and night, and if I had felt, at any time, a desire to pray. I felt forsaken of the whole world, I answered him, and was praying mentally all the while. At such times, said he, the heart of man turns instinctively towards his Maker. In prosperity, and whenever there is nothing to injure or make him afraid, he remembers Him not, and is ready to defy Him; but place him in the midst of dangers, cut him off from human aid, let the grave open before him—then it is, in the time of his tribulation, that the scoffer and unbelieving man turns to God for help, feeling there is no other hope, or refuge, or safety, save in his protecting arm.

So did that benignant man speak to me of this life and of the life hereafter; of the goodness and power of God, and of the vanity of earthly things, as we journeyed along the solitary road towards Bayou Boeuf.

When within some five miles of the plantation, we discovered a horseman at a distance, galloping towards us. As he came near I saw that it was Tibeats! He looked at me a moment, but did not address me, and turning about, rode along side by side with Ford. I trotted silently at their horses' heels, listing to their conversation. Ford informed him of my arrival in the Pine Woods three days before, of the sad plight I was in, and of the difficulties and dangers I had encountered.

"Well," exclaimed Tibeats, omitting his usual oaths in the presence of Ford, "I never saw such running before. I'll bet him against a hundred dollars, he'll beat any nigger in Louisiana. I offered John David Cheney twenty-five dollars to catch him, dead or alive, but he outran his dogs in a fair race. Them Cheney dogs ain't much, after all. Dunwoodie's hounds would have had him down before he touched the palmettoes. Somehow the dogs got off the track, and we had to give up the hunt. We rode the horses as far as we could, and then kept on foot till the water was three feet deep. The boys said he was drowned, sure. I allow I wanted a shot at him mightily. Ever since, I have been riding up and down the bayou, but had'nt much hope of catching him—thought he was dead, *sartin*. Oh, he's a cuss to run—that nigger is!"

In this way Tibeats ran on, describing his search in the swamp, the wonderful speed with which I had fled before the hounds, and when he had finished, Master Ford responded by saying, I had always been a willing and faithful boy with him; that he was sorry we had such trouble; that, according to Platt's story, he had been inhumanly treated, and that he, Tibeats, was himself in fault. Using hatchets and broadaxes upon slaves was shameful, and should not be allowed, he remarked. "This is no way of dealing with them, when first brought into the country. It will have a pernicious influence, and set them all running away. The swamps will be full of them. A little kindness would be far more effectual in restraining them, and rendering them obedient, than the use of weapons. Every planter on the bayou should frown upon such inhumanity. It is for the interest of all to do so. It is evident enough, Mr. Tibeats, that you and Platt cannot live together. You dislike him, and would not hesitate to kill him, and knowing it, he will run from you again through fear of his life. Now, Tibeats, you must sell him, or hire him out, at least. Unless you do so, I shall take measures to get him out of your possession."

In this spirit Ford addressed him the remainder of the distance. I opened not my mouth. On reaching the plantation they entered the great house, while I repaired to Eliza's cabin. The slaves were astonished to find me there, on returning from the field, supposing I was drowned. That night, again, they gathered about the cabin to listen to the story of my adventure. They took it for granted I would be whipped, and that it would be severe, the well-known penalty of running away being five hundred lashes.

"Poor fellow," said Eliza, taking me by the hand, "it would have been better for you if you had drowned. You have a cruel master, and he will kill you yet, I am afraid."

Lawson suggested that it might be, overseer Chapin would be appointed to inflict the punishment, in which case it would not be severe, whereupon Mary, Rachel, Bristol, and others hoped it would be Master Ford, and then it would be no whipping at all. They all pitied me and tried to console me, and were sad in view of the castigation that awaited me, except Kentucky John. There were no bounds to his laughter; he filled the cabin with cachinnations, holding his sides to prevent an explosion, and the cause of his noisy mirth was the idea of my outstripping the hounds. Somehow, he looked at the subject in a comical light. "I *know'd* dey would'nt cotch him, when he run cross de plantation. O, de lor', didn't Platt pick his feet right up, tho', hey? When dem dogs got whar he was, he was'nt *dar*—haw, haw, haw! O, de lor' a'mity!"—and then Kentucky John relapsed into another of his boisterous fits.

Early the next morning, Tibeats left the plantation. In the course of the forenoon, while sauntering about the gin-house, a tall, good-looking man came to me, and inquired if I was Tibeats' boy, that youthful appellation being applied indiscriminately to slaves even though they may have passed the number of three score years and ten. I took off my hat, and answered that I was.

"How would you like to work for me?" he inquired.

"Oh, I would like to, very much," said I, inspired with a sudden hope of getting away from Tibeats.

"You worked under Myers at Peter Tanner's, didn't you?"

I replied I had, adding some complimentary remarks that Myers had made concerning me.

"Well, boy," said he, "I have hired you of your master to work for me in the 'Big Cane Brake,' thirty-eight miles from here, down on Red River."

This man was Mr. Eldret, who lived below Ford's, on the same side of the bayou. I accompanied him to his plantation, and in the morning started with his slave Sam, and a wagonload of provisions, drawn by four mules, for the Big Cane, Eldret and Myers having preceded us on horseback. This Sam was a native of Charleston, where he had a mother, brother and sisters. He "allowed"—a common word among both black and white—that Tibeats was a mean man, and hoped, as I most earnestly did also, that his master would buy me.

We proceeded down the south shore of the bayou, crossing it at Carey's plantation; from thence to Huff Power, passing which, we came upon the Bayou Rouge road, which runs towards Red River. After passing through Bayou Rouge Swamp, and just at sunset, turning from the highway, we struck off into the "Big Cane Brake." We followed an unbeaten track, scarcely wide enough to admit the wagon. The cane, such as are used for fishing rods, were as thick as they could stand. A person could not be seen through them the distance of a rod. The paths of wild beasts run through them in various directions—the bear and the American tiger abounding in these brakes, and wherever there is a basin of stagnant water, it is full of alligators.

We kept on our lonely course through the "Big Cane" several miles, when we entered a clearing, known as "Sutton's Field." Many years before, a man by the name of Sutton had penetrated the wilderness of cane to this solitary place. Tradition has it, that he fled thither, a fugitive, not from service, but from justice. Here he lived alone—recluse and hermit of the swamp—with his own hands planting the seed and gathering in the harvest. One day a band of Indians stole upon his solitude, and after a bloody battle, overpowered and massacred him. For miles the country round, in the slaves' quarters, and on the piazzas of "great houses," where white children listen to superstitious tales, the story goes, that that spot, in the heart of the "Big Cane," is a haunted place. For more than a quarter of a century, human voices had rarely, if ever, disturbed the silence of the clearing. Rank and noxious weeds had overspread the once cultivated field—serpents sunned themselves on the doorway of the crumbling cabin. It was indeed a dreary picture of desolation.

Passing "Sutton's Field," we followed a new-cut road two miles farther, which brought us to its termination. We had now reached the wild lands of Mr. Eldret, where he contemplated clearing up an extensive plantation. We went to work next morning with our cane-knives, and cleared a sufficient space to allow the erection of two cabins—one for Myers and Eldret, the other for Sam, myself, and the slaves that were to join us. We were now in the midst of trees of enormous growth, whose wide-spreading branches almost shut out the light of the sun, while the space between the trunks was an impervious mass of cane, with here and there an occasional palmetto.

The bay and the sycamore, the oak and the cypress, reach a growth unparalleled, in those fertile lowlands bordering the Red River. From every tree, moreover, hang long, large masses of moss, presenting to the eye unaccustomed to them, a striking and singular appearance. This moss, in large quantities, is sent north, and there used for manufacturing purposes.

We cut down oaks, split them into rails, and with these erected temporary cabins. We covered the roofs with the broad palmetto leaf, an excellent substitute for shingles, as long as they last. The greatest annoyance I met with here were small flies, gnats and mosquitoes. They swarmed the air. They penetrated the porches of the ear, the nose, the eyes, the mouth. They sucked themselves beneath the skin. It was impossible to brush or beat them off. It seemed, indeed, as if they would devour us—carry us away piecemeal, in their small tormenting mouths.

A lonelier spot, or one more disagreeable, than the centre

of the "Big Cane Brake," it would be difficult to conceive; yet to me it was a paradise, in comparison with any other place in the company of Master Tibeats. I labored hard, and oft-times was weary and fatigued, yet I could lie down at night in peace, and arise in the morning without fear.

In the course of a fortnight, four black girls came down from Eldret's plantation—Charlotte, Fanny, Cresia and Kelly. They were all large and stout. Axes were put into their hands, and they were sent out with Sam and myself to cut trees. They were excellent choppers, the largest oak or sycamore standing but a brief season before their heavy and well-directed blows. At piling logs, they were equal to any man. There are lumberwomen as well as lumbermen in the forests of the South. In fact, in the region of the Bayou Boeuf they perform their share of all the labor required on the plantation. They plough, drag, drive team, clear wild lands, work on the highway, and so forth. Some planters, owning large cotton and sugar plantations, have none other than the labor of slave women. Such an one is Jim Burns, who lives on the north shore of the bayou, opposite the plantation of John Fogaman.

On our arrival in the brake, Eldret promised me, if I worked well, I might go up to visit my friends at Ford's in four weeks. On Saturday night of the fifth week, I reminded him of his promise, when he told me I had done so well, that I might go. I had set my heart upon it, and Eldret's announcement thrilled me with pleasure. I was to return in time to commence the labors of the day on Tuesday morning.

While indulging the pleasant anticipation of so soon meeting my old friends again, suddenly the hateful form of Tibeats appeared among us. He inquired how Myers and Platt got along together, and was told, very well, and that Platt was going up to Ford's plantation in the morning on a visit.

"Poh, poh!" sneered Tibeats; "it isn't worthwhile—the nigger will get unsteady, he can't go."

But Eldret insisted I had worked faithfully—that he had

given me his promise, and that, under the circumstances, I ought not to be disappointed. They then, it being about dark, entered one cabin and I the other. I could not give up the idea of going; it was a sore disappointment. Before morning I resolved, if Eldret made no objection, to leave at all hazards. At daylight I was at his door, with my blanket rolled up into a bundle, and hanging on a stick over my shoulder, waiting for a pass. Tibeats came out presently in one of his disagreeable moods, washed his face, and going to a stump nearby, sat down upon it, apparently busily thinking with himself. After standing there a long time, impelled by a sudden impulse of impatience, I started off.

"Are you going without a pass?" he cried out to me.

"Yes, master, I thought I would," I answered.

"How do you think you'll get there?" demanded he.

"Don't know," was all the reply I made him.

"You'd be taken and sent to jail, where you ought to be, before you got half-way there," he added, passing into the cabin as he said it. He came out soon with the pass in his hand, and calling me a "d—d nigger that deserved a hundred lashes," threw it on the ground. I picked it up, and hurried away right speedily.

A slave caught off his master's plantation without a pass, may be seized and whipped by any white man whom he meets. The one I now received was dated, and read as follows:

"Platt has permission to go to Ford's plantation,
on Bayou Boeuf, and return by Tuesday morning.
    JOHN M. TIBEATS."

This is the usual form. On the way, a great many demanded it, read it, and passed on. Those having the air and appearance of gentlemen, whose dress indicated the possession of wealth, frequently took no notice of me whatever; but a shabby fellow, an unmistakable loafer, never failed to hail me, and to scrutinize and examine me in the most thorough manner. Catching runaways is sometimes a money-making business. If, after advertising, no owner appears, they may be sold to the highest bidder; and certain fees are allowed the finder for his services, at all events, even if reclaimed. "A mean white," therefore—a name applied to the species loafer—considers it a god-send to meet an unknown negro without a pass.

There are no inns along the highways in that portion of the state where I sojourned. I was wholly destitute of money, neither did I carry any provisions, on my journey from the Big Cane to Bayou Boeuf; nevertheless, with his pass in his hand, a slave need never suffer from hunger or from thirst. It is only necessary to present it to the master or overseer of a plantation, and state his wants, when he will be sent round to the kitchen and provided with food or shelter, as the case may require. The traveler stops at any house and calls for a meal with as much freedom as if it was a public tavern. It is the general custom of the country. Whatever their faults may be, it is certain the inhabitants along Red River, and around the bayous in the interior of Louisiana are not wanting in hospitality.

I arrived at Ford's plantation towards the close of the afternoon, passing the evening in Eliza's cabin, with Lawson, Rachel, and others of my acquaintance. When we left Washington Eliza's form was round and plump. She stood erect, and in her silks and jewels, presented a picture of graceful strength and elegance. Now she was but a thin shadow of her former self. Her face had become ghastly haggard, and the once straight and active form was bowed down, as if bearing the weight of a hundred years. Crouching on her cabin floor, and clad in the coarse garments of a slave, old Elisha Berry would not have recognized the mother of his child. I never saw her afterwards. Having become useless in the cotton field, she was bartered for a trifle, to some man residing in the vicinity of Peter Compton's. Grief had gnawed remorselessly at her heart, until her strength was gone; and for that, her last master, it is said, lashed and abused her most unmercifully. But he could not whip back the departed vigor of her youth, nor straighten up that bended body to its full height, such as it was when her children were around her, and the light of freedom was shining on her path.

I learned the particulars relative to her departure from this world, from some of Compton's slaves, who had come over Red River to the bayou, to assist young Madam Tanner during the "busy season." She became at length, they said, utterly helpless, for several weeks lying on the ground floor in a dilapidated cabin, dependent upon the mercy of her fellow thralls for an occasional drop of water, and a morsel of food. Her master did not "knock her on the head," as is sometimes done to put a suffering animal out of misery, but left her unprovided for, and unprotected, to linger through a life of pain and wretchedness to its natural close. When the hands returned from the field one night they found her dead! During the day, the Angel of the Lord, who moveth invisibly over all the earth, gathering in his harvest of departing souls, had silently entered the cabin of the dying woman, and taken her from thence. She was *free* at last!

Next day, rolling up my blanket, I started on my return to the Big Cane. After traveling five miles, at a place called Huff Power, the ever-present Tibeats met me in the road. He inquired why I was going back so soon, and when informed I was anxious to return by the time I was directed, he said I need go no farther than the next plantation, as he had that day sold me to Edwin Epps. We walked down into the yard, where we met the latter gentleman, who examined me, and asked me the usual questions propounded by purchasers. Having been duly delivered over, I was ordered to the quarters, and at the same time directed to make a hoe and axe handle for myself.

I was now no longer the property of Tibeats—his dog, his brute, dreading his wrath and cruelty day and night; and whoever or whatever my new master might prove to be, I could not, certainly, regret the change. So it was good news when the sale was announced, and with a sigh of relief I sat down for the first time in my new abode.

Tibeats soon after disappeared from that section of the country. Once afterwards, and only once, I caught a glimpse of him. It was many miles from Bayou Boeuf. He was seated in the doorway of a low groggery. I was passing, in a drove of slaves, through St. Mary's parish.

CHAPTER 12

Edwin Epps, of whom much will be said during the remainder of this history, is a large, portly, heavy-bodied man with light hair, high cheek bones, and a Roman nose of extraordinary dimensions. He has blue eyes, a fair complexion, and is, as I should say, full six feet high. He has the sharp, inquisitive expression of a jockey. His manners are repulsive and coarse, and his language gives speedy and unequivocal evidence that he has never enjoyed the advantages of an education. He has the faculty of saying most provoking things, in that respect even excelling old Peter Tanner. At the time I came into his possession, Edwin Epps was fond of the bottle, his "sprees" sometimes extending over the space of two whole weeks. Latterly, however, he had reformed his habits, and when I left him, was as strict a specimen of temperance as could be found on Bayou Boeuf. When "in his cups," Master Epps was a roystering, blustering, noisy fellow, whose chief delight was in dancing with his "niggers," or lashing them about the yard with his long whip, just for the pleasure of hearing them screech and scream, as the great welts were planted on their backs. When sober, he was silent, reserved and cunning, not beating us indiscriminately, as in his drunken moments, but sending the end of his rawhide to some tender spot of a lagging slave, with a sly dexterity peculiar to himself.

He had been a driver and overseer in his younger years, but at this time was in possession of a plantation on Bayou Huff Power, two and a half miles from Holmesville, eighteen from Marksville, and twelve from Cheneyville. It belonged to Joseph B. Roberts, his wife's uncle, and was leased by Epps. His principal business was raising cotton and inasmuch as some may read this book who have never seen a cotton field, a description of the manner of its culture may not be out of place.

The ground is prepared by throwing up beds or ridges, with the plough—back-furrowing, it is called. Oxen and mules, the latter almost exclusively, are used in ploughing. The women as frequently as the men perform this labor, feeding, currying, and taking care of their teams, and in all respects doing the field and stable work, precisely as do the ploughboys of the North.

The beds, or ridges, are six feet wide, that is, from water furrow to water furrow. A plough drawn by one mule is then run along the top of the ridge or center of the bed, making the drill, into which a girl usually drops the seed, which she carries in a bag hung round her neck. Behind her comes a mule and harrow, covering up the seed, so that two mules, three slaves, a plough and harrow, are employed in planting a row of cotton. This is done in the months of March and April. Corn is planted in February. When there are no cold rains, the cotton usually makes its appearance in a week. In the course of eight or ten days afterwards the first hoeing is commenced. This is performed in part, also, by the aid of the plough and mule. The plough passes as near as possible to the cotton on both sides, throwing the furrow from it. Slaves follow with their hoes, cutting up the grass and cotton, leaving hills two feet and a half apart. This is called scraping cotton. In two weeks more commences the second hoeing. This time the furrow is thrown towards the cotton. Only one stalk, the largest, is now left standing in each hill. In another fortnight it is hoed the third time, throwing the furrow towards the cotton in the same manner as before, and killing all the grass between the rows. About the first of July, when it is a foot high or thereabouts, it is hoed the fourth and last time. Now the whole space between the rows is ploughed, leaving a deep water furrow in the center. During all these hoeings the overseer or driver follows the slaves on horseback with a whip, such as has been described. The fastest hoer takes the lead row. He is usually about a rod in advance of his companions. If one of them passes him, he is whipped. If one falls behind or is a moment idle, he is whipped. In fact, the lash is flying from morning until night, the whole day long. The hoeing season thus continues from April until July, a field having no sooner been finished once, than it is commenced again.

In the latter part of August begins the cotton-picking season. At this time each slave is presented with a sack. A strap is fastened to it, which goes over the neck, holding the mouth of the sack breast high, while the bottom reaches nearly to the ground. Each one is also presented with a large basket that will hold about two barrels. This is to put the cotton in when the sack is filled. The baskets are carried to the field and placed at the beginning of the rows. When a new hand, one unaccustomed to the business, is sent for the first time into the field, he is whipped up smartly, and made for that day to pick as fast as he can possibly. At night it is weighed, so that his capability in cotton picking is known He must bring in the same weight each night following. If it falls short, it is considered evidence that he has been laggard, and a greater or less number of lashes is the penalty.

An ordinary day's work is two hundred pounds. A slave who is accustomed to picking, is punished, if he or she brings in a less quantity than that. There is a great difference among them as regards this kind of labor. Some of them seem to have a natural knack, or quickness, which enables them to pick with great celerity, and with both hands, while others, with whatever practice or industry, are utterly unable to come up to the ordinary standard. Such hands are taken from the cotton field and employed in other business. Patsey, of whom I shall have more to say, was known as the most remarkable cotton picker on Bayou Boeuf. She picked with both hands and with such surprising rapidity, that five hundred pounds a day was not unusual for her.

Each one is tasked, therefore, according to his picking abilities, none, however, to come short of two hundred weight. I, being unskillful always in that business, would have satisfied my master by bringing in the latter quantity, while on the other hand, Patsey would surely have been beaten it she failed to produce twice as much.

The cotton grows from five to seven feet high, each stalk having a great many branches, shooting out in all directions, and lapping each other above the water furrow.

There are few sights more pleasant to the eye, than a wide cotton field when it is in the bloom. It presents an appearance of purity, like an immaculate expanse of light, new-fallen snow.

Sometimes the slave picks down one side of a row, and back upon the other, but more usually, there is one on either side, gathering all that has blossomed, leaving the unopened bolls for a succeeding picking. When the sack is tilled, it is emptied into the basket and trodden down. It is necessary to be extremely careful the first time going through the field, in order not to break the branches off the stalks. The cotton will not bloom upon a broken branch. Epps never failed to inflict the severest chastisement on the unlucky servant who, either carelessly or unavoidably, was guilty in the least degree in this respect.

The hands are required to be in the cotton field as soon as it is light in the morning, and, with the exception of ten or fifteen minutes, which is given them at noon to swallow their allowance of cold bacon, they are not permitted to be a moment idle until it is too dark to see, and when the moon is full, they oftentimes labor till the middle of the night. They do not dare to stop even at dinner time, nor return to the quarters, however late it be, until the order to halt is given by the driver.

The day's work over in the field, the baskets are "toted," or in other words, carried to the gin-house, where the cotton is weighed. No matter how fatigued and weary he may be—no matter how much he longs for sleep and rest—a slave never approaches the gin-house with his basket of cotton but with fear. If it falls short in weight—if he has not performed the full task appointed him, he knows that he must suffer. And if he has exceeded it by ten or twenty pounds, in all probability his master will measure the next day's task accordingly. So, whether he has too little or too much, his approach to the gin-house is always with fear and trembling. Most frequently they have too little, and therefore it is they are not anxious to leave the field. After weighing, follow the whippings; and then the baskets are carried to the cotton house, and their contents stored away like hay, all hands being sent in to tramp it down. If the cotton is not dry, instead of taking it to the gin-house at once, it is laid upon platforms, two feet high, and some three times as wide, covered with boards or plank, with narrow walks running between them.

This done, the labor of the day is not yet ended, by any means. Each one must then attend to his respective chores. One feeds the mules, another the swine—another cuts the wood, and so forth; besides, the packing is all done by candlelight. Finally, at a late hour, they reach the quarters, sleepy and overcome with the long day's toil. Then a fire must be kindled in the cabin, the corn ground in the small hand-mill, and supper, and dinner for the next day in the field, prepared. All that is allowed them is corn and bacon, which is given out at the corn crib and smoke-house every Sunday morning. Each one receives, as his weekly allowance, three and a half pounds of bacon, and corn enough to make a peck of meal. That is all—no tea, coffee, sugar, and with the exception of a very scanty sprinkling now and then, no salt. I can say, from a ten years' residence with Master Epps, that no slave of his is ever likely to suffer from the gout, superinduced by excessive high living. Master Epps' hogs were fed on *shelled* corn—it was thrown out to his "niggers" in the ear. The former, he thought, would fatten faster by shelling, and soaking it in the water— the latter, perhaps, if treated in the same manner, might grow too fat to labor. Master Epps was a shrewd calculator, and knew how to manage his own animals, drunk or sober.

The corn mill stands in the yard beneath a shelter. It is like a common coffee mill, the hopper holding about six quarts. There was one privilege which Master Epps granted freely to every slave he had. They might grind their corn nightly, in such small quantities as their daily wants required, or they might grind the whole week's allowance at one time, on Sundays, just as they preferred. A very generous man was Master Epps!

I kept my corn in a small wooden box, the meal in a gourd; and, by the way, the gourd is one of the most con- venient and necessary utensils on a plantation. Besides supplying the place of all kinds of crockery in a slave cabin, it is used for carrying water to the fields. Another, also, contains the dinner. It dispenses with the necessity of pails, dippers, basins, and such tin and wooden superfluities altogether.

When the corn is ground, and fire is made, the bacon is taken down from the nail on which it hangs, a slice cut off and thrown upon the coals to broil. The majority of slaves have no knife, much less a fork. They cut their bacon with the axe at the wood pile. The corn meal is mixed with a little water placed in the fire, and baked. When it is "done brown," the ashes are scraped off, and being placed upon a chip, which answers for a table, the tenant of the slave hut is ready to sit down upon the ground to supper. By this time it is usually midnight. The same fear of punishment with which they approach the gin-house, possesses them again on lying down to get a snatch of rest. It is the fear of oversleeping in the morning. Such an offence would certainly be attended with not less than twenty lashes. With a prayer that he may be on his feet and wide awake at the first sound of the horn, he sinks to his slumbers nightly.

The softest couches in the world are not to be found in the log mansion of the slave. The one whereon I reclined year after year, was a plank twelve inches wide and ten feet long. My pillow was a stick of wood. The bedding was a coarse blanket, and not a rag or shred beside. Moss might be used, were it not that it directly breeds a swarm of fleas.

The cabin is constructed of logs, without floor or window. The latter is altogether unnecessary, the crevices between the logs admitting sufficient light. In stormy weather the rain drives through them, rendering it comfortless and extremely disagreeable. The rude door hangs on great wooden hinges. In one end is constructed an awkward fireplace.

An hour before daylight the horn is blown. Then the slaves arouse, prepare their breakfast, fill a gourd with water, in another deposit their dinner of cold bacon and corn cake, and hurry to the field again. It is an offence invariably followed by a flogging, to be found at the quarters after daybreak. Then the fears and labors of another day begin; and until its close there is no such thing as rest. He fears he will be caught lagging through the day; he fears to approach the gin-house with his basket-load of cotton at night; he fears, when he lies down, that he will over-sleep himself in the morning. Such is a true, faithful, unexaggerated picture and description of the slave's daily life, during the time of cotton picking, on the shores of Bayou Boeuf.

In the month of January, generally, the fourth and last picking is completed. Then commences the harvesting of corn.

This is considered a secondary crop, and receives far less attention than the cotton. It is planted, as already mentioned, in February. Corn is grown in that region for the purpose of fattening hogs and feeding slaves; very little, if any, being sent to market. It is the white variety, the ear of great size, and the stalk growing to the height of eight, and oftentimes ten feet. In August the leaves are stripped off, dried in the sun, bound in small bundles, and stored away as provender for the mules and oxen. After this the slaves go through the field, turning down the ear, for the purpose of keeping the rains from penetrating to the grain. It is left in this condition until after cotton picking is over, whether earlier or later. Then the ears are separated from the stalks, and deposited in the corn crib with the husks on; otherwise, stripped of the husks, the weevil would destroy it. The stalks are left standing in the field.

The Carolina, or sweet potato, is also grown in that region to some extent. They are not fed, however, to hogs or cattle, and are considered but of small importance. They are preserved by placing them upon the surface of the ground, with a slight covering of earth or cornstalks. There is not a cellar on Bayou Boeuf. The ground is so low it would fill with water. Potatoes are worth from two to three "bits," or shillings a barrel; corn, except when there is an unusual scarcity, can be purchased at the same rate.

As soon as the cotton and corn crops are secured, the stalks are pulled up, thrown into piles and burned. The ploughs are started at the same time, throwing up the beds again, preparatory to another planting. The soil, in the parishes of Rapides and Avoyelles, and throughout the whole country, so far as my observation extended, is of exceeding richness and fertility. It is a kind of marl, of a brown or reddish color. It does not require those invigorating composts necessary to more barren lands, and on the same field the same crop is grown for many successive years.

Ploughing, planting, picking cotton, gathering the corn, and pulling and burning stalks, occupies the whole of the four seasons of the year. Drawing and cutting wood, pressing cotton, fattening and killing hogs, are but incidental labors.

In the month of September or October, the hogs are run out of the swamps by dogs, and confined in pens. On a cold morning, generally about New Year's Day, they are slaughtered. Each carcass is cut into six parts, and piled one above the other in salt, upon large tables in the smokehouse. In this condition it remains a fortnight, when it is hung up, and a fire built, and continued more than half the time during the remainder of the year. This thorough smoking is necessary to prevent the bacon from becoming infested with worms. In so warm a climate it is difficult to preserve it, and very many times myself and my companions have received our weekly allowance of three pounds and a half, when it was full of these disgusting vermin.

Although the swamps are overrun with cattle, they are never made the source of profit, to any considerable extent. The planter cuts his mark upon the ear, or brands his initials upon the side, and turns them into the swamps, to roam unrestricted within their almost limitless confines. They are the Spanish breed, small and spike-horned. I have known of droves being taken from Bayou Boeuf, but it is of very rare occurrence. The value of the best cows is about five dollars each. Two quarts at one milking, would be considered an unusual large quantity. They furnish little tallow, and that of a soft, inferior quality. Notwithstanding the great number of cows that throng the swamps, the planters are indebted to the North for their cheese and butter, which is purchased in the New Orleans market. Salted beef is not an article of food either in the great house, or in the cabin.

Master Epps was accustomed to attend shooting matches for the purpose of obtaining what fresh beef he required. These sports occurred weekly at the neighboring village of

Holmesville. Fat beeves are driven thither and shot at, a stipulated price being demanded for the privilege. The lucky marksman divides the flesh among his fellows, and in this manner the attending planters are supplied.

The great number of tame and untamed cattle which swarm the woods and swamps of Bayou Boeuf, most probably suggested that appellation to the French, inasmuch as the term, translated, signifies the creek or river of the wild ox.

Garden products, such as cabbages, turnips and the like, are cultivated for the use of the master and his family. They have greens and vegetables at all times and seasons of the year. "The grass withereth and the flower fadeth" before the desolating winds of autumn in the chill northern latitudes, but perpetual verdure overspreads the hot lowlands, and flowers bloom in the heart of winter, in the region of Bayou Boeuf.

There are no meadows appropriated to the cultivation of the grasses. The leaves of the corn supply a sufficiency of food for the laboring cattle, while the rest provide for themselves all the year in the ever-growing pasture.

There are many other peculiarities of climate, habit, custom, and of the manner of living and laboring at the South, but the foregoing, it is supposed, will give the reader an insight and general idea of life on a cotton plantation in Louisiana. The mode of cultivating cane, and the process of sugar manufacturing will be mentioned in another place.

CHAPTER 13

On my arrival at Master Epps', in obedience to his order, the first business upon which I entered was the making of an axe-helve. The handles in use there are simply a round, straight stick. I made a crooked one, shaped like those to which I had been accustomed at the North. When finished, and presented to Epps, he looked at it with astonishment, unable to determine exactly what it was. He had never before seen such a handle, and when I explained its conveniences, he was forcibly struck with the novelty of the idea. He kept it in the house a long time, and when his friends called, was wont to exhibit it as a curiosity.

It was now the season of hoeing. I was first sent into the cornfield, and afterwards set to scraping cotton. In this employment I remained until hoeing time was nearly passed, when I began to experience the symptoms of approaching illness. I was attacked with chills, which were succeeded by a burning fever. I became weak and emaciated, and frequently so dizzy that it caused me to reel and stagger like a drunken man. Nevertheless I was compelled to keep up my row. When in health I found little difficulty in keeping pace with my fellow laborers, but now it seemed to be an utter impossibility. Often I fell behind, when the driver's lash was sure to greet my back, infusing into my sick and drooping body a little temporary energy. I continued to decline until at length the whip became entirely ineffectual. The sharpest sting of the rawhide could not arouse me. Finally, in September, when the busy season of cotton picking was at hand, I was unable to leave my cabin. Up to this time I had received no medicine, nor any attention from my master or mistress. The old cook visited me occasionally, preparing me corn-coffee, and sometimes boiling a bit of bacon, when I had grown too feeble to accomplish it myself.

When it was said that I would die, Master Epps, unwilling to bear the loss, which the death of an animal worth a thousand dollars would bring upon him, concluded to incur the expense of sending to Holmesville for Dr. Wines. He announced to Epps that it was the effect of the climate, and there was a probability of his losing me. He directed me to eat no meat, and to partake of no more food than was absolutely necessary to sustain life. Several weeks elapsed, during which time, under the scanty diet to which was subjected, I had partially recovered. One morning, long before I was in a proper condition to labor, Epps appeared at the cabin door, and, presenting me a sack, ordered me to the cotton field. At this time I had had no experience whatever in cotton picking. It was an awkward business indeed. While others used both hands, snatching the cotton and depositing it in the mouth of the sack, with a precision and dexterity that was incomprehensible to me, I had to seize the boll with one hand, and deliberately draw out the white, gushing blossom with the other.

Depositing the cotton in the sack, moreover, was a difficulty that demanded the exercise of both hands and eyes. I was compelled to pick it from the ground where it would fall, nearly as often as from the stalk where it had grown. I made havoc also with the branches, loaded with the yet unbroken bolls, the long, cumbersome sack swinging from side to side in a manner not allowable in the cotton field. After a most laborious day I arrived at the gin-house with my load. When the scale determined its weight to be only ninety-five pounds, not half the quantity required of the poorest picker, Epps threatened the severest flogging, but in consideration of my being a "raw hand," concluded to pardon me on that occasion The following day, and many days succeeding, I returned at night with no better success—I was evidently not designed for that kind of labor. I had not the gift—the dexterous fingers and quick motion of Patsey, who could fly along one side of a row of cotton, stripping it of its undefiled and fleecy whiteness miraculously fast. Practice and whipping were alike unavailing, and Epps, satisfied of it at last, swore I was a disgrace—that I was not fit to associate with a cotton-picking "nigger"—that I could not pick enough in a day to pay the trouble of weighing it, and that I should go into the cotton field no more. I was now employed in cutting and hauling wood, drawing cotton from the field to the gin-house, and performed whatever other service was required. Suffice to say, I was never permitted to be idle.

It was rarely that a day passed by without one or more whippings. This occurred at the time the cotton was weighed. The delinquent, whose weight had fallen short, was taken out, stripped, made to lie upon the ground, face downwards, when he received a punishment proportioned to his offence. It is the literal, unvarnished truth, that the crack of the lash, and the shrieking of the slaves, can be heard from dark till bed time, on Epps' plantation, any day almost during the entire period of the cotton-picking season.

The number of lashes is graduated according to the nature of the case. Twenty-five are deemed a mere brush, inflicted, for instance, when a dry leaf or piece of boll is found in the cotton, or when a branch is broken in the field; fifty is the ordinary penalty following all delinquencies of the next higher grade; one hundred is called severe: it is the punishment inflicted for the serious offence of standing idle in the field;

from one hundred and fifty to two hundred is bestowed upon him who quarrels with his cabin-mates, and five hundred, well laid on, besides the mangling of the dogs, perhaps, is certain to consign the poor, unpitied runaway to weeks of pain and agony.

During the two years Epps remained on the plantation at Bayou Huff Power, he was in the habit, as often as once in a fortnight at least, of coming home intoxicated from Holmesville. The shooting matches almost invariably concluded with a debauch. At such times he was boisterous and half-crazy. Often he would break the dishes, chairs, and whatever furniture he could lay his hands on. When satisfied with his amusement in the house, he would seize the whip and walk forth into the yard. Then it behooved the slaves to be watchful and exceeding wary. The first one who came within reach felt the smart of his lash. Sometimes for hours he would keep them running in all directions, dodging around the corners of the cabins. Occasionally he would come upon one unawares, and if he succeeded in inflicting a fair, round blow, it was a feat that much delighted him. The younger children, and the aged, who had become inactive, suffered then. In the midst of the confusion he would slyly take his stand behind a cabin, waiting with raised whip, to dash it into the first black face that peeped cautiously around the corner.

At other times he would come home in a less brutal humor. Then there must be a merrymaking. They all must move to the measure of a tune. Then Master Epps must needs regale his melodious ears with the music of a fiddle. Then did he become buoyant, elastic, gaily "tripping the light fantastic toe" around the piazza and all through the house.

Tibeats, at the time of my sale, had informed him I could play on the violin. He had received his information from Ford. Through the importunities of Mistress Epps, her husband had been induced to purchase me one during a visit to New Orleans. Frequently I was called into the house to play before the family, mistress being passionately fond of music.

All of us would be assembled in the large room of the great house, whenever Epps came home in one of his dancing moods. No matter how worn out and tired we were, there must be a general dance. When properly stationed on the floor, I would strike up a tune, "Dance, you d—d niggers, dance," Epps would shout.

Then there must be no halting or delay, no slow or languid movements; all must be brisk, and lively, and alert. "Up and down, heel and toe, and away we go," was the order of the hour. Epps' portly form mingled with those of his dusky slaves, moving rapidly through all the mazes of the dance.

Usually his whip was in his hand, ready to fall about the ears of the presumptuous thrall, who dared to rest a moment, or even stop to catch his breath. When he was himself exhausted, there would be a brief cessation, but it would be very brief. With a slash, and crack, and flourish of the whip, he would shout again, "Dance, niggers, dance," and away they would go once more, pell-mell, while I, spurred by an occasional sharp touch of the lash, sat in a corner, extracting from my violin a marvelous quick-stepping tune. The mistress often upbraided him, declaring she would return to her father's house at Cheneyville; nevertheless, there were times she could not restrain a burst of laughter, on witnessing his uproarious pranks. Frequently, we were thus detained until almost morning. Bent with excessive toil—actually suffering for a little refreshing rest, and feeling rather as if we could cast ourselves upon the earth and weep, many a night in the house of Edwin Epps have his unhappy slaves been made to dance and laugh.

Notwithstanding these deprivations in order to gratify the whim of an unreasonable master, we had to be in the field as soon as it was light, and during the day perform the ordinary and accustomed task. Such deprivations could not be urged at the scales in extenuation of any lack of weight, or in the cornfield for not hoeing with the usual rapidity. The whippings were just as severe as if we'd gone forth in the morning, strengthened and invigorated by a night's repose. Indeed, after such frantic revels, he was always more sour and savage than before, punishing for slighter causes, and using the whip with increased and more vindictive energy.

Ten years I toiled for that man without reward. Ten years of my incessant labor has contributed to increase the bulk of his possessions. Ten years I was compelled to address him with downcast eyes and uncovered head—in the attitude and language of a slave. I am indebted to him for nothing, save undeserved abuse and stripes.

Beyond the reach of his inhuman thong, and standing on the soil of the free state where I was born, thanks be to Heaven, I can raise my head once more among men. I can speak of the wrongs I have suffered, and of those who inflicted them, with upraised eyes. But I have no desire to speak of him or any other one otherwise than truthfully. Yet to speak truthfully of Edwin Epps would be to say—he is a man in whose heart the quality of kindness or of justice is not found. A rough, rude energy, united with an uncultivated mind and an avaricious spirit, are his prominent characteristics. He is known as a "nigger breaker," distinguished for his faculty of subduing the spirit of the slave, and priding himself upon his reputation in this respect, as a jockey boasts of his skill in managing a refractory horse. He looked upon a colored man, not as a human being, responsible to his Creator for the small talent entrusted to him, but as a "chattel personal," as mere live property, no better, except in value, than his mule or dog. When the evidence, clear and indisputable, was laid before him that I was a free man, and as much entitled to my liberty as he—when, on the day I left, he was informed that I had a wife and children, as dear to me as his babes to him, he only raved and swore, denouncing the law that tore me from him, and declaring he would find out the man who had forwarded the letter that disclosed the place of my captivity, if there was any virtue or power in money, and would take his life. He thought of nothing but his loss, and cursed me for having been born free. He could have stood unmoved and seen the tongues of his poor slaves torn out by the roots—he could have seen them burned to ashes over a slow fire, or gnawed to death by dogs, if it only brought him profit. Such a hard, cruel, unjust man is Edwin Epps.

There was but one greater savage on Bayou Boeuf than he. Jim Burns' plantation was cultivated, as already mentioned, exclusively by women. That barbarian kept their backs so sore and raw, that they could not perform the customary labor demanded daily of the slave. He boasted of his cruelty, and through all the country round was accounted a more thorough-going, energetic man than even Epps. A brute himself, Jim Burns had not a particle of mercy for his subject brutes, and like a fool, whipped and scourged away the very strength upon which depended his amount of gain.

Epps remained on Huff Power two years, when, having accumulated a considerable sum of money, he expended it in the purchase of the plantation on the east bank of Bayou Boeuf, where he still continues to reside. He took possession of it in 1845, after the holidays were passed. He carried thither with him nine slaves, all of whom, except myself, and Susan, who has since died, remain there yet. He made no addition to this force, and for eight years the following were my companions in his quarters, viz: Abram, Wiley, Phebe, Bob, Henry, Edward, and Patsey. All these, except Edward, born since, were purchased out of a drove by Epps during the time he was overseer for Archy B. Williams, whose plantation is situated on the shore of Red River, not far from Alexandria.

Abram was tall, standing a full head above any common man. He is sixty years of age, and was born in Tennessee. Twenty years ago, he was purchased by a trader, carried into

South Carolina, and sold to James Buford, of Williamsburgh county, in that state. In his youth he was renowned for his great strength, but age and unremitting toil have somewhat shattered his powerful frame and enfeebled his mental faculties.

Wiley is forty-eight. He was born on the estate of William Tassle, and for many years took charge of that gentleman's ferry over the Big Black River, in South Carolina.

Phebe was a slave of Buford, Tassle's neighbor, and having married Wiley, he bought the latter, at her instigation. Buford was a kind master, sheriff of the county, and in those days a man of wealth.

Bob and Henry are Phebe's children, by a former husband, their father having been abandoned to give place to Wiley. That seductive youth had insinuated himself into Phebe's affections, and therefore the faithless spouse had gently kicked her first husband out of her cabin door. Edward had been born to them on Bayou Huff Power.

Patsey is twenty-three—also from Buford's plantation. She is in no wise connected with the others, but glories in the fact that she is the offspring of a "Guinea nigger," brought over to Cuba in a slave ship, and in the course of trade transferred to Buford, who was her mother's owner.

This, as I learned from them, is a genealogical account of my master's slaves. For years they had been together. Often they recalled the memories of other days, and sighed to retrace their steps to the old home in Carolina. Troubles came upon their master Buford, which brought far greater troubles upon them. He became involved in debt, and unable to bear up against his failing fortunes, was compelled to sell these, and others of his slaves. In a chain gang they had been driven from beyond the Mississippi to the plantation of Archy B. Williams. Edwin Epps, who, for a long while had been his driver and overseer, was about establishing himself in business on his own account, at the time of their arrival, and accepted them in payment of his wages.

Old Abram was a kind-hearted being—a sort of patriarch among us, fond of entertaining his younger brethren with grave and serious discourse. He was deeply versed in such philosophy as is taught in the cabin of the slave; but the great absorbing hobby of Uncle Abram was General Jackson, whom his young master in Tennessee had followed to the wars. He loved to wander back, in imagination, to the place where he was born, and to recount the scenes of his youth during those stirring times when the nation was in arms. He had been athletic, and more keen and powerful than the generality of his race, but now his eye had become dim, and his natural force abated. Very often indeed, while discussing the best method of baking the hoecake, or expatiating at large upon the glory of Jackson, he would forget where he left his hat, or his hoe, or his basket; and then would the old man be laughed at, if Epps was absent, and whipped if he was present. So was he perplexed continually, and sighed to think that he was growing aged and going to decay. Philosophy and Jackson and forgetfulness had played the mischief with him, and it was evident that all of them combined were fast bringing down the gray hairs of Uncle Abram to the grave.

Aunt Phebe had been an excellent field hand, but latterly was put into the kitchen, where she remained, except occasionally, in a time of uncommon hurry. She was a sly old creature, and when not in the presence of her mistress or her master, was garrulous in the extreme.

Wiley, on the contrary, was silent. He performed his task without murmur or complaint, seldom indulging in the luxury of speech, except to utter a wish that he was away from Epps, and back once more in South Carolina.

Bob and Henry had reached the ages of twenty and twenty-three, and were distinguished for nothing extraordinary or unusual, while Edward, a lad of thirteen, not yet able to maintain his row in the corn or the cotton field, was kept in the great house, to wait on the little Eppses.

Patsey was slim and straight. She stood erect as the human form is capable of standing. There was an air of loftiness in her movement, that neither labor, nor weariness, nor punishment could destroy. Truly, Patsey was a splendid animal, and were it not that bondage had enshrouded her intellect in utter and everlasting darkness, would have been chief among ten thousand of her people. She could leap the highest fences, and a fleet hound it was indeed, that could outstrip her in a race. No horse could fling her from his back. She was a skillful teamster. She turned as true a furrow as the best, and at splitting rails there were none who could excel her. When the order to halt was heard at night, she would have her mules at the crib, unharnessed, fed and curried, before Uncle Abram had found his hat. Not, however, for all or any of these, was she chiefly famous. Such lightning-like motion was in her fingers as no other fingers ever possessed, and therefore it was, that in cotton-picking time, Patsey was queen of the field.

She had a genial and pleasant temper, and was faithful and obedient. Naturally, she was a joyous creature, a laughing, light-hearted girl, rejoicing in the mere sense of existence. Yet Patsey wept oftener, and suffered more, than any of her companions. She had been literally excoriated. Her back bore the scars of a thousand stripes; not because she was backward in her work, nor because she was of an unmindful and rebellious spirit, but because it had fallen to her lot to be the slave of a licentious master and a jealous mistress. She shrank before the lustful eye of the one, and was in danger even of her life at the hands of the other, and between the two, she was indeed accursed. In the great house, for days together, there were high and angry words, poutings and estrangement, whereof she was the innocent cause. Nothing delighted the mistress so much as to see her suffer, and more than once, when Epps had refused to sell her, has she tempted me with bribes to put her secretly to death and bury her body in some lonely place in the margin of the swamp. Gladly would Patsey have appeased this unforgiving spirit, if it had been in her power, but not like Joseph, dared she escape from Master Epps, leaving her garment in his hand. Patsey walked under a cloud. If she uttered a word in opposition to her master's will, the lash was resorted to at once, to bring her to subjection; if she was not watchful when about her cabin, or when walking in the yard, a billet of wood, or a broken bottle perhaps, hurled from her mistress' hand, would smite her unexpectedly in the face. The enslaved victim of lust and hate, Patsey had no comfort of her life.

These were my companions and fellow slaves, with whom I was accustomed to be driven to the field, and with whom it has been my lot to dwell for ten years in the log cabins of Edwin Epps. They, if living, are yet toiling on the banks of Bayou Boeuf, never destined to breathe, as I now do, the blessed air of liberty, nor to shake off the heavy shackles that enthrall them, until they shall lie down forever in the dust.

CHAPTER 14

The first year of Epps' residence on the bayou, 1845, the caterpillars almost totally destroyed the cotton crop throughout that region. There was little to be done, so that the slaves were necessarily idle half the time. However, there came a rumor to Bayou Boeuf that wages were high, and laborers in great demand on the sugar plantations in St. Mary's parish. This parish is situated on the coast of the Gulf of Mexico, about one hundred and forty miles from Avoyelles. The Rio Teche, a considerable stream, flows through St. Mary's to the gulf.

It was determined by the planters, on the receipt of this intelligence, to make up a drove of slaves to be sent down to Tuckapaw in St. Mary's, for the purpose of hiring them out in the cane fields. Accordingly, in the month of September, there were one hundred and forty-seven collected at Holmesville, Abram, Bob and myself among the number. Of these about one-half were women. Epps, Alonson Pierce, Henry Toler, and Addison Roberts, were the white men, selected to accompany, and take charge of the drove. They had a two-horse carriage and two saddle horses for their use. A large wagon, drawn by four horses, and driven by John, a boy belonging to Mr. Roberts, carried the blankets and provisions.

About two o'clock in the afternoon, having been fed, preparations were made to depart. The duty assigned me was, to take charge of the blankets and provisions, and see that none were lost by the way. The carriage proceeded in advance, the wagon following; behind this the slaves were arranged, while the two horsemen brought up the rear, and in this order the procession moved out of Holmesville.

That night we reached a Mr. McCrow's plantation, a distance of ten or fifteen miles, when we were ordered to halt. Large fires were built, and each one spreading his blanket on the ground, laid down upon it. The white men lodged in the great house. An hour before day we were aroused by the drivers coming among us, cracking their whips and ordering us to arise. Then the blankets were rolled up, and being severally delivered to me and deposited in the wagon, the procession set forth again.

The following night it rained violently. We were all drenched, our clothes saturated with mud and water. Reaching an open shed, formerly a gin-house, we found beneath it such shelter as it afforded. There was not room for all of us to lay down. There we remained, huddled together, through the night, continuing our march, as usual, in the morning. During the journey we were fed twice a day, boiling our bacon and baking our corn cake at the fires in the same manner as in our huts. We passed through La Fayetteville, Mountsville, New-Town, to Centreville, where Bob and Uncle Abram were hired. Our number decreased as we advanced—nearly every sugar plantation requiring the services of one or more.

On our route we passed the Grand Coteau or prairie, a vast space of level, monotonous country, without a tree, except an occasional one which had been transplanted near some dilapidated dwelling. It was once thickly populated, and under cultivation, but for some cause had been abandoned. The business of the scattered inhabitants that now dwell upon it is principally raising cattle. Immense herds were feeding upon it as we passed. In the centre of the Grand Coteau one feels as if he were on the ocean, out of sight of land. As far as the eye can see, in all directions, it is but a ruined and deserted waste.

I was hired to Judge Turner, a distinguished man and extensive planter, whose large estate is situated on Bayou Salle, within a few miles of the gulf. Bayou Salle is a small stream flowing into the bay of Atchafalaya. For some days I was employed at Turner's in repairing his sugar house, when a cane knife was put into my hand, and with thirty or forty others, I was sent into the field. I found no such difficulty in learning the art of cutting cane that I had in picking cotton. It came to me naturally and intuitively, and in a short time I was able to keep up with the fastest knife. Before the cutting was over, however, Judge Tanner transferred me from the field to the sugar house, to act there in the capacity of driver. From the time of the commencement of sugar making to the close, the grinding and boiling does not cease day or night. The whip was given me with directions to use it upon any one who was caught standing idle. If I failed to obey them to the letter, there was another one for my own back. In addition to this my duty was to call on and off the different gangs at the proper time. I had no regular periods of rest, and could never snatch but a few moments of sleep at a time.

It is the custom in Louisiana, as I presume it is in other slave states, to allow the slave to retain whatever compensation he may obtain for services performed on Sundays. In this way, only, are they able to provide themselves with any luxury or convenience whatever. When a slave, purchased, or kidnapped in the North, is transported to a cabin on Bayou Boeuf, he is furnished with neither knife, nor fork nor dish, nor kettle, nor any other thing in the shape of crockery, or furniture of any nature or description. He is furnished with a blanket before he reaches there, and wrapping that around him, he can either stand up, or lie down upon the ground, or on a board, if his master has no use for it. He is at liberty to find a gourd in which to keep his meal, or he can eat his corn from the cob, just as he pleases. To ask the master for a knife, or skillet, or any small convenience of the kind, would be answered with a kick, or laughed at as a joke. Whatever necessary article of this nature is found in a cabin has been purchased with Sunday money. However injurious to the morals, it is certainly a blessing to the physical condition of the slave, to be permitted to break the Sabbath. Otherwise there would be no way to provide himself with any utensils, which seem to be indispensable to him who is compelled to be his own cook.

On cane plantations in sugar time, there is no distinction as to the days of the week. It is well understood that all hands must labor on the Sabbath, and it is equally well understood that those especially who are hired, as I was to Judge Turner, and others in succeeding years, shall receive remuneration for it. It is usual, also, in the most hurrying time of cotton-picking, to require the same extra service. From this source, slaves generally are afforded an opportunity of earning sufficient to purchase a knife a kettle, tobacco and so forth. The females, discarding the latter luxury, are apt to expend their little revenue in the purchase of gaudy ribbons, wherewithal to deck their hair in the merry season of the holidays.

I remained in St. Mary's until the first of January, during which time my Sunday money amounted to ten dollars. I met with other good fortune, for which I was indebted to my violin, my constant companion, the source of profit, and soother of my sorrows during years of servitude. There was a grand party of whites assembled at Mr. Yarney's, in Centreville, a hamlet in the vicinity of Turner's plantation. I was employed to play for them, and so well pleased were the merrymakers with my performance, that a contribution was taken for my benefit, which amounted to seventeen dollars.

With this sum in possession, I was looked upon by my fellows as a millionaire. It afforded me great pleasure to look at it—to count it over and over again, day after day. Visions of cabin furniture, of water pails, of pocket knives, new shoes and coats and hats, floated through my fancy, and up through all rose the triumphant contemplation, that I was the wealthiest "nigger" on Bayou Boeuf.

Vessels run up the Rio Teche to Centreville. While there, I was bold enough one day to present myself before the captain of a steamer, and beg permission to hide myself among the freight. I was emboldened to risk the hazard of such a step, from overhearing a conversation, in the course of which I ascertained he was a native of the North. I did not relate to him the particulars of my history, but only expressed an ardent desire to escape from slavery for a free state. He pitied me, but said it would be impossible to avoid the vigilant custom house officers in New Orleans, and that detection would subject him to punishment, and his vessel to confiscation. My earnest entreaties evidently excited his sympathies, and doubtless he would have yielded to them, could he have done so with any kind of safety. I was compelled to smother the sudden flame that lighted up my bosom with sweet hopes of liberation, and turn my steps once more towards the increasing darkness of despair.

Immediately after this event the drove assembled at Centreville, and several of the owners having arrived and collected the monies due for our services, we were driven back to Bayou Boeuf. It was on our return, while passing through a small village, that I caught sight of Tibeats, seated in the door of a dirty grocery, looking somewhat seedy and out of repair. Passion and poor whisky, I doubt not, have ere this laid him on the shelf.

During our absence, I learned from Aunt Phebe and Patsey, that the latter had been getting deeper and deeper into trouble. The poor girl was truly an object of pity. "Old Hogjaw," the name by which Epps was called, when the slaves were by themselves, had beaten her more severely and frequently than ever. As surely as he came from Holmesville, elated with liquor—and it was often in those days—he would whip her, merely to gratify the mistress; would punish her to an extent almost beyond endurance, for an offence of which he himself was the sole and irresistible cause. In his sober moments he could not always be prevailed upon to indulge his wife's insatiable thirst for vengeance.

To be rid of Patsey—to place her beyond sight or reach, by sale, or death, or in any other manner, of late years, seemed to be the ruling thought and passion of my mistress. Patsey had been a favorite when a child, even in the great house. She had been petted and admired for her uncommon sprightliness and pleasant disposition. She had been fed many a time, so Uncle Abram said, even on biscuit and milk, when the madam, in her younger days, was wont to call her to the piazza, and fondle her as she would a playful kitten. But a sad change had come over the spirit of the woman. Now, only black and angry fiends ministered in the temple of her heart, until she could look on Patsey but with concentrated venom.

Mistress Epps was not naturally such an evil woman, after all. She was possessed of the devil, jealousy, it is true, but aside from that, there was much in her character to admire. Her father, Mr. Roberts, resided in Cheneyville, an influential and honorable man, and as much respected throughout the parish as any other citizen. She had been well educated at some institution this side the Mississippi; was beautiful, accomplished, and usually good-humored. She was kind to all of us but Patsey—frequently, in the absence of her husband, sending out to us some little dainty from her own table. In other situations—in a different society from that which exists on the shores of Bayou Boeuf, she would have been pronounced an elegant and fascinating woman. An ill wind it was that blew her into the arms of Epps.

He respected and loved his wife as much as a coarse nature like his is capable of loving, but supreme selfishness always overmastered conjugal affection.

"He loved as well as baser natures can,
But a mean heart and soul were in that man."

He was ready to gratify any whim—to grant any request she made, provided it did not cost too much. Patsey was equal to any two of his slaves in the cotton field. He could not replace her with the same money she would bring. The idea of disposing of her, therefore, could not be entertained. The mistress did not regard her at all in that light. The pride of the haughty woman was aroused; the blood of the fiery southern boiled at the sight of Patsey, and nothing less than trampling out the life of the helpless bondwoman would satisfy her.

Sometimes the current of her wrath turned upon him whom she had just cause to hate. But the storm of angry words would pass over at length, and there would be a season of calm again. At such times Patsey trembled with fear, and cried as if her heart would break, for she knew from painful experience, that if mistress should work herself to the red-hot pitch of rage, Epps would quiet her at last with a promise that Patsey should be flogged—a promise he was sure to keep. Thus did pride, and jealousy, and vengeance war with avarice and brute-passion in the mansion of my master, filling it with daily tumult and contention. Thus, upon the head of Patsey—the simple-minded slave, in whose heart God had implanted the seeds of virtue—the force of all these domestic tempests spent itself at last.

During the summer succeeding my return from St Mary's parish, I conceived a plan of providing myself with food, which, though simple, succeeded beyond expectation. It has been followed by many others in my condition, up and down the bayou, and of such benefit has it become that I am almost persuaded to look upon myself as a benefactor. That summer the worms got into the bacon. Nothing but ravenous hunger could induce us to swallow it. The weekly allowance of meal scarcely sufficed to satisfy us. It was customary with us, as it is with all in that region, where the allowance is exhausted before Saturday night, or is in such a state as to render it nauseous and disgusting, to hunt in the swamps for coon and opossum. This, however, must be done at night, after the day's work is accomplished. There are planters whose slaves, for months at a time, have no other meat than such as is obtained in this manner. No objections are made to hunting, inasmuch as it dispenses with drafts upon the smoke-house, and because every marauding coon that is killed is so much saved from the standing corn. They are hunted with dogs and clubs, slaves not being allowed the use of firearms.

The flesh of the coon is palatable, but verily there is nothing in all butcherdom so delicious as a roasted possum. They are a round, rather long-bodied, little animal, of a whitish color, with nose like a pig, and caudal extremity like a rat. They burrow among the roots and in the hollows of the gum tree, and are clumsy and slow of motion. They are deceitful and cunning creatures. On receiving the slightest tap of a stick, they will roll over on the ground and feign death. If the hunter leaves him, in pursuit of another, without first taking particular pains to break his neck, the chances are, on his return, he is not to be found. The little animal has outwitted the enemy—has "played possum"—and is off.

But after a long and hard day's work, the weary slave feels little like going to the swamp for his supper, and half the time prefers throwing himself on the cabin floor without it. It is for the interest of the master that the servant should not suffer in health from starvation, and it is also for his interest that he should not become gross from overfeeding. In the estimation of the owner, a slave is the most serviceable when in rather a lean and lank condition, such a condition as the racehorse is in, when fitted for the course, and in that condition they are generally to be found on the sugar and cotton plantations along Red River.

My cabin was within a few rods of the bayou bank, and necessity being indeed the mother of invention, I resolved upon a mode of obtaining the requisite amount of food, without the trouble of resorting nightly to the woods. This was to construct a fish trap. Having, in my mind, conceived the manner in which it could be done, the next Sunday I set about putting it into practical execution. It may be impossible for me to convey to the reader a full and correct idea of its construction, but the following will serve as a general description:

A frame between two and three feet square is made, and of a greater or less height, according to the depth of water. Boards or slats are nailed on three sides of this frame, not so closely, however, as to prevent the water circulating freely through it. A door is fitted into the fourth side, in such manner that it will slide easily up and down in the grooves cut in the two posts. A movable bottom is then so fitted that it can be raised to the top of the frame without difficulty. In the centre of the movable bottom an auger hole is bored, and into this one end of a handle or round stick is fastened on the underside so loosely that it will turn. The handle ascends from the centre of the movable bottom to the top of the frame, or as much higher as is desirable. Up and down this handle, in a great many places, are gimlet holes, through which small sticks are inserted, extending to opposite sides of the frame. So many of these small sticks are running out from the handle in all directions, that a fish of any considerable dimensions cannot pass through without hitting one of them. The frame is then placed in the water and made stationary.

The trap is "set" by sliding or drawing up the door, and kept in that position by another stick, one end of which rests in a notch on the inner side, the other end in a notch made in the handle, running up from the centre of the movable bottom. The trap is baited by rolling a handful of wet meal and cotton together until it becomes hard, and depositing it in the back part of the frame. A fish swimming through the upraised door towards the bait, necessarily strikes one of the small sticks turning the handle, which displacing the stick supporting the door, the latter falls, securing the fish within the frame. Taking hold of the top of the handle, the movable bottom is then drawn up to the surface of the water, and the fish taken out. There may have been other such traps in use before mine was constructed, but if there were I had never happened to see one. Bayou Boeuf abounds in fish of large size and excellent quality, and after this time I was very rarely in want of one for myself, or for my comrades. Thus a mine was opened—a new resource was developed, hitherto unthought of by the enslaved children of Africa, who toil and hunger along the shores of that sluggish, but prolific stream.

About the time of which I am now writing, an event occurred in our immediate neighborhood, which made a deep impression upon me, and which shows the state of society existing there, and the manner in which affronts are oftentimes avenged. Directly opposite our quarters, on the other side of the bayou, was situated the plantation of Mr. Marshall. He belonged to a family among the most wealthy and aristocratic in the country. A gentleman from the vicinity of Natchez had been negotiating with him for the purchase of the estate. One day a messenger came in great haste to our plantation, saying that a bloody and fearful battle was going on at Marshall's—that blood had been spilled—and unless the combatants were forthwith separated, the result would be disastrous.

On repairing to Marshall's house, a scene presented itself that beggars description. On the floor of one of the rooms lay the ghastly corpse of the man from Natchez, while Marshall, enraged and covered with wounds and blood, was stalking back and forth, "breathing out threatenings and slaughter." A difficulty had arisen in the course of their negotiation, high words ensued, when drawing their weapons, the deadly strife began that ended so unfortunately. Marshall was never placed in confinement. A sort of trial or investigation was had at Marksville, when he was acquitted, and returned to his plantation, rather more respected, as I thought, than ever, from the fact that the blood of a fellow being was on his soul.

Epps interested himself in his behalf, accompanying him to Marksville, and on all occasions loudly justifying him, but his services in this respect did not afterwards deter a kinsman of this same Marshall from seeking his life also. A brawl occurred between them over a gambling table, which terminated in a deadly feud. Riding up on horseback in front of the house one day, armed with pistols and bowie knife, Marshall challenged him to come forth and make a final settlement of the quarrel, or he would brand him as a coward, and shoot him like a dog the first opportunity. Not through cowardice, nor from any conscientious scruples, in my opinion, but through the influence of his wife, he was restrained from accepting the challenge of his enemy. A reconciliation, however, was effected afterward, since which time they have been on terms of the closest intimacy.

Such occurrences, which would bring upon the parties

concerned in them merited and condign punishment in the Northern States, are frequent on the bayou, and pass without notice, and almost without comment. Every man carries his bowie knife, and when two fall out, they set to work hacking and thrusting at each other, more like savages than civilized and enlightened beings.

The existence of slavery in its most cruel form among them has a tendency to brutalize the humane and finer feelings of their nature. Daily witnesses of human suffering—listening to the agonizing screeches of the slave—beholding him writhing beneath the merciless lash—bitten and torn by dogs—dying without attention, and buried without shroud or coffin it cannot otherwise be expected, than that they should become brutified and reckless of human life. It is true there are many kind-hearted and good men in the parish of Avoyelles—such men as William Ford—who can look with pity upon the sufferings of a slave, just as there are, over all the world, sensitive and sympathetic spirits, who cannot look with indifference upon the sufferings of any creature which the Almighty has endowed with life. It is not the fault of the slaveholder that he is cruel, so much as it is the fault of the system under which he lives. He cannot withstand the influence of habit and associations that surround him. Taught from earliest childhood, by all that he sees and hears, that the rod is for the slave's back, he will not be apt to change his opinions in maturer years.

There may be humane masters, as there certainly are inhuman ones—there may be slaves well-clothed, well-fed, and happy, as there surely are those half-clad, half-starved and miserable; nevertheless, the institution that tolerates such wrong and inhumanity as I have witnessed, is a cruel, unjust, and barbarous one. Men may write fictions portraying lowly life as it is, or as it is not—may expatiate with owlish gravity upon the bliss of ignorance—discourse flippantly from armchairs of the pleasures of slave life; but let them toil with him in the field—sleep with him in the cabin—feed with him on husks; let them behold him scourged, hunted, trampled on, and they will come back with another story in their mouths. Let them know the *heart* of the poor slave—learn his secret thoughts—thoughts he dare not utter in the hearing of the white man; let them sit by him in the silent watches of the night—converse with him in trustful confidence, of "life, liberty, and the pursuit of happiness," and they will find that ninety-nine out of every hundred are intelligent enough to understand their situation, and to cherish in their bosoms the love of freedom, as passionately as themselves.

CHAPTER 15

In consequence of my inability in cotton picking, Epps was in the habit of hiring me out on sugar plantations during the season of cane-cutting and sugar-making. He received for my services a dollar a day, with the money supplying my place on his cotton plantation. Cutting cane was an employment that suited me, and for three successive years I held the lead row at Hawkins, leading a gang of from fifty to an hundred hands.

In a previous chapter the mode of cultivating cotton is described. This may be the proper place to speak of the manner of cultivating cane.

The ground is prepared in beds, the same as it is prepared for the reception of the cotton seed, except it is ploughed deeper. Drills are made in the same manner. Planting commences in January, and continues until April. It is necessary to plant a sugar field only once in three years. Three crops are taken before the seed or plant is exhausted.

Three gangs are employed in the operation. One draws the cane from the rick, or stack, cutting the top and flags from the stalk, leaving only that part which is sound and healthy. Each joint of the cane has an eye, like the eye of a potato, which sends forth a sprout when buried in the soil. Another gang lays the cane in the drill, placing two stalks side by side in such manner that joints will occur once in four or six inches. The third gang follows with hoes, drawing earth upon the stalks, and covering them to the depth of three inches.

In four weeks, at the farthest, the sprouts appear above the ground, and from this time forward grow with great rapidity. A sugar field is hoed three times, the same as cotton, save that a greater quantity of earth is drawn to the roots. By the first of August hoeing is usually over. About the middle of September, whatever is required for seed is cut and stacked in ricks, as they are termed. In October it is ready for the mill or sugar-house, and then the general cutting begins. The blade of a cane-knife is fifteen inches long, three inches wide in the middle, and tapering towards the point and handle. The blade is thin, and in order to be at all serviceable must be kept very sharp. Every third hand takes the lead of two others, one of whom is on each side of him. The lead hand, in the first place, with a blow of his knife shears the flags from the stalk. He next cuts off the top down as far as it is green. He must be careful to sever all the green from the ripe part, inasmuch as the juice of the former sours the molasses, and renders it unsalable. Then he severs the stalk at the root, and lays it directly behind him. His right and left hand companions lay their stalks, when cut in the same manner, upon his. To every three hands there is a cart, which follows, and the stalks are thrown into it by the younger slaves, when it is drawn to the sugar-house and ground.

If the planter apprehends a frost, the cane is winrowed. Winrowing is cutting the stalks at an early period and throwing them lengthwise in the water farrow in such a manner that the tops will cover the butts of the stalks. They will remain in this condition three weeks or a month without souring, and secure from frost. When the proper time arrives, they are taken up, trimmed and carted to the sugar-house.

In the month of January the slaves enter the field again

to prepare for another crop. The ground is now strewn with the tops, and flags cut from the past year's cane. On a dry day fire is set to this combustible refuse, which sweeps over the field, leaving it bare and clean, and ready for the hoes. The earth is loosened about the roots of the old stubble, and in process of time another crop springs up from the last year's seed. It is the same the year following; but the third year the seed has exhausted its strength, and the field must be ploughed and planted again. The second year the cane is sweeter and yields more than the first, and the third year more than the second.

During the three seasons I labored on Hawkins' plantation, I was employed a considerable portion of the time in the sugar-house. He is celebrated as the producer of the finest variety of white sugar. The following is a general description of his sugar-house and the process of manufacture:

The mill is an immense brick building, standing on the shore of the bayou. Running out from the building is an open shed, at least an hundred feet in length and forty or fifty feet in width. The boiler in which the steam is generated is situated outside the main building; the machinery and engine rest on a brick pier, fifteen feet above the floor, within the body of the building. The machinery turns two great iron rollers, between two and three feet in diameter and six or eight feet in length. They are elevated above the brick pier, and roll in towards each other. An endless carrier, made of chain and wood, like leathern belts used in small mills, extends from the iron rollers out of the main building and through the entire length of the open shed. The carts in which the cane is brought from the field as fast as it is cut, are unloaded at the sides of the shed. All along the endless carrier are ranged slave children, whose business it is to place the cane upon it, when it is conveyed through the shed into the main building, where it falls between the rollers, is crushed, and drops upon another carrier that conveys it out of the main building in an opposite direction, depositing it in the top of a chimney upon a fire beneath, which consumes it. It is necessary to burn it in this manner, because otherwise it would soon fill the building, and more especially because it would soon sour and engender disease. The juice of the cane falls into a conductor underneath the iron rollers, and is carried into a reservoir. Pipes convey it from thence into five filterers, holding several hogsheads each. These filterers are filled with bone-black, a substance resembling pulverized charcoal. It is made of bones calcinated in close vessels, and is used for the purpose of decolorizing, by filtration, the cane juice before boiling. Through these five filterers it passes in succession, and then runs into a large reservoir underneath the ground floor, from whence it is carried up, by means of a steam pump, into a clarifier made of sheet iron, where it is heated by steam until it boils. From the first clarifier it is carried in pipes to a second and a third, and thence into close iron pans, through which tubes pass, filled with steam. While in a boiling state it flows through three pans in succession, and is then carried in other pipes down to the coolers on the ground floor. Coolers are wooden boxes with sieve bottoms made of the finest wire. As soon as the syrup passes into the coolers, and is met by the air, it grains, and the molasses at once escapes through the sieves into a cistern below. It is then white or loaf sugar of the finest kind—clear, clean, and as white as snow. When cool, it is taken out, packed in hogsheads, and is ready for market. The molasses is then carried from the cistern into the upper story again, and by another process converted into brown sugar.

There are larger mills, and those constructed differently from the one thus imperfectly described, but none, perhaps, more celebrated than this anywhere on Bayou Boeuf. Lambert, of New Orleans, is a partner of Hawkins. He is a man of vast wealth, holding, as I have been told, an interest in over forty different sugar plantations in Louisiana.

*   *   *

The only respite from constant labor the slave has through the whole year, is during the Christmas holidays. Epps allowed us three—others allow four, five and six days, according to the measure of their generosity. It is the only time to which they look forward with any interest or pleasure. They are glad when night comes, not only because it brings them a few hours repose, but because it brings them one day nearer Christmas. It is hailed with equal delight by the old and the young; even Uncle Abram ceases to glorify Andrew Jackson, and Patsey forgets her many sorrows, amid the general hilarity of the holidays. It is the time of feasting, and frolicking, and fiddling—the carnival season with the children of bondage. They are the only days when they are allowed a little restricted liberty, and heartily indeed do they enjoy it.

It is the custom for one planter to give a "Christmas supper," inviting the slaves from neighboring plantations to join his own on the occasion; for instance, one year it is given by Epps, the next by Marshall, the next by Hawkins, and so on. Usually from three to five hundred are assembled, coming together on foot, in carts, on horseback, on mules, riding double and triple, sometimes a boy and girl, at others a girl and two boys, and at others again a boy, a girl and an old woman. Uncle Abram astride a mule, with Aunt Phebe and Patsey behind him, trotting towards a Christmas supper, would be no uncommon sight on Bayou Boeuf.

Then, too, "of all days i' the year," they array themselves in their best attire. The cotton coat has been washed clean, the stump of a tallow candle has been applied to the shoes, and if so fortunate as to possess a rimless or a crownless hat, it is placed jauntily on the head. They are welcomed with equal cordiality, however, if they come bare-headed and bare-footed to the feast. As a general thing, the women wear handkerchiefs tied about their heads, but if chance has thrown in their way a fiery red ribbon, or a cast-off bonnet of their mistress' grandmother, it is sure to be worn on such occasions.

Red—the deep blood red is decidedly the favorite color among the enslaved damsels of my acquaintance. If a red ribbon does not encircle the neck, you will be certain to find all the hair of their woolly heads tied up with red strings of one sort or another.

The table is spread in the open air, and loaded with varieties of meat and piles of vegetables. Bacon and corn meal at such times are dispensed with. Sometimes the cooking is performed in the kitchen on the plantation, at others in the shade of wide branching trees. In the latter case, a ditch is dug in the ground, and wood laid in and burned until it is filled with glowing coals, over which chickens, ducks, turkeys, pigs, and not infrequently the entire body of a wild ox, are roasted. They are furnished also with flour, of which biscuits are made, and often with peach and other preserves, with tarts, and every manner and description of pies, except the mince, that being an article of pastry as yet unknown among them. Only the slave who has lived all the years on his scanty allowance of meal and bacon, can appreciate such suppers. White people in great numbers assemble to witness the gastronomical enjoyments.

They seat themselves at the rustic table—the males on one side, the females on the other. The two between whom there may have been an exchange of tenderness, invariably manage to sit opposite; for the omnipresent Cupid disdains not to hurl his arrows into the simple hearts of slaves. Unalloyed and exulting happiness lights up the dark faces of them all. The ivory teeth, contrasting with their black complexions, exhibit two long, white streaks the whole extent of the table. All round the bountiful board a multitude of eyes roll in ecstasy. Giggling and laughter and the clattering of cutlery and crockery succeed. Cuffee's elbow hunches his neighbor's side, impelled by an involuntary impulse of delight; Nelly shakes her finger at Sambo and laughs, she knows not why, and so the fun and merriment flows on.

When the viands have disappeared, and the hungry maws of the children of toil are satisfied, then, next in the order of amusement, is the Christmas dance. My business on these gala days always was to play on the violin. The African race is a music-loving one, proverbially; and many there were among my fellow bondsmen whose organs of tune were strikingly developed, and who could thumb the banjo with dexterity; but at the expense of appearing egotistical, I must, nevertheless, declare, that I was considered the Ole Bull of Bayou Boeuf. My master often received letters, sometimes from a distance of ten miles, requesting him to send me to play at a ball or festival of the whites. He received his compensation, and usually I also returned with many picayunes jingling in my pockets—the extra contributions of those to whose delight I had administered. In this manner I became more acquainted than I otherwise would, up and down the bayou. The young men and maidens of Holmesville always knew there was to be a jollification somewhere, whenever Platt Epps was seen passing through the town with his fiddle in his hand. "Where are you going now, Platt?" and "What is coming off tonight, Platt?" would be interrogatories issuing from every door and window, and many a time when there was no special hurry, yielding to pressing importunities, Platt would draw his bow, and sitting astride his mule, perhaps, discourse musically to a crowd of delighted children, gathered around him in the street.

Alas! had it not been for my beloved violin, I scarcely can conceive how I could have endured the long years of bondage. It introduced me to great houses—relieved me of many days' labor in the field—supplied me with conveniences for my cabin—with pipes and tobacco, and extra pairs of shoes, and oftentimes led me away from the presence of a hard master, to witness scenes of jollity and mirth. It was my companion—the friend of my bosom—triumphing loudly when I was joyful, and uttering its soft, melodious consolations when I was sad. Often, at midnight, when sleep had fled affrighted from the cabin, and my soul was disturbed and troubled with the contemplation of my fate, it would sing me a song of peace. On holy Sabbath days, when an hour or two of leisure was allowed, it would accompany me to some quiet place on the bayou bank, and, lifting up its voice, discourse kindly and pleasantly indeed. It heralded my name round the country—made me friends, who, otherwise would not have noticed me—gave me an honored seat at the yearly feasts, and secured the loudest and heartiest welcome of them all at the Christmas dance. The Christmas dance! Oh, ye pleasure-seeking sons and daughters of idleness, who move with measured step, listless and snail-like, through the slow-winding cotillion, if ye wish to look upon the celerity, if not the "poetry of motion"—upon genuine happiness, rampant and unrestrained—go down to Louisiana, and see the slaves dancing in the starlight of a Christmas night.

On that particular Christmas I have now in my mind, a description whereof will serve as a description of the day generally, Miss Lively and Mr. Sam the first belonging to Stewart, the latter to Roberts, started the ball. It was well known that Sam cherished an ardent passion for Lively, as also did one of Marshall's and another of Carey's boys; for Lively was *lively* indeed, and a heartbreaking coquette withal. It was a victory for Sam Roberts, when, rising from the repast, she gave him her hand for the first "figure" in preference to either of his rivals. They were somewhat crestfallen, and, shaking their heads angrily, rather intimated they would like to pitch into Mr. Sam and hurt him badly. But not an emotion of wrath ruffled the placid bosom of Samuel as his legs flew like drumsticks down the outside and up the middle, by the side of his bewitching partner. The whole company cheered them vociferously, and, excited with the applause, they continued "tearing down" after all the others had become exhausted and halted a moment to recover breath. But Sam's superhuman exertions overcame him finally, leaving Lively alone, yet whirling like a top. Thereupon one of Sam's rivals,

Pete Marshall, dashed in, and, with might and main, leaped and shuffled and threw himself into every conceivable shape, as if determined to show Miss Lively and all the world that Sam Roberts was of no account.

Pete's affection, however, was greater than his discretion. Such violent exercise took the breath out of him directly, and he dropped like an empty bag. Then was the time for Harry Carey to try his hand; but Lively also soon out-winded him, amidst hurrahs and shouts, fully sustaining her well-earned reputation of being the "fastest gal" on the bayou.

One "set" off, another takes its place, he or she remaining longest on the floor receiving the most uproarious commendation, and so the dancing continues until broad daylight. It does not cease with the sound of the fiddle, but in that case they set up a music peculiar to themselves. This is called "patting," accompanied with one of those unmeaning songs, composed rather for its adaptation to a certain time or measure, than for the purpose of expressing any distinct idea. The patting is performed by striking the hands on the knees, then striking the hands together, then striking the right shoulder with one hand, the left with the other all the while keeping time with the feet, and singing, perhaps, this song:

> "Harper's creek and roarin' ribber,
> Thar, my dear, we'll live forebber;
> Den we'll go to de Ingin nation,
> All I want in dis creation,
> Is pretty little wife and big plantation.

> *Chorus.* Up dat oak and down dat ribber,
>   Two overseers and one little nigger."

Or, if these words are not adapted to the tune called for, it may be that "Old Hog Eye" *is*—a rather solemn and startling specimen of versification, not, however, to be appreciated unless heard at the South. It runneth as follows:

"Who's been here since I've been gone?
Pretty little gal wid a josey on.
　　　　Hog Eye!
　　　　Old Hog Eye,
　　　　And Hosey too!

Never see de like since I was born,
Here come a little gal wid a josey on.
　　　　Hog Eye!
　　　　Old Hog Eye!
　　　　And Hosey too!"

Or, may be the following, perhaps, equally nonsensical, but full of melody, nevertheless, as it flows from the negro's mouth:

"Ebo Dick and Jurdan's Jo,
Them two niggers stole my yo'.
　　Chorus. Hop Jim along,
　　　　Walk Jim along,
　　　　Talk Jim along, etc.

Old black Dan, as black as tar,
He dam glad he was not dar.
　　　　Hop Jim along," etc.

During the remaining holidays succeeding Christmas, they are provided with passes, and permitted to go where they please within a limited distance, or they may remain and labor on the plantation, in which case they are paid for it. It is very rarely, however, that the latter alternative is accepted. They may be seen at these times hurrying in all directions, as happy looking mortals as can be found on the face of the earth. They are different beings from what they are in the field; the temporary relaxation, the brief deliverance from fear, and from the lash, producing an entire metamorphosis in their appearance and demeanor. In visiting, riding, renewing old friendships, or, perchance, reviving some old attachment, or pursuing whatever pleasure may suggest itself, the time is occupied. Such is "southern life as it is," *three days in the year*, as I found it—the other three hundred and sixty-two being days of weariness, and fear, and suffering, and unremitting labor.

Marriage is frequently contracted during the holidays, if such an institution may be said to exist among them. The only ceremony required before entering into that "holy estate," is to obtain the consent of the respective owners. It is usually encouraged by the masters of female slaves. Either party can have as many husbands or wives as the owner will permit, and either is at liberty to discard the other at pleasure. The law in relation to divorce, or to bigamy, and so forth, is not applicable to property of course. If the wife does not belong on the same plantation with the husband, the latter is permitted to visit her on Saturday nights, if the distance is not too far. Uncle Abram's wife lived seven miles from Epps', on Bayou Huff Power. He had permission to visit her once a fortnight, but he was growing old, as has been said, and truth to say, had latterly well-nigh forgotten her. Uncle Abram had no time to spare from his meditations on General Jackson— connubial dalliance being well enough for the young and thoughtless, but unbecoming a grave and solemn philosopher like himself.

CHAPTER 16

With the exception of my trip to St. Mary's parish, and my absence during the cane-cutting seasons, I was constantly employed on the plantation of Master Epps. He was considered but a small planter, not having a sufficient number of hands to require the services of an overseer, acting in the latter capacity himself. Not able to increase his force, it was his custom to hire during the hurry of cotton picking.

On larger estates, employing fifty or a hundred, or perhaps two hundred hands, an overseer is deemed indispensable. These gentlemen ride into the field on horseback, without an exception, to my knowledge armed with pistols, bowie knife, whip, and accompanied by several dogs. They follow, equipped in this fashion, in rear of the slaves, keeping a sharp lookout upon them all. The requisite qualifications in an overseer are utter heartlessness, brutality and cruelty. It is his business to produce large crops, and if that is accomplished, no matter what amount of suffering it may have cost. The presence of the dogs are necessary to overhaul a fugitive who may take to his heels as is sometimes the case, when faint or sick, he is unable to maintain his row, and unable, also, to endure the whip. The pistols are reserved for any dangerous emergency, there having been instances when such weapons were necessary. Goaded into uncontrollable madness, even the slave will sometimes turn upon his oppressor. The gallows were standing at Marksville last January, upon which one was executed a year ago for killing his overseer. It occurred not many miles from Epps' plantation on Red River. The slave was given his task at splitting rails. In the course of the day the overseer sent him on an errand, which occupied so much time that it was not possible for him to perform the task. The next day he was called to an account, but the loss of time occasioned by the errand was no excuse, and he was ordered to kneel and bare his back for the reception of the lash. They were in the woods alone—beyond the reach of sight or hearing. The boy submitted until maddened at such injustice, and insane with pain, he sprang to his feet, and seizing an axe, literally chopped the overseer in pieces. He made no attempt whatever at concealment, but hastening to his master, related the whole affair, and declared himself ready to expiate the wrong by the sacrifice of his life. He was led to the scaffold, and while the rope was around his neck, maintained an undismayed and fearless bearing, and with his last words justified the act.

Besides the overseer, there are drivers under him the number being in proportion to the number of hands in the field. The drivers are black, who, in addition to the performance of their equal share of work, are compelled to do the whipping of their several gangs. Whips hang around their necks, and if they fail to use them thoroughly, are whipped themselves. They have a few privileges, however; for example, in cane-cutting the hands are not allowed to sit down long enough to eat their dinners. Carts filled with corn cake, cooked at the kitchen, are driven into the field at noon. The cake is distributed by the drivers, and must be eaten with the least possible delay.

When the slave ceases to perspire, as he often does when taxed beyond his strength, he falls to the ground and becomes entirely helpless. It is then the duty of the driver to drag him into the shade of the standing cotton or cane, or of a neighboring tree, where he dashes buckets of water upon him, and uses other means of bringing out perspiration again, when he is ordered to his place, and compelled to continue his labor.

At Huff Power, when I first came to Epps', Tom, one of Roberts' negroes, was driver. He was a burly fellow, and severe in the extreme. After Epps' removal to Bayou Boeuf, that distinguished honor was conferred upon myself. Up to the time of my departure I had to wear a whip about my neck in the field. If Epps was present, I dared not show any lenity, not having the Christian fortitude of a certain well-known Uncle Tom sufficiently to brave his wrath by refusing to perform the office. In that way, only, I escaped the immediate martyrdom he suffered, and, withal, saved my companions much suffering, as it proved in the end. Epps, I soon found, whether actually in the field or not, had his eyes pretty generally upon us. From the piazza, from behind some adjacent tree, or other concealed point of observation, he was perpetually on the watch. If one of us had been backward or idle through the day, we were apt to be told all about it on returning to the quarters, and as it was a matter of principle with him to reprove every offence of that kind that came within his knowledge, the offender not only was certain of receiving a castigation for his tardiness, but I likewise was punished for permitting it.

If, on the other hand, he had seen me use the lash freely, the man was satisfied. "Practice makes perfect," truly; and during my eight years' experience as a driver, I learned to handle the whip with marvelous dexterity and precision, throwing the lash within a hair's breadth of the back, the ear, the nose, without, however, touching either of them. If Epps was observed at a distance, or we had reason to apprehend he was sneaking somewhere in the vicinity, I would commence plying the lash vigorously, when, according to arrangement, they would squirm and screech as if in agony, although not one of them had in fact been even grazed. Patsey would take occasion, if he made his appearance presently, to mumble in his hearing some complaints that Platt was lashing them the whole time, and Uncle Abram, with an appearance of honesty peculiar to himself, would declare roundly I had just whipped them worse than General Jackson whipped the enemy at New Orleans. If Epps was not drunk, and in one of his beastly humors, this was, in general, satisfactory. If he was, some one or more of us must suffer, as a matter of course. Sometimes his violence assumed a dangerous form, placing the lives of his human stock in jeopardy. On one occasion the drunken madman thought to amuse himself by cutting my throat.

He had been absent at Holmesville, in attendance at a shooting match, and none of us were aware of his return. While hoeing by the side of Patsey, she exclaimed, in a low voice, suddenly, "Platt, d'ye see old Hog-Jaw beckoning me to come to him?"

Glancing sideways, I discovered him in the edge of the field, motioning and grimacing, as was his habit when half-intoxicated. Aware of his lewd intentions, Patsey began to cry. I whispered her not to look up, and to continue at her work, as if she had not observed him. Suspecting the truth of the matter, however, he soon staggered up to me in a great rage.

"What did you say to Pats?" he demanded, with an oath. I made him some evasive answer, which only had the effect of increasing his violence.

"How long have you owned this plantation, *say*, you d—d nigger?" he inquired, with a malicious sneer, at the same time taking hold of my shirt collar with one hand, and thrusting the other into his pocket. "Now I'll cut your black throat; that's what I'll do," drawing his knife from his pocket as he said it. But with one hand he was unable to open it, until finally seizing the blade in his teeth, I saw he was about to succeed, and felt the necessity of escaping from him, for in his present reckless state, it was evident he was not joking, by any means. My shirt was open in front, and as I turned round quickly and sprang from him, while he still retained his grip, it was stripped entirely from my back. There was no difficulty now in eluding him. He would chase me until out of breath, then stop until it was recovered, swear, and renew the chase again. Now he would command me to come to him, now endeavor to coax me, but I was careful to keep at a respectful distance. In this manner we made the circuit of the field several times, he making desperate plunges, and I always dodging them, more amused than frightened, well knowing that when his sober senses returned, he would laugh at his own drunken folly. At length I observed the mistress standing by the yard fence, watching our half-serious, half-comical manoeuvres. Shooting past him, I ran directly to her. Epps, on discovering her, did not follow. He remained about the field an hour or more, during which time I stood by the mistress, having related the particulars of what had taken place. Now, *she* was aroused again, denouncing her husband and Patsey about equally. Finally, Epps came towards the house, by this time nearly sober, walking demurely, with his hands behind his back, and attempting to look as innocent as a child.

As he approached, nevertheless, Mistress Epps began to berate him roundly, heaping upon him many rather disrespectful epithets, and demanding for what reason he had attempted to cut my throat. Epps made wondrous strange of it all, and to my surprise, swore by all the saints in the calendar he had not spoken to me that day.

"Platt, you lying nigger, *have* I?" was his brazen appeal to me.

It is not safe to contradict a master, even by the assertion of a truth. So I was silent, and when he entered the house I returned to the field, and the affair was never after alluded to.

Shortly after this time a circumstance occurred that came

nigh divulging the secret of my real name and history, which I had so long and carefully concealed, and upon which I was convinced depended my final escape. Soon after he purchased me, Epps asked me if I could write and read, and on being informed that I had received some instruction in those branches of education, he assured me, with emphasis, if he ever caught me with a book, or with pen and ink, he would give me a hundred lashes. He said he wanted me to understand that he bought "niggers" to work and not to educate. He never inquired a word of my past life, or from whence I came. The mistress, however, cross-examined me frequently about Washington, which she supposed was my native city, and more than once remarked that I did not talk nor act like the other "niggers," and she was sure I had seen more of the world than I admitted.

My great object always was to invent means of getting a letter secretly into the post office, directed to some of my friends or family at the North. The difficulty of such an achievement cannot be comprehended by one unacquainted with the severe restrictions imposed upon me. In the first place, I was deprived of pen, ink, and paper. In the second place, a slave cannot leave his plantation without a pass, nor will a postmaster mail a letter for one without written instructions from his owner. I was in slavery nine years, and always watchful and on the alert, before I met with the good fortune of obtaining a sheet of paper. While Epps was in New Orleans, one winter, disposing of his cotton, the mistress sent me to Holmesville, with an order for several articles, and among the rest a quantity of foolscap. I appropriated a sheet concealing it in the cabin, under the board on which I slept.

After various experiments I succeeded in making ink, by boiling white maple bark, and with a feather from the wing of a duck, manufactured a pen. When all were asleep in the cabin, by the light of the coals, lying upon my plank couch, I managed to complete a somewhat lengthy epistle. It was directed to an old acquaintance at Sandy Hill, stating my condition, and urging him to take measures to restore me to liberty. This letter I kept a long time, contriving measures by which it could be safely deposited in the post office. At length, a low fellow, by the name of Armsby, hitherto a stranger, came into the neighborhood, seeking a situation as overseer. He applied to Epps, and was about the plantation for several days. He next went over to Shaw's, nearby, and remained with him several weeks. Shaw was generally surrounded by such worthless characters, being himself noted as a gambler and unprincipled man. He had made a wife of his slave Charlotte, and a brood of young mulattoes were growing up in his house. Armsby became so much reduced at last, that he was compelled to labor with the slaves. A white man working in the field is a rare and unusual spectacle on Bayou Boeuf. I improved every opportunity of cultivating his acquaintance privately, desiring to obtain his confidence so far as to be willing to entrust the letter to his keeping. He visited Marksville repeatedly, he informed me, a town some twenty miles distant, and there, I proposed to myself, the letter should be mailed.

Carefully deliberating on the most proper manner of approaching him on the subject, I concluded finally to ask him simply if he would deposit a letter for me in the Marksville post office the next time he visited that place, without disclosing to him that the letter was written, or any of the particulars it contained; for I had fears that he might betray me, and knew that some inducement must be held out to him of a pecuniary nature, before it would be safe to confide in him. As late as one o'clock one night I stole noiselessly from my cabin, and, crossing the field to Shaw's, found him sleeping on the piazza. I had but a few picayunes—the proceeds of my fiddling performances, but all I had in the world I promised him if he would do me the favor required. I begged him not to expose me if he could not grant the request. He assured me, upon his honor, he would deposit it in the Marksville post office, and that he would keep it an inviolable secret forever. Though the letter was in my pocket at the time, I dared not then deliver it to him, but stating I would have it written in a day or two, bade him good night, and returned to my cabin. It was impossible for me to expel the suspicions I entertained, and all night I lay awake, revolving in my mind the safest course to pursue. I was willing to risk a great deal to accomplish my purpose, but should the letter by any means fall into the hands of Epps, it would be a death-blow to my aspirations. I was "perplexed in the extreme."

My suspicions were well-founded, as the sequel demonstrated. The next day but one, while scraping cotton in the field, Epps seated himself on the line fence between Shaw's plantation and his own, in such a position as to overlook the scene of our labors. Presently Armsby made his appearance, and, mounting the fence, took a seat beside him. They remained two or three hours, all of which time I was in an agony of apprehension.

That night, while broiling my bacon, Epps entered the cabin with his rawhide in his hand.

"Well, boy," said he, "I understand I've got a larned nigger, that writes letters, and tries to get white fellows to mail 'em. Wonder if you know who he is?"

My worst fears were realized, and although it may not be considered entirely creditable, even under the circumstances, yet a resort to duplicity and downright falsehood was the only refuge that presented itself.

"Don't know nothing about it, Master Epps," I answered him, assuming an air of ignorance and surprise; "Don't know nothing at all about it, sir."

"Wan't you over to Shaw's night before last?" he inquired.

"No, master," was the reply.

"Haven't you asked that fellow, Armsby, to mail a letter for you at Marksville?"

"Why, Lord, master, I never spoke three words to him in all my life. I don't know what you mean."

"Well," he continued, "Armsby told me today the devil was among my niggers; that I had one that needed close watching or he would run away; and when I axed him why, he said you come over to Shaw's, and waked him up in the night, and wanted him to carry a letter to Marksville. What have you got to say to that, ha?"

"All I've got to say, master," I replied, "is, there is no truth in it. How could I write a letter without any ink or paper. There is nobody I want to write to, 'cause I hain't got no friends living as I know of. That Armsby is a lying, drunken fellow, they say, and nobody believes him anyway. You know I always tell the truth, and that I never go off the plantation without a pass. Now, master, I can see what that Armsby is after, plain enough. Did'nt he want you to hire him for an overseer?"

"Yes, he wanted me to hire him," answered Epps.

"That's it," said I, "he wants to make you believe we're all going to run away, and then he thinks you'll hire an overseer to watch us. He just made that story out of whole cloth, 'cause he wants to get a situation. It's all a lie, master, you may depend on't."

Epps mused awhile, evidently impressed with the plausibility of my theory, and exclaimed,

"I'm d—d, Platt, if I don't believe you tell the truth. He must take me for a soft, to think he can come it over me with them kind of yarns, mustn't he? Maybe he thinks he can fool me; maybe he thinks I don't know nothing—can't take care of my own niggers, eh! Soft soap old Epps, eh! Ha, ha, ha! D—n Armsby! Set the dogs on him, Platt," and with many other comments descriptive of Armsby's general character, and his capability of taking care of his own business, and attending to his own "niggers," Master Epps left the cabin. As soon as he was gone I threw the letter in the fire, and, with a desponding and despairing heart, beheld the epistle which had cost me so much anxiety and thought, and which I fondly hoped would have been my forerunner to the land of freedom, writhe and shrivel on its bed of coals, and dissolve into smoke and ashes. Armsby, the treacherous wretch, was driven from Shaw's plantation not long subsequently, much to my relief, for I feared he might renew his conversation, and perhaps induce Epps to credit him.

I knew not now whither to look for deliverance. Hopes sprang up in my heart only to be crushed and blighted. The summer of my life was passing away; I felt I was growing prematurely old; that a few years more, and toil, and grief, and the poisonous miasmas of the swamps would accomplish their work upon me—would consign me to the grave's embrace, to moulder and be forgotten. Repelled, betrayed, cut off from the hope of succor, I could only prostrate myself upon the earth and groan in unutterable anguish. The hope of rescue was the only light that cast a ray of comfort on my heart. That was now flickering, faint and low; another breath of disappointment would extinguish it altogether, leaving me to grope in midnight darkness to the end of life.

CHAPTER 17

The year 1850, down to which time I have now arrived, omitting many occurrences uninteresting to the reader, was an unlucky year for my companion Wiley, the husband of Phebe, whose taciturn and retiring nature has thus far kept him in the background. Notwithstanding Wiley seldom opened his mouth, and revolved in his obscure and unpretending orbit without a grumble, nevertheless the warm elements of sociality were strong in the bosom of that silent "nigger." In the exuberance of his self-reliance, disregarding the philosophy of Uncle Abram, and setting the counsels of Aunt Phebe utterly at naught, he had the foolhardiness to essay a nocturnal visit to a neighboring cabin without a pass.

So attractive was the society in which he found himself, that Wiley took little note of the passing hours, and the light began to break in the east before he was aware. Speeding homeward as fast as he could run, he hoped to reach the quarters before the horn would sound; but, unhappily, he was spied on the way by a company of patrollers.

How it is in other dark places of slavery, I do not know, but on Bayou Boeuf there is an organization of patrollers, as they are styled, whose business it is to seize and whip any slave they may find wandering from the plantation. They ride on horseback, headed by a captain, armed, and accompanied by dogs. They have the right, either by law, or by general consent, to inflict discretionary chastisement upon a black man caught beyond the boundaries of his master's estate without a pass, and even to shoot him, if he attempts to escape. Each company has a certain distance to ride up and down the bayou. They are compensated by the planters, who contribute in proportion to the number of slaves they own. The clatter of their horses' hoofs dashing by can be heard at all hours of the night, and frequently they may be seen driving a slave before them, or leading him by a rope fastened around his neck, to his owner's plantation.

Wiley fled before one of these companies, thinking he could reach his cabin before they could overtake him; but one of their dogs, a great ravenous hound, gripped him by the leg, and held him fast. The patrollers whipped him severely, and brought him, a prisoner, to Epps. From him he received another flagellation still more severe, so that the cuts of the lash and the bites of the clog rendered him sore, stiff and miserable, insomuch he was scarcely able to move. It was impossible in such a state to keep up his row and consequently there was not an hour in the day but Wiley felt the sting of his master's rawhide on his raw and bleeding back. His sufferings became intolerable, and finally he resolved to run away. Without disclosing his intentions to run away even to his wife Phebe, he proceeded to make arrangements for carrying his plan into execution. Having cooked his whole week's allowance, he cautiously left the cabin on a Sunday night, after the inmates of the quarters were asleep. When the horn sounded in the morning, Wiley did not make his appearance. Search was made for him in the cabins, in the corn crib, in the cotton house, and in every nook and corner of the premises. Each of us was examined, touching any knowledge we might have that could throw light upon his sudden disappearance or present whereabouts. Epps raved and stormed, and mounting his horse, galloped to neighboring plantations, making inquiries in all directions. The search was fruitless. Nothing whatever was elicited, going to show what had become of the missing man. The dogs were led to the swamp, but were unable to strike his trail. They would circle away through the forest, their noses to the ground, but invariably returned in a short time to the spot from whence they started.

Wiley had escaped, and so secretly and cautiously as to elude and baffle all pursuit. Days and even weeks passed away, and nothing could be heard of him. Epps did nothing but curse and swear. It was the only topic of conversation among us when alone. We indulged in a great deal of speculation in regard to him, one suggesting he might have been drowned in some bayou, inasmuch as he was a poor swimmer; another, that perhaps he might have been devoured by alligators, or stung by the venomous moccasin, whose bite is certain and sudden death. The warm and hearty sympathies of us all, however, were with poor Wiley, wherever he might be. Many an earnest prayer ascended from the lips of Uncle Abram, beseeching safety for the wanderer.

In about three weeks, when all hope of ever seeing him again was dismissed, to our surprise, he one day appeared among us. On leaving the plantation, he informed us, it was his intention to make his way back to South Carolina—to the old quarters of Master Buford. During the day he remained secreted, sometimes in the branches of a tree, and at night pressed forward through the swamps. Finally, one morning, just at dawn, he reached the shore of Red River. While standing on the bank, considering how he could cross it, a white man accosted him, and demanded a pass. Without one, and evidently a runaway, he was taken to Alexandria, the shire town of the parish of Rapides, and confined in prison. It happened several days after that Joseph B. Roberts, uncle of Mistress Epps, was in Alexandria, and going into the jail, recognized him. Wiley had worked on his plantation, when Epps resided at Huff Power. Paying the jail fee, and writing him a pass, underneath which was a note to Epps, requesting him not to whip him on his return, Wiley was sent back to Bayou Boeuf. It was the hope that hung upon this request, and which Roberts assured him would be respected by his master, that sustained him as he approached the house. The request, however, as may be readily supposed, was entirely disregarded. After being kept in suspense three days, Wiley was stripped, and compelled to endure one of those inhuman floggings to which the poor slave is so often subjected. It was the first and last attempt of Wiley to run away. The long scars upon his back, which he would carry with him to the grave, perpetually remind him of the dangers of such a step.

There was not a day throughout the ten years I belonged to Epps that I did not consult with myself upon the prospect of escape. I laid many plans, which at the time I considered excellent ones, but one after the other they were all abandoned. No man who has never been placed in such a situation, can comprehend the thousand obstacles thrown in the way of the flying slave. Every white man's hand is raised against him—the patrollers are watching for him—the hounds are ready to follow on his track, and the nature of the country is such as renders it impossible to pass through it with any safety. I thought, however, that the time might come, perhaps, when I should be running through the swamps again. I concluded, in that case, to be prepared for Epps' dogs, should they pursue me. He possessed several, one of which was a notorious slave-hunter, and the most fierce and savage of his breed. While out hunting the coon or the opossum, I never allowed an opportunity to escape, when alone, of whipping them severely. In this manner I succeeded at length in subduing them completely. They feared me, obeying my voice at once when others had no control over them whatever. Had they followed and overtaken me, I doubt not they would have shrank from attacking me.

Notwithstanding the certainty of being captured, the woods and swamps are, nevertheless, continually filled with runaways. Many of them, when sick, or so worn out as to be unable to perform their tasks, escape into the swamps, willing to suffer the punishment inflicted for such offences, in order to obtain a day or two of rest.

While I belonged to Ford, I was unwittingly the means of disclosing the hiding-place of six or eight, who had taken up their residence in the "Great Pine Woods." Adam Taydem frequently sent me from the mills over to the opening after provisions. The whole distance was then a thick pine forest. About ten o'clock of a beautiful moonlight night, while walking along the Texas road, returning to the mills, carrying a dressed pig in a bag swung over my shoulder, I heard footsteps behind me, and turning round, beheld two black men in the dress of slaves approaching at a rapid pace. When within a short distance, one of them raised a club, as if intending to strike me; the other snatched at the bag. I managed to dodge them both, and seizing a pine knot, hurled it with such force against the head of one of them that he was prostrated apparently senseless to the ground. Just then two more made their appearance from one side of the road. Before they could grapple me, however, I succeeded in passing them, and taking to my heels, fled, much affrighted, towards the mills. When Adam was informed of the adventure, he hastened straightway to the Indian village, and arousing Cascalla and several of his tribe, started in pursuit of the highwaymen. I accompanied them to the scene of attack, when we discovered a puddle of blood in the road, where the man whom I had smitten with the pine knot had fallen. After searching carefully through the woods a long time, one of Cascalla's men discovered a smoke curling up through the branches of several prostrate pines, whose tops had fallen together. The rendezvous was cautiously surrounded, and all of them taken prisoners. They had escaped from a plantation in the vicinity of Lamourie, and had been secreted there three weeks. They had no evil design upon me, except to frighten me out of my pig. Having observed me passing towards Ford's just at nightfall, and suspecting the nature of my errand, they had followed me, seen me butcher and dress the porker, and start on my return. They had been pinched for food, and were driven to this extremity by necessity. Adam conveyed them to the parish jail, and was liberally rewarded.

Not infrequently the runaway loses his life in the attempt to escape. Epps' premises were bounded on one side by Carey's, a very extensive sugar plantation. He cultivates annually at least fifteen hundred acres of cane, manufacturing twenty-two or twenty-three hundred hogsheads of sugar; an hogshead and a half being the usual yield of an acre. Besides this he also cultivates five or six hundred acres of corn and cotton. He owned last year one hundred and fifty-three field hands, besides nearly as many children, and yearly hires a drove during the busy season from this side the Mississippi.

One of his negro drivers, a pleasant, intelligent boy, was named Augustus. During the holidays, and occasionally while at work in adjoining fields, I had an opportunity of making his acquaintance, which eventually ripened into a warm and mutual attachment. Summer before last he was so unfortunate as to incur the displeasure of the overseer, a coarse, heartless brute, who whipped him most cruelly. Augustus ran away. Reaching a cane rick on Hawkins' plantation, he secreted himself in the top of it. All Carey's dogs were put upon his track—some fifteen of them—and soon scented his footsteps to the hiding place. They surrounded the rick, baying and scratching, but could not reach him.

Presently, guided by the clamor of the hounds, the pursuers rode up, when the overseer, mounting on to the rick, drew him forth. As he rolled down to the ground the whole pack plunged upon him, and before they could be beaten off, had gnawed and mutilated his body in the most shocking manner, their teeth having penetrated to the bone in an hundred places. He was taken up, tied upon a mule, and carried home. But this was Augustus' last trouble. He lingered until the next day, when death sought the unhappy boy, and kindly relieved him from his agony.

It was not unusual for slave women as well as slave men to endeavor to escape. Nelly, Eldret's girl, with whom I lumbered for a time in the "Big Cane Brake," lay concealed in Epps' corn crib three days. At night, when his family were asleep, she would steal into the quarters for food, and return to the crib again. We concluded it would no longer be safe for us to allow her to remain, and accordingly she retraced her steps to her own cabin.

But the most remarkable instance of a successful evasion of dogs and hunters was the following: Among Carey's girls was one by the name of Celeste. She was nineteen or twenty, and far whiter than her owner, or any of his offspring. It required a close inspection to distinguish in her features the slightest trace of African blood. A stranger would never have dreamed that she was the descendant of slaves. I was sitting in my cabin late at night, playing a low air on my violin, when the door opened carefully, and Celeste stood before me. She was pale and haggard. Had an apparition arisen from the earth, I could not have been more startled.

"Who are you?" I demanded, after gazing at her a moment.

"I'm hungry; give me some bacon," was her reply.

My first impression was that she was some deranged young mistress, who, escaping from home, was wandering, she knew not whither, and had been attracted to my cabin by the sound of the violin. The coarse cotton slave dress she wore, however, soon dispelled such a supposition.

"What is your name?" I again interrogated.

"My name is Celeste," she answered. "I belong to Carey, and have been two days among the palmettoes. I am sick and can't work, and would rather die in the swamp than be whipped to death by the overseer. Carey's dogs won't follow me. They have tried to set them on. There's a secret between them and Celeste, and they won't mind the devilish orders of the overseer. Give me some meat—I'm starving."

I divided my scanty allowance with her, and while partaking of it, she related how she had managed to escape, and described the place of her concealment. In the edge of the swamp, not half a mile from Epps' house, was a large space, thousands of acres in extent, thickly covered with palmetto. Tall trees, whose long arms interlocked each other, formed a canopy above them, so dense as to exclude the beams of the sun. It was like twilight always, even in the middle of the brightest day. In the centre of this great space, which nothing but serpents very often explore—a sombre and solitary spot—Celeste had erected a rude hut of dead branches that had fallen to the ground, and covered it with the leaves of the palmetto. This was the abode she had selected. She had no fear of Carey's dogs, any more than I had of Epps. It is a fact, which I have never been able to explain, that there are those whose tracks the hounds will absolutely refuse to follow. Celeste was one of them.

For several nights she came to my cabin for food. On one occasion our dogs barked as she approached, which aroused Epps, and induced him to reconnoitre the premises. He did not discover her, but after that it was not deemed prudent for her to come to the yard. When all was silent I carried provisions to a certain spot agreed upon, where she would find them.

In this manner Celeste passed the greater part of the

summer. She regained her health, and became strong and hearty. At all seasons of the year the howlings of wild animals can be heard at night along the borders of the swamps. Several times they had made her a midnight call, awakening her from slumber with a growl. Terrified by such unpleasant salutations, she finally concluded to abandon her lonely dwelling; and, accordingly, returning to her master, was scourged, her neck meanwhile being fastened in the stocks, and sent into the field again.

The year before my arrival in the country there was a concerted movement among a number of slaves on Bayou Boeuf, that terminated tragically indeed. It was, I presume, a matter of newspaper notoriety at the time, but all the knowledge I have of it, has been derived from the relation of those living at that period in the immediate vicinity of the excitement. It has become a subject of general and unfailing interest in every slave hut on the bayou, and will doubtless go down to succeeding generations as their chief tradition. Lew Cheney, with whom I became acquainted—a shrewd, cunning negro, more intelligent than the generality of his race, but unscrupulous and full of treachery—conceived the project of organizing a company sufficiently strong to fight their way against all opposition, to the neighboring territory of Mexico.

A remote spot, far within the depths of the swamp back of Hawkins' plantation, was selected as the rallying point. Lew flitted from one plantation to another, in the dead of night, preaching a crusade to Mexico, and, like Peter the Hermit, creating a furor of excitement wherever he appeared. At length a large number of runaways were assembled; stolen mules, and corn gathered from the fields, and bacon filched from smoke-houses, had been conveyed into the woods. The expedition was about ready to proceed, when their hiding place was discovered. Lew Cheney, becoming convinced of the ultimate failure of his project, in order to curry favor with his master, and avoid the consequences which he foresaw would follow, deliberately determined to sacrifice all his companions. Departing secretly from the encamp, he proclaimed among the planters the number collected in the swamp, and, instead of stating truly the object they had in view, asserted their intention was to emerge from their seclusion the first favorable opportunity, and murder every white person along the bayou.

Such an announcement, exaggerated as it passed from mouth to mouth, filled the whole country with terror. The fugitives were surrounded and taken prisoners, carried in chains to Alexandria, and hung by the populace. Not only those, but many who were suspected, though entirely innocent, were taken from the field and from the cabin, and without the shadow of process or form of trial, hurried to the scaffold. The planters on Bayou Boeuf finally rebelled against such reckless destruction of property, but it was not until a regiment of soldiers had arrived from some fort on the Texan frontier, demolished the gallows, and opened the doors of the Alexandria prison, that the indiscriminate slaughter was stayed. Lew Cheney escaped, and was even rewarded for his treachery. He is still living, but his name is despised and execrated by all his race throughout the parishes of Rapides and Avoyelles.

Such an idea as insurrection, however, is not new among the enslaved population of Bayou Boeuf. More than once I have joined in serious consultation, when the subject has been discussed, and there have been times when a word from me would have placed hundreds of my fellow bondsmen in an attitude of defiance. Without arms or ammunition, or even with them, I saw such a step would result in certain defeat, disaster and death, and always raised my voice against it.

During the Mexican war I well remember the extravagant hopes that were excited. The news of victory filled the great house with rejoicing, but produced only sorrow and disappointment in the cabin. In my opinion—and I have had opportunity to know something of the feeling of which I speak—there are not fifty slaves on the shores of Bayou Boeuf, but would hail with unmeasured delight the approach of an invading army.

They are deceived who flatter themselves that the ignorant and debased slave has no conception of the magnitude of his wrongs. They are deceived who imagine that he arises from his knees, with back lacerated and bleeding, cherishing only a spirit of meekness and forgiveness. A day may come—it *will* come, if his prayer is heard—a terrible day of vengeance, when the master in his turn will cry in vain for mercy.

CHAPTER 18

Wiley suffered severely at the hands of Master Epps, as has been related in the preceding chapter, but in this respect he fared no worse than his unfortunate companions. "Spare the rod," was an idea scouted by our master. He was constitutionally subject to periods of ill-humor, and at such times, however little provocation there might be, a certain amount of punishment was inflicted. The circumstances attending the last flogging but one that I received, will show how trivial a cause was sufficient with him for resorting to the whip.

A Mr. O'Niel, residing in the vicinity of the Big Pine Woods, called upon Epps for the purpose of purchasing me. He was a tanner and currier by occupation, transacting an extensive business, and intended to place me at service in some department of his establishment, provided he bought me. Aunt Phebe, while preparing the dinner table in the great house, overheard their conversation. On returning to the yard at night, the old woman ran to meet me, designing, of course, to overwhelm me with the news. She entered into a minute repetition of all she had heard, and Aunt Phebe was one whose ears never failed to drink in every word of conversation uttered in her hearing. She enlarged upon the fact that "Massa Epps was g'wine to sell me to a tanner ober in de Pine Woods," so long and loudly as to attract the attention of the mistress, who, standing unobserved on the piazza at the time, was listening to our conversation.

"Well, Aunt Phebe," said I, "I'm glad of it. I'm tired of scraping cotton, and would rather be a tanner. I hope he'll buy me."

O'Niel did not effect a purchase, however, the parties differing as to price, and the morning following his arrival, departed homewards. He had been gone but a short time, when Epps made his appearance in the field. Now nothing will more violently enrage a master, especially Epps, than the intimation of one of his servants that he would like to leave him. Mistress Epps had repeated to him my expressions to Aunt Phebe the evening previous, as I learned from the latter afterwards, the mistress having mentioned to her that she had overheard us. On entering the field, Epps walked directly to me.

"So, Platt, you're tired of scraping cotton, are you? You would like to change your master, eh? You're fond of moving round—traveler—ain't ye? Ah, yes—like to travel for your health, may be? Feel above cotton-scraping, I s'pose. So you're going into the tanning business? Good business—devilish fine business. Enterprising nigger! B'lieve I'll go into that business myself. Down on your knees, and strip that rag off your back! I'll try my hand at tanning."

I begged earnestly, and endeavored to soften him with excuses, but in vain. There was no other alternative; so kneeling down, I presented my bare back for the application of the lash.

"How do you like *tanning*?" he exclaimed, as the rawhide descended upon my flesh. "How do you like *tanning*?" he repeated at every blow. In this manner he gave me twenty or thirty lashes, incessantly giving utterance to the word "tanning," in one form of expression or another. When sufficiently "tanned," he allowed me to arise, and with a half-malicious laugh assured me, if I still fancied the business, he would give me further instruction in it whenever I desired. This time, he remarked, he had only given me a short lesson in "*tanning*"—the next time he would "curry me down."

Uncle Abram, also, was frequently treated with great brutality, although he was one of the kindest and most faithful creatures in the world. He was my cabin-mate for years. There was a benevolent expression in the old man's face, pleasant to behold, He regarded us with a kind of parental feeling, always counseling us with remarkable gravity and deliberation.

Returning from Marshall's plantation one afternoon, whither I had been sent on some errand of the mistress, I found him lying on the cabin floor, his clothes saturated with blood. He informed me that he been stabbed! While spreading cotton on the scaffold, Epps came home intoxicated from Holmesville. He found fault with everything, giving many orders so directly contrary that it was impossible to execute any of them. Uncle Abram, whose faculties were growing dull, became confused, and committed some blunder of no particular consequence. Epps was so enraged thereat, that, with drunken recklessness, he flew upon the old man, and stabbed him in the back. It was a long, ugly wound, but did not happen to penetrate far enough to result fatally. It was sewed up by the mistress, who censured her husband with extreme severity, not only denouncing his inhumanity, but declaring that she expected nothing else than that he would bring the family to poverty—that he would kill all the slaves on the plantation in some of his drunken fits.

It was no uncommon thing with him to prostrate Aunt Phebe with a chair or stick of wood; but the most cruel whipping that ever I was doomed to witness—one I can never recall with any other emotion than that of horror—was inflicted on the unfortunate Patsey.

It has been seen that the jealousy and hatred of Mistress Epps made the daily life of her young and agile slave completely miserable. I am happy in the belief that on numerous occasions I was the means of averting punishment from the inoffensive girl. In Epps' absence the mistress often ordered me to whip her without the remotest provocation. I would refuse, saying that I feared my master's displeasure, and several times ventured to remonstrate with her against the treatment Patsey received. I endeavored to impress her with the truth that the latter was not responsible for the acts of which she complained, but that she being a slave, and subject entirely to her master's will, he alone was answerable.

At length "the green-eyed monster" crept into the soul of Epps also, and then it was that he joined with his wrathful wife in an infernal jubilee over the girl's miseries.

On a Sabbath day in hoeing time, not long ago, we were on the bayou bank, washing our clothes, as was our usual custom. Presently Patsey was missing. Epps called aloud, but there was no answer. No one had observed her leaving the yard, and it was a wonder with us whither she had gone. In the course of a couple of hours she was seen approaching from the direction of Shaw's. This man, as has been intimated, was a notorious profligate, and withal not on the most friendly terms with Epps. Harriet, his black wife, knowing Patsey's troubles, was kind to her, in consequence of which the latter was in the habit of going over to see her every opportunity. Her visits were prompted by friendship merely, but the suspicion gradually entered the brain of Epps, that another and a baser passion led her thither—that it was not Harriet she desired to meet, but rather the unblushing libertine, his neighbor. Patsey found her master in a fearful rage on her return. His violence so alarmed her that at first she attempted to evade direct answers to his questions, which only served to increase his suspicions. She finally, however, drew herself up proudly, and in a spirit of indignation boldly denied his charges.

"Missus don't give me soap to wash with, as she does the rest," said Patsey, "and you know why. I went over to Harriet's to get a piece," and saying this, she drew it forth from a pocket in her dress and exhibited it to him. "That's what I went to Shaw's for, Massa Epps," continued she; "the Lord knows that was all."

"You lie, you black wench!" shouted Epps.

"I *don't* lie, massa. If you kill me, I'll stick to that."

"Oh! I'll fetch you down. I'll learn you to go to Shaw's. I'll take the starch out of ye," he muttered fiercely through his shut teeth.

Then turning to me, he ordered four stakes to be driven into the ground, pointing with the toe of his boot to the places where he wanted them. When the stakes were driven down, he ordered her to be stripped of every article of dress. Ropes were then brought, and the naked girl was laid upon her face, her wrists and feet each tied firmly to a stake. Stepping to the piazza, he took down a heavy whip, and placing it in my hands, commanded me to lash her. Unpleasant as it was, I was compelled to obey him. Nowhere that day, on the face of the whole earth, I venture to say, was there such a demoniac exhibition witnessed as then ensued.

Mistress Epps stood on the piazza among her children, gazing on the scene with an air of heartless satisfaction. The slaves were huddled together at a little distance, their countenances indicating the sorrow of their hearts. Poor Patsey prayed piteously for mercy, but her prayers were vain. Epps ground his teeth, and stamped upon the ground, screaming at me, like a mad fiend, to strike *harder*.

"Strike harder, or *your* turn will come next, you scoundrel," he yelled.

"Oh, mercy, massa!—oh! have mercy, *do*. Oh, God! pity me," Patsey exclaimed continually, struggling fruitlessly, and the flesh quivering at every stroke.

When I had struck her as many as thirty times, I stopped, and turned round toward Epps, hoping he was satisfied; but with bitter oaths and threats, he ordered me to continue. I inflicted ten or fifteen blows more. By this time her back was covered with long welts, intersecting each other like net work. Epps was yet furious and savage as ever, demanding if she would like to go to Shaw's again, and swearing he would flog her until she wished she was in h—l. Throwing down the whip, I declared I could punish her no more. He ordered me to go on, threatening me with a severer flogging than she had received, in case of refusal. My heart revolted at the inhuman scene, and risking the consequences, I absolutely refused to raise the whip. He then seized it himself, and applied it with ten-fold greater force than I had. The painful cries and shrieks of the tortured Patsey, mingling with the loud and angry curses of Epps, loaded the air. She was terribly lacerated—I may say, without exaggeration, literally flayed. The lash was wet with blood, which flowed down her sides and dropped upon the ground. At length she ceased struggling. Her head sank listlessly on the ground. Her screams and supplications gradually decreased and died away into a low moan. She no longer writhed and shrank beneath the lash when it bit out small pieces of her flesh. I thought that she was dying!

It was the Sabbath of the Lord. The fields smiled in the warm sunlight—the birds chirped merrily amidst the foliage of the trees—peace and happiness seemed to reign everywhere, save in the bosoms of Epps and his panting victim and the silent witnesses around him. The tempestuous emotions that were raging there were little in harmony with the calm and quiet beauty of the day. I could look on Epps only with unutterable loathing and abhorrence, and thought within myself—"Thou devil, sooner or later, somewhere in the course of eternal justice, thou shalt answer for this sin!"

Finally, he ceased whipping from mere exhaustion, and ordered Phebe to bring a bucket of salt and water. After washing her thoroughly with this, I was told to take her to her cabin. Untying the ropes, I raised her in my arms. She was unable to stand, and as her head rested on my shoulder, she repeated many times, in a faint voice scarcely perceptible, "Oh, Platt—oh, Platt!" but nothing further. Her dress was replaced, but it clung to her back, and was soon stiff with blood. We laid her on some boards in the hut, where she remained a long time, with eyes closed and groaning in agony. At night Phebe applied melted tallow to her wounds, and so far as we were able, all endeavored to assist and console her. Day after day she lay in her cabin upon her face, the sores preventing her resting in any other position.

A blessed thing it would have been for her—days and weeks and months of misery it would have saved her—had she never lifted up her head in life again. Indeed, from that time forward she was not what she had been. The burden of a deep melancholy weighed heavily on her spirits. She no longer moved with that buoyant and elastic step—there was not that mirthful sparkle in her eyes that formerly distinguished her. The bounding vigor—the sprightly, laughter-loving spirit of her youth, were gone. She fell into a mournful and desponding mood, and oftentimes would start up in her sleep, and with raised hands, plead for mercy. She became more silent than she was, toiling all day in our midst, not uttering a word. A careworn, pitiful expression settled on her face, and it was her humor now to weep, rather than rejoice. If ever there was a broken heart—one crushed and blighted by the rude grasp of suffering and misfortune—it was Patsey's.

She had been reared no better than her master's beast—looked upon merely as a valuable and handsome animal—and consequently possessed but a limited amount of knowledge. And yet a faint light cast its rays over her intellect, so that it was not wholly dark. She had a dim perception of God and of eternity, and a still more dim perception of a Saviour who had died even for such as her. She entertained but confused notions of a future life not—comprehending the distinction between the corporeal and spiritual existence. Happiness, in her mind, was exemption from stripes—from labor—from the cruelty of masters and overseers. Her idea of the joy of heaven was simply *rest*, and is fully expressed in these lines of a melancholy bard:

> "I ask no paradise on high,
> With cares on earth oppressed,
> The only heaven for which I sigh,
> Is rest, eternal rest."

It is a mistaken opinion that prevails in some quarters, that the slave does not understand the term—does not comprehend the idea of freedom. Even on Bayou Boeuf, where I conceive slavery exists in its most abject and cruel form—where it exhibits features altogether unknown in more northern states—the most ignorant of them generally know full well its meaning. They understand the privileges and exemptions that belong to it—that it would bestow upon them the fruits of their own labors, and that it would secure to them the enjoyment of domestic happiness. They do not fail to observe the difference between their own condition and the meanest white man's, and to realize the injustice of the laws which place it in his power not only to appropriate the profits of their industry, but to subject them to unmerited and unprovoked punishment, without remedy, or the right to resist, or to remonstrate.

Patsey's life, especially after her whipping, was one long dream of liberty. Far away, to her fancy an immeasurable distance, she knew there was a land of freedom. A thousand times she had heard that somewhere in the distant North there were no slaves—no masters. In her imagination it was an enchanted region, the Paradise of the earth. To dwell where the black man may work for himself—live in his own cabin—till his own soil, was a blissful dream of Patsey's—a dream, alas! the fulfillment of which she can never realize.

The effect of these exhibitions of brutality on the household of the slave-holder, is apparent. Epps' oldest son is an intelligent lad of ten or twelve years of age. It is pitiable, sometimes, to see him chastising, for instance, the venerable Uncle Abram. He will call the old man to account, and if in his childish judgment it is necessary, sentence him to a certain number of lashes, which he proceeds to inflict with much gravity and deliberation. Mounted on his pony, he often rides into the field with his whip, playing the overseer, greatly to his father's delight. Without discrimination, at such times, he applies the rawhide, urging the slaves forward with shouts, and occasional expressions of profanity, while the old man laughs, and commends him as a thorough-going boy.

"The child is father to the man," and with, such training, whatever may be his natural disposition, it cannot well be otherwise than that, on arriving at maturity, the sufferings and miseries of the slave will be looked upon with entire indifference. The influence of the iniquitous system necessarily fosters an unfeeling and cruel spirit, even in the bosoms of those who, among their equals, are regarded as humane and generous.

Young Master Epps possessed some noble qualities, yet no process of reasoning could lead him to comprehend, that in the eye of the Almighty there is no distinction of color. He looked upon the black man simply as an animal, differing in no respect from any other animal, save in the gift of speech and the possession of somewhat higher instincts, and, therefore, the more valuable. To work like his father's mules—to be whipped and kicked and scourged through life—to address the white man with hat in hand, and eyes bent servilely on the earth, in his mind, was the natural and proper destiny of the slave. Brought up with such ideas—in the notion that we stand without the pale of humanity—no wonder the oppressors of my people are a pitiless and unrelenting race.

CHAPTER 19

In the month of June, 1852, in pursuance of a previous contract, Mr. Avery, a carpenter of Bayou Rouge, commenced the erection of a house for Master Epps. It has previously been stated that there are no cellars on Bayou Boeuf; on the other hand, such is the low and swampy nature of the ground, the great houses are usually built upon spiles. Another peculiarity is, the rooms are not plastered, but the ceiling and sides are covered with matched cypress boards, painted such color as most pleases the owner's taste. Generally the plank and boards are sawed by slaves with whipsaws, there being no water-power upon which mills might be built within many miles. When the planter erects for himself a dwelling, therefore, there is plenty of extra work for his slaves. Having had some experience under Tibeats as a carpenter, I was taken from the field altogether, on the arrival of Avery and his hands.

Among them was one to whom I owe an immeasurable debt of gratitude. Only for him, in all probability, I should have ended my days in slavery. He was my deliverer—a man whose true heart overflowed with noble and generous emotions. To the last moment of my existence I shall remember him with feelings of thankfulness. His name was

Bass, and at that time he resided in Marksville. It will be difficult to convey a correct impression of his appearance or character. He was a large man, between forty and fifty years old, of light complexion and light hair. He was very cool and self-possessed, fond of argument, but always speaking with extreme deliberation. He was that kind of person whose peculiarity of manner was such that nothing he uttered ever gave offence. What would be intolerable, coming from the lips of another, could be said by him with impunity. There was not a man on Red River, perhaps, that agreed with him on the subject of politics or religion, and not a man, I venture to say, who discussed either of those subjects half as much. It seemed to be taken for granted that he would espouse the unpopular side of every local question, and it always created amusement rather than displeasure among his auditors, to listen to the ingenious and original manner in which he maintained the controversy. He was a bachelor—an "old bachelor," according to the true acceptation of the term—having no kindred living, as he knew of, in the world. Neither had he any permanent abiding place—wandering from one state to another, as his fancy dictated. He had lived in Marksville three or four years, and in the prosecution of his business as a carpenter; and in consequence, likewise, of his peculiarities, was quite extensively known throughout the parish of Avoyelles. He was liberal to a fault; and his many acts of kindness and transparent goodness of heart rendered him popular in the community, the sentiment of which he unceasingly combated.

He was a native of Canada, from whence he had wandered in early life, and after visiting all the principal localities in the northern and western states, in the course of his peregrinations, arrived in the unhealthy region of the Red River. His last removal was from Illinois. Whither he has now gone, I regret to be obliged to say, is unknown to me. He gathered up his effects and departed quietly from Marksville the day before I did, the suspicions of his instrumentality in procuring my liberation rendering such a step necessary. For the commission of a just and righteous act he would undoubtedly have suffered death, had he remained within reach of the slave-whipping tribe on Bayou Boeuf.

One day, while working on the new house, Bass and Epps became engaged in a controversy, to which, as will be readily supposed, I listened with absorbing interest. They were discussing the subject of slavery.

"I tell you what it is, Epps," said Bass, "It's all wrong— all wrong, sir—there's no justice nor righteousness in it. I wouldn't own a slave if I was rich as Croesus, which I am not, as is perfectly well understood, more particularly among my creditors. *There's* another humbug—the credit system— humbug, sir; no credit—no debt. Credit leads a man into temptation. Cash down is the only thing that will deliver him from evil. But this question of *slavery*; what *right* have you to your niggers when you come down to the point?"

"What right!" said Epps, laughing; "why, I bought 'em, and paid for 'em."

"Of *course* you did; the law says you have the right to hold a nigger, but begging the law's pardon, it *lies*. Yes, Epps, when the law says that it's a *liar*, and the truth is not in it. Is everything right because the law allows it? Suppose they'd pass a law taking away your liberty and making you a slave?"

"Oh, that ain't a supposable case," said Epps, still laughing; "hope you don't compare me to a nigger, Bass."

"Well," Bass answered gravely, "no, not exactly. But I have seen niggers before now as good as I am, and I have no acquaintance with any white man in these parts that I consider a whit better than myself. Now, in the sight of God, what is the difference, Epps, between a white man and a black one?"

"All the difference in the world," replied Epps. "You might as well ask what the difference is between a white man and a baboon. Now, I've seen one of them critters in

Orleans that knowed just as much as any nigger I've got. You'd call them feller citizens, I s'pose?"—and Epps indulged in a loud laugh at his own wit.

"Look here, Epps," continued his companion; "you can't laugh me down in that way. Some men are witty, and some ain't so witty as they think they are. Now let me ask you a question. Are all men created free and equal as the Declaration of Independence holds they are?"

"Yes," responded Epps, "but all men, niggers, and monkeys *ain't*;" and hereupon he broke forth into a more boisterous laugh than before.

"There are monkeys among white people as well as black, when you come to that," coolly remarked Bass. "I know some white men that use arguments no sensible monkey would. But let that pass. These niggers are human beings. If they don't know as much as their masters, whose fault is it? They are not *allowed* to know anything. You have books and papers, and can go where you please, and gather intelligence in a thousand ways. But your slaves have no privileges. You'd whip one of them if caught reading a book. They are held in bondage, generation after generation, deprived of mental improvement, and who can expect them to possess much knowledge? If they are not brought down to a level with the brute creation, you slaveholders will never be blamed for it. If they are baboons, or stand no higher in the scale of intelligence than such animals, you and men like you will have to answer for it. There's a sin, a fearful sin, resting on this nation, that will not go unpunished forever. There will be a reckoning yet—yes, Epps, there's a day coming that will burn as an oven. It may be sooner or it may be later, but it's a coming as sure as the Lord is just."

"If you lived up among the Yankees in New England," said Epps, "I expect you'd be one of them cursed fanatics that know more than the constitution, and go about peddling clocks and coaxing niggers to run away."

"If I was in New England," returned Bass, "I would be just what I am here. I would say that slavery was an iniquity, and ought to be abolished. I would say there was no reason nor justice in the law, or the constitution that allows one man to hold another man in bondage. It would be hard for you to lose your property, to be sure, but it wouldn't be half as hard as it would be to lose your liberty. You have no more right to your freedom, in exact justice, than Uncle Abram yonder. Talk about black skin, and black blood; why, how many slaves are there on this bayou as white as either of us? And what difference is there in the color of the soul? Pshaw! the whole system is as absurd as it is cruel. You may own niggers and be hanged, but I wouldn't own one for the best plantation in Louisiana."

"You like to hear yourself talk, Bass, better than any man I know of. You would argue that black was white or white black, if anybody would contradict you. Nothing suits you in this world, and I don't believe you will be satisfied with the next, if you should have your choice in them."

Conversations substantially like the foregoing were not unusual between the two after this; Epps drawing him out more for the purpose of creating a laugh at his expense, than with a view of fairly discussing the merits of the question. He looked upon Bass, as a man ready to say anything merely for the pleasure of hearing his own voice; as somewhat self-conceited, perhaps, contending against his faith and judgment, in order, simply, to exhibit his dexterity in argumentation.

He remained at Epps' through the summer, visiting Marksville generally once a fortnight. The more I saw of him, the more I became convinced he was a man in whom I could confide. Nevertheless, my previous ill-fortune had taught me to be extremely cautious. It was not my place to speak to a white except when spoken to, but I omitted no opportunity of throwing myself in his way, and endeavored constantly in every possible manner to attract his attention. In the early part of August he and myself were at work alone in the house, the other carpenters having left, and Epps being absent in the field. Now was the time, if ever, to broach the subject, and I resolved to do it, and submit to whatever consequences might ensue. We were busily at work in the afternoon, when I stopped suddenly and said—

"Master Bass, I want to ask you what part of the country you came from?"

"Why, Platt, what put that into your head?" he answered. "You wouldn't know if I should tell you." After a moment or two he added—"I was born in Canada; now guess where that is."

"Oh, I know where Canada is," said I, "I have been there myself."

"Yes, I expect you are well acquainted all through that country," he remarked, laughing incredulously.

"As sure as I live, Master Bass," I replied, "I have been there. I have been in Montreal and Kingston, and Queenston, and a great many places in Canada, and I have been in York State, too—in Buffalo, and Rochester, and Albany, and can tell you the names of the villages on the Erie Canal and the Champlain Canal."

Bass turned round and gazed at me a long time without uttering a syllable.

"How came you here?" he inquired, at length.

"Master Bass," I answered, "if justice had been done, I never would have been here."

"Well, how's this?" said he. "Who are you? You have been in Canada sure enough; I know all the places you mention. How did you happen to get here? Come, tell me all about it."

"I have no friends here," was my reply, "that I can put confidence in. I am afraid to tell you, though I don't believe you would tell Master Epps if I should."

He assured me earnestly he would keep every word I might speak to him a profound secret, and his curiosity was evidently strongly excited. It was a long story, I informed him, and would take some time to relate it. Master Epps would be back soon, but if he would see me that night after all were asleep, I would repeat it to him. He consented readily to the arrangement, and directed me to come into the building where we were then at work, and I would find him there. About midnight, when all was still and quiet I crept cautiously from my cabin, and silently entering the unfinished building, found him awaiting me.

After further assurances on his part that I should not be betrayed, I began a relation of the history of my life and misfortunes. He was deeply interested, asking numerous questions in reference to localities and events. Having ended my story I besought him to write to some of my friends at the North, acquainting them with my situation, and begging them to forward free papers, or take such steps as they might consider proper to secure my release. He promised to do so, but dwelt upon the danger of such an act in case of detection, and now impressed upon me the great necessity of strict silence and secrecy. Before we parted our plan of operation was arranged.

We agreed to meet the next night at a specified place among the high weeds on the bank of the bayou some distance from master's dwelling. There he was to write down on paper the names and address of several persons, old friends in the North, to whom he would direct letters during his next visit to Marksville. It was not deemed prudent to meet in the new house, inasmuch as the light it would be necessary to use might possibly be discovered. In the course of the day I managed to obtain a few matches and a piece of candle, unperceived, from the kitchen, during a temporary absence of Aunt Phebe. Bass had pencil and paper in his tool chest.

At the appointed hour we met on the bayou bank, and creeping among the high weeds, I lighted the candle, while he drew forth pencil and paper and prepared for business. I gave him the names of William Perry, Cephas Parker and Judge Marvin, all of Saratoga Springs, Saratoga county, New York. I had been employed by the latter in the United States Hotel, and had transacted business with the former to a considerable extent, and trusted that at least one of them would be still living at that place. He carefully wrote the names, and then remarked, thoughtfully—

"It is so many years since you left Saratoga, all these men may be dead, or may have removed. You say you obtained papers at the custom house in New York. Probably there is a record of them there, and I think it would be well to write and ascertain."

I agreed with him, and again repeated the circumstances related heretofore, connected with my visit to the custom house with Brown and Hamilton. We lingered on the bank of the bayou an hour or more, conversing upon the subject which now engrossed our thoughts. I could no longer doubt his fidelity, and freely spoke to him of the many sorrows I had borne in silence, and so long. I spoke of my wife and children, mentioning their names and ages, and dwelling upon the unspeakable happiness it would be to clasp them to my heart once more before I died. I caught him by the hand, and with tears and passionate entreaties implored him to befriend me—to restore me to my kindred and to liberty—promising I would weary Heaven the remainder of my life with prayers that it would bless and prosper him. In the enjoyment of freedom—surrounded by the associations of youth, and restored to the bosom of my family—that promise is not yet forgotten, nor shall it ever be so long as I have strength to raise my imploring eyes on high.

"Oh, blessings on his kindly voice and on his silver hair,

And blessings on his whole life long, until he meet
me there."

He overwhelmed me with assurances of friendship and
faithfulness, saying he had never before taken so deep an
interest in the fate of any one. He spoke of himself in a somewhat mournful tone, as a lonely man, a wanderer about the
world—that he was growing old, and must soon reach the end
of his earthly journey, and lie down to his final rest without
kith or kin to mourn for him, or to remember him—that his
life was of little value to himself, and henceforth should be
devoted to the accomplishment of my liberty, and to an
unceasing warfare against the accursed shame of slavery.

After this time we seldom spoke to, or recognized each
other. He was, moreover, less free in his conversation with
Epps on the subject of slavery. The remotest suspicion that
there was any unusual intimacy—any secret understanding
between us—never once entered the mind of Epps, or any
other person, white or black, on the plantation.

I am often asked, with an air of incredulity, how I
succeeded so many years in keeping from my daily and
constant companions the knowledge of my true name and
history. The terrible lesson Burch taught me, impressed indel-
ibly upon my mind the danger and uselessness of asserting I
was a freeman. There was no possibility of any slave being
able to assist me, while, on the other hand, there *was* a possibility of his exposing me. When it is recollected the whole
current of my thoughts, for twelve years, turned to the
contemplation of escape, it will not be wondered at, that I
was always cautious and on my guard. It would have been an
act of folly to have proclaimed my *right* to freedom; it would
only have subjected me to severer scrutiny—probably have
consigned me to some more distant and inaccessible region
than even Bayou Boeuf. Edwin Epps was a person utterly
regardless of a black man's rights or wrongs—utterly destitute

of any natural sense of justice, as I well knew. It was important, therefore, not only as regarded my hope of deliverance, but also as regarded the few personal privileges I was permitted to enjoy, to keep from him the history of my life.

The Saturday night subsequent to our interview at the water's edge, Bass went home to Marksville. The next day, being Sunday, he employed himself in his own room writing letters. One he directed to the Collector of Customs at New York, another to Judge Marvin, and another to Messrs. Parker and Perry jointly. The latter was the one which led to my recovery. He subscribed my true name, but in the postscript intimated I was not the writer. The letter itself shows that he considered himself engaging in a dangerous undertaking— no less than running "the risk of his life, if detected." I did not see the letter before it was mailed, but have since obtained a copy, which is here inserted:

"Bayou Boeuf, August 15, 1852
"Mr. WILLIAM PERRY or Mr. CEPHAS PARKER:

"Gentlemen—It having been a long time since I
have seen or heard from you, and not knowing
that you are living, it is with uncertainty that I
write to you, but the necessity of the case must
be my excuse.

"Having been born free, just across the
river from you, I am certain you must know me,
and I am here now a slave. I wish you to obtain
free papers for me, and forward them to me at
Marksville, Louisiana, Parish of Avoyelles, and
oblige

"Yours,
SOLOMON NORTHUP

"The way I came to be a slave, I was taken sick
in Washington City, and was insensible for some
time. When I recovered my reason, I was robbed
of my free papers, and in irons on my way to
this state, and have never been able to get
anyone to write for me until now; and he that is
writing for me runs the risk of his life if
detected."

The allusion to myself in the work recently issued, entitled
A Key to Uncle Tom's Cabin, contains the first part of this
letter, omitting the postscript. Neither are the full names of
the gentlemen to whom it is directed correctly stated, there
being a slight discrepancy, probably a typographical error. To
the postscript more than to the body of the communication
am I indebted for my liberation, as will presently be seen.

When Bass returned from Marksville he informed me
of what he had done. We continued our midnight consulta-
tions, never speaking to each other through the day, excepting
as it was necessary about the work. As nearly as he was able
to ascertain, it would require two weeks for the letter to
reach Saratoga in due course of mail, and the same length
of time for an answer to return. Within six weeks, at the
farthest, we concluded, an answer would arrive, if it arrived
at all. A great many suggestions were now made, and a great
deal of conversation took place between us, as to the most
safe and proper course to pursue on receipt of the free papers.
They would stand between him and harm, in case we were
overtaken and arrested leaving the country altogether. It
would be no infringement of law, however much it might
provoke individual hostility, to assist a freeman regain his
freedom.

At the end of four weeks he was again at Marksville,
but no answer had arrived. I was sorely disappointed, but
still reconciled myself with the reflection that sufficient

length of time had not yet elapsed—that there might have been delays—and that I could not reasonably expect one so soon. Six, seven, eight, and ten weeks passed by, however, and nothing came. I was in a fever of suspense whenever Bass visited Marksville, and could scarcely close my eyes until his return. Finally my master's house was finished, and the time came when Bass must leave me. The night before his departure I was wholly given up to despair. I had clung to him as a drowning man clings to the floating spar, knowing if it slips from his grasp he must forever sink beneath the waves. The all-glorious hope, upon which I had laid such eager hold, was crumbling to ashes in my hands. I felt as if sinking down, down, amidst the bitter waters of slavery, from the unfathomable depths of which I should never rise again.

The generous heart of my friend and benefactor was touched with pity at the sight of my distress. He endeavored to cheer me up, promising to return the day before Christmas, and if no intelligence was received in the meantime, some further step would be under taken to effect our design. He exhorted me to keep up my spirits—to rely upon his continued efforts in my behalf, assuring me, in most earnest and impressive language, that my liberation should, from thenceforth, be the chief object of his thoughts.

In his absence the time passed slowly indeed. I looked forward to Christmas with intense anxiety and impatience. I had about given up the expectation of receiving any answer to the letters. They might have miscarried, or might have been misdirected. Perhaps those at Saratoga, to whom they had been addressed, were all dead; perhaps, engaged in their pursuits, they did not consider the fate of an obscure, unhappy black man of sufficient importance to be noticed. My whole reliance was in Bass. The faith I had in him was continually reassuring me, and enabled me to stand up against the tide of disappointment that had overwhelmed me.

So wholly was I absorbed in reflecting upon my situation and prospects, that the hands with whom I labored in the field often observed it. Patsey would ask me if I was sick, and Uncle Abram, and Bob, and Wiley frequently expressed a curiosity to know what I could be thinking about so steadily. But I evaded their inquiries with some light remark, and kept my thoughts locked closely in my breast.

CHAPTER 20

Faithful to his word, the day before Christmas, just at night-fall, Bass came riding into the yard.

"How are you," said Epps, shaking him by the hand, "glad to see you."

He would not have been *very* glad had he known the object of his errand.

"Quite well, quite well," answered Bass. "Had some business out on the bayou, and concluded to call and see you, and stay overnight."

Epps ordered one of the slaves to take charge of his horse, and with much talk and laughter they passed into the house together; not, however, until Bass had looked at me significantly, as much as to say, "Keep dark, we understand each other." It was ten o'clock at night before the labors of the day were performed, when I entered the cabin. At that time Uncle Abram and Bob occupied it with me. I laid down upon my board and feigned I was asleep. When my companions had fallen into a profound slumber, I moved stealthily out of the door, and watched, and listened attentively for some sign or sound from Bass. There I stood until long after midnight, but nothing could be seen or heard. As I suspected, he dared not leave the house, through fear of exciting the suspicion of some of the family. I judged, correctly, he would rise earlier than was his custom, and take the opportunity of seeing me before Epps was up. Accordingly I aroused Uncle Abram an hour sooner than usual, and sent him into the house to build a fire, which, at that season of the year, is a part of Uncle Abram's duties.

I also gave Bob a violent shake, and asked him if he intended to sleep till noon, saying master would be up before the mules were fed. He knew right well the consequence that would follow such an event, and, jumping to his feet, was at the horse-pasture in a twinkling.

Presently, when both were gone, Bass slipped into the cabin.

"No letter yet, Platt," said he. The announcement fell upon my heart like lead.

"Oh, *do* write again, Master Bass," I cried; "I will give you the names of a great many I know. Surely they are not all dead. Surely someone will pity me."

"No use," Bass replied, "no use. I have made up my mind to that. I fear the Marksville postmaster will mistrust something, I have inquired so often at his office. Too uncertain—too dangerous."

"Then it is all over," I exclaimed. "Oh, my God, how can I end my days here!"

"You're not going to end them here," he said, "unless you die very soon. I've thought this matter all over, and have come to a determination. There are more ways than one to manage this business, and a better and surer way than writing letters. I have a job or two on hand which can be completed by March or April. By that time I shall have a considerable sum of money, and then, Platt, I am going to Saratoga myself."

I could scarcely credit my own senses as the words fell from his lips. But he assured me, in a manner that left no doubt of the sincerity of his intention, that if his life was spared until spring, he should certainly undertake the journey.

"I have lived in this region long enough," he continued; "I may as well be in one place as another. For a long time I have been thinking of going back once more to the place where I was born. I'm tired of slavery as well as you. If I can succeed in getting you away from here, it will be a good act that I shall like to think of all my life. And I *shall* succeed. Platt; I'm *bound* to do it. Now let me tell you what I want. Epps will be up soon, and it won't do to be caught here. Think of a great many men at Saratoga and Sandy Hill, and in that neighborhood, who once knew you. I shall make excuse to come here again in the course of the winter, when I will write down their names. I will then know who to call on when I go north. Think of all you can. Cheer up! Don't be discouraged. I'm with you, life or death. Good-bye. God bless you," and saying this he left the cabin quickly, and entered the great house.

It was Christmas morning—the happiest day in the whole year for the slave. That morning he need not hurry to the field, with his gourd and cotton bag. Happiness sparkled in the eyes and overspread the countenances of all. The time of feasting and dancing had come. The cane and cotton fields were deserted. That day the clean dress was to be donned—the red ribbon displayed; there were to be reunions, and joy and laughter, and hurrying to and fro. It was to be a day of *liberty* among the children of slavery. Wherefore they were happy, and rejoiced.

After breakfast Epps and Bass sauntered about the yard, conversing upon the price of cotton, and various other topics.

"Where do your niggers hold Christmas?" Bass inquired.

"Platt is going to Tanner's today. His fiddle is in great demand. They want him at Marshall's Monday, and Miss Mary McCoy, on the old Norwood plantation, writes me a note that she wants him to play for her niggers Tuesday."

"He is rather a smart boy, ain't he?" said Bass. "Come here, Platt," he added, looking at me as I walked up to them, as if he had never thought before to take any special notice of me.

"Yes," replied Epps, taking hold of my arm and feeling it, "there isn't a bad joint in him. There ain't a boy on the bayou worth more than he is—perfectly sound, and no bad tricks. D—n him, he isn't like other niggers; doesn't look like 'em—don't act like 'em. I was offered seventeen hundred dollars for him last week."

"And didn't take it?" Bass inquired, with an air of surprise.

"Take it—no; devilish clear of it. Why, he's a reg'lar genius; can make a plough beam, wagon tongue—anything, as well as you can. Marshall wanted to put up one of his niggers agin him and raffle for them, but I told him I would see the devil have him first."

"I don't see anything remarkable about him," Bass observed.

"Why, just feel of him, now," Epps rejoined. "You don't see a boy very often put together any closer than he is. He's a thin-skin'd cuss, and won't bear as much whipping as some; but he's got the muscle in him, and no mistake."

Bass felt of me, turned me round, and made a thorough examination, Epps all the while dwelling on my good points. But his visitor seemed to take but little interest finally in the subject, and consequently it was dropped. Bass soon departed, giving me another sly look of recognition and significance, as he trotted out of the yard.

When he was gone I obtained a pass, and started for Tanner's—not Peter Tanner's, of whom mention has previously been made, but a relative of his. I played during the day and most of the night, spending the next day, Sunday, in my cabin. Monday I crossed the bayou to Douglas Marshall's, all Epps' slaves accompanying me, and on Tuesday went to the old Norwood place, which is the third plantation above Marshall's, on the same side of the water.

This estate is now owned by Miss Mary McCoy, a lovely girl, some twenty years of age. She is the beauty and the glory of Bayou Boeuf. She owns about a hundred working hands, besides a great many house servants, yard boys, and young children. Her brother-in-law, who resides on the adjoining estate, is her general agent. She is beloved by all her slaves, and good reason indeed have they to be thankful that they have fallen into such gentle hands. Nowhere on the bayou are there such feasts, such merrymaking, as at young Madam McCoy's. Thither, more than to any other place, do the old and the young for miles around love to repair in the time of the Christmas holidays; for nowhere else can they find such delicious repasts; nowhere else can they hear a voice speaking to them so pleasantly. No one is so well beloved—no one fills so large a space in the hearts of a thousand slaves, as young Madam McCoy, the orphan mistress of the old Norwood estate.

On my arrival at her place, I found two or three hundred had assembled. The table was prepared in a long building, which she had erected expressly for her slaves to dance in. It was covered with every variety of food the country afforded, and was pronounced by general acclamation to be the rarest of dinners. Roast turkey, pig, chicken, duck, and all kinds of meat, baked, boiled, and broiled, formed a line the whole length of the extended table, while the vacant spaces were filled with tarts, jellies, and frosted cake, and pastry of many kinds. The young mistress walked around the table, smiling and saying a kind word to each one, and seemed to enjoy the scene exceedingly.

When the dinner was over the tables were removed to make room for the dancers. I tuned my violin and struck up a lively air; while some joined in a nimble reel, others patted and sang their simple but melodious songs, filling the great room with music mingled with the sound of human voices and the clatter of many feet.

In the evening the mistress returned, and stood in the door a long time, looking at us. She was magnificently arrayed. Her dark hair and eyes contrasted strongly with her clear and delicate complexion. Her form was slender but commanding, and her movement was a combination of unaffected and grace. As she stood there, clad in her rich apparel, her face animated with pleasure, I thought I had never looked upon a human being half as beautiful. I dwell with delight upon the description of this fair and gentle lady, not only because she inspired me with emotions of gratitude and admiration, but because I would have the reader understand that all slave-owners on Bayou Boeuf are not like Epps, or Tibeats, or Jim Burns. Occasionally can be found, rarely it may be, indeed, a good man like William Ford, or an angel of kindness like young Mistress McCoy.

Tuesday concluded the three holidays Epps yearly allowed us. On my way home, Wednesday morning, while passing the plantation of William Pierce, that gentleman hailed me, saying he had received a line from Epps, brought down by William Varnell, permitting him to detain me for the purpose of playing for his slaves that night. It was the last time I was destined to witness a slave dance on the shores of Bayou Boeuf. The party at Pierce's continued their jollification until broad daylight, when I returned to my master's house, somewhat wearied with the loss of rest, but rejoicing in the possession of numerous bits and picayunes, which the whites, who were pleased with my musical performances, had contributed.

On Saturday morning, for the first time in years, I overslept myself. I was frightened on coming out of the cabin to find the slaves were already in the field. They had preceded me some fifteen minutes. Leaving my dinner and water-gourd, I hurried after them as fast as I could move. It was not yet sunrise, but Epps was on the piazza as I left the hut, and cried out to me that it was a pretty time of day to be getting up. By extra exertion my row was up when he came out after breakfast. This, however, was no excuse for the offence of oversleeping. Bidding me strip and lie down, he gave me ten or fifteen lashes, at the conclusion of which he inquired if I thought, after that, I could get up sometime in the *morning*. I expressed myself quite positively that I *could*, and, with back stinging with pain, went about my work.

The following day, Sunday, my thoughts were upon Bass, and the probabilities and hopes which hung upon his action and determination. I considered the uncertainty of life; that if it should be the will of God that he should die, my prospect of deliverance, and all expectation of happiness in this world, would be wholly ended and destroyed. My sore back, perhaps, did not have a tendency to render me unusually cheerful. I felt downhearted and unhappy all day long, and when I laid down upon the hard board at night, my heart was oppressed with such a load of grief, it seemed that it must break.

Monday morning, the third of January, 1853, we were in the field betimes. It was a raw, cold morning, such as is unusual in that region. I was in advance, Uncle Abram next to me, behind him Bob, Patsey and Wiley, with our cotton bags about our necks. Epps happened (a rare thing, indeed,) to come out that morning without his whip. He swore, in a manner that would shame a pirate, that we were doing nothing. Bob ventured to say that his fingers were so numb with cold he couldn't pick fast. Epps cursed himself for not having brought his rawhide, and declared that when he came out again he would warm us well; yes, he would make us all hotter than that fiery realm in which I am sometimes compelled to believe he will himself eventually reside.

With these fervent expressions, he left us. When out of hearing, we commenced talking to each other, saying how hard it was to be compelled to keep up our tasks with numb fingers; how unreasonable master was, and speaking of him generally in no flattering terms. Our conversation was interrupted by a carriage passing rapidly towards the house.

Looking up, we saw two men approaching us through the cotton field.

Having now brought down this narrative to the last hour I was to spend on Bayou Boeuf—having gotten through my last cotton picking, and about to bid Master Epps farewell—I must beg the reader to go back with me to the month of August; to follow Bass's letter on its long journey to Saratoga; to learn the effect it produced—and that, while I was repining and despairing in the slave hut of Edwin Epps, through the friendship of Bass and the goodness of Providence, all things were working together for my deliverance.

CHAPTER 21

I am indebted to Mr. Henry B. Northup and others for many of the particulars contained in this chapter.

The letter written by Bass, directed to Parker and Perry, and which was deposited in the post office in Marksville on the fifteenth day of August, 1852, arrived at Saratoga in the early part of September. Sometime previous to this, Anne had removed to Glens Falls, Warren County, where she had charge of the kitchen in Carpenter's Hotel. She kept house, however, lodging with our children, and was only absent from them during such time as the discharge of her duties in the hotel required.

Messrs. Parker and Perry, on receipt of the letter forwarded it immediately to Anne. On reading it the children were all excitement, and without delay hastened to the neighboring village of Sandy Hill, to consult Henry B. Northup, and obtain his advice and assistance in the matter.

Upon examination, that gentleman found among the statutes of the state an act providing for the recovery of free citizens from slavery. It was passed May 14, 1840, and is entitled "An act more effectually to protect the free citizens of this State from being kidnapped or reduced to slavery." It provides that it shall be the duty of the Governor, upon the receipt of satisfactory information that any free citizen or inhabitant of this State, is wrongfully held in another State or Territory of the United States, upon the allegation or pretence that such person is a slave, or by color of any usage or rule of law is deemed or taken to be a slave, to take such measures to procure the restoration of such person to liberty, as he shall deem necessary. And to that end, he is authorized to appoint and employ an agent, and directed to furnish him with such credentials and instructions as will be likely to accomplish the object of his appointment. It requires the agent so appointed to proceed to collect the proper proof to establish the right of such person to his freedom; to perform such journeys, take such measures, institute such legal proceedings, etc., as may be necessary to return such person to this State, and charges all expenses incurred in carrying the act into effect, upon moneys not otherwise appropriated in the treasury.

It was necessary to establish two facts to the satisfaction of the Governor: First, that I was a free citizen of New York; and secondly, that I was wrongfully held in bondage. As to the first point, there was no difficulty, all the older inhabitants in the vicinity being ready to testify to it. The second point rested entirely upon the letter to Parker and Perry, written in an unknown hand, and upon the letter penned on board the brig *Orleans*, which, unfortunately, had been mislaid or lost.

A memorial was prepared, directed to his excellency, Governor Hunt, setting forth her marriage, my departure to Washington city; the receipt of the letters; that I was a free citizen, and such other facts as were deemed important, and was signed and verified by Anne. Accompanying this memorial were several affidavits of prominent citizens of Sandy Hill and Fort Edward, corroborating fully the statements it contained, and also a request of several well-known gentlemen to the Governor, that Henry B. Northup be appointed agent under the legislative act.

On reading the memorial and affidavits, his excellency took a lively interest in the matter, and on the twenty-third day of November, 1852, under the seal of the state, "constituted, appointed and employed Henry B. Northup, Esq., an agent, with full power to effect my restoration, and to take such measures as would be most likely to accomplish it, and instructing him to proceed to Louisiana with all convenient dispatch.

The pressing nature of Mr. Northup's professional and political engagements delayed his departure until December. On the fourteenth day of that month he left Sandy Hill, and proceed to Washington. The Hon. Pierre Soule, Senator in Congress from Louisiana, Hon. Mr. Conrad, Secretary of War, and Judge Kelson, of the Supreme Court of the United States, upon hearing a statement of the facts, and examining his commission, and certified copies of the memorial and affidavits, furnished him with open letters to gentlemen in Louisiana, strongly urging their assistance in accomplishing the object, of his appointment.

Senator Soule especially interested himself in the matter, insisting, in forcible language, that it was the duty and interest of every planter in his state to aid in restoring me to freedom, and trusted the sentiments of honor and justice in the bosom of every citizen of the commonwealth would enlist him at once in my behalf. Having obtained these valuable letters, Mr. Northup returned to Baltimore, and proceeded from thence to Pittsburgh. It was his original intention, under advice of friends at Washington, to go directly to New Orleans, and consult the authorities of that city. Providentially, however, on arriving at the mouth of Red River, he changed his mind. Had he continued on, he would not have met with Bass, in which case the search for me would probably have been fruitless.

Taking passage on the first steamer that arrived, he pursued his journey up Red River, a sluggish, winding stream, flowing through a vast region of primitive forests and impenetrable swamps, almost wholly destitute of inhabitants. About nine o'clock in the forenoon, January 1st, 1853, he left the steamboat at Marksville, and proceeded directly to Marksville Court House, a small village four miles in the interior.

From the fact that the letter to Messrs. Parker and Perry was postmarked at Marksville, it was supposed by him that I was in that place or its immediate vicinity. On reaching this town, he at once laid his business before the Hon. John P. Waddill, a legal gentleman of distinction, and a man of fine genius and most noble impulses. After reading the letters and documents presented him, and listening to a representation of the circumstances under which I had been carried away into captivity, Mr. Waddill at once proffered his services, and entered into the affair with great zeal and earnestness. He, in common with others of like elevated character, looked upon the kidnapper with abhorrence. The title of his fellow parishioners and clients to the property which constituted the larger proportion of their wealth, not only depended upon the good faith in which slave sales were transacted, but he was a man in whose honorable heart emotions of indignation were aroused by such an instance of injustice.

Marksville, although occupying a prominent position, and standing out in impressive italics on the map of Louisiana, is, in fact, but a small and insignificant hamlet. Aside from the tavern, kept by a jolly and generous boniface, the court house, inhabited by lawless cows and swine in the seasons of vacation, and a high gallows, with its dissevered rope dangling in the air, there is little to attract the attention of the stranger.

Solomon Northup was a name Mr. Waddill had never heard, but he was confident that if there was a slave bearing that appellation in Marksville or vicinity, his black boy Tom would know him. Tom was accordingly called, but in all his extensive circle of acquaintances there was no such personage.

The letter to Parker and Perry was dated at Bayou Boeuf.

At this place, therefore, the conclusion was, I must be sought. But here a difficulty suggested itself, of a very grave character indeed. Bayou Boeuf, at its nearest point, was twenty-three miles distant, and was the name applied to the section of country extending between fifty and a hundred miles, on both sides of that stream. Thousands and thousands of slaves resided upon its shores, the remarkable richness and fertility of the soil having attracted thither a great number of planters. The information in the letter was so vague and indefinite as to render it difficult to conclude upon any specific course of proceeding. It was finally determined, however, as the only plan that presented any prospect of success, that Northup and the brother of Waddill, a student in the office of the latter, should repair to the Bayou, and traveling up one side and down the other its whole length, inquire at each plantation for me. Mr. Waddill tendered the use of his carriage, and it was definitely arranged that they should start upon the excursion early Monday morning.

It will be seen at once that this course, in all probability, would have resulted unsuccessfully. It would have been impossible for them to have gone into the fields and examine all the gangs at work. They were not aware that I was known only as Platt; and had they inquired of Epps himself, he would had stated truly that he knew nothing of Solomon Northup.

The arrangement being adopted, however, there was nothing further to be done until Sunday had elapsed. The conversation between Messrs. Northup and Waddill, in the course of the afternoon, turned upon New York politics.

"I can scarcely comprehend the nice distinctions and shades of political parties in your state," observed Mr. Waddill. "I read of soft-shells and hard-shells, hunkers and barnburners, woolly-heads and silver-grays, and am unable to understand the precise difference between them. Pray, what is it?"

Mr. Northup, re-filling his pipe, entered into quite an elaborate narrative of the origin of the various sections of parties, and concluded by saying there was another party in New York, known as free-soilers or abolitionists. "You have seen none of those in this part of the country, I presume?" Mr. Northup remarked.

"Never, but one," answered Waddill, laughingly. "We have one here in Marksville, an eccentric creature, who preaches abolitionism as vehemently as any fanatic at the North. He is a generous, inoffensive man, but always maintaining the wrong side of an argument. It affords us a deal of amusement. He is an excellent mechanic, and almost indispensable in this community. He is a carpenter. His name is Bass."

Some further good-natured conversation was had at the expense of Bass' peculiarities, when Waddill all at once fell into a reflective mood, and asked for the mysterious letter again.

"Let me see—l-e-t m-e s-e-e!" he repeated, thoughtfully to himself, running his eyes over the letter once more. "'Bayou Boeuf, August 15.' August 15—postmarked here. 'He that is writing for me—' Where did Bass work last summer?" he inquired, turning suddenly to his brother. His brother was unable to inform him, but rising, left the office, and soon returned with the intelligence that "Bass worked last summer somewhere on Bayou Boeuf."

"He is the man," bringing down his hand emphatically on the table, "who can tell us all about Solomon Northup," exclaimed Waddill.

Bass was immediately searched for, but could not be found. After some inquiry, it was ascertained he was at the landing on Red River. Procuring a conveyance, young Waddill and Northup were not long in traversing the few miles to the latter place. On their arrival, Bass was found, just on the point of leaving, to be absent a fortnight or more. After an introduction, Northup begged the privilege of speaking to him privately a moment. They walked together towards the river, when the following conversation ensued:

"Mr. Bass," said Northup, "allow me to ask you if you were on Bayou Boeuf last August?"

"Yes, sir, I was there in August," was the reply.

"Did you write a letter for a colored man at that place to some gentleman in Saratoga Springs?"

"Excuse me, sir, if I say that is none of your business," answered Bass, stopping and looking his interrogator searchingly in the face.

"Perhaps I am rather hasty, Mr. Bass; I beg your pardon; but I have come from the state of New York to accomplish the purpose the writer of a letter dated the fifteenth of August, postmarked at Marksville, had in view. Circumstances have led me to think that you are perhaps the man who wrote it. I am in search of Solomon Northup. If you know him, I beg you to inform me frankly where he is, and I assure you the source of any information you may give me shall not be divulged, if you desire it not to be."

A long time Bass looked his new acquaintance steadily in the eyes, without opening his lips. He seemed to be doubting in his own mind if there was not an attempt to practise some deception upon him. Finally he said, deliberately:

"I have done nothing to be ashamed of. I am the man who wrote the letter. If you have come to rescue Solomon Northup, I am glad to see you."

"When did you last see him, and where is he?" Northup inquired.

"I last saw him Christmas, a week ago today. He is the slave of Edwin Epps, a planter on Bayou Boeuf, near Holmesville. He is not known as Solomon Northup; he is called Platt."

The secret was out—the mystery was unraveled. Through the thick, black cloud, amid whose dark and dismal shadows I had walked twelve years, broke the star that was to light me back to liberty. All mistrust and hesitation were soon thrown aside, and the two men conversed long and freely upon the subject uppermost in their thoughts. Bass expressed the interest he had taken in my behalf—his intention of going north in the spring, and declaring that he had resolved to accomplish my emancipation, if it were in his power. He described the commencement and progress of his acquaintance with me, and listened with eager curiosity to the account given him of my family, and the history of my early life. Before separating, he drew a map of the bayou on a strip of paper with a piece of red chalk, showing the locality of Epps' plantation, and the road leading most directly to it.

Northup and his young companion returned to Marksville, where it was determined to commence legal proceedings to test the question of my right to freedom. I was made plaintiff, Mr. Northup acting as my guardian, and Edwin Epps defendant. The process to be issued was in the nature of replevin, directed to the sheriff of the parish, commanding him to take me into custody, and detain me until the decision of the court. By the time the papers were duly drawn up, it was twelve o'clock at night—too late to obtain the necessary signature of the judge, who resided some distance out of town. Further business was therefore suspended until Monday morning.

Everything, apparently, was moving along swimmingly, until Sunday afternoon, when Waddill called at Northup's room to express his apprehension of difficulties they had not expected to encounter. Bass had become alarmed, and had placed his affairs in the hands of a person at the landing, communicating to him his intention of leaving the State. This person had betrayed the confidence reposed in him to a certain extent, and a rumor began to float about the town, that the stranger at the hotel, who had been observed in the company of lawyer Waddill, was after one of old Epps' slaves, over on the bayou. Epps was known at Marksville, having frequent occasion to visit that place during the session of the courts, and the fear entertained by Mr. Northup's adviser was, that intelligence would be conveyed to him in the night, giving him an opportunity of secreting me before the arrival of the sheriff.

This apprehension had the effect of expediting matters considerably. The sheriff, who lived in one direction from the village, was requested to hold himself in readiness immediately after midnight, while the judge was informed he would be called upon at the same time. It is but justice to say, that the authorities at Marksville cheerfully rendered all the assistance in their power.

As soon after midnight as bail could be perfected, and the Judge's signature obtained, a carriage, containing Mr. Northup and the sheriff, driven by the landlord's son, rolled rapidly out of the village of Marksville, on the road towards Bayou Boeuf.

It was supposed that Epps would contest the issue involving my right to liberty, and it therefore suggested itself to Mr. Northup, that the testimony of the sheriff, describing my first meeting with the former, might perhaps become material on the trial. It was accordingly arranged during the ride, that before I had an opportunity of speaking to Mr. Northup, the sheriff should propound to me certain questions agreed upon, such as the number and names of my children, the name of my wife before marriage, of places I knew at the North, and so forth. If my answers corresponded with the statements given him, the evidence must necessarily be considered conclusive.

At length, shortly after Epps had left the field, with the consoling assurance that he would soon return and *warm* us, as was stated in the conclusion of the preceding chapter, they came in sight of the plantation, and discovered us at work. Alighting from the carriage, and directing the driver to proceed to the great house, with instructions not to mention to any one the object of their errand until they met again, Northup and the sheriff turned from the highway, and came towards us across the cotton field. We observed them, on looking up at the carriage—one several rods in advance of the other. It was a singular and unusual thing to see white men approaching us in that manner, and especially at that early hour in the morning, and Uncle Abram and Patsey made some remarks, expressive of their astonishment. Walking up to Bob, the sheriff inquired:

"Where's the boy they call Platt?"

"Thar he is, massa," answered Bob, pointing to me, and twitching off his hat.

I wondered to myself what business he could possibly have with me, and turning round, gazed at him until he had approached within a step. During my long residence on the bayou, I had become familiar with the face of every planter within many miles; but this man was an utter stranger— certainly I had never seen him before.

"Your name is Platt, is it?" he asked.

"Yes, master," I responded.

Pointing towards Northup, standing a few rods distant, he demanded—"Do you know that man?"

I looked in the direction indicated, and as my eyes rested on his countenance, a world of images thronged my brain; a multitude of well-known faces—Anne's, and the dear children's, and my old dead father's; all the scenes and associations of childhood and youth; all the friends of other and happier days, appeared and disappeared, flitting and floating like dissolving shadows before the vision of my imagination, until at last the perfect memory of the man recurred to me, and throwing up my hands towards Heaven, I exclaimed, in a voice louder than I could utter in a less exciting moment—

"*Henry B. Northup!* Thank God—thank God!"

In an instant I comprehended the nature of his business, and felt that the hour of my deliverance was at hand. I started towards him, but the sheriff stepped before me.

"Stop a moment," said he; "have you any other name than Platt?"

"Solomon Northup is my name, master," I replied.

"Have you a family?" he inquired.

"I *had* a wife and three children."

"What were your children's names?"

"Elizabeth, Margaret and Alonzo."

"And your wife's name before her marriage?"

"Anne Hampton."

"Who married you?"

"Timothy Eddy, of Fort Edward."

"Where does that gentleman live?" again pointing to Northup, who remained standing in the same place where I had first recognized him.

"He lives in Sandy Hill, Washington county, New York," was the reply.

He was proceeding to ask further questions, but I pushed past him, unable longer to restrain myself. I seized my old acquaintance by both hands. I could not speak. I could not refrain from tears.

"Sol," he said at length, "I'm glad to see you."

I essayed to make some answer, but emotion choked all utterance, and I was silent. The slaves, utterly confounded, stood gazing upon the scene, their open mouths and rolling eyes indicating the utmost wonder and astonishment. For ten years I had dwelt among them, in the field and in the cabin, borne the same hardships, partaken the same fare, mingled my griefs with theirs, participated in the same scanty joys; nevertheless, not until this hour, the last I was to remain among them, had the remotest suspicion of my true name, or the slightest knowledge of my real history, been entertained by any one of them.

Not a word was spoken for several minutes, during which time I clung fast to Northup, looking up into his face, fearful I should awake and find it all a dream.

"Throw down that sack," Northup added, finally, "your cotton-picking days are over. Come with us to the man you live with."

I obeyed him, and walking between him and the sheriff, we moved towards the great house. It was not until we had proceeded some distance that I had recovered my voice sufficiently to ask if my family were all living. He informed me he had seen Anne, Margaret and Elizabeth but a short time previously; that Alonzo was still living, and all were well. My mother, however, I could never see again. As I began to recover in some measure from the sudden and great excitement which so overwhelmed me, I grew faint and weak, insomuch it was with difficulty I could walk. The sheriff took hold of my arm and assisted me, or I think I should have fallen. As we entered the yard, Epps stood by the gate, conversing with the driver. That young man, faithful to his instructions, was entirely unable to give him the least information in answer to his repeated inquiries of what was going on. By the time we reached him he was almost as much amazed and puzzled as Bob or Uncle Abram. Shaking hands with the sheriff, and receiving an introduction to Mr. Northup, he invited them into the house, ordering me, at the same time, to bring in some wood. It was some time before I succeeded in cutting an armful, having, somehow, unaccountably lost the power of wielding the axe with any manner of precision. When I entered with it at last, the table was strewn with papers, from one of which Northup was reading. I was probably longer than necessity required, in placing the sticks upon the fire, being particular as to the exact position of each individual one of them. I heard the words, "the said Solomon Northup," and "the deponent further says," and "free citizen of New York," repeated frequently, and from these expressions understood that the secret I had so long retained from Master and Mistress Epps, was finally developing. I lingered as long as prudence permitted, and was about leaving the room, when Epps inquired,

"Platt, do you know this gentleman? "

"Yes, master," I replied, "I have known him as long as I can remember."

"Where does he live?"

"He lives in New York."

"Did you ever live there?"

"Yes, master—born and bred there."

"You was free, then. Now you d—d nigger," he exclaimed, "why did you not tell me that when I bought you? "

"Master Epps," I answered, in a somewhat different tone than the one in which I had been accustomed to address him—"Master Epps, you did not take the trouble to ask me; besides, I told one of my owners—the man that kidnapped me—that I was free, and was whipped almost to death for it."

"It seems there has been a letter written for you by somebody. Now, who is it?" he demanded, authoritatively. I made no reply.

"I say, who wrote that letter?" he demanded again.

"Perhaps I wrote it myself," I said.

"You haven't been to Marksville post office and back before light, I know."

He insisted upon my informing him, and I insisted I would not. He made many vehement threats against the man, whoever he might be, and intimated the bloody and savage vengeance he would wreak upon him, when he found him out. His whole manner and language exhibited a feeling of anger towards the unknown person who had written for me, and of fretfulness at the idea of losing so much property. Addressing Mr. Northup, he swore if he had only had an hour's notice of his coming, he would have saved him the trouble of taking me back to New York; that he would have run me into the swamp, or some other place out of the way, where all the sheriffs on earth couldn't have found me.

I walked out into the yard, and was entering the kitchen door, when something struck me in the back. Aunt Phebe, emerging from the back door of the great house with a pan of potatoes, had thrown one of them with unnecessary violence, thereby giving me to understand that she wished to speak to me a moment confidentially. Running up to me, she whispered in my ear with great earnestness,

"Lor a'mity, Platt! what d'ye think? Dem two men come after ye. Heard 'em tell massa you free—got wife and tree children back thar whar you come from. Goin' wid 'em? Fool if ye don't—wish I could go," and Aunt Phebe ran on in this manner at a rapid rate.

Presently Mistress Epps made her appearance in the kitchen. She said many things to me, and wondered why I had not told her who I was. She expressed her regret, complimenting me by saying she had rather lose any other servant on the plantation. Had Patsey that day stood in my place, the measure of my mistress' joy would have overflowed. Now there was no one left who could mend a chair or a piece of furniture—no one who was of any use about the house—no one who could play for her on the violin—and Mistress Epps was actually affected to tears.

Epps had called to Bob to bring up his saddle horse. The other slaves, also, overcoming their fear of the penalty, had left their work and come to the yard. They were standing behind the cabins, out of sight of Epps. They beckoned me to come to them, and with all the eagerness of curiosity, excited to the highest pitch, conversed with and questioned me. If I could repeat the exact words they uttered, with the same emphasis— if I could paint their several attitudes, and the expression of their countenances—it would be indeed an interesting picture. In their estimation, I had suddenly arisen to an immeasurable height—had become a being of immense importance.

The legal papers having been served, and arrangements made with Epps to meet them the next day at Marksville, Northup and the sheriff entered the carriage to return to the latter place. As I was about mounting to the driver's seat, the sheriff said I ought to bid Mr. and Mrs. Epps good-bye. I ran back to the piazza where they were standing, and taking off my hat, said,

"Good-bye, missis."

"Good-bye, Platt," said Mrs. Epps, kindly.

"Good-bye, master."

"Ah! you d—d nigger," muttered Epps, in a surly malicious tone of voice, "you needn't feel so cussed tickled—you ain't gone yet—I'll see about this business at Marksville tomorrow."

I was only a "*nigger*" and knew my place, but felt as strongly as if I had been a white man, that it would have been an inward comfort, had I dared to have given him a parting kick. On my way back to the carriage, Patsey ran from behind a cabin and threw her arms about my neck.

"Oh? Platt," she cried, tears streaming down her face, "you're goin' to be free—you're goin' way off yonder, where we'll nebber see ye any more. You've saved me a good many whippins, Platt; I'm glad you're goin' to be free—but oh! de Lord, de Lord! What'll become of me?"

I disengaged myself from her, and entered the carriage. The driver cracked his whip and away we rolled. I looked back and saw Patsey, with drooping head, half reclining on the ground; Mrs. Epps was on the piazza; Uncle Abram, and Bob, and Wiley, and Aunt Phebe stood by the gate, gazing after me. I waved my hand, but the carriage turned a bend of the bayou, hiding them from my eyes forever.

We stopped a moment at Carey's sugar house, where a great number of slaves were at work, such an establishment being a curiosity to a Northern man. Epps dashed by us on horseback at full speed—on the way, as we learned next day, to the "Pine Woods," to see William Ford, who had brought me into the country.

Tuesday, the fourth of January, Epps and his counsel, the Hon. H. Taylor Northup, Waddill, the Judge and sheriff of Avoyelles, and myself, met in a room in the village of Marksville. Mr. Northup stated the facts in regard to me, and presented his commission, and the affidavits accompanying it. The sheriff described the scene in the cotton field. I was also interrogated at great length. Finally, Mr. Taylor assured his client that he was satisfied, and that litigation would not only be expensive, but utterly useless. In accordance with his advice, a paper was drawn up and signed by the proper parties, wherein Epps acknowledged he was satisfied of my right to freedom, and formally surrendered me to the authorities of New York. It was also stipulated that it be entered of record in the recorder's office of Avoyelles.

Mr. Northup and myself immediately hastened to the landing, and taking passage on the first steamer that arrived, were soon floating down Red River, up which, with such desponding thoughts, I had been borne twelve years before.

CHAPTER 22

As the steamer glided on its way towards New Orleans, *perhaps* I was not happy—*perhaps* there was no difficulty in restraining myself from dancing round the deck—perhaps I did not feel grateful to the man who had come so many hundred miles for me—perhaps I did not light his pipe, and wait and watch his word, and run at his slightest bidding. If I didn't—well, no matter.

We tarried at New Orleans two days. During that time I pointed out the locality of Freeman's slave pen, and the room in which Ford purchased me. We happened to meet Theophilus in the street, but I did not think it worthwhile to renew acquaintance with him. From respectable citizens we ascertained he had become a low, miserable rowdy—a broken-down, disreputable man.

We also visited the recorder, Mr. Genois, to whom Senator Scale's letter was directed, and found him a man well deserving the wide and honorable reputation that he bears. He very generously furnished us with a sort of legal pass, over his signature and seal of office, and as it contains the recorder's description of my personal appearance, it may not be amiss to insert it here. The following is a copy:

"*State of Louisiana—City of New Orleans*:
Recorder's Office, Second District.

"To all to whom these presents shall come—

"This is to certify that Henry B. Northup,
Esquire, of the county of Washington, New York,
has produced before me due evidence of the
freedom of Solomon, a mulatto man, aged about
forty-two years, five feet, seven inches and six
lines, woolly hair, and chestnut eyes, who is a
native born of the State of New York. That the
said Northup, being about bringing the said
Solomon to his native place, through the southern
routes, the civil authorities are requested to let
the aforesaid colored man Solomon pass
unmolested, he demeaning well and properly.

"Given under my hand and the seal of the city
of New Orleans this 7th January, 1853.
"TH. GENOIS, Recorder."

On the eighth we came to Lake Pontchartrain, by railroad, and, in due time, following the usual route, reached
Charleston. After going on board the steamboat, and paying
our passage at this city, Mr. Northup was called upon by a
custom-house officer to explain why he had not registered
his servant. He replied that he had no servant—that, as the
agent of New York, he was accompanying a free citizen of
that state from slavery to freedom, and did not desire nor
intend to make any registry whatever. I conceived from his
conversation and manner, though I may perhaps be entirely
mistaken, that no great pains would be taken to avoid whatever difficulty the Charleston officials might deem proper
to create. At length, however, we were permitted to proceed,

and, passing through Richmond, where I caught a glimpse of Goodin's pen, arrived in Washington January 17th, 1853.

We ascertained that both Burch and Radburn were still residing in that city. Immediately a complaint was entered with a police magistrate of Washington, against James H. Burch, for kidnapping and selling me into slavery. He was arrested upon a warrant issued by Justice Goddard, and returned before Justice Mansel, and held to bail in the sum of three thousand dollars. When first arrested, Burch was much excited, exhibiting the utmost fear and alarm, and before reaching the justice's office on Louisiana Avenue, and before knowing the precise nature of the complaint, begged the police to permit him to consult Benjamin O. Shekels, a slave trader of seventeen years' standing, and his former partner. The latter became his bail.

At ten o'clock, the eighteenth of January, both parties appeared before the magistrate. Senator Chase, of Ohio, Hon. Orville Clark, of Sandy Hill, and Mr. Northup acted as counsel for the prosecution, and Joseph H. Bradley for the defence.

Gen. Orville Clark was called and sworn as a witness, and testified that he had known me from childhood, and that I was a free man, as was my father before me. Mr. Northup then testified to the same, and proved the facts connected with his mission to Avoyelles.

Ebenezer Radburn was then sworn for the prosecution, and testified he was forty-eight years old; that he was a resident of Washington, and had known Burch fourteen years; that in 1841 he was keeper of Williams' slave pen; that he remembered the fact of my confinement in the pen that year. At this point it was admitted by the defendant's counsel, that I had been placed in the pen by Burch in the spring of 1841, and hereupon the prosecution rested.

Benjamin O. Shekels was then offered as a witness by the prisoner. Benjamin is a large, coarse-featured man, and the reader may perhaps get a somewhat correct conception of him by reading the exact language he used in answer to the first question of defendant's lawyer. He was asked the place of his nativity, and his reply, uttered in a sort of rowdyish way, was in these very words—

"I was born in Ontario county, New York, and *weighed fourteen pounds!*"

Benjamin was a prodigious baby! He further testified that he kept the Steamboat Hotel in Washington in 1841, and saw me there in the spring of that year. He was proceeding to state what he had heard two men say, when Senator Chase raised a legal objection, to wit, that the sayings of third persons, being hearsay, was improper evidence. The objection was overruled by the Justice, and Shekels continued, stating that two men came to his hotel and represented they had a colored man for sale; that they had an interview with Burch; that they stated they came from Georgia, but he did not remember the county; that they gave a full history of the boy, saying he was a bricklayer, and played on the violin; that Burch remarked he would purchase if they could agree; that they went out and brought the boy in, and that I was the same person. He further testified, with as much unconcern as if it was the truth, that I represented I was born and bred in Georgia; that one of the young men with me was my master; that I exhibited a great deal of regret at parting with him, and he believed "got into tears!"— nevertheless, that I insisted my master had a right to sell me; that he *ought* to sell me; and the remarkable reason I gave was, according to Shekels, because he, my master, "had been gambling and on a spree!"

He continued, in these words, copied from the minutes taken on the examination: "Burch interrogated the boy in the usual manner, told him if he purchased him he should send him south. The boy said he had no objection, that in fact he would like to go south. Burch paid $650 for him, to my knowledge: I don't know what name was given him, but think it was not Solomon. Did not know the name of either of the two men. They were in my tavern two or three hours, during which time the boy played on the violin. The bill of sale was signed in my bar-room. It was a *printed blank, filled up by Burch*. Before 1838 Burch was my partner. Our business was buying and selling slaves. After that time he was a partner of Theophilus Freeman, of New Orleans. Burch bought here—Freeman sold there!"

Shekels, before testifying, had heard my relation of the circumstances connected with the visit to Washington with Brown and Hamilton, and therefore, it was, undoubtedly, he spoke of "two men," and of my playing on the violin. Such was his fabrication, utterly untrue, and yet there was found in Washington a man who endeavored to corroborate him.

Benjamin A. Thorn testified he was at Shekels' in 1841, and saw a colored boy playing on a fiddle. "Shekels said he was for sale. Heard his master tell him he should sell him. The boy acknowledged to me he was a slave. I was not present when the money was paid. Will not swear positively this is the boy. The master came near *shedding tears: I think the boy did!* I have been engaged in the business of taking slaves south, off and on, for twenty years. When I can't do that I do something else."

I was then offered as a witness, but, objection being made, the court decided my evidence inadmissible. It was rejected solely on the ground that I was a colored man—the fact of my being a free citizen of New York not being disputed.

Shekels having testified there was a bill of sale executed, Burch was called upon by the prosecution to produce it, inasmuch as such a paper would corroborate the testimony of Thorn and Shekels. The prisoner's counsel saw the necessity of exhibiting it, or giving some reasonable explanation for its non-production. To effect the latter, Burch himself was offered as a witness in his own behalf. It was contended by counsel for the people, that such testimony should not be allowed—that it was in contravention of every rule of evidence, and if permitted would defeat the ends of justice. His testimony, however, was received by the court! He made oath that such a bill of sale had been drawn up and signed, *but he had lost it, and did not know what had become of it!* Thereupon the magistrate was requested to dispatch a police officer to Burch's residence, with directions to bring his books, containing his bills of sales for the year 1841. The request was granted, and before any measure could be taken to prevent it, the officer had obtained possession of the books, and brought them into court. The sales for the year 1841 were found, and carefully examined, but no sale of myself, by any name, was discovered!

Upon this testimony the court held the fact to be established, that Burch came innocently and honestly by me, and accordingly he was discharged.

An attempt was then made by Burch and his satellites, to fasten upon me the charge that I had conspired with the two white men to defraud him—with what success, appears in an extract taken from an article in the *New York Times*, published a day or two subsequent to the trial: "The counsel for the defendant had drawn up, before the defendant was discharged, an affidavit, signed by Burch, and had a warrant out against the colored man for a conspiracy with the two white men before referred to, to defraud Burch out of six hundred and twenty-five dollars. The warrant was served, and the colored man arrested and brought before Officer Goddard. Burch and his witnesses appeared in court, and H. B. Northup appeared as counsel for the colored man, stating he was ready to proceed as counsel on the part of the defendant, and asking no delay whatever. Burch, after consulting privately a short time with Shekels, stated to the magistrate that he wished him to dismiss the complaint, as he would not proceed farther with it. Defendant's counsel stated to the magistrate that if the complaint was withdrawn, it must be without the request or consent of the defendant. Burch then asked the magistrate to let him have the complaint and the warrant, and he took them. The counsel for the defendant objected to his receiving them, and insisted they should remain as part of the records of the court, and that the court should endorse the proceedings which had been had under the process. Burch delivered them up, and the court rendered a judgment of discontinuance by the request of the prosecutor, and filed it in his office."

There may be those who will affect to believe the statement of the slave trader—those, in whose minds his allegations will weigh heavier than mine. I am a poor colored man—one of a downtrodden and degraded race, whose humble voice may not be heeded by the oppressor—but *knowing* the truth, and with a full sense of my accountability, I do solemnly declare before men, and before God, that any charge or assertion, that I conspired directly or indirectly with any person or persons to sell myself; that any other account of my visit to Washington, my capture and imprisonment in Williams' slave pen, than is contained in these pages, is utterly and absolutely false. I never played on the violin in Washington. I never was in the Steamboat Hotel, and never saw Thorn or Shekels, to my knowledge, in my life, until last January. The story of the trio of slave traders is a fabrication as absurd as it is base and unfounded. Were it true, I should not have turned aside on my way back to liberty for the purpose of prosecuting Burch. I should have *avoided* rather than sought him. I should have known that such a step would have resulted in rendering me infamous. Under the circumstances—longing as I did to behold my family, and elated with the prospect of returning home—it is an outrage upon probability to suppose I would have run the hazard, not only of exposure, but of a criminal prosecution and conviction, by voluntarily placing myself in the position I did, if the statements of Burch and his confederates contain a particle of truth. I took pains to seek him out, to confront him in a court of law, charging him with the crime of kidnapping; and the only motive that impelled me to this step, was a burning sense of the wrong he had inflicted upon me, and a desire to bring him to justice. He was acquitted, in the manner, and by such means as have been described. A human tribunal has permitted him to escape; but there is another and a higher tribunal, where false testimony will not prevail, and where I am willing, so far at least as these statements are concerned, to be judged at last.

We left Washington on the twentieth of January, and proceeding by the way of Philadelphia, New York, and Albany, reached Sandy Hill in the night of the 21st. My heart overflowed with happiness as I looked around upon old familiar scenes, and found myself in the midst of friends of other days. The following morning I started, in company with several acquaintances, for Glens Falls, the residence of Anne and our children.

As I entered their comfortable cottage, Margaret was the first that met me. She did not recognize me. When I left her, she was but seven years old, a little prattling girl, playing with her toys. Now she was grown to woman-hood—was married, with a bright-eyed boy standing by her side. Not forgetful of his enslaved, unfortunate grand-father, she had named the child Solomon Northup Staunton. When told who I was, she was overcome with emotion, and unable to speak. Presently Elizabeth entered the room, and Anne came running from the hotel, having been informed of my arrival. They embraced me, and with tears flowing down their cheeks, hung upon my neck. But I draw a veil over a scene which can better be imagined than described.

When the violence of our emotions had subsided to a sacred joy—when the household gathered round the fire, that sent out its warm and crackling comfort through the room, we conversed of the thousand events that had occurred—the hopes and fears, the joys and sorrows, the trials and troubles we had each experienced during the long separation. Alonzo was absent in the western part of the State. The boy had written to his mother a short time previous, of the prospect of his obtaining sufficient money to purchase my freedom. From his earliest years, that had been the chief object of his thoughts and his ambition. They knew I was in bondage. The letter written on board the brig, and Clem Kay himself, had given them that information. But where I was, until the arrival of Bass' letter, was a matter of conjecture. Elizabeth and Margaret once returned from school—so Anne informed me—weeping bitterly. On inquiring the cause of the children's sorrow, it was found that, while studying geography, their attention had been attracted to the picture of slaves working in the cotton field, and an overseer following them with his whip. It reminded them of the sufferings their father might be, and, as it happened, actually was, enduring in the South. Numerous incidents, such as these, were related—incidents showing they still held me in constant remembrance, but not, perhaps, of sufficient interest to the reader, to be recounted.

My narrative is at an end. I have no comments to make upon the subject of slavery. Those who read this book may form their own opinions of the "peculiar institution." What it may be in other States, I do not profess to know; what it is in the region of Red River, is truly and faithfully delineated in these pages. This is no fiction, no exaggeration. If I have failed in anything, it has been in presenting to the reader too prominently the bright side of the picture. I doubt not hundreds have been as unfortunate as myself; that hundreds of free citizens have been kidnapped and sold into slavery, and are at this moment wearing out their lives on plantations in Texas and Louisiana. But I forbear. Chastened and subdued in spirit by the sufferings I have borne, and thankful to that good Being through whose mercy I have been restored to happiness and liberty, I hope henceforward to lead an upright though lowly life, and rest at last in the church yard where my father sleeps.

Appendix A

Chap. 375

An act more effectually to protect the free citizens of this Staff from being kidnapped, or reduced to slavery.
[Passed May 14, 1840]

The People of the State of New York, represented in Senate and Assembly, do enact as follows:

1. Whenever the Governor of this State shall receive information satisfactory to him that any free citizen or any inhabitant of this State has been kidnapped or transported away out of this State, into any other State or Territory of the United States, for the purpose of being there held in slavery; or that such free citizen or inhabitant is wrongfully seized, imprisoned or held in slavery in any of the States or Territories of the United States, on the allegation or pretence that such a person is a slave, or by color of any usage or rule of law prevailing in such State or Territory, is deemed or taken to be a slave, or not entitled of right to the personal liberty belonging to a citizen; it shall be the duty of the said Governor to

take such measures as he shall deem necessary to procure such person to be restored to his liberty and returned to this State. The Governor is hereby authorized to appoint and employ such agent or agents as he shall deem necessary to effect the restoration and return of such person; and shall furnish the said agent with such credentials and instructions as will be likely to accomplish the object of his appointment. The Governor may determine the compensation to be allowed to such agent for his services besides his necessary expenses.

2. Such agent shall proceed to collect the proper proof to establish the right of such person to his freedom, and shall perform such journeys, take such measures, institute and procure to be prosecuted such legal proceedings, under the direction of the Governor, as shall be necessary to procure such person to be restored to his liberty and returned to this State.

3. The accounts for all services and expenses incurred in carrying this act into effect shall be audited by the Comptroller, and paid by the Treasurer on his warrant, out of any moneys in the treasury of this State not otherwise appropriated. The Treasurer may advance, on the warrant of the Comptroller, to such agent, such sum or sums as the Governor shall certify to be reasonable advances to enable him to accomplish the purposes of his appointment, for which advance such agent shall account, on the final audit of his warrant.

4. This act shall take effect immediately.

Appendix B—Memorial of Anne

To His Excellency, the Governor of the State of New York:

The memorial of Anne Northup, of the village of Gleria Falls, in the county of Warren, State aforesaid, respectfully sets forth—

That your memorialist, whose maiden name was Anne Hampton, was forty-four years old on the fourteenth day of March last, and was married to Solomon Northup, then of Fort Edward, in the county of Washington and State aforesaid, on the twenty-fifth day of December, A. D. 1828, by Timothy Eddy, then a Justice of the Peace. That the said Solomon, after such marriage, lived and kept house with your memorialist in said town until 1830, when he removed with his said family to the town of Kingsbury in said county, and remained there about three years, and then removed to Saratoga Springs in the State aforesaid, and continued to reside in said Saratoga Springs and the adjoining town until about the year 1841, as near as the time can be recollected, when the said Solomon started to go to the city of Washington, in the District of Columbia, since which time your memorialist has never seen her said husband.

And your memorialist further states, that in the year 1841 she received information by a letter directed to Henry B.

Northup, Esq., of Sandy Hill, Washington County, New York, and postmarked at New Orleans, that said Solomon had been kidnapped in Washington, put on board of a vessel, and was then in such vessel in New Orleans, but could not tell how he came in that situation, nor what his destination was.

That your memorialist ever since the last mentioned period has been wholly unable to obtain any information of where the said Solomon was, until the month of September last, when another letter was received from the said Solomon, postmarked at Marksville, in the parish of Avoyelles, in the State of Louisiana, stating that he was held there as a slave, which statement your memorialist believes to be true.

That the said Solomon is about forty-five years of age, and never resided out of the State of New York, in which State he was born, until the time he went to Washington city, as before stated. That the said Solomon Northup is a free citizen of the State of New York, and is now wrongfully held in slavery, in or near Marksville, in the parish of Avoyelles, in the State of Louisiana, one of the United States of America, on the allegation or pretence that the said Solomon is a slave.

And your memorialist further states that Mintus Northup was the reputed father of said Solomon, and was a negro, and died at Fort Edward, on the twenty-second day of November, 1829; that the mother of said Solomon was a mulatto, or three quarters white, and died in the county of Oswego, New York some five or six years ago, as your memorialist was informed and believes, and never was a slave.

That your memorialist and her family are poor and wholly unable to pay or sustain any portion of the expenses of restoring the said Solomon to his freedom.

Your excellency is entreated to employ such agent or agents as shall be deemed necessary to effect the restoration and return of said Solomon Northup, in pursuance of an act of the Legislature of the State of New York, passed May 14th, 1840, entitled "An act more effectually to protect the free citizens of this State from being kidnapped or reduced to slavery." And your memorialist will ever pray.

(Signed,)
ANNE NORTHUP

Dated November 19, 1852

STATE OF NEW YORK:
Washington county, ss.

Anne Northup, of the village of Glens Falls, in the county of Warren, in said state, being duly sworn, doth depose and say that she signed the above memorial, and that the statements therein contained are true.

(Signed,)
ANNE NORTHUP

Subscribed and sworn before me this
19th November, 1852
CHARLES HUGHES, Justice Peace

We recommend that the Governor appoint Henry B. Northup, of the village of Sandy Hill, Washington County, New York, as one of the agents to procure the restoration and return of Solomon Northup, named in the foregoing memorial of Anne Northup.

Dated at Sandy Hill, Washington Co., N.Y., November 20, 1852 (Signed,)

PETEE HOLBKOOK
DANIEL SWEET
B. F. HOAG
ALMON CLARK

CHARLES HUGHES
BENJAMIN FERRIS
E. D. BAKER
JOSIAH H. BROWN
ORVILLE CLARK

STATE OF NEW YORK:
Washington County, ss:

Josiah Hand, of the village of Sandy Hill, in said county, being duly sworn, says, he is fifty-seven years old, and was born in said village, and has always resided there; that he has known Mintus Northup and his son Solomon, named in the annexed memorial of Anne Northup, since previous to the year 1816; that Mintus Northup then, and until the time of his death, cultivated a farm in the towns of Kingsbury and Fort Edward, from the time deponent first knew him until he died; that said Mintus and his wife, the mother of said Solomon Northup, were reported to be free citizens of New York, and deponent believes they were so free; that said Solomon Northup was born in said county of Washington, as deponent believes, and was married Dec. 25th, 1828, in Fort Edward aforesaid, and his said wife and three children—two daughters and one son—are now living in Glens Falls, Warren County, New York, and that the said Solomon Northup always resided in said county of Washington, and its immediate vicinity, until about 1841, since which time deponent has not seen him, but deponent has been credibly informed, and as he verily believes truly the said Solomon is now wrongfully held as a slave in the State of Louisiana. And deponent further says that Anne Northup, named in the said memorial, is entitled to credit, and deponent believes the statements contained in her said memorial are true.

(Signed,)
JOSIAH HAND

Subscribed and sworn before me this
19th day of November, 1852,
CHARLES HUGHES, Justice Peace

STATE OF NEW YORK:
Washington County, ss:

Timothy Eddy, of Fort Edward, in said county, being duly
sworn, says he is now over — years old, and has been a
resident of said town more than — years past, and that
he was well acquainted with Solomon Northup, named in the
annexed memorial of Anne Northup, and with his father,
Mintus Northup, who was a negro—the wife of said Mintus
was a mulatto woman; that said Mintus Northup and his
said wife and family, two sons, Joseph and Solomon, resided
in said town of Fort Edward for several years before the
year 1828, and said Mintus died in said town A.D. 1829, as
deponent believes. And deponent further says that he was a
Justice of the Peace in said town in the year 1828, and as such
Justice of the Peace, he, on the twenty-fifth day of December,
1828, joined the said Solomon Northup in marriage with
Anne Hampton, who is the same person who has subscribed
the annexed memorial. And deponent expressly says, that
said Solomon was a free citizen of the State of New York, and
always lived in said State, until about the year A.D. 1840,
since which time deponent has not seen him, but has recently
been informed, and as deponent believes truly, that said
Solomon Northup is wrongfully held in slavery in or near
Marksvillle, in the parish of Avoyelles, in the State of Louisiana.
And deponent further says, that said Mintus Northup was
nearly sixty years old at the time of his death, and was, for
more than thirty years next prior to his death, a free citizen
of the State of New York.

And this deponent further says, that Anne Northup, the
wife of said Solomon Northup, is of good character and

reputation, and her statements, as contained in the memorial hereto annexed, are entitled to full credit.
(Signed,)
TIMOTHY EDDY

Subscribed and sworn before me this
19th day of November, 1852,
TIM'Y STOUGHTON, Justice

STATE OF NEW YORK:
Washington County, ss:

Henry B. Northup, of the village of Sandy Hill, in said county, being duly sworn, says, that he is forty-seven years old, and has always lived in said county; that he knew Mintus Northup, named in the annexed memorial, from deponent's earliest recollection until the time of his death, which occurred at Fort Edward, in said county, in 1829; that deponent knew the children of said Mintus, viz, Solomon and Joseph; that they were both born in the county of Washington aforesaid, as deponent believes; that deponent was well acquainted with said Solomon, who is the same person named in the annexed memorial of Anne Northup, from his childhood; and that said Solomon always resided in said county of Washington and the adjoining counties until about the year 1841; that said Solomon could read and write; that said Solomon and his mother and father were free citizens of the State of New York; that sometime about the year 1841 this deponent received a letter from said Solomon, postmarked New Orleans, stating that while on business at Washington city, he had been kidnapped, and his free papers taken from him, and he was then on board a vessel, in irons, and was claimed as a slave, and that he did not know his destination, which the deponent believes to be true, and he urged this deponent to assist in procuring his restoration to freedom; that deponent has lost or mislaid said letter, and cannot find it; that deponent has since endeavored to find where said Solomon was, but could get no farther trace of him until Sept. last, when this deponent ascertained by a letter purporting to have been written by the direction of said Solomon, that said Solomon was held and claimed as a slave in or near Marksville, in the parish of Avoyelles, Louisiana, and that this deponent verily believes that such information is true, and that said Solomon is now wrongfully held in slavery at Marksville aforesaid.

(Signed,)
HENRY B. NORTHUP

Subscribed and sworn to before me
this 20th day of November, 1852,
CHARLES HUGHES, J. P.

STATE OF NEW YORK:
Washington County, ss:

Nicholas C. Northup, of the village of Sandy Hill, in said county, being duly sworn, doth depose and say, that he is now fifty-eight years of age, and has known Solomon Northup, mentioned in the annexed memorial of Anne Northup, ever since he was born. And this deponent saith that said Solomon is now about forty-five years old, and was born in the county of Washington aforesaid, or in the county of Essex, in said State, and always resided in the State of New York until about the year 1841, since which time deponent has not seen him or known where he was, until a few weeks since, deponent was informed, and believes truly, that said Solomon was held in slavery in the State of Louisiana. Deponent further says, that said Solomon was married in the town of Fort Edward, in said county, about twenty-four years ago, and that his wife and two daughters and one son now reside in the village of

Glens Falls, county of Warren, in said State of New York. And this deponent swears positively that said Solomon Northup is a citizen of said State of New York, and was born free, and from his earliest infancy lived and resided in the counties of Washington, Essex, Warren and Saratoga, in the State of New York, and that his said wife and children have never resided out of said counties since the time said Solomon was married; that deponent knew the father of said Solomon Northup; that said father was a negro, named Mintus Northup, and died in the town of Fort Edward, in the county of Washington, State of New York, on the twenty-second day of November, A.D. 1829, and was buried in the graveyard in Sandy Hill aforesaid; that for more than thirty years before his death he lived in the counties of Essex, Washington and Rensselaer and State of New York, and left a wife and two sons, Joseph and the said Solomon, him surviving; that the mother of said Solomon was a mulatto woman, and is now dead, and died, as deponent believes, in Oswego county, New York, within five or six years past. And this deponent further states, that the mother of the said Solomon Northup was not a slave at the time of the birth of said Solomon Northup, and has not been a slave at any time within the last fifty years.

(Signed,)
N. C. NORTHUP

Subscribed and sworn before me this 19th day of November, 1852,
CHARLES HUGHES, Justice Peace

STATE OF NEW YORK:
Washington County, ss.

Orville Clark, of the village of Sandy Hill, in the county of Washington, State of New York, being duly sworn, doth depose and say—that he, this deponent, is over fifty years of age; that in the years 1810 and 1811, or most of the time of those years, this deponent resided at Sandy Hill, aforesaid, and at Glens Falls; that this deponent then knew Mintus Northup, a black or colored man; he was then a free man, as this deponent believes and always understood; that the wife of said Mintus Northup, and mother of Solomon, was a free woman; that from the year 1818 until the time of the death of said Mintus Northup, about the year 1829, this deponent was very well acquainted with the said Mintus Northup; that he was a respectable man in the community in which he resided, and was a free man, so taken and esteemed by all his acquaintances; that this deponent has also been and was acquainted with his son Solomon Northup, from the said year 1818 until he left this part of the country, about the year 1840 or 1841; that he married Anne Hampton, daughter of William Hampton, a near neighbor of this deponent; that the said Anne, wife of said Solomon, is now living and resides in this vicinity; that the said Mintus Northup and William Hampton were both reputed and esteemed in this community as respectable men. And this deponent saith that the said Mintus Northup and his family, and the said William Hampton and his family, from the earliest recollection and acquaintance of this deponent with him (as far back as 1810), were always reputed, esteemed, and taken to be, and this deponent believes, truly so, free citizens of the State of New York. This deponent knows the said William Hampton, under the laws of this State, was entitled to vote at our elections, and he believes the said Mintus Northup also was entitled as a free citizen with the property qualification. And this deponent further saith, that the said Solomon Northup, son of said Mintus, and husband of said Anne Hampton, when he left this State, was at the time thereof a free citizen of the State of New York. And this deponent further saith, that said Anne Hampton, wife of Solomon Northup, is a respectable woman, of good character, and I would believe her statements, and do believe the facts set forth in her memorial to his excellency, the Governor, in relation to her said husband, are true.

(Signed,)
ORVILLE CLARK

Sworn before me,
November 19th, 1852
U.G. PARIS, Justice of the Peace

STATE OF NEW YORK:
Washington County, ss.

Benjamin Ferns, of the village of Sandy Hill, in said county, being duly sworn, doth depose and say—that he is now fifty-seven years old, and has resided in said village forty-five years; that he was well acquainted with Mintus Northup, named in the annexed memorial of Anne Northup, from the year 1810 to the time of his death, which occurred at Fort Edward, in the fall of 1829; that he knew the children of the said Mintus, namely, Joseph Northup and Solomon Northup, and that the said Solomon is the same person named in said memorial; that said Mintus resided in the said county of Washington to the time of his death, and was, during all that time, a free citizen of the said State of New York, deponent verily believes: that said memorialist, Anne Northup, is a woman of good character, and the statement contained in her memorial is entitled to credit.

(Signed)
BENJAMIN FERRIS

Sworn before me,

November 19th, 1852
U.G. PARIS, Justice of the Peace

STATE OF NEW YORK:
Executive Chamber, Albany, Nov. 30, 1852

I hereby certify that the foregoing is a correct copy of certain proofs filed in the Executive Department, upon which have appointed Henry B. Northup an Agent of this State, to take proper proceedings in behalf of Solomon Northup, therein mentioned.

(Signed,)
WASHINGTON HUNT

By the Governor
J. F. R., Private Secretary

STATE OF NEW YORK:
Executive Department
WASHINGTON HUNT, *Governor of the State of New York*

To whom it may concern, greeting:

Whereas, I have received information on oath, which is satisfactory to me, that Solomon Northup, who is a free citizen of this State, is wrongfully held in slavery, in the State of Louisiana:

And whereas, it is made my duty, by the laws of this State, to take such measures as I shall deem necessary to procure any citizen so wrongfully held in slavery, to be restored to his liberty and returned to this State:

Be it known, that in pursuance of chapter 375 of the laws of this State, passed in 1840, I have constituted, appointed and employed Henry B. Northup, Esquire, of the county of Washington, this State, an Agent, with full power to effect the restoration of said Solomon Northup, and the said Agent is hereby authorized and empowered to institute such proper and legal proceedings, to procure such evidence, retain such counsel, and finally to take such measures as will be most likely to accomplish the object of his said appointment.

He is also instructed to proceed to the State of Louisiana with all convenient dispatch, to execute the agency hereby created.

In witness whereof, I have hereunto subscribed my name, and affixed the privy seal of the State, at Albany, this twenty-third day of November, in the year of our Lord 1852.

(Signed,)
WASHINGTON HUNT

JAMES F. RUGGLES, Private Secretary

Appendix C

STATE OF LOUISIANA:

Parish of Avoyelles.

Before me, Aristide Barbin, Recorder of the parish of Avoyelles, personally came and appeared Henry B. Northup, of the county of Washington, State of New York, who hath declared that by virtue of a commission to him as agent of the State of New York, given and granted by his excellency, Washington Hunt, Governor of the said State of New York, bearing date the 23d day of November, 1852, authorizing and empowering him, the said Northup, to pursue and recover from slavery a free man of color, called Solomon Northup, who is a free citizen of the State of New York, and who was kidnapped and sold into slavery, in the State of Louisiana, and now in the possession of Edwin Epps, of the State of Louisiana, of the parish of Avoyelles; he, the said agent, hereto signing, acknowledges that the said Edwin has this day given and surrendered to him as such agent, the said Solomon Northup, free man of color, as afore said, in order that he be restored to his freedom, and carried back to the said State of New York, pursuant to said commission, the said Edwin Epps being satisfied from the proofs produced by said agent, that the said Solomon Northup is entitled to his freedom, the parties consenting that a certified copy of said power of attorney be annexed to this act.

Done and signed at Marksville, parish of Avoyelles, this fourth day of January, one thousand eight hundred and fifty three, in the presence of the undersigned, legal and competent witnesses, who have also hereto signed.

(Signed,)
HENRY B. NORTHUP

EDWIN EPPS
ADE. BARBIN, Recorder

Witnesses:
H. TAYLOR,
JOHN P. WADDILL

STATE OF LOUISIANA:
Parish of Avoyelles.

I do hereby certify the foregoing to be a true and correct copy of the original on file and of record in my office.

Given under my hand and seal of office as Recorder in and for the parish of Avoyelles, this 4th day of January, A.D. 1853.

(Signed,)
ADE. BARBIN, Recorder

CLASSIC LITERATURE: WORDS AND PHRASES
adapted from the Collins English Dictionary

Accoucheur NOUN a male midwife or doctor ❏ *I think my sister must have had some general idea that I was a young offender whom an Accoucheur Policemen had taken up (on my birthday) and delivered over to her* (*Great Expectations* by Charles Dickens)

addled ADJ confused and unable to think properly ❏ *But she counted and counted till she got that addled* (*The Adventures of Huckleberry Finn* by Mark Twain)

admiration NOUN amazement or wonder ❏ *lifting up his hands and eyes by way of admiration* (*Gulliver's Travels* by Jonathan Swift)

afeard ADJ afeard means afraid ❏ *shake it–and don't be afeard* (*The Adventures of Huckleberry Finn* by Mark Twain)

affected VERB affected means to assume the appearance of ❏ *Hadst thou affected sweet divinity* (*Doctor Faustus 5.2* by Christopher Marlowe)

aground ADV when a boat runs aground, it touches the ground in a shallow part of the water and gets stuck ❏ *what kep' you?–boat get aground?* (*The Adventures of Huckleberry Finn* by Mark Twain)

ague NOUN a fever in which the patient has alternate hot and cold shivering fits ❏ *his exposure to the wet and cold had brought on fever and ague* (*Oliver Twist* by Charles Dickens)

alchemy ADJ false or worthless ❏ *all wealth alchemy* (*The Sun Rising* by John Donne)

all alike PHRASE the same all the time ❏ *Love, all alike* (*The Sun Rising* by John Donne)

alow and aloft PHRASE alow means in the lower part or bottom, and aloft means on the top, so alow and aloft means on the top and in the bottom or throughout ❏ *Someone's turned the chest out alow and aloft* (*Treasure Island* by Robert Louis Stevenson)

ambuscade NOUN ambuscade is not a proper word. Tom means an ambush, which is when a group of people attack their enemies, after hiding and waiting for them ❏ *and so we would lie in ambuscade, as he called it* (*The Adventures of Huckleberry Finn* by Mark Twain)

amiable ADJ likeable or pleasant ❏ *Such amiable qualities must speak for themselves* (*Pride and Prejudice* by Jane Austen)

amulet NOUN an amulet is a charm thought to drive away evil spirits. ❏ *uttered phrases at once occult and familiar, like the amulet worn on the heart* (*Silas Marner* by George Eliot)

amusement NOUN here amusement means a strange and disturbing puzzle ❏ *this was an amusement the other way* (*Robinson Crusoe* by Daniel Defoe)

ancient NOUN an ancient was the flag displayed on a ship to show which country it belongs to. It is also called the ensign ❏ *her ancient and pendants out* (*Robinson Crusoe* by Daniel Defoe)

antic ADJ here antic means horrible or grotesque ❏ *armed and dressed after a very antic manner* (*Gulliver's Travels* by Jonathan Swift)

antics NOUN antics is an old word meaning clowns, or people who do silly things to make other people laugh ❏ *And point like antics at his triple crown* (*Doctor Faustus 3.2* by Christopher Marlowe)

appanage NOUN an appanage is a living

allowance ❑ *As if loveliness were not the special prerogative of woman–her legitimate appanage and heritage!* (*Jane Eyre* by Charlotte Brontë)

appended VERB appended means attached or added to ❑ *and these words appended* (*Treasure Island* by Robert Louis Stevenson)

approver NOUN an approver is someone who gives evidence against someone he used to work with ❑ *Mr. Noah Claypole: receiving a free pardon from the Crown in consequence of being admitted approver against Fagin* (*Oliver Twist* by Charles Dickens)

areas NOUN the areas is the space, below street level, in front of the basement of a house ❑ *The Dodger had a vicious propensity, too, of pulling the caps from the heads of small boys and tossing them down areas* (*Oliver Twist* by Charles Dickens)

argument NOUN theme or important idea or subject which runs through a piece of writing ❑ *Thrice needful to the argument which now* (*The Prelude* by William Wordsworth)

artificially ADV artfully or cleverly ❑ *and he with a sharp flint sharpened very artificially* (*Gulliver's Travels* by Jonathan Swift)

artist NOUN here artist means a skilled workman ❑ *This man was a most ingenious artist* (*Gulliver's Travels* by Jonathan Swift)

assizes NOUN assizes were regular court sessions which a visiting judge was in charge of ❑ *you shall hang at the next assizes* (*Treasure Island* by Robert Louis Stevenson)

attraction NOUN gravitation, or Newton's theory of gravitation ❑ *he predicted the same fate to attraction* (*Gulliver's Travels* by Jonathan Swift)

aver VERB to aver is to claim something strongly ❑ *for Jem Rodney, the mole catcher, averred that one evening as he was returning homeward* (*Silas Marner* by George Eliot)

baby NOUN here baby means doll, which is a child's toy that looks like a small person ❑ *and skilful dressing her baby* (*Gulliver's Travels* by Jonathan Swift)

bagatelle NOUN bagatelle is a game rather like billiards and pool ❑ *Breakfast had been ordered at a pleasant little tavern, a mile or so away upon the rising ground beyond the green; and there was a bagatelle board in the room, in case we should desire to unbend our minds after the solemnity.* (*Great Expectations* by Charles Dickens)

bah EXCLAM Bah is an exclamation of frustration or anger ❑ *"Bah," said Scrooge.* (*A Christmas Carol* by Charles Dickens)

bairn NOUN a northern word for child ❑ *Who has taught you those fine words, my bairn?* (*Wuthering Heights* by Emily Brontë)

bait VERB to bait means to stop on a journey to take refreshment ❑ *So, when they stopped to bait the horse, and ate and drank and enjoyed themselves, I could touch nothing that they touched, but kept my fast unbroken.* (*David Copperfield* by Charles Dickens)

balustrade NOUN a balustrade is a row of vertical columns that form railings ❑ *but I mean to say you might have got a hearse up that staircase, and taken it broadwise, with the splinter-bar towards the wall, and the door towards the balustrades: and done it easy* (*A Christmas Carol* by Charles Dickens)

bandbox NOUN a large lightweight box for carrying bonnets or hats ❑ *I am glad I bought my bonnet, if it is only for the fun of having another bandbox* (*Pride and Prejudice* by Jane Austen)

barren NOUN a barren here is a stretch or expanse of barren land ❑ *a line of upright stones, continued the* *length of the barren* (*Wuthering Heights* by Emily Brontë)

basin NOUN a basin was a cup without a handle ❑ *who is drinking his tea out of a basin* (*Wuthering Heights* by Emily Brontë)

battalia NOUN the order of battle ❑ *till I saw part of his army in battalia* (*Gulliver's Travels* by Jonathan Swift)

battery NOUN a Battery is a fort or a place where guns are positioned ❑ *You bring the lot to me, at that old Battery over yonder* (*Great Expectations* by Charles Dickens)

battledore and shuttlecock NOUN The game battledore and shuttlecock was an early version of the game now known as badminton. The aim of the early game was simply to keep the shuttlecock from hitting the ground. ❑ *Battledore and shuttlecock's a wery good game vhen you an't the shuttlecock and two lawyers the battledores, in which case it gets too excitin' to be pleasant* (*Pickwick Papers* by Charles Dickens)

beadle NOUN a beadle was a local official who had power over the poor ❑ *But these impertinences were speedily checked by the evidence of the surgeon, and the testimony of the beadle* (*Oliver Twist* by Charles Dickens)

bearings NOUN the bearings of a place are the measurements or directions that are used to find or locate it ❑ *the bearings of the island* (*Treasure Island* by Robert Louis Stevenson)

beaufet NOUN a beaufet was a sideboard ❑ *and sweet-cake from the beaufet* (*Emma* by Jane Austen)

beck NOUN a beck is a small stream ❑ *a beck which follows the bend of the glen* (*Wuthering Heights* by Emily Brontë)

bedight VERB decorated ❑ *and bedight with Christmas holly stuck into the top.* (*A Christmas Carol* by Charles Dickens).

Bedlam NOUN Bedlam was a lunatic asylum in London which had statues carved by Caius Gabriel Cibber at its entrance ❑ *Bedlam, and those carved maniacs at the gates* (*The Prelude* by William Wordsworth)

beeves NOUN oxen or castrated bulls which are animals used for pulling vehicles or carrying things ❑ *to deliver in every morning six beeves* (*Gulliver's Travels* by Jonathan Swift)

begot VERB created or caused ❑ *Begot in thee* (*On His Mistress* by John Donne)

behoof NOUN behoof means benefit ❑ *"Yes, young man," said he, releasing the handle of the article in question, retiring a step or two from my table, and speaking for the behoof of the landlord and waiter at the door* (*Great Expectations* by Charles Dickens)

berth NOUN a berth is a bed on a boat ❑ *this is the berth for me* (*Treasure Island* by Robert Louis Stevenson)

bevers NOUN a bever was a snack, or small portion of food, eaten between main meals ❑ *that buys me thirty meals a day and ten bevers* (*Doctor Faustus 2.1* by Christopher Marlowe)

bilge water NOUN the bilge is the widest part of a ship's bottom, and the bilge water is the dirty water that collects there ❑ *no gush of bilge-water had turned it to fetid puddle* (*Jane Eyre* by Charlotte Brontë)

bills NOUN bills is an old term meaning prescription. A prescription is the piece of paper on which your doctor writes an order for medicine and which you give to a chemist to get the medicine ❑ *Are not thy bills hung up as monuments* (*Doctor Faustus 1.1* by Christopher Marlowe)

black cap NOUN a judge wore a black cap when he was about to sentence a prisoner to death ❑ *The judge assumed the black cap, and the* *prisoner still stood with the same air and gesture.* (*Oliver Twist* by Charles Dickens)

boot-jack NOUN a wooden device to help take boots off ❏ *The speaker appeared to throw a boot-jack, or some such article, at the person he addressed* (*Oliver Twist* by Charles Dickens)

booty NOUN booty means treasure or prizes ❏ *would be inclined to give up their booty in payment of the dead man's debts* (*Treasure Island* by Robert Louis Stevenson)

Bow Street runner PHRASE Bow Street runners were the first British police force, set up by the author Henry Fielding in the eighteenth century ❏ *as would have convinced a judge or a Bow Street runner* (*Treasure Island* by Robert Louis Stevenson)

brawn NOUN brawn is a dish of meat which is set in jelly ❏ *Heaped up upon the floor, to form a kind of throne, were turkeys, geese, game, poultry, brawn, great joints of meat, sucking-pigs* (*A Christmas Carol* by Charles Dickens)

bray VERB when a donkey brays, it makes a loud, harsh sound ❏ *and she doesn't bray like a jackass* (*The Adventures of Huckleberry Finn* by Mark Twain)

break VERB in order to train a horse you first have to break it ❏ *"If a high-mettled creature like this," said he, "can't be broken by fair means, she will never be good for anything"* (*Black Beauty* by Anna Sewell)

bullyragging VERB bullyragging is an old word which means bullying. To bullyrag someone is to threaten or force someone to do something they don't want to do ❏ *and a lot of loafers bullyragging him for sport* (*The Adventures of Huckleberry Finn* by Mark Twain)

but PREP except for (this) ❏ *but this, all pleasures fancies be* (*The Good-Morrow* by John Donne)

by hand PHRASE by hand was a common expression of the time meaning that baby had been fed either using a spoon or a bottle rather than by breast-feeding ❏ *My sister, Mrs. Joe Gargery, was more than twenty years older than I, and had established a great reputation with herself . . . because she had bought me up "by hand"* (*Great Expectations* by Charles Dickens)

bye-spots NOUN bye-spots are lonely places ❏ *and bye-spots of tales rich with indigenous produce* (*The Prelude* by William Wordsworth)

calico NOUN calico is plain white fabric made from cotton ❏ *There was two old dirty calico dresses* (*The Adventures of Huckleberry Finn* by Mark Twain)

camp-fever NOUN camp-fever was another word for the disease typhus ❏ *during a severe camp-fever* (*Emma* by Jane Austen)

cant NOUN cant is insincere or empty talk ❏ *"Man," said the Ghost, "if man you be in heart, not adamant, forbear that wicked cant until you have discovered What the surplus is, and Where it is."* (*A Christmas Carol* by Charles Dickens)

canty ADJ canty means lively, full of life ❏ *My mother lived til eighty, a canty dame to the last* (*Wuthering Heights* by Emily Brontë)

canvas VERB to canvas is to discuss ❏ *We think so very differently on this point Mr Knightley, that there can be no use in canvassing it* (*Emma* by Jane Austen)

capital ADJ capital means excellent or extremely good ❏ *for it's capital, so shady, light, and big* (*Little Women* by Louisa May Alcott)

capstan NOUN a capstan is a device used on a ship to lift sails and anchors ❏ *capstans going, ships going out to sea, and unintelligible* *sea creatures roaring curses over the bulwarks at respondent lightermen* (*Great Expectations* by Charles Dickens)

case-bottle NOUN a square bottle designed to fit with others into a case ❏ *The spirit being set before him in a huge case-bottle, which had originally come out of some ship's locker* (*The Old Curiosity Shop* by Charles Dickens)

casement NOUN casement is a word meaning window. The teacher in *Nicholas Nickleby* misspells window showing what a bad teacher he is ❏ *W-i-n, win, d-e-r, der, winder, a casement.* (*Nicholas Nickleby* by Charles Dickens)

cataleptic ADJ a cataleptic fit is one in which the victim goes into a trance-like state and remains still for a long time ❏ *It was at this point in their history that Silas's cataleptic fit occurred during the prayer-meeting* (*Silas Marner* by George Eliot)

cauldron NOUN a cauldron is a large cooking pot made of metal ❏ *stirring a large cauldron which seemed to be full of soup* (*Alice's Adventures in Wonderland* by Lewis Carroll)

cephalic ADJ cephalic means to do with the head ❏ *with ink composed of a cephalic tincture* (*Gulliver's Travels* by Jonathan Swift)

chaise and four NOUN a closed four-wheel carriage pulled by four horses ❏ *he came down on Monday in a chaise and four to see the place* (*Pride and Prejudice* by Jane Austen)

chamberlain NOUN the main servant in a household ❏ *In those times a bed was always to be got there at any hour of the night, and the chamberlain, letting me in at his ready wicket, lighted the candle next in order on his shelf* (*Great Expectations* by Charles Dickens)

characters NOUN distinguishing marks ❏ *Impressed upon all forms the characters* (*The Prelude* by William Wordsworth)

chary ADJ cautious ❏ *I should have been chary of discussing my guardian too freely even with her* (*Great Expectations* by Charles Dickens)

cherishes VERB here cherishes means cheers or brightens ❏ *some philosophic song of Truth that cherishes our daily life* (*The Prelude* by William Wordsworth)

chickens' meat PHRASE chickens' meat is an old term which means chickens' feed or food ❏ *I had shook a bag of chickens' meat out in that place* (*Robinson Crusoe* by Daniel Defoe)

chimeras NOUN a chimera is an unrealistic idea or a wish which is unlikely to be fulfilled ❏ *with many other wild impossible chimeras* (*Gulliver's Travels* by Jonathan Swift)

chines NOUN chine is a cut of meat that includes part or all of the backbone of the animal ❏ *and they found hams and chines uncut* (*Silas Marner* by George Eliot)

chits NOUN chits is a slang word which means girls ❏ *I hate affected, niminy-piminy chits!* (*Little Women* by Louisa May Alcott)

chopped VERB chopped means come suddenly or accidentally ❏ *if I had chopped upon them* (*Robinson Crusoe* by Daniel Defoe)

chute NOUN a narrow channel ❏ *One morning about day-break, I found a canoe and crossed over a chute to the main shore* (*The Adventures of Huckleberry Finn* by Mark Twain)

circumspection NOUN careful observation of events and circumstances; caution ❏ *I honour your circumspection* (*Pride and Prejudice* by Jane Austen)

clambered VERB clambered means to climb somewhere with difficulty, usually using your hands and your feet ❏ *he clambered up and down stairs* (*Treasure Island* by Robert Louis Stevenson)

clime NOUN climate ❏ *no season knows nor clime* (*The Sun Rising* by John Donne)

clinched VERB clenched ❏ *the tops whereof I could but just reach with my fist clinched* (*Gulliver's Travels* by Jonathan Swift)

close chair NOUN a close chair is a sedan chair, which is an covered chair which has room for one person. The sedan chair is carried on two poles by two men, one in front and one behind ❏ *persuaded even the Empress herself to let me hold her in her close chair* (*Gulliver's Travels* by Jonathan Swift)

clown NOUN clown here means peasant or person who lives off the land ❏ *In ancient days by emperor and clown* (*Ode on a Nightingale* by John Keats)

coalheaver NOUN a coalheaver loaded coal onto ships using a spade ❏ *Good, strong, wholesome medicine, as was given with great success to two Irish labourers and a coalheaver* (*Oliver Twist* by Charles Dickens)

coal-whippers NOUN men who worked at docks using machines to load coal onto ships ❏ *here, were colliers by the score and score, with the coal-whippers plunging off stages on deck* (*Great Expectations* by Charles Dickens)

cobweb NOUN a cobweb is the net which a spider makes for catching insects ❏ *the walls and ceilings were all hung round with cobwebs* (*Gulliver's Travels* by Jonathan Swift)

coddling VERB coddling means to treat someone too kindly or protect them too much ❏ *and I've been coddling the fellow as if I'd been his grand-mother* (*Little Women* by Louisa May Alcott)

coil NOUN coil means noise or fuss or disturbance ❏ *What a coil is there?* (*Doctor Faustus 4.7* by Christopher Marlowe)

collared VERB to collar something is a

slang term which means to capture. In this sentence, it means he stole it [the money] ❏ *he collared it* (*The Adventures of Huckleberry Finn* by Mark Twain)

colling VERB colling is an old word which means to embrace and kiss ❏ *and no clasping and colling at all* (*Tess of the D'Urbervilles* by Thomas Hardy)

colloquies NOUN colloquy is a formal conversation or dialogue ❏ *Such colloquies have occupied many a pair of pale-faced weavers* (*Silas Marner* by George Eliot)

comfit NOUN sugar-covered pieces of fruit or nut eaten as sweets ❏ *and pulled out a box of comfits* (*Alice's Adventures in Wonderland* by Lewis Carroll)

coming out VERB when a girl came out in society it meant she was of marriageable age. In order to "come out" girls were expecting to attend balls and other parties during a season ❏ *The younger girls formed hopes of coming out a year or two sooner than they might otherwise have done* (*Pride and Prejudice* by Jane Austen)

commit VERB commit means arrest or stop ❏ *Commit the rascals* (*Doctor Faustus 4.7* by Christopher Marlowe)

commodious ADJ commodious means convenient ❏ *the most commodious and effectual ways* (*Gulliver's Travels* by Jonathan Swift)

commons NOUN commons is an old term meaning food shared with others ❏ *his pauper assistants ranged them-selves behind him; the gruel was served out; and a long grace was said over the short commons.* (*Oliver Twist* by Charles Dickens)

complacency NOUN here complacency means a desire to please others. To-day complacency means feeling pleased with oneself without good reason. ❏ *Twas thy power that raised the first complacency in me* (*The Prelude* by William Wordsworth)

complaisance NOUN complaisance was eagerness to please ❏ *we cannot wonder at his complaisance* (*Pride and Prejudice* by Jane Austen)

complaisant ADJ complaisant means polite ❏ *extremely cheerful and complaisant to their guest* (*Gulliver's Travels* by Jonathan Swift)

conning VERB conning means learning by heart ❏ *Or conning more* (*The Prelude* by William Wordsworth)

consequent NOUN consequence ❏ *as avarice is the necessary consequent of old age* (*Gulliver's Travels* by Jonathan Swift)

consorts NOUN concerts ❏ *The King, who delighted in music, had frequent consorts at Court* (*Gulliver's Travels* by Jonathan Swift)

conversible ADJ conversible meant easy to talk to, companionable ❏ *He can be a conversible companion* (*Pride and Prejudice* by Jane Austen)

copper NOUN a copper is a large pot that can be heated directly over a fire ❏ *He gazed in stupefied astonishment on the small rebel for some seconds, and then clung for support to the copper* (*Oliver Twist* by Charles Dickens)

copper-stick NOUN a copper-stick is the long piece of wood used to stir washing in the copper (or boiler) which was usually the biggest cooking pot in the house ❏ *It was Christmas Eve, and I had to stir the pudding for next day, with a copper-stick, from seven to eight by the Dutch clock* (*Great Expectations* by Charles Dickens)

counting-house NOUN a counting-house is a place where accountants work ❏ *Once upon a time–of all the good days in the year, on Christmas Eve–old Scrooge sat busy in his counting-house* (*A Christmas Carol* by Charles Dickens)

courtier NOUN a courtier is someone who attends the king or queen–a member of the court ❏ *next the ten courtiers;* (*Alice's Adventures in Wonderland* by Lewis Carroll)

covies NOUN covies were flocks of partridges ❏ *and will save all of the best covies for you* (*Pride and Prejudice* by Jane Austen)

cowed VERB cowed means frightened or intimidated ❏ *it cowed me more than the pain* (*Treasure Island* by Robert Louis Stevenson)

cozened VERB cozened means tricked or deceived ❏ *Do you remember, sir, how you cozened me* (*Doctor Faustus 4.7* by Christopher Marlowe)

cravats NOUN a cravat is a folded cloth that a man wears wrapped around his neck as a decorative item of clothing ❏ *we'd 'a' slept in our cravats to-night* (*The Adventures of Huckleberry Finn* by Mark Twain)

crock and dirt PHRASE crock and dirt is an old expression meaning soot and dirt ❏ *and the mare catching cold at the door, and the boy grimed with crock and dirt* (*Great Expectations* by Charles Dickens)

crockery NOUN here crockery means pottery ❏ *By one of the parrots was a cat made of crockery* (*The Adventures of Huckleberry Finn* by Mark Twain)

crooked sixpence PHRASE it was considered unlucky to have a bent sixpence ❏ *You've got the beauty, you see, and I've got the luck, so you must keep me by you for your crooked sixpence* (*Silas Marner* by George Eliot)

croquet NOUN croquet is a traditional English summer game in which players try to hit wooden balls through hoops ❏ *and once she remembered trying to box her own ears for having cheated herself in a game of croquet* (*Alice's Adventures in Wonderland* by Lewis Carroll)

cross PREP across ❏ *The two great streets, which run cross and divide it into four quarters* (*Gulliver's Travels* by Jonathan Swift)

culpable ADJ if you are culpable for something it means you are to blame ❑ *deep are the sorrows that spring from false ideas for which no man is culpable.* (*Silas Marner* by George Eliot)

cultured ADJ cultivated ❑ *Nor less when spring had warmed the cultured Vale* (*The Prelude* by William Wordsworth)

cupidity NOUN cupidity is greed ❑ *These people hated me with the hatred of cupidity and disappointment.* (*Great Expectations* by Charles Dickens)

curricle NOUN an open two-wheeled carriage with one seat for the driver and space for a single passenger ❑ *and they saw a lady and a gentleman in a curricle* (*Pride and Prejudice* by Jane Austen)

cynosure NOUN a cynosure is something that strongly attracts attention or admiration ❑ *Then I thought of Eliza and Georgiana; I beheld one the cynosure of a ballroom, the other the inmate of a convent cell* (*Jane Eyre* by Charlotte Brontë)

dalliance NOUN someone's dalliance with something is a brief involvement with it ❑ *nor sporting in the dalliance of love* (*Doctor Faustus Chorus* by Christopher Marlowe)

darkling ADV darkling is an archaic way of saying in the dark ❑ *Darkling I listen* (*Ode on a Nightingale* by John Keats)

delf-case NOUN a sideboard for holding dishes and crockery ❑ *at the pewter dishes and delf-case* (*Wuthering Heights* by Emily Brontë)

determined ■ VERB here determined means ❑ *and be out of vogue when that was determined* (*Gulliver's Travels* by Jonathan Swift) ■ VERB determined can mean to have been learned or found especially by investigation or experience ❑ *All the sensitive feelings it wounded so cruelly, all the shame and misery it kept alive within my breast, became more poignant as I*

thought of this; and I determined that the life was unendurable (*David Copperfield* by Charles Dickens)

Deuce NOUN a slang term for the Devil ❑ *Ah, I dare say I did. Deuce take me, he added suddenly, I know I did. I find I am not quite unscrewed yet.* (*Great Expectations* by Charles Dickens)

diabolical ADJ diabolical means devilish or evil ❑ *and with a thousand diabolical expressions* (*Treasure Island* by Robert Louis Stevenson)

direction NOUN here direction means address ❑ *Elizabeth was not surprised at it, as Jane had written the direction remarkably ill* (*Pride and Prejudice* by Jane Austen)

discover VERB to make known or announce ❑ *the Emperor would discover the secret while I was out of his power* (*Gulliver's Travels* by Jonathan Swift)

dissemble VERB hide or conceal ❑ *Dissemble nothing* (*On His Mistress* by John Donne)

dissolve VERB dissolve here means to release from life, to die ❑ *Fade far away, dissolve, and quite forget* (*Ode on a Nightingale* by John Keats)

distrain VERB to distrain is to seize the property of someone who is in debt in compensation for the money owed ❑ *for he's threatening to distrain for it* (*Silas Marner* by George Eliot)

Divan NOUN a Divan was originally a Turkish council of state–the name was transferred to the couches they sat on and is used to mean this in English ❑ *Mr Brass applauded this picture very much, and the bed being soft and comfortable, Mr Quilp determined to use it, both as a sleeping place by night and as a kind of Divan by day.* (*The Old Curiosity Shop* by Charles Dickens)

divorcement NOUN separation ❑ *By all pains which want and divorcement* *hath* (*On His Mistress* by John Donne)

dog in the manger, PHRASE this phrase describes someone who prevents you from enjoying something that they themselves have no need for ❑ *You are a dog in the manger, Cathy, and desire no one to be loved but yourself* (*Wuthering Heights* by Emily Brontë)

dolorifuge NOUN dolorifuge is a word which Thomas Hardy invented. It means pain-killer or comfort ❑ *as a species of dolorifuge* (*Tess of the D'Urbervilles* by Thomas Hardy)

dome NOUN building ❑ *that river and that mouldering dome* (*The Prelude* by William Wordsworth)

domestic NOUN here domestic means a person's management of the house ❑ *to give some account of my domestic* (*Gulliver's Travels* by Jonathan Swift)

dunce NOUN a dunce is another word for idiot ❑ *Do you take me for a dunce? Go on?* (*Alice's Adventures in Wonderland* by Lewis Carroll)

Ecod EXCLAM a slang exclamation meaning "oh God!" ❑ *"Ecod," replied Wemmick, shaking his head, "that's not my trade."* (*Great Expectations* by Charles Dickens)

egg-hot NOUN an egg-hot (see also "flip" and "negus") was a hot drink made from beer and eggs, sweetened with nutmeg ❑ *She fainted when she saw me return, and made a little jug of egg-hot afterwards to console us while we talked it over.* (*David Copperfield* by Charles Dickens)

encores NOUN an encore is a short extra performance at the end of a longer one, which the entertainer gives because the audience has enthusiastically asked for it ❑ *we want a little something to answer encores with, anyway* (*The Adventures of Huckleberry Finn* by Mark Twain)

equipage NOUN an elegant and impressive carriage ❑ *and besides, the equipage did not answer to any of*

their neighbours (*Pride and Prejudice* by Jane Austen)

exordium NOUN an exordium is the opening part of a speech ❑ *"Now, Handel," as if it were the grave beginning of a portentous business exordium, he had suddenly given up that tone* (*Great Expectations* by Charles Dickens)

expect VERB here expect means to wait for ❑ *to expect his farther commands* (*Gulliver's Travels* by Jonathan Swift)

familiars NOUN familiars means spirits or devils who come to someone when they are called ❑ *I'll turn all the lice about thee into familiars* (*Doctor Faustus 1.4* by Christopher Marlowe)

fantods NOUN a fantod is a person who fidgets or can't stop moving nervously ❑ *It most give me the fantods* (*The Adventures of Huckleberry Finn* by Mark Twain)

farthing NOUN a farthing is an old unit of British currency which was worth a quarter of a penny ❑ *Not a farthing less. A great many back-payments are included in it, I assure you.* (*A Christmas Carol* by Charles Dickens)

farthingale NOUN a hoop worn under a skirt to extend it ❑ *A bell with an old voice–which I dare say in its time had often said to the house, Here is the green farthingale* (*Great Expectations* by Charles Dickens)

favours NOUN here favours is an old word which means ribbons ❑ *A group of humble mourners entered the gate: wearing white favours* (*Oliver Twist* by Charles Dickens)

feigned VERB pretend or pretending ❑ *not my feigned page* (*On His Mistress* by John Donne)

fence ■ NOUN a fence is someone who receives and sells stolen goods ❑ *What are you up to? Ill-treating the boys, you covetous, avaricious, in-sa-ti-a-ble old fence?* (*Oliver Twist* by

Charles Dickens) ■ NOUN defence or protection ❏ *but honesty hath no fence against superior cunning* (*Gulliver's Travels* by Jonathan Swift)

fess ADJ fess is an old word which means pleased or proud ❏ *You'll be fess enough, my poppet* (*Tess of the D'Urbervilles* by Thomas Hardy)

fettered ADJ fettered means bound in chains or chained ❏ *"You are fettered," said Scrooge, trembling. "Tell me why?"* (*A Christmas Carol* by Charles Dickens)

fidges VERB fidges means fidgets, which is to keep moving your hands slightly because you are nervous or excited ❏ *Look, Jim, how my fingers fidges* (*Treasure Island* by Robert Louis Stevenson)

finger-post NOUN a finger-post is a sign-post showing the direction to different places ❏ *"The gallows," continued Fagin, "the gallows, my dear, is an ugly finger-post, which points out a very short and sharp turning that has stopped many a bold fellow's career on the broad highway."* (*Oliver Twist* by Charles Dickens)

fire-irons NOUN fire-irons are tools kept by the side of the fire to either cook with or look after the fire ❏ *the fire-irons came first* (*Alice's Adventures in Wonderland* by Lewis Carroll)

fire-plug NOUN a fire-plug is another word for a fire hydrant ❏ *The pony looked with great attention into a fire-plug, which was near him, and appeared to be quite absorbed in contemplating it* (*The Old Curiosity Shop* by Charles Dickens)

flank NOUN flank is the side of an animal ❏ *And all her silken flanks with garlands dressed* (*Ode on a Grecian Urn* by John Keats)

flip NOUN a flip is a drink made from warmed ale, sugar, spice and beaten egg ❏ *The events of the day, in combination with the twins, if not with the flip, had made Mrs.*

Micawber *hysterical, and she shed tears as she replied* (*David Copperfield* by Charles Dickens)

flit VERB flit means to move quickly ❏ *and if he had meant to flit to Thrushcross Grange* (*Wuthering Heights* by Emily Brontë)

floorcloth NOUN a floorcloth was a hard-wearing piece of canvas used instead of carpet ❏ *This avenging phantom was ordered to be on duty at eight on Tuesday morning in the hall (it was two feet square, as charged for floorcloth)* (*Great Expectations* by Charles Dickens)

fly-driver NOUN a fly-driver is a carriage drawn by a single horse ❏ *The fly-drivers, among whom I inquired next, were equally jocose and equally disrespectful* (*David Copperfield* by Charles Dickens)

fob NOUN a small pocket in which a watch is kept ❏ *"Certain," replied the man, drawing a gold watch from his fob* (*Oliver Twist* by Charles Dickens)

folly NOUN folly means foolishness or stupidity ❏ *the folly of beginning a work* (*Robinson Crusoe* by Daniel Defoe)

fond ADJ fond means foolish ❏ *Fond worldling* (*Doctor Faustus 5.2* by Christopher Marlowe)

fondness NOUN silly or foolish affection ❏ *They have no fondness for their colts or foals* (*Gulliver's Travels* by Jonathan Swift)

for his fancy PHRASE for his fancy means for his liking or as he wanted ❏ *and as I did not obey quick enough for his fancy* (*Treasure Island* by Robert Louis Stevenson)

forlorn ADJ lost or very upset ❏ *you are from that day forlorn* (*Gulliver's Travels* by Jonathan Swift)

foster-sister NOUN a foster-sister was someone brought up by the same nurse or in the same household ❏ *I had been his foster-sister* (*Wuthering Heights* by Emily Brontë)

fox-fire NOUN fox-fire is a weak glow that is given off by decaying, rotten wood ❏ *what we must have was a lot of them rotten chunks that's called fox-fire* (*The Adventures of Huckleberry Finn* by Mark Twain)

frozen sea PHRASE the Arctic Ocean ❏ *into the frozen sea* (*Gulliver's Travels* by Jonathan Swift)

gainsay VERB to gainsay something is to say it isn't true or to deny it ❏ *"So she had," cried Scrooge. "You're right. I'll not gainsay it, Spirit. God forbid!"* (*A Christmas Carol* by Charles Dickens)

gaiters NOUN gaiters were leggings made of a cloth or piece of leather which covered the leg from the knee to the ankle ❏ *Mr Knightley was hard at work upon the lower buttons of his thick leather gaiters* (*Emma* by Jane Austen)

galluses NOUN galluses is an old spelling of gallows, and here means suspenders. Suspenders are straps worn over someone's shoulders and fastened to their trousers to prevent the trousers falling down ❏ *and home-knit galluses* (*The Adventures of Huckleberry Finn* by Mark Twain)

galoot NOUN a sailor but also a clumsy person ❏ *and maybe a galoot on it chopping* (*The Adventures of Huckleberry Finn* by Mark Twain)

gayest ADJ gayest means the most lively and bright or merry ❏ *Beth played her gayest march* (*Little Women* by Louisa May Alcott)

gem NOUN here gem means jewellery ❏ *the mountain shook off turf and flower, had only heath for raiment and crag for gem* (*Jane Eyre* by Charlotte Brontë)

giddy ADJ giddy means dizzy ❏ *and I wish you wouldn't keep appearing and vanishing so suddenly; you make one quite giddy.* (*Alice's Adventures in Wonderland* by Lewis Carroll)

gig NOUN a light two-wheeled carriage ❏ *when a gig drove up to the garden gate: out of which there jumped a fat gentleman* (*Oliver Twist* by Charles Dickens)

gladsome ADJ gladsome is an old word meaning glad or happy ❏ *Nobody ever stopped him in the street to say, with gladsome looks* (*A Christmas Carol* by Charles Dickens)

glen NOUN a glen is a small valley; the word is used commonly in Scotland ❏ *a beck which follows the bend of the glen* (*Wuthering Heights* by Emily Brontë)

gravelled VERB gravelled is an old term which means to baffle or defeat someone ❏ *Gravelled the pastors of the German Church* (*Doctor Faustus 1.1* by Christopher Marlowe)

grinder NOUN a grinder was a private tutor ❏ *but that when he had had the happiness of marrying Mrs Pocket very early in his life, he had impaired his prospects and taken up the calling of a Grinder* (*Great Expectations* by Charles Dickens)

gruel NOUN gruel is a thin, watery cornmeal or oatmeal soup ❏ *and the little saucepan of gruel (Scrooge had a cold in his head) upon the hob.* (*A Christmas Carol* by Charles Dickens)

guinea, half a NOUN half a guinea was ten shillings and sixpence ❏ *but lay out half a guinea at Ford's* (*Emma* by Jane Austen)

gull VERB gull is an old term which means to fool or deceive someone ❏ *Hush, I'll gull him supernaturally* (*Doctor Faustus 3.4* by Christopher Marlowe)

gunnel NOUN the gunnel, or gunwale, is the upper edge of a boat's side ❏ *But he put his foot on the gunnel and rocked her* (*The Adventures of Huckleberry Finn* by Mark Twain)

gunwale NOUN the side of a ship ❏ *He dipped his hand in the water over the boat's gunwale* (*Great Expectations* by Charles Dickens)

Gytrash NOUN a Gytrash is an omen of misfortune to the superstitious, usually taking the form of a hound ❑ *I remembered certain of Bessie's tales, wherein figured a North-of-England spirit, called a "Gytrash"* (*Jane Eyre* by Charlotte Brontë)

hackney-cabriolet NOUN a two-wheeled carriage with four seats for hire and pulled by a horse ❑ *A hackney-cabriolet was waiting; with the same vehemence which she had exhibited in addressing Oliver, the girl pulled him in with her, and drew the curtains close.* (*Oliver Twist* by Charles Dickens)

hackney-coach NOUN a four-wheeled horse-drawn vehicle for hire ❑ *The twilight was beginning to close in, when Mr. Brownlow alighted from a hackney-coach at his own door, and knocked softly.* (*Oliver Twist* by Charles Dickens)

haggler NOUN a haggler is someone who travels from place to place selling small goods and items ❑ *when I be plain Jack Durbeyfield, the haggler* (*Tess of the D'Urbervilles* by Thomas Hardy)

halter NOUN a halter is a rope or strap used to lead an animal or to tie it up ❑ *I had of course long been used to a halter and a headstall* (*Black Beauty* by Anna Sewell)

hamlet NOUN a hamlet is a small village or a group of houses in the countryside ❑ *down from the hamlet* (*Treasure Island* by Robert Louis Stevenson)

hand-barrow NOUN a hand-barrow is a device for carrying heavy objects. It is like a wheelbarrow except that it has handles, rather than wheels, for moving the barrow ❑ *his sea chest following behind him in a hand-barrow* (*Treasure Island* by Robert Louis Stevenson)

handspike NOUN a handspike was a stick which was used as a lever ❑ *a bit of stick like a handspike* (*Treasure Island* by Robert Louis Stevenson)

haply ADV haply means by chance or perhaps ❑ *And haply the Queen-Moon is on her throne* (*Ode on a Nightingale* by John Keats)

harem NOUN the harem was the part of the house where the women lived ❑ *mostly they hang round the harem* (*The Adventures of Huckleberry Finn* by Mark Twain)

hautboys NOUN hautboys are oboes ❑ *sausages and puddings resembling flutes and hautboys* (*Gulliver's Travels* by Jonathan Swift)

hawker NOUN a hawker is someone who sells goods to people as he travels rather than from a fixed place like a shop ❑ *to buy some stockings from a hawker* (*Treasure Island* by Robert Louis Stevenson)

hawser NOUN a hawser is a rope used to tie up or tow a ship or boat ❑ *Again among the tiers of shipping, in and out, avoiding rusty chain-cables, frayed hempen hawsers* (*Great Expectations* by Charles Dickens)

headstall NOUN the headstall is the part of the bridle or halter that goes around a horse's head ❑ *I had of course long been used to a halter and a headstall* (*Black Beauty* by Anna Sewell)

hearken VERB hearken means to listen ❑ *though we sometimes stopped to lay hold of each other and hearken* (*Treasure Island* by Robert Louis Stevenson)

heartless ADJ here heartless means without heart or dejected ❑ *I am not heartless* (*The Prelude* by William Wordsworth)

hebdomadal ADJ hebdomadal means weekly ❑ *It was the hebdomadal treat to which we all looked forward from Sabbath to Sabbath* (*Jane Eyre* by Charlotte Brontë)

highwaymen NOUN highwaymen were people who stopped travellers and robbed them ❑ *We are high-waymen* (*The Adventures of Huckleberry Finn* by Mark Twain)

hinds NOUN hinds means farm hands, or people who work on a farm ❏ *He called his hinds about him* (*Gulliver's Travels* by Jonathan Swift)

histrionic ADJ if you refer to someone's behaviour as histrionic, you are being critical of it because it is dramatic and exaggerated ❏ *But the histrionic muse is the darling* (*The Adventures of Huckleberry Finn* by Mark Twain)

hogs NOUN hogs is another word for pigs ❏ *Tom called the hogs "ingots"* (*The Adventures of Huckleberry Finn* by Mark Twain)

horrors NOUN the horrors are a fit, called delirium tremens, which is caused by drinking too much alcohol ❏ *I'll have the horrors* (*Treasure Island* by Robert Louis Stevenson)

huffy ADJ huffy means to be obviously annoyed or offended about something ❏ *They will feel that more than angry speeches or huffy actions* (*Little Women* by Louisa May Alcott)

hulks NOUN hulks were prison-ships ❏ *The miserable companion of thieves and ruffians, the fallen outcast of low haunts, the associate of the scourings of the jails and hulks* (*Oliver Twist* by Charles Dickens)

humbug NOUN humbug means nonsense or rubbish ❏ *"Bah," said Scrooge. "Humbug!"* (*A Christmas Carol* by Charles Dickens)

humours NOUN it was believed that there were four fluids in the body called humours which decided the temperament of a person depending on how much of each fluid was present ❏ *other peccant humours* (*Gulliver's Travels* by Jonathan Swift)

husbandry NOUN husbandry is farming animals ❏ *bad husbandry were plentifully anointing their wheels* (*Silas Marner* by George Eliot)

huswife NOUN a huswife was a small sewing kit ❏ *but I had put my huswife on it* (*Emma* by Jane Austen)

ideal ADJ ideal in this context means imaginary ❏ *I discovered the yell was not ideal* (*Wuthering Heights* by Emily Brontë)

If our two PHRASE if both our ❏ *If our two loves be one* (*The Good-Morrow* by John Donne)

ignis-fatuus NOUN ignis-fatuus is the light given out by burning marsh gases, which lead careless travellers into danger ❏ *it is madness in all women to let a secret love kindle within them, which, if unreturned and unknown, must devour the life that feeds it; and, if discovered and responded to, must lead ignis-fatuus-like, into miry wilds whence there is no extrication.* (*Jane Eyre* by Charlotte Brontë)

imaginations NOUN here imaginations means schemes or plans ❏ *soon drove out those imaginations* (*Gulliver's Travels* by Jonathan Swift)

impressible ADJ impressible means open or impressionable ❏ *for Marner had one of those impressible, self-doubting natures* (*Silas Marner* by George Eliot)

in good intelligence PHRASE friendly with each other ❏ *that these two persons were in good intelligence with each other* (*Gulliver's Travels* by Jonathan Swift)

inanity NOUN inanity is silliness or dull stupidity ❏ *Do we not wile away moments of inanity* (*Silas Marner* by George Eliot)

incivility NOUN incivility means rudeness or impoliteness ❏ *if it's only for a piece of incivility like to-night's* (*Treasure Island* by Robert Louis Stevenson)

indigenae NOUN indigenae means natives or people from that area ❏ *an exotic that the surly indigenae will not recognise for kin* (*Wuthering Heights* by Emily Brontë)

indocible ADJ unteachable ❏ *so they were the most restive and indocible* (*Gulliver's Travels* by Jonathan Swift)

ingenuity NOUN inventiveness ❏ *entreated me to give him something as an encouragement to ingenuity* (*Gulliver's Travels* by Jonathan Swift)

ingots NOUN an ingot is a lump of a valuable metal like gold, usually shaped like a brick ❏ *Tom called the hogs "ingots"* (*The Adventures of Huckleberry Finn* by Mark Twain)

inkstand NOUN an inkstand is a pot which was put on a desk to contain either ink or pencils and pens ❏ *throwing an inkstand at the Lizard as she spoke* (*Alice's Adventures in Wonderland* by Lewis Carroll)

inordinate ADJ without order. To-day inordinate means "excessive". ❏ *Though yet untutored and inordinate* (*The Prelude* by William Wordsworth)

intellectuals NOUN here intellectuals means the minds (of the workmen) ❏ *those instructions they give being too refined for the intellectuals of their workmen* (*Gulliver's Travels* by Jonathan Swift)

interview NOUN meeting ❏ *By our first strange and fatal interview* (*On His Mistress* by John Donne)

jacks NOUN jacks are rods for turning a spit over a fire ❏ *It was a small bit of pork suspended from the kettle hanger by a string passed through a large door key, in a way known to primitive housekeepers unpossessed of jacks* (*Silas Marner* by George Eliot)

jews-harp NOUN a jews-harp is a small, metal, musical instrument that is played by the mouth ❏ *A jews-harp's plenty good enough for a rat* (*The Adventures of Huckleberry Finn* by Mark Twain)

jorum NOUN a large bowl ❏ *while Miss Skiffins brewed such a jorum of tea, that the pig in the back premises became strongly excited* (*Great Expectations* by Charles Dickens)

jostled VERB jostled means bumped or pushed by someone or some people

❏ *being jostled himself into the kennel* (*Gulliver's Travels* by Jonathan Swift)

keepsake NOUN a keepsake is a gift which reminds someone of an event or of the person who gave it to them. ❏ *books and ornaments they had in their boudoirs at home: keepsakes that different relations had presented to them* (*Jane Eyre* by Charlotte Brontë)

kenned VERB kenned means knew ❏ *though little kenned the lamplighter that he had any company but Christmas!* (*A Christmas Carol* by Charles Dickens)

kennel NOUN kennel means gutter, which is the edge of a road next to the pavement, where rain water collects and flows away ❏ *being jostled himself into the kennel* (*Gulliver's Travels* by Jonathan Swift)

knock-knee ADJ knock-knee means slanted, at an angle. ❏ *LOT 1 was marked in whitewashed knock-knee letters on the brewhouse* (*Great Expectations* by Charles Dickens)

ladylike ADJ to be ladylike is to behave in a polite, dignified and graceful way ❏ *No, winking isn't ladylike* (*Little Women* by Louisa May Alcott)

lapse NOUN flow ❏ *Stealing with silent lapse to join the brook* (*The Prelude* by William Wordsworth)

larry NOUN larry is an old word which means commotion or noisy celebration ❏ *That was all a part of the larry!* (*Tess of the D'Urbervilles* by Thomas Hardy)

laths NOUN laths are strips of wood ❏ *The panels shrunk, the windows cracked; fragments of plaster fell out of the ceiling, and the naked laths were shown instead* (*A Christmas Carol* by Charles Dickens)

leer NOUN a leer is an unpleasant smile ❏ *with a kind of leer* (*Treasure Island* by Robert Louis Stevenson)

lenitives NOUN these are different kinds of drugs or medicines: lenitives and palliatives were pain relievers; aperitives were laxatives; abstersives caused vomiting; corrosives destroyed human tissue; restringents caused constipation; cephalalgics stopped headaches; icterics were used as medicine for jaundice; apophlegmatics were cough medicine, and acoustics were cures for the loss of hearing ❑ *lenitives, aperitives, abstersives, corrosives, restringents, palliatives, laxatives, cephalalgics, icterics, apophlegmatics, acoustics* (*Gulliver's Travels* by Jonathan Swift)

lest CONJ in case. If you do something lest something (usually) unpleasant happens you do it to try to prevent it happening ❑ *She went in without knocking, and hurried upstairs, in great fear lest she should meet the real Mary Ann* (*Alice's Adventures in Wonderland* by Lewis Carroll)

levee NOUN a levee is an old term for a meeting held in the morning, shortly after the person holding the meeting has got out of bed ❑ *I used to attend the King's levee once or twice a week* (*Gulliver's Travels* by Jonathan Swift)

life-preserver NOUN a club which had lead inside it to make it heavier and therefore more dangerous ❑ *and with no more suspicious articles displayed to view than two or three heavy bludgeons which stood in a corner, and a "life-preserver" that hung over the chimney-piece.* (*Oliver Twist* by Charles Dickens)

lighterman NOUN a lighterman is another word for sailor ❑ *in and out, hammers going in ship-builders' yards, saws going at timber, clashing engines going at things unknown, pumps going in leaky ships, capstans going, ships going out to sea, and unintelligible sea creatures roaring curses over the bulwarks at respondent lightermen* (*Great Expectations* by Charles Dickens)

livery NOUN servants often wore a uniform known as a livery ❑

suddenly a footman in livery came running out of the wood (*Alice's Adventures in Wonderland* by Lewis Carroll)

livid ADJ livid means pale or ash coloured. Livid also means very angry ❑ *a dirty, livid white* (*Treasure Island* by Robert Louis Stevenson)

lottery-tickets NOUN a popular card game ❑ *and Mrs. Philips protested that they would have a nice comfortable noisy game of lottery tickets* (*Pride and Prejudice* by Jane Austen)

lower and upper world PHRASE the earth and the heavens are the lower and upper worlds ❑ *the changes in the lower and upper world* (*Gulliver's Travels* by Jonathan Swift)

lustres NOUN lustres are chandeliers. A chandelier is a large, decorative frame which holds light bulbs or candles and hangs from the ceiling ❑ *the lustres, lights, the carving and the guilding* (*The Prelude* by William Wordsworth)

lynched VERB killed without a criminal trial by a crowd of people ❑ *He'll never know how nigh he come to getting lynched* (*The Adventures of Huckleberry Finn* by Mark Twain)

malingering VERB if someone is malingering they are pretending to be ill to avoid working ❑ *And you stand there malingering* (*Treasure Island* by Robert Louis Stevenson)

managing PHRASE treating with consideration ❑ *to think the honour of my own kind not worth managing* (*Gulliver's Travels* by Jonathan Swift)

manhood PHRASE manhood means human nature ❑ *concerning the nature of manhood* (*Gulliver's Travels* by Jonathan Swift)

man-trap NOUN a man-trap is a set of steel jaws that snap shut when trodden on and trap a person's leg

❏ *"Don't go to him," I called out of the window, "he's an assassin! A man-trap!"* (*Oliver Twist* by Charles Dickens)

maps NOUN charts of the night sky ❏ *Let maps to others, worlds on worlds have shown* (*The Good-Morrow* by John Donne)

mark VERB look at or notice ❏ *Mark but this flea, and mark in this* (*The Flea* by John Donne)

maroons NOUN A maroon is someone who has been left in a place which it is difficult for them to escape from, like a small island ❏ *if schooners, islands, and maroons* (*Treasure Island* by Robert Louis Stevenson)

mast NOUN here mast means the fruit of forest trees ❏ *a quantity of acorns, dates, chestnuts, and other mast* (*Gulliver's Travels* by Jonathan Swift)

mate VERB defeat ❏ *Where Mars did mate the warlike Carthigens* (*Doctor Faustus Chorus* by Christopher Marlowe)

mealy ADJ Mealy when used to describe a face meant pallid, pale or colourless ❏ *I only know two sorts of boys. Mealy boys, and beef-faced boys* (*Oliver Twist* by Charles Dickens)

middling ADV fairly or moderately ❏ *she worked me middling hard for about an hour* (*The Adventures of Huckleberry Finn* by Mark Twain)

mill NOUN a mill, or treadmill, was a device for hard labour or punishment in prison ❏ *Was you never on the mill?* (*Oliver Twist* by Charles Dickens)

milliner's shop NOUN a milliner's sold fabrics, clothing, lace and accessories; as time went on they specialized more and more in hats ❏ *to pay their duty to their aunt and to a milliner's shop just over the way* (*Pride and Prejudice* by Jane Austen)

minching un' munching PHRASE how people in the north of England used to describe the way people

from the south speak ❏ *Minching un' munching!* (*Wuthering Heights* by Emily Brontë)

mine NOUN gold ❏ *Whether both th'Indias of spice and mine* (*The Sun Rising* by John Donne)

mire NOUN mud ❏ *Tis my fate to be always ground into the mire under the iron heel of oppression* (*The Adventures of Huckleberry Finn* by Mark Twain)

miscellany NOUN a miscellany is a collection of many different kinds of things ❏ *under that, the miscellany began* (*Treasure Island* by Robert Louis Stevenson)

mistarshers NOUN mistarshers means moustache, which is the hair that grows on a man's upper lip ❏ *when he put his hand up to his mistarshers* (*Tess of the D'Urbervilles* by Thomas Hardy)

morrow NOUN here good-morrow means tomorrow and a new and better life ❏ *And now good-morrow to our waking souls* (*The Good-Morrow* by John Donne)

mortification NOUN mortification is an old word for gangrene which is when part of the body decays or "dies" because of disease ❏ *Yes, it was a mortification–that was it* (*The Adventures of Huckleberry Finn* by Mark Twain)

mought VERB mought is an old spelling of might ❏ *what you mought call me? You mought call me captain* (*Treasure Island* by Robert Louis Stevenson)

move VERB move me not means do not make me angry ❏ *Move me not, Faustus* (*Doctor Faustus 2.1* by Christopher Marlowe)

muffin-cap NOUN a muffin-cap is a flat cap made from wool ❏ *the old one, remained stationary in the muffin-cap and leathers* (*Oliver Twist* by Charles Dickens)

mulatter NOUN a mulatter was another word for mulatto, which is a person with parents who are from different races ❏ *a mulatter, most as white as a white man* (*The Adventures of Huckleberry Finn* by Mark Twain)

mummery NOUN mummery is an old word that meant meaningless (or pretentious) ceremony ❏ *When they were all gone, and when Trabb and his men–but not his boy: I looked for him–had crammed their mummery into bags, and were gone too, the house felt wholesomer.* (*Great Expectations* by Charles Dickens)

nap NOUN the nap is the woolly surface on a new item of clothing. Here the surface has been worn away so it looks bare ❏ *like an old hat with the nap rubbed off* (*The Adventures of Huckleberry Finn* by Mark Twain)

natural ■ NOUN a natural is a person born with learning difficulties ❏ *though he had been left to his particular care by their deceased father, who thought him almost a natural.* (*David Copperfield* by Charles Dickens) ■ ADJ natural meant illegitimate ❏ *Harriet Smith was the natural daughter of some-body* (*Emma* by Jane Austen)

navigator NOUN a navigator was origi-nally someone employed to dig canals. It is the origin of the word "navvy" meaning a labourer ❏ *She ascertained from me in a few words what it was all about, comforted Dora, and gradually convinced her that I was not a labourer–from my manner of stating the case I believe Dora concluded that I was a navi-gator, and went balancing myself up and down a plank all day with a wheelbarrow–and so brought us together in peace.* (*David Copperfield* by Charles Dickens)

necromancy NOUN necromancy means a kind of magic where the magician speaks to spirits or ghosts to find out what will happen in the future ❏ *He surfeits upon cursed necro-mancy* (*Doctor Faustus chorus* by Christopher Marlowe)

negus NOUN a negus is a hot drink made from sweetened wine and water ❏ *He sat placidly perusing the newspaper, with his little head on one side, and a glass of warm sherry negus at his elbow.* (*David Copperfield* by Charles Dickens)

nice ADJ discriminating. Able to make good judgements or choices ❏ *consequently a claim to be nice* (*Emma* by Jane Austen)

nigh ADV nigh means near ❏ *He'll never know how nigh he come to getting lynched* (*The Adventures of Huckleberry Finn* by Mark Twain)

nimbleness NOUN nimbleness means being able to move very quickly or skilfully ❏ *and with incredible accuracy and nimbleness* (*Treasure Island* by Robert Louis Stevenson)

noggin NOUN a noggin is a small mug or a wooden cup ❏ *you'll bring me one noggin of rum* (*Treasure Island* by Robert Louis Stevenson)

none ADJ neither ❏ *none can die* (*The Good-Morrow* by John Donne)

notices NOUN observations ❏ *Arch are his notices* (*The Prelude* by William Wordsworth)

occiput NOUN occiput means the back of the head ❏ *saw off the occiput of each couple* (*Gulliver's Travels* by Jonathan Swift)

officiously ADV kindly ❏ *the governess who attended Glumdalclitch very officiously lifted me up* (*Gulliver's Travels* by Jonathan Swift)

old salt PHRASE old salt is a slang term for an experienced sailor ❏ *a "true sea-dog", and a "real old salt"* (*Treasure Island* by Robert Louis Stevenson)

or ere PHRASE before ❏ *or ere the Hall was built* (*The Prelude* by William Wordsworth)

ostler NOUN one who looks after horses at an inn ❏ *The bill paid, and the waiter remembered, and the ostler not forgotten, and the chambermaid taken into consideration* (*Great Expectations* by Charles Dickens)

ostry NOUN an ostry is an old word for a pub or hotel ❑ *lest I send you into the ostry with a vengeance* (*Doctor Faustus 2.2* by Christopher Marlowe)

outrunning the constable PHRASE outrunning the constable meant spending more than you earn ❑ *but I shall by this means be able to check your bills and to pull you up if I find you outrunning the constable.* (*Great Expectations* by Charles Dickens)

over ADV across ❑ *It is in length six yards, and in the thickest part at least three yards over* (*Gulliver's Travels* by Jonathan Swift)

over the broomstick PHRASE this is a phrase meaning "getting married without a formal ceremony" ❑ *They both led tramping lives, and this woman in Gerrard-street here, had been married very young, over the broomstick (as we say), to a tramping man, and was a perfect fury in point of jealousy.* (*Great Expectations* by Charles Dickens)

own VERB own means to admit or to acknowledge ❑ *It's my old girl that advises. She has the head. But I never own to it before her. Discipline must be maintained* (*Bleak House* by Charles Dickens)

page NOUN here page means a boy employed to run errands ❑ *not my feigned page* (*On His Mistress* by John Donne)

paid pretty dear PHRASE paid pretty dear means paid a high price or suffered quite a lot ❑ *I paid pretty dear for my monthly fourpenny piece* (*Treasure Island* by Robert Louis Stevenson)

pannikins NOUN pannikins were small tin cups ❑ *of lifting light glasses and cups to his lips, as if they were clumsy pannikins* (*Great Expectations* by Charles Dickens)

pards NOUN pards are leopards ❑ *Not charioted by Bacchus and his pards* (*Ode on a Nightingale* by John Keats)

parlour boarder NOUN a pupil who lived with the family ❑ *and somebody had lately raised her from the condition of scholar to parlour boarder* (*Emma* by Jane Austen)

particular, a London PHRASE London in Victorian times and up to the 1950s was famous for having very dense fog–which was a combination of real fog and the smog of pollution from factories ❑ *This is a London particular . . . A fog, miss* (*Bleak House* by Charles Dickens)

patten NOUN pattens were wooden soles which were fixed to shoes by straps to protect the shoes in wet weather ❑ *carrying a basket like the Great Seal of England in plaited straw, a pair of pattens, a spare shawl, and an umbrella, though it was a fine bright day* (*Great Expectations* by Charles Dickens)

paviour NOUN a paviour was a labourer who worked on the street pavement ❑ *the paviour his pickaxe* (*Oliver Twist* by Charles Dickens)

peccant ADJ peccant means unhealthy ❑ *other peccant humours* (*Gulliver's Travels* by Jonathan Swift)

penetralium NOUN penetralium is a word used to describe the inner rooms of the house ❑ *and I had no desire to aggravate his impatience previous to inspecting the penetralium* (*Wuthering Heights* by Emily Brontë)

pensive ADV pensive means deep in thought or thinking seriously about something ❑ *and she was leaning pensive on a tomb-stone on her right elbow* (*The Adventures of Huckleberry Finn* by Mark Twain)

penury NOUN penury is the state of being extremely poor ❑ *Distress, if not penury, loomed in the distance* (*Tess of the D'Urbervilles* by Thomas Hardy)

perspective NOUN telescope ❑ *a pocket perspective* (*Gulliver's Travels* by Jonathan Swift)

phaeton NOUN a phaeton was an open carriage for four people ❑ *often* condescends to drive by my humble abode in her little phaeton and ponies (*Pride and Prejudice* by Jane Austen)

phantasm NOUN a phantasm is an illusion, something that is not real. It is sometimes used to mean ghost ❑ *Experience had bred no fancies in him that could raise the phantasm of appetite* (*Silas Marner* by George Eliot)

physic NOUN here physic means medicine ❑ *there I studied physic two years and seven months* (*Gulliver's Travels* by Jonathan Swift)

pinioned VERB to pinion is to hold both arms so that a person cannot move them ❑ *But the relentless Ghost pinioned him in both his arms, and forced him to observe what happened next.* (*A Christmas Carol* by Charles Dickens)

piquet NOUN piquet was a popular card game in the C18th ❑ *Mr Hurst and Mr Bingley were at piquet* (*Pride and Prejudice* by Jane Austen)

plaister NOUN a plaister is a piece of cloth on which an apothecary (or pharmacist) would spread ointment. The cloth is then applied to wounds or bruises to treat them ❑ *Then, she gave the knife a final smart wipe on the edge of the plaister, and then sawed a very thick round off the loaf: which she finally, before separating from the loaf, hewed into two halves, of which Joe got one, and I the other.* (*Great Expectations* by Charles Dickens)

plantations NOUN here plantations means colonies, which are countries controlled by a more powerful country ❑ *besides our plantations in America* (*Gulliver's Travels* by Jonathan Swift)

plastic ADJ here plastic is an old term meaning shaping or a power that was forming ❑ *A plastic power abode with me* (*The Prelude* by William Wordsworth)

players NOUN actors ❑ *of players which upon the world's stage be* (*On His Mistress* by John Donne)

plump ADV all at once, suddenly ❑ *But it took a bit of time to get it well round, the change come so uncommon plump, didn't it?* (*Great Expectations* by Charles Dickens)

plundered VERB to plunder is to rob or steal from ❑ *These crosses stand for the names of ships or towns that they sank or plundered* (*Treasure Island* by Robert Louis Stevenson)

pommel ■ VERB to pommel someone is to hit them repeatedly with your fists ❑ *hug him round the neck, pommel his back, and kick his legs in irrepressible affection!* (*A Christmas Carol* by Charles Dickens) ■ NOUN a pommel is the part of a saddle that rises up at the front ❑ *He had his gun across his pommel* (*The Adventures of Huckleberry Finn* by Mark Twain)

poor's rates NOUN poor's rates were property taxes which were used to support the poor ❑ *"Oh!" replied the undertaker; "why, you know, Mr. Bumble, I pay a good deal towards the poor's rates."* (*Oliver Twist* by Charles Dickens)

popular ADJ popular means ruled by the people, or Republican, rather than ruled by a monarch ❑ *With those of Greece compared and popular Rome* (*The Prelude* by William Wordsworth)

porringer NOUN a porringer is a small bowl ❑ *Of this festive composition each boy had one porringer, and no more* (*Oliver Twist* by Charles Dickens)

postboy NOUN a postboy was the driver of a horse-drawn carriage ❑ *He spoke to a postboy who was dozing under the gateway* (*Oliver Twist* by Charles Dickens)

post-chaise NOUN a fast carriage for two or four passengers ❑ *Looking round, he saw that it was a post-chaise, driven at great speed* (*Oliver Twist* by Charles Dickens)

postern NOUN a small gate usually at the back of a building ❑ *The little servant happening to be entering the* *fortress with two hot rolls, I passed through the postern and crossed the drawbridge, in her company* (*Great Expectations* by Charles Dickens)

pottle NOUN a pottle was a small basket ❏ *He had a paper-bag under each arm and a pottle of strawberries in one hand . . .* (*Great Expectations* by Charles Dickens)

pounce NOUN pounce is a fine powder used to prevent ink spreading on untreated paper ❏ *in that grim atmosphere of pounce and parchment, red-tape, dusty wafers, inkjars, brief and draft paper, law reports, writs, declarations, and bills of costs* (*David Copperfield* by Charles Dickens)

pox NOUN pox means sexually transmitted diseases like syphilis ❏ *how the pox in all its consequences and denominations* (*Gulliver's Travels* by Jonathan Swift)

prelibation NOUN prelibation means a foretaste of or an example of something to come ❏ *A prelibation to the mower's scythe* (*The Prelude* by William Wordsworth)

prentice NOUN an apprentice ❏ *and Joe, sitting on an old gun, had told me that when I was 'prentice to him regularly bound, we would have such Larks there!* (*Great Expectations* by Charles Dickens)

presently ADV immediately ❏ *I presently knew what they meant* (*Gulliver's Travels* by Jonathan Swift)

pumpion NOUN pumpkin ❏ *for it was almost as large as a small pumpion* (*Gulliver's Travels* by Jonathan Swift)

punctual ADJ kept in one place ❏ *was not a punctual presence, but a spirit* (*The Prelude* by William Wordsworth)

quadrille ■ NOUN a quadrille is a dance invented in France which is usually performed by four couples ❏ *However, Mr Swiveller had Miss Sophy's hand for the first quadrille* (*country-dances being low, were utterly proscribed*) (*The Old Curiosity Shop* by Charles Dickens) ■ NOUN quadrille was a card game for four people ❏ *to make up her pool of quadrille in the evening* (*Pride and Prejudice* by Jane Austen)

quality NOUN gentry or upper-class people ❏ *if you are with the quality* (*The Adventures of Huckleberry Finn* by Mark Twain)

quick parts PHRASE quick-witted ❏ *Mr Bennet was so odd a mixture of quick parts* (*Pride and Prejudice* by Jane Austen)

quid NOUN a quid is something chewed or kept in the mouth, like a piece of tobacco ❏ *rolling his quid* (*Treasure Island* by Robert Louis Stevenson)

quit VERB quit means to avenge or to make even ❏ *But Faustus's death shall quit my infamy* (*Doctor Faustus 4.3* by Christopher Marlowe)

rags NOUN divisions ❏ *Nor hours, days, months, which are the rags of time* (*The Sun Rising* by John Donne)

raiment NOUN raiment means clothing ❏ *the mountain shook off turf and flower, had only heath for raiment and crag for gem* (*Jane Eyre* by Charlotte Brontë)

rain cats and dogs PHRASE an expression meaning rain heavily. The origin of the expression is unclear ❏ *But it'll perhaps rain cats and dogs to-morrow* (*Silas Marner* by George Eliot)

raised Cain PHRASE raised Cain means caused a lot of trouble. Cain is a character in the Bible who killed his brother Abel ❏ *and every time he got drunk he raised Cain around town* (*The Adventures of Huckleberry Finn* by Mark Twain)

rambling ADJ rambling means confused and not very clear ❏ *my head began to be filled very early with rambling thoughts* (*Robinson Crusoe* by Daniel Defoe)

raree-show NOUN a raree-show is an old term for a peep-show or a fairground entertainment ❏ *A raree-show is here, with children gathered round* (*The Prelude* by William Wordsworth)

recusants NOUN people who resisted authority ❏ *hardy recusants* (*The Prelude* by William Wordsworth)

redounding VERB eddying. An eddy is a movement in water or air which goes round and round instead of flowing in one direction ❏ *mists and steam-like fogs redounding everywhere* (*The Prelude* by William Wordsworth)

redundant ADJ here redundant means overflowing but Wordsworth also uses it to mean excessively large or too big ❏ *A tempest, a redundant energy* (*The Prelude* by William Wordsworth)

reflex NOUN reflex is a shortened version of reflexion, which is an alternative spelling of reflection ❏ *To cut across the reflex of a star* (*The Prelude* by William Wordsworth)

Reformatory NOUN a prison for young offenders/criminals ❏ *Even when I was taken to have a new suit of clothes, the tailor had orders to make them like a kind of Reformatory, and on no account to let me have the free use of my limbs.* (*Great Expectations* by Charles Dickens)

remorse NOUN pity or compassion ❏ *by that remorse* (*On His Mistress* by John Donne)

render VERB in this context render means give. ❏ *and Sarah could render no reason that would be sanctioned by the feeling of the community.* (*Silas Marner* by George Eliot)

repeater NOUN a repeater was a watch that chimed the last hour when a button was pressed—as a result it was useful in the dark ❏ *And his watch is a gold repeater, and worth a hundred pound if it's worth a penny.* (*Great Expectations* by Charles Dickens)

repugnance NOUN repugnance means a strong dislike of something or someone ❏ *overcoming a strong repugnance* (*Treasure Island* by Robert Louis Stevenson)

reverence NOUN reverence means bow. When you bow to someone, you briefly bend your body towards them as a formal way of showing them respect ❏ *made my reverence* (*Gulliver's Travels* by Jonathan Swift)

reverie NOUN a reverie is a daydream ❏ *I can guess the subject of your reverie* (*Pride and Prejudice* by Jane Austen)

revival NOUN a religious meeting held in public ❏ *well I'd ben a-running' a little temperance revival thar' bout a week* (*The Adventures of Huckleberry Finn* by Mark Twain)

revolt VERB revolt means turn back or stop your present course of action and go back to what you were doing before ❏ *Revolt, or I'll in piecemeal tear thy flesh* (*Doctor Faustus 5.1* by Christopher Marlowe)

rheumatics/rheumatism NOUN rheumatics [rheumatism] is an illness that makes your joints or muscles stiff and painful ❏ *a new cure for the rheumatics* (*Treasure Island* by Robert Louis Stevenson)

riddance NOUN riddance is usually used in the form good riddance which you say when you are pleased that something has gone or been left behind ❏ *I'd better go into the house, and die and be a riddance* (*David Copperfield* by Charles Dickens)

rimy ADJ rimy is an adjective which means covered in ice or frost ❏ *It was a rimy morning, and very damp* (*Great Expectations* by Charles Dickens)

riper ADJ riper means more mature or older ❏ *At riper years to Wittenberg he went* (*Doctor Faustus chorus* by Christopher Marlowe)

rubber NOUN a set of games in whist or backgammon ❏ *her father was sure of his rubber* (*Emma* by Jane Austen)

ruffian NOUN a ruffian is a person who behaves violently ❏ *and when the ruffian had told him* (*Treasure Island* by Robert Louis Stevenson)

sadness NOUN sadness is an old term meaning seriousness ❏ *But I prithee tell me, in good sadness* (*Doctor Faustus 2.2* by Christopher Marlowe)

sailed before the mast PHRASE this phrase meant someone who did not look like a sailor ❏ *he had none of the appearance of a man that sailed before the mast* (*Treasure Island* by Robert Louis Stevenson)

scabbard NOUN a scabbard is the covering for a sword or dagger ❏ *Girded round its middle was an antique scabbard; but no sword was in it, and the ancient sheath was eaten up with rust* (*A Christmas Carol* by Charles Dickens)

schooners NOUN A schooner is a fast, medium-sized sailing ship ❏ *if schooners, islands, and maroons* (*Treasure Island* by Robert Louis Stevenson)

science NOUN learning or knowledge ❏ *Even Science, too, at hand* (*The Prelude* by William Wordsworth)

scrouge VERB to scrouge means to squeeze or to crowd ❏ *to scrouge in and get a sight* (*The Adventures of Huckleberry Finn* by Mark Twain)

scrutore NOUN a scrutore, or escritoire, was a writing table ❏ *set me gently on my feet upon the scrutore* (*Gulliver's Travels* by Jonathan Swift)

scutcheon/escutcheon NOUN an escutcheon is a shield with a coat of arms, or the symbols of a family name, engraved on it ❏ *On the scutcheon we'll have a bend* (*The Adventures of Huckleberry Finn* by Mark Twain)

sea-dog PHRASE sea-dog is a slang term for an experienced sailor or pirate ❏ *a "true sea-dog", and a "real old salt,"* (*Treasure Island* by Robert Louis Stevenson)

see the lions PHRASE to see the lions was to go and see the sights of London. Originally the phrase referred to the menagerie in the Tower of London and later in Regent's Park ❏ *We will go and see the lions for an hour or two–it's something to have a fresh fellow like you to show them to, Copperfield* (*David Copperfield* by Charles Dickens)

self-conceit NOUN self-conceit is an old term which means having too high an opinion of oneself, or deceiving yourself ❏ *Till swollen with cunning, of a self-conceit* (*Doctor Faustus chorus* by Christopher Marlowe)

seneschal NOUN a steward ❏ *where a grey-headed seneschal sings a funny chorus with a funnier body of vassals* (*Oliver Twist* by Charles Dickens)

sensible ADJ if you were sensible of something you are aware or conscious of something ❏ *If my children are silly I must hope to be always sensible of it* (*Pride and Prejudice* by Jane Austen)

sessions NOUN court cases were heard at specific times of the year called sessions ❏ *He lay in prison very ill, during the whole interval between his committal for trial, and the coming round of the Sessions.* (*Great Expectations* by Charles Dickens)

shabby ADJ shabby places look old and in bad condition ❏ *a little bit of a shabby village named Pikesville* (*The Adventures of Huckleberry Finn* by Mark Twain)

shay-cart NOUN a shay-cart was a small cart drawn by one horse ❏ *"I were at the Bargemen t'other night, Pip;" whenever he subsided into affection, he called me Pip, and whenever he relapsed into politeness he called me Sir; "when there come up in his* *shay-cart Pumblechook."* (*Great Expectations* by Charles Dickens)

shilling NOUN a shilling is an old unit of currency. There were twenty shillings in every British pound ❑ *"Ten shillings too much," said the gentleman in the white waistcoat.* (*Oliver Twist* by Charles Dickens)

shines NOUN tricks or games ❑ *well, it would make a cow laugh to see the shines that old idiot cut* (*The Adventures of Huckleberry Finn* by Mark Twain)

shirking VERB shirking means not doing what you are meant to be doing, or evading your duties ❑ *some of you shirking lubbers* (*Treasure Island* by Robert Louis Stevenson)

shiver my timbers PHRASE shiver my timbers is an expression which was used by sailors and pirates to express surprise ❑ *why, shiver my timbers, if I hadn't forgotten my score!* (*Treasure Island* by Robert Louis Stevenson)

shoe-roses NOUN shoe-roses were roses made from ribbons which were stuck on to shoes as decoration ❑ *the very shoe-roses for Netherfield were got by proxy* (*Pride and Prejudice* by Jane Austen)

singular ADJ singular means very great and remarkable or strange ❑ *"Singular dream," he says* (*The Adventures of Huckleberry Finn* by Mark Twain)

sire NOUN sire is an old word which means lord or master or elder ❑ *She also defied her sire* (*Little Women* by Louisa May Alcott)

sixpence NOUN a sixpence was half of a shilling ❑ *if she had only a shilling in the world, she would be very lilkely to give away sixpence of it* (*Emma* by Jane Austen)

slavey NOUN the word slavey was used when there was only one servant in a house or boarding-house–so she had to perform all the duties of a larger staff ❑ *Two distinct knocks, sir, will produce the slavey at any*

time (*The Old Curiosity Shop* by Charles Dickens)

slender ADJ weak ❑ *In slender accents of sweet verse* (*The Prelude* by William Wordsworth)

slop-shops NOUN slop-shops were shops where cheap ready-made clothes were sold. They mainly sold clothes to sailors ❑ *Accordingly, I took the jacket off, that I might learn to do without it; and carrying it under my arm, began a tour of inspection of the various slop-shops.* (*David Copperfield* by Charles Dickens)

sluggard NOUN a lazy person ❑ *"Stand up and repeat 'Tis the voice of the sluggard,'" said the Gryphon.* (*Alice's Adventures in Wonderland* by Lewis Carroll)

smallpox NOUN smallpox is a serious infectious disease ❑ *by telling the men we had smallpox aboard* (*The Adventures of Huckleberry Finn* by Mark Twain)

smalls NOUN smalls are short trousers ❑ *It is difficult for a large-headed, small-eyed youth, of lumbering make and heavy countenance, to look dignified under any circumstances; but it is more especially so, when superadded to these personal attractions are a red nose and yellow smalls* (*Oliver Twist* by Charles Dickens)

sneeze-box NOUN a box for snuff was called a sneeze-box because sniffing snuff makes the user sneeze ❑ *To think of Jack Dawkins — lummy Jack — the Dodger — the Artful Dodger — going abroad for a common twopenny-halfpenny sneeze-box!* (*Oliver Twist* by Charles Dickens)

snorted VERB slept ❑ *Or snorted we in the Seven Sleepers' den?* (*The Good-Morrow* by John Donne)

snuff NOUN snuff is tobacco in powder form which is taken by sniffing ❑ *as he thrust his thumb and fore-finger into the proffered snuff-box of the undertaker: which was an* *ingenious little model of a patent coffin.* (*Oliver Twist* by Charles Dickens)

soliloquized VERB to soliloquize is when an actor in a play speaks to himself or herself rather than to another actor ❑ *"A new servitude! There is something in that," I soliloquized (mentally, be it understood; I did not talk aloud)* (*Jane Eyre* by Charlotte Brontë)

sough NOUN a sough is a drain or a ditch ❑ *as you may have noticed the sough that runs from the marshes* (*Wuthering Heights* by Emily Brontë)

spirits NOUN a spirit is the nonphysical part of a person which is believed to remain alive after their death ❑ *that I might raise up spirits when I please* (*Doctor Faustus 1.5* by Christopher Marlowe)

spleen ■ NOUN here spleen means a type of sadness or depression which was thought to only affect the wealthy ❑ *yet here I could plainly discover the true seeds of spleen* (*Gulliver's Travels* by Jonathan Swift) ■ NOUN irritability and low spirits ❑ *Adieu to disappointment and spleen* (*Pride and Prejudice* by Jane Austen)

spondulicks NOUN spondulicks is a slang word which means money ❑ *not for all his spondulicks and as much more on top of it* (*The Adventures of Huckleberry Finn* by Mark Twain)

stalled of VERB to be stalled of something is to be bored with it ❑ *I'm stalled of doing naught* (*Wuthering Heights* by Emily Brontë)

stanchion NOUN a stanchion is a pole or bar that stands upright and is used as a building support ❑ *and slid down a stanchion* (*The Adventures of Huckleberry Finn* by Mark Twain)

stang NOUN stang is another word for pole which was an old measurement ❑ *These fields were intermingled with woods of half a stang* (*Gulliver's Travels* by Jonathan Swift)

starlings NOUN a starling is a wall built around the pillars that support a bridge to protect the pillars ❑ *There were states of the tide when, having been down the river, I could not get back through the eddy-chafed arches and starlings of old London Bridge* (*Great Expectations* by Charles Dickens)

startings NOUN twitching or night-time movements of the body ❑ *with midnight's startings* (*On His Mistress* by John Donne)

stomacher NOUN a panel at the front of a dress ❑ *but send her aunt the pattern of a stomacher* (*Emma* by Jane Austen)

stoop VERB swoop ❑ *Once a kite hovering over the garden made a stoop at me* (*Gulliver's Travels* by Jonathan Swift)

succedaneum NOUN a succedaneum is a substitute ❑ *But as a succedaneum* (*The Prelude* by William Wordsworth)

suet NOUN a hard animal fat used in cooking ❑ *and your jaws are too weak For anything tougher than suet* (*Alice's Adventures in Wonderland* by Lewis Carroll)

sultry ADJ sultry weather is hot and damp. Here sultry means unpleasant or risky ❑ *for it was getting pretty sultry for us* (*The Adventures of Huckleberry Finn* by Mark Twain)

summerset NOUN summerset is an old spelling of somersault. If someone does a somersault, they turn over completely in the air ❑ *I have seen him do the summerset* (*Gulliver's Travels* by Jonathan Swift)

supper NOUN supper was a light meal taken late in the evening. The main meal was dinner which was eaten at four or five in the afternoon ❑ *and the supper table was all set out* (*Emma* by Jane Austen)

surfeits VERB to surfeit in something is to have far too much of it, or to overindulge in it to an unhealthy degree ❑ *He surfeits upon cursed* necromancy (*Doctor Faustus chorus* by Christopher Marlowe)

surtout NOUN a surtout is a long close-fitting overcoat ❏ *He wore a long black surtout reaching nearly to his ankles* (*The Old Curiosity Shop* by Charles Dickens)

swath NOUN swath is the width of corn cut by a scythe ❏ *while thy hook Spares the next swath* (*Ode to Autumn* by John Keats)

sylvan ADJ sylvan means belonging to the woods ❏ *Sylvan historian* (*Ode on a Grecian Urn* by John Keats)

taction NOUN taction means touch. This means that the people had to be touched on the mouth or the ears to get their attention ❏ *without being roused by some external taction upon the organs of speech and hearing* (*Gulliver's Travels* by Jonathan Swift)

Tag and Rag and Bobtail PHRASE the riff-raff, or lower classes. Used in an insulting way ❏ *"No," said he; "not till it got about that there was no protection on the premises, and it come to be considered dangerous, with convicts and Tag and Rag and Bobtail going up and down."* (*Great Expectations* by Charles Dickens)

tallow NOUN tallow is hard animal fat that is used to make candles and soap ❏ *and a lot of tallow candles* (*The Adventures of Huckleberry Finn* by Mark Twain)

tan VERB to tan means to beat or whip ❏ *and if I catch you about that school I'll tan you good* (*The Adventures of Huckleberry Finn* by Mark Twain)

tanyard NOUN the tanyard is part of a tannery, which is a place where leather is made from animal skins ❏ *hid in the old tanyard* (*The Adventures of Huckleberry Finn* by Mark Twain)

tarry ADJ tarry means the colour of tar or black ❏ *his tarry pig-tail* (*Treasure Island* by Robert Louis Stevenson)

thereof PHRASE from there ❏ *By all desires which thereof did ensue* (*On His Mistress* by John Donne)

thick with, be PHRASE if you are "thick with someone" you are very close, sharing secrets–it is often used to describe people who are planning something secret ❏ *Hasn't he been thick with Mr Heathcliff lately?* (*Wuthering Heights* by Emily Brontë)

thimble NOUN a thimble is a small cover used to protect the finger while sewing ❏ *The paper had been sealed in several places by a thimble* (*Treasure Island* by Robert Louis Stevenson)

thirtover ADJ thirtover is an old word which means obstinate or that someone is very determined to do want they want and can not be persuaded to do something in another way ❏ *I have been living on in a thirtover, lackadaisical way* (*Tess of the D'Urbervilles* by Thomas Hardy)

timbrel NOUN timbrel is a tambourine ❏ *What pipes and timbrels?* (*Ode on a Grecian Urn* by John Keats)

tin NOUN tin is slang for money/cash ❏ *Then the plain question is, an't it a pity that this state of things should continue, and how much better would it be for the old gentleman to hand over a reasonable amount of tin, and make it all right and comfortable* (*The Old Curiosity Shop* by Charles Dickens)

tincture NOUN a tincture is a medicine made with alcohol and a small amount of a drug ❏ *with ink composed of a cephalic tincture* (*Gulliver's Travels* by Jonathan Swift)

tithe NOUN a tithe is a tax paid to the church ❏ *and held farms which, speaking from a spiritual point of view, paid highly-desirable tithes* (*Silas Marner* by George Eliot)

towardly ADJ a towardly child is

dutiful or obedient ❏ *and a towardly child* (*Gulliver's Travels* by Jonathan Swift)

toys NOUN trifles are things which are considered to have little importance, value, or significance ❏ *purchase my life from them bysome bracelets, glass rings, and other toys* (*Gulliver's Travels* by Jonathan Swift)

tract NOUN a tract is a religious pamphlet or leaflet ❏ *and Joe Harper got a hymn-book and a tract* (*The Adventures of Huckleberry Finn* by Mark Twain)

train-oil NOUN train-oil is oil from whale blubber ❏ *The train-oil and gunpowder were shoved out of sight in a minute* (*Wuthering Heights* by Emily Brontë)

tribulation NOUN tribulation means the suffering or difficulty you experience in a particular situation ❏ *Amy was learning this distinction through much tribulation* (*Little Women* by Louisa May Alcott)

trivet NOUN a trivet is a three-legged stand for resting a pot or kettle ❏ *a pocket-knife in his right; and a pewter pot on the trivet* (*Oliver Twist* by Charles Dickens)

trot line NOUN a trot line is a fishing line to which a row of smaller fishing lines are attached ❏ *when he got along I was hard at it taking up a trot line* (*The Adventures of Huckleberry Finn* by Mark Twain)

troth NOUN oath or pledge ❏ *I wonder, by my troth* (*The Good-Morrow* by John Donne)

truckle NOUN a truckle bedstead is a bed that is on wheels and can be slid under another bed to save space ❏ *It rose under my hand, and the door yielded. Looking in, I saw a lighted candle on a table, a bench, and a mattress on a truckle bedstead.* (*Great Expectations* by Charles Dickens)

trump NOUN a trump is a good, reliable person who can be trusted ❏ *This lad Hawkins is a trump, I perceive*

(*Treasure Island* by Robert Louis Stevenson)

tucker NOUN a tucker is a frilly lace collar which is worn around the neck ❏ *Whereat Scrooge's niece's sister—the plump one with the lace tucker: not the one with the roses—blushed.* (*A Christmas Carol* by Charles Dickens)

tureen NOUN a large bowl with a lid from which soup or vegetables are served ❏ *Waiting in a hot tureen!* (*Alice's Adventures in Wonderland* by Lewis Carroll)

turnkey NOUN a prison officer; jailer ❏ *As we came out of the prison through the lodge, I found that the great importance of my guardian was appreciated by the turnkeys, no less than by those whom they held in charge.* (*Great Expectations* by Charles Dickens)

turnpike NOUN the upkeep of many roads of the time was paid for by tolls (fees) collected at posts along the road. There was a gate to prevent people travelling further along the road until the toll had been paid. ❏ *Traddles, whom I have taken up by appointment at the turnpike, presents a dazzling combination of cream colour and light blue; and both he and Mr. Dick have a general effect about them of being all gloves.* (*David Copperfield* by Charles Dickens)

twas PHRASE it was ❏ *twas but a dream of thee* (*The Good-Morrow* by John Donne)

tyrannized VERB tyrannized means bullied or forced to do things against their will ❏ *for people would soon cease coming there to be tyrannized over and put down* (*Treasure Island* by Robert Louis Stevenson)

'un NOUN 'un is a slang term for one—usually used to refer to a person ❏ *She's been thinking the old 'un* (*David Copperfield* by Charles Dickens)

undistinguished ADJ undiscriminating or incapable of making a distinction between good and bad things ❏

their undistinguished appetite to devour everything (*Gulliver's Travels* by Jonathan Swift)

use NOUN habit ❑ *Though use make you apt to kill me* (*The Flea* by John Donne)

vacant ADJ vacant usually means empty, but here Wordsworth uses it to mean carefree ❑ *To vacant musing, unreproved neglect* (*The Prelude* by William Wordsworth)

valetudinarian NOUN one too concerned with his or her own health. ❑ *for having been a valetudinarian all his life* (*Emma* by Jane Austen)

vamp VERB vamp means to walk or tramp to somewhere ❑ *Well, vamp on to Marlott, will 'ee* (*Tess of the D'Urbervilles* by Thomas Hardy)

vapours NOUN the vapours is an old term which means unpleasant and strange thoughts, which make the person feel nervous and unhappy ❑ *and my head was full of vapours* (*Robinson Crusoe* by Daniel Defoe)

vegetables NOUN here vegetables means plants ❑ *the other vegetables are in the same proportion* (*Gulliver's Travels* by Jonathan Swift)

venturesome ADJ if you are venturesome you are willing to take risks ❑ *he must be either hopelessly stupid or a venturesome fool* (*Wuthering Heights* by Emily Brontë)

verily ADV verily means really or truly ❑ *though I believe verily* (*Robinson Crusoe* by Daniel Defoe)

vicinage NOUN vicinage is an area or the residents of an area ❑ *and to his thought the whole vicinage was haunted by her.* (*Silas Marner* by George Eliot)

victuals NOUN victuals means food ❑ *grumble a little over the victuals* (*The Adventures of Huckleberry Finn* by Mark Twain)

vintage NOUN vintage in this context means wine ❑ *Oh, for a draught of*

vintage! (*Ode on a Nightingale* by John Keats)

virtual ADJ here virtual means powerful or strong ❑ *had virtual faith* (*The Prelude* by William Wordsworth)

vittles NOUN vittles is a slang word which means food ❑ *There never was such a woman for givin' away vittles and drink* (*Little Women* by Louisa May Alcott)

voided straight PHRASE voided straight is an old expression which means emptied immediately ❑ *see the rooms be voided straight* (*Doctor Faustus 4.1* by Christopher Marlowe)

wainscot NOUN wainscot is wood panel lining in a room so wainscoted means a room lined with wooden panels ❑ *in the dark wainscoted parlor* (*Silas Marner* by George Eliot)

walking the plank PHRASE walking the plank was a punishment in which a prisoner would be made to walk along a plank on the side of the ship and fall into the sea, where they would be abandoned ❑ *about hanging, and walking the plank* (*Treasure Island* by Robert Louis Stevenson)

want VERB want means to be lacking or short of ❑ *The next thing wanted was to get the picture framed* (*Emma* by Jane Austen)

wanting ADJ wanting means lacking or missing ❑ *wanting two fingers of the left hand* (*Treasure Island* by Robert Louis Stevenson)

wanting, I was not PHRASE I was not wanting means I did not fail ❑ *I was not wanting to lay a foundation of religious knowledge in his mind* (*Robinson Crusoe* by Daniel Defoe)

ward NOUN a ward is, usually, a child who has been put under the protection of the court or a guardian for his or her protection ❑ *I call the Wards in Jarndcye. The*

are caged up with all the others.
(*Bleak House* by Charles Dickens)

waylay VERB to waylay someone is to lie in wait for them or to intercept them ❑ *I must go up the road and waylay him* (*The Adventures of Huckleberry Finn* by Mark Twain)

weazen NOUN weazen is a slang word for throat. It actually means shrivelled ❑ *You with an uncle too! Why, I knowed you at Gargery's when you was so small a wolf that I could have took your weazen betwixt this finger and thumb and chucked you away dead* (*Great Expectations* by Charles Dickens)

wery ◼ ADV very ❑ *Be wery careful o' vidders all your life* (*Pickwick Papers* by Charles Dickens) ◼ *See* wibrated

wherry NOUN wherry is a small swift rowing boat for one person ❑ *It was flood tide when Daniel Quilp sat himself down in the wherry to cross to the opposite shore.* (*The Old Curiosity Shop* by Charles Dickens)

whether PREP whether means which of the two in this example ❑ *we came in full view of a great island or continent (for we knew not whether)* (*Gulliver's Travels* by Jonathan Swift)

whetstone NOUN a whetstone is a stone used to sharpen knives and other tools ❑ *I dropped pap's whetstone there too* (*The Adventures of Huckleberry Finn* by Mark Twain)

wibrated VERB in Dickens's use of the English language "w" often replaces "v" when he is reporting speech. So here "wibrated" means "vibrated". In *Pickwick Papers* a judge asks Sam Weller (who constantly confuses the two letters) "Do you spell it with a 'v' or a 'w'?" to which Weller replies 'That depends upon the taste and fancy of the speller, my Lord' ❑ *There are strings . . . in the human heart that had better not be wibrated* (*Barnaby Rudge* by Charles Dickens)

wicket NOUN a wicket is a little door in a larger entrance ❑ *Having rested here, for a minute or so, to collect a good burst of sobs and an imposing show of tears and terror, he knocked loudly at the wicket* (*Oliver Twist* by Charles Dickens)

without CONJ without means unless ❑ *You don't know about me, without you have read a book by the name of The Adventures of Tom Sawyer* (*The Adventures of Huckleberry Finn* by Mark Twain)

wittles ◼ NOUN vittles is a slang word which means food ❑ *I live on broken wittles–and I sleep on the coals* (*David Copperfield* by Charles Dickens) ◼ *See* wibrated

woo VERB courts or forms a proper relationship with ❑ *before it woo* (*The Flea* by John Donne)

words, to have PHRASE if you have words with someone you have a disagreement or an argument ❑ *I do not want to have words with a young thing like you.* (*Black Beauty* by Anna Sewell)

workhouse NOUN workhouses were places where the homeless were given food and a place to live in return for doing very hard work ❑ *And the Union workhouses? demanded Scrooge. Are they still in operation?* (*A Christmas Carol* by Charles Dickens)

yawl NOUN a yawl is a small boat kept on a bigger boat for short trips. Yawl is also the name for a small fishing boat ❑ *She sent out her yawl, and we went aboard* (*The Adventures of Huckleberry Finn* by Mark Twain)

yeomanry NOUN the yeomanry was a collective term for the middle classes involved in agriculture ❑ *The yeomanry are precisely the order of people with whom I feel I can have nothing to do* (*Emma* by Jane Austen)

yonder ADV yonder means over there ❑ *all in the same second we seem to hear low voices in yonder!* (*The Adventures of Huckleberry Finn* by Mark Twain)